EVERY LAST DEVIL

A DCI ROBERT KETT NOVEL

ALEX SMITH

EVERY LAST DEVIL
Published Worldwide by Relentless Media.
This edition published in 2024.

Edited by Hanna Elizabeth

16.0.4

www.alexsmithbooks.com
relentless.media

ALSO BY ALEX SMITH

The DCI Robert Kett Thrillers

Paper Girls

Bad Dog

Three Little Pigs

Whip Crack

Run Rabbit Run

Stone Cold Dead

Every Mother's Son

Sweet Briar Rose

Jaw Breaker

Knock Knock

King Rat

Knuckle Bones

Lucky Number Seven

Unholy Saints

Truly Madly Deadly

Every Last Devil

Red Line

Cry Baby: A Novella

Other Books

Six Days, Six Hours, Six Minutes

The Harder They Fall

For everyone at KDP.
Thanks for changing my life!

PROLOGUE

Monday

THEY'D LEFT THE WORLD BEHIND THEM FIFTEEN minutes ago, civilisation a distant memory. Charlie Ford half thought they'd driven through a portal into the past, because when she stared through the foggy window in the backseat of the Nissan Micra, she saw nothing but rolling dunes topped with wisps of seagrass, all drenched in early morning mist.

The sea cowered behind them, too frightened to show itself to the newcomers, but the sky was making up for it. It was a true Norfolk sky, too big and too blue to be real, the sun dazzling even though it wasn't yet eight in the morning. The gulls did their best to fill the space where the clouds should have been, wheeling in lazy circles, their calls lost behind the tinny voice of Taylor Swift as she bemoaned yet another breakup.

It was beautiful, sure. But Charlie felt a little terrified

too, because the last house she'd seen along the coastal road had been a mile or so back, and the state of the place made her pretty sure a serial killer lived there.

The Micra, dubbed Donkey by its owner, Aggie Clegg, wasn't handling the heat very well, the engine clanking like somebody was locked in there with a steel drum. Every time Charlie peeked past Aggie's shoulder to check the time, she noticed that the little temperature needle was deeper into the red. The air conditioning had stopped blowing cold five minutes after they'd left Norwich, blasting them with warm dust ever since.

If Donkey died all the way out here, in this wasteland that seemed somehow untouched by human exploration, in this little corner of Norfolk where there was absolutely zero phone reception, then they were all screwed.

There was also the small matter of the fact that she was about to pee herself.

"Are we nearly there?" she asked, leaning between the two front seats. She caught sight of herself in the mirror, her pasty complexion made even worse by a sheen of sweat, her lifeless hair plastered to her cheeks.

"I think so," said Aggie, craning over the wheel to peer through the dusty windscreen.

Charlie had no idea how Aggie looked so fresh, her skin sandpaper dry, every wisp of hair in place. Aggie was four months younger than her, not even eighteen until tomorrow, but she carried herself like a proper grownup. Charlie didn't know her that well, because they didn't have too many classes together, but it had always been obvious how put together she was. Charlie felt like her awkward, clumsy child, moaning in the back seat.

"It's around here somewhere," said Aggie. Her voice was blunt, a hint of annoyance. Charlie wasn't sure if it had anything to do with her, but she'd been grumpy since they'd picked her up that morning. "Matthew?"

Matt Kamau was busy drumming his hands on his thighs in the passenger seat, singing the words to *Cruel Summer* beneath his breath. The morning light caught in the curls of his hair, made his dark skin glow, and Charlie felt the temperature in the car rise by about four hundred degrees.

"Matt?" said Aggie, and when he still didn't respond she poked him in the side of his head.

"Huh?" he said, spinning in his chair. "We there?"

"That's what I want you to tell me," said Aggie, slowing the Micra to twenty as she took another sharp turn in the narrow road. "Since you're the navigator."

"Oh, right," said Matt, pulling his phone from the compartment in the door. He squinted at it for a few seconds before shrugging. "No signal."

"That's very useful," said Aggie.

"You're the one who insists on using *What3Words* every time we go anywhere," said Matt. "It only works if you've got a signal."

"You didn't bring a map?"

"Map," he said, frowning. "Map... I know the word, can't think what it means. Because I'm not, like, a hundred years old."

He flashed a grin at Charlie, and she offered a reluctant smile back. Her bladder was like an overfilled balloon, and she sat back in her seat to take some of the pressure off. They'd entered a tunnel of trees that seemed to have gathered night beneath their heavy branches.

"I don't know why you bother coming sometimes," said Aggie, speeding up a little. "I don't know why either of you did."

"Because everyone knows I'm the brains of the outfit," said Matt, doing his best to keep the tone light. "And the beauty. The beauty and the brains of the *Paranormal Norfolk* YouTube channel."

"You think?" said Aggie. "What does that make me, then?"

"You're the one with the car," said Matt, and he screamed like Fay Wray as Aggie slapped him with the back of her hand. The car wobbled for a few seconds before she got control again. "I'm joking," Matt told her. "Calm down."

"Did you seriously just tell this woman to calm down?" said Aggie, flashing him a look with barely concealed rage.

Matt retreated as far into his seat as it was possible to go.

"Those words left my mouth, but I did not give them permission," he said. "Naughty words."

The road curved ahead, shafts of sunlight forming ghostly pillars where they broke through the trees—so bright that Charlie almost didn't see the sign. It stood on the verge, a wooden post topped by an arrow.

"Is that it?" she asked.

Aggie and Matt were still bickering, and she had to say it again before they heard her. By the time Aggie had applied the brakes, the Micra had zipped past the sign.

"Hang on," said Aggie. "Charlie, hit the floor, will you?"

She peered into the mirror, and Charlie ducked down to get out of her way. The Micra whined backwards, the steel drum engine playing louder than ever. When Charlie sat up again, she saw that they were close enough to the sign to read what it said.

"St Mary's ruins," said Aggie. "We're here."

She hesitated for a moment, her hands flexing around the wheel as she stared into the dark trees. Then she turned off the main road, squeezing between overgrown verges. Another sign jutted out at an angle, pointing into the woods.

There was no car park, but a lay-by rested beside the road and Aggie manoeuvred the Micra into it. She switched off the engine and silence roared into the car like seawater, loud enough to drown in. It filled Charlie with a panic she didn't understand, and she reached for the handle before remembering the car only had two doors. She had to bite her lip to stem the rush of panic, and the pressure in her bladder grew more painful still.

Hurry up, hurry up, hurry up, she thought, one hand on the lever that would move Aggie's chair forward. She was so desperate now she'd happily fold the other girl in two if it meant escaping.

Aggie pushed her hands against the ceiling, groaning dramatically as she stretched. Then, *thank God,* she cranked open her door and stepped out into the dappled daylight.

"Grab the stuff," she said.

Charlie fiddled with the lever but the seat wouldn't budge.

"Little help?" she asked, but Aggie had walked to the boot.

"You have to jiggle it," said Matt.

"I am jiggling it," said Charlie, jiggling with all her might.

"No, like *jiggle* jiggle."

"I'm jiggling!"

If she jiggled any harder then she was going to leave a puddle in the back of the car.

"Here," said Matt, leaning over the gearstick and reaching for the clasp. His hand touched hers, what felt like an electric shock passing through their fingers, and for a moment Charlie almost lost all control. "Just a sec," he said, oblivious. "It's almost..."

He pulled the lever and Charlie's weight snapped the chair forward, almost taking his hand off. She shouted an apology as she clambered out of the car, her feet catching on something and depositing her on her hands. She crawled onto the hot road like a dog, standing up to see Aggie staring at her. The look on her face was not kind.

"Toilet?" was all Charlie could manage.

Aggie opened her arms and directed them to the trees along the side of the road.

"Take your pick, mate."

Charlie hopped up the verge, struggling through the tangled undergrowth. The trees weren't particularly thick, and no matter where she went, she could still see the car and her friends. But neither of them seemed interested in watching her pee, so after half a dozen false starts she squatted beside a straggly bush and let rip.

It was, without doubt, one of the best moments of her life.

What felt like fifteen minutes and four gallons later, she stood up, pulling everything back into place. When she looked towards where she thought the road was, though, she couldn't see any sign of it. She turned the other way, finding nothing but trees. They spoke to her, creaking like crones in the gentle wind. Deeper in the whispering shade, a woodpecker drummed, and her entire body seemed to crunch into goosebumps.

She spun around again, wondering how she'd managed to get so lost when she'd only walked a handful of yards from the road. Even the light seemed to have changed, as if the trees had placed her under a spell and she'd only just woken after a hundred years.

"Aggie?" she said, too quietly for anyone to hear her. She cleared her throat, tried again. "Matt?"

"You done?" came Aggie's reply, and when Charlie turned in the direction of the voice she saw both of her friends stomping through the weeds a stone's throw away. Past them was the Micra, the sunlight catching the roof and flashing like a lighthouse beacon.

How the hell had she missed it?

"Don't forget the rules of the countryside," said Matt, clutching a black camera bag to his broad chest. He broke into song. "Pick off a leaf and wipe your underneath, in an English country garden."

"Matt, leave it!" said Aggie, who had a bag of her own.

"Dig a little hole and do it on a mole, in an English country garden," Matt went on, even louder. Despite herself, Charlie laughed—more to do with the relief of seeing them than the quality of the joke. "What was the next one? Something about ants?"

"Pull down your pants and widdle on the ants," Charlie told him, and he grinned at her.

"I knew you'd fit right in," he said. "Pull down your pants and—"

Aggie used her free hand to smack him into silence.

"I said leave it! We've got a job to do."

She scanned the trees again, pulling out her phone to check the time.

"What's the problem?" said Matt. "You're never normally this stressed."

"Because we don't normally have a sponsor to impress," she said. "This is big for us, this episode could change everything."

Matt shrugged.

"Just supposed to be a bit of fun, Ag."

"For *you*, maybe," said Aggie, shooting him a look before turning her sour face to Charlie. "Since you're here, you might as well grab this."

She held out the bag and Charlie took it, holding it with both sweaty hands. She moved to let Aggie pass, almost tumbling onto her backside in the tangled roots. Matt steadied her with a hand and she nodded her thanks.

"You okay?" he asked.

"Yeah, just got the feeling I'm not wanted."

"You are," said Matt, staring at Aggie's back. "She's just foul in the mornings, and she's stressed about turning eighteen tomorrow. Nobody wants to be an adult these days."

He gave her a brotherly pat on the shoulder and walked away. Charlie heaved out a sigh before following them both along a poor excuse for a path. The trees closed in, crowding them in twilight even though it wasn't even midday yet. Nearby, the woodpecker hammered, as if announcing their presence to the spirits of the woods, to the ghosts who dwelled here, to the mighty Green Man.

Goosebumps broke out on Charlie's arms, a shiver that felt like a breath running down the nape of her neck. She knew she shouldn't look back, but she did anyway, and once again the car had been erased from the world, swallowed whole by the greenery.

There was nothing here but age, she thought as she struggled on, the branches catching on the bag like the trees were trying to grab hold of it. It even smelled wrong. Not unpleasant, just alien, a scent she'd never encountered before, one she couldn't even begin to describe. It was the stench of a place that would literally eat her if she strayed too far down its throat. If she fell here, she would sink into the mulch where the bugs and the worms would break her into pieces. Then she'd be gulped up by the trees, digested there for the rest of time.

"You okay?" Matt asked again, his voice almost punching a scream from her.

He and Aggie had stopped up ahead, and she couldn't figure out why because there was still nothing but trees.

Then her eyes drifted up and she saw it.

It was as if the church had grown out of the ground, an organic monstrosity of flint and ivy. She couldn't see where the structure ended and the forest began. All she could make out was an archway that stood between the trees like a glitch in reality, one that didn't have any right to be there. It led, as if by magic, into the stone-walled interior of a church where the sun danced like candlelight.

And growing right in the middle of the ruined nave was an oak tree.

"Pretty cool, right?" said Matt, his neck craned back as he studied the tower of the church. "You been out here before?"

"No," said Charlie, her voice muted by the spectacle before her.

She'd done her research, though. She'd come prepared, and maybe that was why she felt so unnerved, because she knew the story that went with this church.

"Right, let's get the kit sorted," said Aggie. "Mic's in the bag. I'm assuming you know how it works."

"Yeah, I think so," said Charlie, ripping her eyes from the archway and attempting a smile. "Haven't gone through two years of A-Level media studies for nothing."

Aggie wasn't listening, pulling the camera from the case that Matt was holding. She clicked her fingers until Charlie figured out what she was asking, opening the bag and removing the microphone. She trotted over and handed it to her, watching as she fixed it to the mount at the top. She passed the camera to Charlie.

"Don't drop it."

I won't, Charlie thought, and then very nearly dropped it. The camera was a Canon DSLR, and thankfully she knew how to operate it. She switched it on, studying the little screen when it came to life.

"This isn't the camera we usually use," said Matt. "Dougie has his own kit. But they're pretty easy to figure out, everything should be ready to go."

"Sounds good," she replied, attempting to sound as casual as possible and hoping he wouldn't hear her pounding heart. Her hands were so sweaty it was a struggle to hold onto the heavy camera, and everything she'd learned at school seemed to drain out of her stupid, sweaty head.

She really, *really* didn't want to mess this up. She'd only stepped in this morning because Dougie's mum had fallen ill and Matt had called her, frantically asking for help. But if she played her cards right, then this episode of *Paranormal Norfolk* could be the first entry on her CV, and a perfect calling card for university.

"Right," said Aggie, her knees cracking as she stood up. She glanced at her phone again, her brow furrowing. "Here's good. Make sure you get as much of the archway in as possible, but I don't want to reveal the tree until we step to the side. Yeah?"

"Yeah," said Charlie, scrubbing her hand down her shorts.

"We want a little shake, but not tremors, okay? Think early MTV."

Charlie couldn't remember what MTV was, but she nodded.

"We get it done quick, no mistakes," said Aggie. "You good?"

"I'm good," said Charlie.

"Get over here, Matthew, before the whole world beats us to the punch."

The whole world had beaten them to it already, Charlie knew. When she'd Googled St Mary's ruins she'd found dozens of videos exposing the 'secret' ruin and its terrifying legend—everything from school trips to an episode of the insufferable Norman Balls and his conspiracy theory website. She kept her thoughts to herself, hoiking the camera up and pressing the record button.

"Hold up a second," she said, manually adjusting the zoom and then the focus until both Aggie and Matt were crystal clear. She took a couple of steps back, angling the camera so that the shot almost reached the top of the arch. "Okay, in five, four, three..."

She mouthed the rest of the countdown, watching Aggie's face open up into a smile before she started speaking.

"Hi guys, and welcome to another episode of..."

Matt joined in at this point, both doing jazz hands.

"Paranormal Norfolk!"

"Today we're in one of the most haunted places in the whole county," Aggie went on, and Charlie leaned in to make her the focal point of the shot. A flicker of annoyance crossed Aggie's face, but she didn't stop. "The ruins of the Church of St Mary, in East Somerton."

She paused, and Charlie let the camera rise slowly to take in the full drama of the arch, and past that, the tower. She hadn't been told to, but she'd watched enough episodes of the show to know that's what Dougie would have done. When she'd finished, she panned back out to the presenters.

Matt took over the talking, his eyes wide with theatrical terror.

"Built over five hundred years ago, the church lies deep in the forest, just a stone's throw from the sea. The trees have done their best to erase this building from existence, to bury the horrors of its past. But no true act of wickedness can ever be truly forgotten. Because, oh—"

"Because," Aggie said at the same time, barely able to conceal her irritation. "Because what happened here, in these stone walls, really was evil. And the truth of this tale is one of the reasons why so many people come here looking for answers, and leave wishing they hadn't found them. What is the truth of St Mary's? To answer that, we have to turn to the witch's tree."

Aggie and Matt stepped aside and Charlie moved forward instinctively, zooming in on the tree that grew in the middle of the church. She held the shot there until Matt whooped.

"That was amazing, well done!"

Charlie thought he was talking to Aggie, but when she looked up from the viewscreen she saw that he was smiling at her. He jogged over, wiping the sweat from his brow as he leaned in.

Close enough to kiss, thought Charlie, but instead he pulled the camera strap over her head so that he could take it from her. There was a bleep as he pressed play, then the muffled sound of her own voice as she counted them in.

"There was a little too much movement there," said Aggie, her face stern. "We don't want to make anyone motion sick. Less is more with a camera."

"Right, sorry," said Charlie. "Shall we do it again?"

"No time," said Aggie.

"Mate, it's *perfect*," said Matt, squinting at the screen.

"She's a natural, Ag. This is literally better than anything Dougie does. Wanna see?"

He offered Aggie the camera but she shook her head.

"It will have to do, and Matt, remember your lines, yeah? It looks shit when we talk over each other."

Aggie walked off towards the arch, and Matt threw Charlie a look like they were two naughty siblings being told off by a parent. Charlie giggled, almost dropping the camera as Matt passed it to her. She looped the strap over her neck again as Matt followed Aggie into the dark interior of the ruin.

Charlie hesitated for a moment more, the chill of the forest settling into her bones. The trees sang their whispering song, and there was something about it that made her want to turn around and walk away, head back to the car, head back to civilisation. Because the rules were different here, weren't they? In the old places of the world, like this one, anything was possible.

Quit it! she told herself, pinching the flesh of her upper thigh to goad her body into moving. She crunched through the dry undergrowth, passing through the archway, trying to ignore the way her ears popped as if she'd just dived too deep in a swimming pool.

The church was so much bigger than it seemed from the outside, as if it had taken a breath when she'd entered, inflating itself. The walls craned upwards like cliff edges, leading to a roof that was forged from the dancing trees. The nave was a giant space broken only by the oak tree that sat dead centre. Something about it made Charlie feel like it was watching her.

Past that was a door that led into the church's bell tower. It was so dark through there that the world might have ended right on its threshold.

She shivered, the goosebumps returning. The church felt like a fridge, even though shafts of sunlight broke through the shifting canopies, spearing the dirt floor. Flies buzzed everywhere, landing on her face to taste her, trying to crawl into her ears and nose.

"Gross," said Aggie, almost at the tree. She waved her arms to chase the flies away, spitting into the dirt.

Don't, Charlie almost said. *Don't spit on her grave.*

Because there *was* a grave here. A body buried deep beneath their feet, woven into the knotted roots of the old oak.

"Right, this will do," said Aggie, turning her back to the tree. "Let's get it over with. Reeks in here."

Matt joined her, and Charlie took up a position in front of them, lifting the camera until they appeared on the screen. They stood in a dark spot between two sunbeams, almost invisible, as if the ruins had turned them into ghosts. She adjusted the light settings until they looked a little more solid. Whatever Aggie had smelled had reached Charlie's nose, and she felt it wrinkle. It stank like the bins at school when they hadn't been emptied for a while.

"Ready?" Aggie asked, and Charlie pressed record.

"Five, four, three..."

She nodded the last two beats, watching Aggie's face light up again.

"We're now inside the church, and right below us is something so horrible you'd struggle to imagine it."

"No, not mud," said Matt. "A body."

"The body of..."

They said the next bit together, and for a reason Charlie didn't understand, they both did the jazz hands again.

"A witch!"

"Legends tell the story of a woman who lived in the

village hundreds of years ago," Aggie went on. "She had a wooden leg, and the locals accused her of being a witch."

"They dragged her kicking and screaming into the church," Matt went on with a morbid grin. He had to shake his hand at a fly that kept trying to land on his cheek. "And killed her in the most horrific way."

"They dug a hole," Aggie said, her voice quieter now. Charlie zoomed in a little for dramatic effect.

"And threw her in it," said Matt, his eyes wide. "They covered her up while she was screaming for help."

"They buried her..." said Aggie, and this time Charlie zoomed right in on her. "Alive."

Something exploded through the door at the back of the church, a thunderous flap of wings that made a jolt of pure panic rip through Charlie's body. Aggie screamed, Matt wheeling around with his arms up as if the witch herself was rising from the earth.

It wasn't her, though, it was a bird of some kind, a big one, which flapped awkwardly up and over the lip of the roof. Only when it chattered its outrage like a machine gun did Charlie realise it was a magpie, although she couldn't ever remember seeing one that size before.

"Fuck," said Aggie, a hand on her heart. "That almost killed me. Did you get it?"

Charlie nodded, the camera still recording. Matt laughed.

"People are gonna love that," he said. "We staying here or moving?"

"Staying," said Aggie. "You ready, Charlie?"

Charlie ended the shot, then started recording again to create a new clip.

"Back up a bit," said Aggie, flapping her hands. "I want to try something."

Charlie did as she was asked, zooming out a little to take in as much of the tree as possible.

"Five, four, three..."

She gave another nod, but this time Aggie didn't smile.

"The legend states that the witch's wooden leg sprouted into a monstrous oak tree," she said, gesturing behind her. "Which grew so quickly that it demolished the church."

Charlie took a moment to pan up the full height of the tree, through the missing roof and into the canopy above. The branches seemed even more agitated than they had a moment ago, sweeping back and forth as if trying to warn them. She swallowed another unpleasant thump of fear, returning the shot earthwards.

"Here's where it gets really interesting," said Matt. "And this is what we're here to prove today. The witch lies beneath us, trapped in an eternal sleep. But there is a way to wake her."

"There's a way to bring her back," said Aggie, her eyes wild.

There were more flies here than ever, five or six of them crawling on Charlie's hands as she fought to keep the camera steady. She could see them boiling in the air over her friends' heads.

"All you have to do to release the witch from her slumber, to set her free," said Matt, "is walk around the tree three times."

"Has anyone ever been brave enough to try it?" asked Aggie.

"Not that I know of," added Matt, and Charlie had to agree with him, because in all the videos she'd seen of this place, not one person had been stupid enough to walk around the oak more than twice.

"Are we brave enough to try it?" said Aggie.

Don't, Charlie thought, as if it would make any difference at all.

"I don't know," said Matt. "Are we?"

He turned to the camera.

"What do you think?"

Charlie thought he was asking her, but she couldn't work her dry tongue into a reply. In the end, though, it turned out he wasn't.

"I think they're saying yes," he said to Aggie.

"They're definitely saying yes," she replied. "Together?"

Matt held out a hand and Aggie took it. Then they glanced at Charlie.

"You can come with us," said Matt. "Let's go."

They set off like lovers, hand in hand, Matt almost skipping as they walked around the ancient tree. They circled the trunk once before stopping.

"Cut," said Aggie, glaring at Charlie. "You have to follow us around or it won't work."

"I don't want to," said Charlie, her voice small. She lowered the camera but kept it running. "What if it's... you know?"

They didn't know, according to their frowns.

"What if it's *true*?"

Matt laughed. Aggie didn't.

"I mean, I know it's not true," Charlie went on, the heat blazing in her cheeks. "But..."

She didn't have anything to add. She lifted the camera again.

"Sorry," she said.

"Okay, let's try that again," said Aggie. "Ready?"

Charlie nodded, counting down.

"Are we brave enough to try it?" Aggie said.

"I don't know. Are we? What do you think?"

I think something bad is about to happen, Charlie answered him silently.

"You can come with us. Let's do it!"

They set off again, although this time they weren't holding hands. Charlie sucked in air as she followed them, doing her best to keep them in the viewscreen as she struggled on the uneven ground. She passed the door to the bell tower as she went, cold air reaching out and running its fingers down her cheek. There was a sound from inside like somebody humming and her skin shuddered so hard she almost sloughed it off in one go.

It's just your imagination, she told herself. *It's not real.*

"One!" yelled Aggie as they reached the starting point. She set off on the second lap without stopping, faster now, fast enough that Charlie had to trot to keep up. She was already dizzy, the church seeming to sway around her, the trees overhead in a frenzy.

Aggie and Matt were already out of sight by the time Charlie had reached the back of the tree again, but this time she didn't hurry to catch them. Instead, she found herself stopping beside that rectangle of darkness that led into the bell tower, ensnared by the same inhuman hum that seemed to come from inside.

"Two!" yelled Aggie, as if from a million miles away. "Charlie? For fuck's sake."

Aggie traipsed back the way she'd come, planting her hands on her hips as she scowled at Charlie.

"Uh, hello? Anytime today, mate."

Charlie didn't reply, angling the camera towards the door of the bell tower.

"What?" snapped Aggie.

"What is it?" added Matt, as he walked up to her.

"You don't hear that?" she replied, just a whisper. "The humming?"

Even as she said it, she realised it wasn't a human voice. It was an insect hum, a swarm of buzzing flies. There had to have been thousands of them to make that noise. Tens of thousands.

It was still too dark to see what sat in the tower—too dark for human eyes, anyway. Charlie angled the camera, using the zoom to float through the door. She heard the click and whirr of the autofocus as it struggled to find something, the viewfinder blurring, then clearing, blurring and clearing, and finally clicking home.

A man stared at her from the floor of the tower, his eyes inky black pits in his head, his mouth open in a silent scream. He, like the witch, had been buried alive in the dirt, although in his case, it was up to the neck. He looked like he'd been swallowed almost whole.

It was as though somebody had wrapped Charlie in a frozen blanket, the sudden chill paralysing her. All she could do was stand there, staring at the image on the little screen of the camera, waiting for a scream to tear its way out of the man's gaping mouth—or from her own.

In the end, it was Aggie who broke the silence.

"Fuck! Fuck! Is that..."

The click of her torch, scattering the shadows of the bell tower like they were crows, revealing the dead man in sickening detail.

Because there was no doubt at all now that he was dead.

For one, he had no eyes. The sockets were empty other than what might have been a handful of black pebbles collected in the drooping hollows. His skin was parchment pale and streaked with dirt, a crust of crimson around the ragged mess of his throat.

He hadn't been buried up to the neck, Charlie realised. The head had been cut from its shoulders and planted on a bed of loosened soil. Even as she watched, a beetle scurried up from the ravaged flesh and vanished into the mouth, hiding itself amongst yellow teeth and yet more stones.

"Fuck me," Matt said again, retreating. "He's fucking *dead*."

"You think?" said Aggie, bending down to get a better look. "You getting this, Charlie?"

Charlie felt numb, as if her own head had been removed.

"Hey!"

Aggie stood up and pulled the camera from Charlie's hands, almost garrotting her with the strap. She aimed the lens at the head, zooming in.

"This has never been seen before," she said. "This is exclusive to *Paranormal Norfolk*, guys. A dead body beneath the witch's tree. Look at it."

"Aggie," said Charlie. "Leave it, please."

Aggie swept the camera back, the lens flashing in a shaft of sunlight. She looked ecstatic.

"Even our camera crew are shocked," she said. "They can't believe what they just found."

"Aggie," yelled Matt. He'd retreated to the far end of the church. "Come on, we can't be here. What if—"

He was cut off by the crack of a branch from outside the church, another explosion of wings. Three or four enormous magpies tore into the trees, blistering the quiet with their cries.

The adrenaline reminded Charlie's legs what they were supposed to be doing, and she staggered away, one shoulder thumping into the witch's tree and jarring her spine. She broke into a jog as she neared the towering archway they'd entered through, Matt waiting for her there. He took her arm in both hands as soon as she was close enough to touch.

"That wasn't real," he said. "That can't have been real."

Another branch cracked nearby, the sound of somebody walking fast on the other side of the wall. Charlie's blood was boiling, her head ringing as if the bell still tolled in the crumbling tower. She couldn't see anything through the flint walls, past the tangled mess of the woods.

"Aggie!" yelled Matt. "Fuck this, I'm going."

He bolted down the path until the trees swallowed him. Charlie hesitated, torn between her fear and her need to make this all okay, to find sense in the insanity, to realise that it was a joke, or a hoax, or a trick that Aggie and Matt had set up just so they could catch her reaction on film.

The footsteps crunched louder, and a woman ran out from behind the crumbling wall of the church.

Not a woman, thought Charlie. *A witch.*

Because who else could it be—her ancient face sagging beneath a mop of grey hair, her mouth too wide, not a single tooth in her red-raw gums, her eyes as dead as the man they'd found in the tower—and that was all Charlie had time to think as the woman ploughed towards her, grunting hard, her legs like pistons beneath the filthy fabric of her dress, her too-long arm raised like a club.

"No!" Charlie said.

The witch reached her, carrying the stench of the grave, the reek of death, grunting like a boar as she swung her arm through the air.

The punch struck Charlie on the side of her head and the world shattered into endless pieces. She didn't know if she had fallen, didn't know if she was still alive, because there was no pain, just an awful disconnect, a spiralling kaleidoscope of light and dark that made her feel as though she was spinning through a void.

Move, she screamed at herself. *Move!*

Because if she didn't, she was going to die here, and the trees were going to feast on her.

She pushed down with her hand, grabbing a fistful of dirt, grounding herself. She blinked the forest back into focus, her vision shuddering like old VHS tapes. She was on the ground, the archway of the church right in front of her, the trees shaking themselves into a frenzy overhead, that infernal bell still ringing in her skull.

The witch was a spectre who flitted through the dark interior of the church, whose laughter seemed to rise even over the roar of blood in Charlie's ears. She vanished into the shadows behind the tree, and a second later a scream howled its way from the church.

Move, Aggie! Charlie called out inside her head, too weak to shout. *Run!*

She thought Aggie had heard her, because her friend lurched out from behind the tree, her face contorted by terror. She reached for Charlie as she ran, and even though she was too far away to touch, Charlie reached back.

As if she'd been tied to the end of a string, Aggie jerked backwards, vanishing in less time than it took Charlie to open her mouth and cry her name.

She staggered back into sight, her hands to her face, blood pouring from her nose. Then she was yanked back again.

This time, she fell silent.

No, no, no.

The witch stepped out from behind the tree, cocking her head like a dog and studying Charlie with those sagging, lifeless eyes. Her mouth fell open, and even though her voice was like the gentle scratch of a fingernail, it still carried.

"I see you."

The witch lifted her head as if to howl at the sky, then crumpled into nothing, burrowing herself feet first into the muck and the dirt, vanishing in the blink of an eye.

Charlie counted her breaths, waiting for the witch to accordion herself from the soil right next to her, to worm her way free. But there was just the empty forest, and the wild call of the crows.

She took her chance, pushing herself onto her hands and knees for all of a second before her brain gave in. A fireworks show of sparks lit up the forest like fairy lights, and with a final silent plea, Charlie fell into the dark.

CHAPTER ONE

"You sure you're ready for this, mate?"

DC Kate Savage stood in the cramped bedroom of her flat, watching her boyfriend Aaron Duke groan his way out of bed.

Not boyfriend, she reminded herself, the way she'd had to do every single day for the last few months, ever since he'd popped the question in the back of a burning lorry.

Fiancé.

Savage lifted her left hand, seeing the little ring that circled her finger. The diamond—quite possibly the smallest one she had ever seen, although she couldn't have cared less—winked at her, reflecting the soft glow of the morning light that filtered through the net curtains.

"Yeah," said Duke, stretching himself to his full height, his head knocking the paper lampshade and making it swing. He reached up and steadied it, and Savage could see the way his hands trembled. They never had before the Jack Valentine case, but then almost dying had a funny way of messing with your neurology.

She knew that well enough herself.

Duke smiled at her, one side of his beard still patchy where the hair had been scorched away. The burns on his cheek had healed, but there was a scar an inch or so beneath his right eye from the piece of shrapnel that had almost blinded him. The eyebrow on that side of his face still hadn't grown back, which—weirdly—was the thing he was most upset about.

He saw her looking.

"Anything?"

"No, sorry," she said, standing on her tiptoes and running her fingers along the smooth skin of his brow. "Still as bare as a baby's bottom."

Duke pouted, but only for as long as it took her to plant a kiss on his lips. She knew it was just her imagination, but she could still taste smoke on his skin, and she was pulled back to that night in the field with such vertiginous force that she could have been on a roller coaster. She felt her stomach buckle, and Duke wrapped his arms around her waist, squeezing the horror from her, bringing her back.

"I'm fine," he said. "We're fine. It's all fine."

And before she could reply, he lifted her off the ground and spun her around so fast the laughter exploded out of her. He dropped her down, and she slapped him gently on the shoulder.

"You'll put your back out," she said.

"You're not heavy enough for that, Kate. You're like a chicken."

"A *chicken*?"

He grinned that enormous grin again, pulling off his T-shirt to reveal his chiselled torso. He'd only just been given the all-clear to return, and the delay had nothing to do with his physical state. He'd been in the gym almost every day since he'd been released from hospital. It was the psychiatrist who had held back from signing the paperwork, and Savage wasn't sure why. As close as they were, Duke still hadn't spoken much about that night in the lorry.

About the explosion that had almost ended him.

"I'm good to go," he said, seeing the doubt in her expression. "I'm excited to be back. I miss it."

She nodded, although part of her felt like barricading the door so he couldn't leave, so he wouldn't be in danger again.

"Besides, I have to be there today. They're filming."

Savage laughed.

"I still can't believe you agreed to that," she said as Duke opened the wardrobe. "I don't know why anyone would want a film crew following them around all day."

"That's the price of being famous," he said, slipping into a shirt.

"You're not famous," said Savage. "You were on the news one time."

"Yeah, for like a month."

"A week, if that."

"I was on BBC Breakfast!" he declared. "They called me Britain's bravest copper, remember?"

"I haven't forgotten, Aaron. You printed off a screenshot and framed it. I see it every time I make a bloody cup of tea."

He walked over and kissed her on the forehead.

"You'd have done the same, if you were Britain's bravest copper."

She slapped him again, dodging another kiss.

"I'm going to put the kettle on. You focus on getting dressed. Last thing you want is to trip over your own feet and lose your other eyebrow."

"Ouch!" he said as she walked out of the bedroom. "Low blow, Kate."

She made her way down the corridor into the microscopic kitchen, glancing at the photo that had been mounted over the sink. Duke sat on the sofa opposite Sally Nugent and Jon Kay, dressed in uniform and still wearing a bandage around his head. Beneath them was the caption, *Is This Britain's Bravest Copper?*

As much as she hated to admit it, the explosion *had* made him a little famous. He'd been on several news reports after the explosion, and the invite from the BBC had happened a month or so later. It had been a bit of a car crash, in all honesty, because Duke had been so starstruck that he'd forgotten how to talk, spending most of the interview grinning at the camera like an idiot and grunting the occasional answer to their increasingly desperate questions.

Which made it all the more surprising that Channel 5 had approached him last month about a TV show following his journey back to work.

Savage filled the kettle, studying the photo as she waited for the water to boil. She was proud of him, of course, but all the picture really did was remind her how close she had come to losing him.

And how dangerous the job really was.

Because *she'd* almost died in that explosion too. She could still feel the blistering heat of it, the fist of smoke down her throat, the nightmare of what Jack Valentine had wanted them to do to each other.

It had taken her a while to go back to work too.

But it was like her granddad had always said. *The job is the job is the job.*

Everyone goes back eventually.

"How do I look?" asked Duke from behind her, and she

turned to see him standing in the doorway. The scar on his face caught the light the same way the diamond in her ring did, a reminder that horrendous pressure wasn't always a bad thing, that it could make something beautiful.

"You look like Britain's bravest copper," she told him, straightening his collar.

She picked up a Biro from the top of the fridge, holding it up.

"But let me draw that eyebrow back on before you leave, yeah?"

CHAPTER TWO

DCI Robert Kett was midway through one of the longest yawns of his life as he steered his Volvo through the gates of Norfolk Constabulary's headquarters, and because of this he almost didn't spot the van that was parked in the middle of the road. He slammed on the brakes and snapped his mouth shut so fast he caught the tip of his tongue between his teeth, muttering beneath his breath as the car shuddered to a halt.

"Come on," he said quietly, trying to work up another yawn to replace the one he'd lost. It had been a long night, both Evie and Moira full of cold and dosed up on Calpol to the point where they'd been wandering the house like zombies. He'd finally got to sleep just after two, and the bastard summer sun had woken him less than three hours later.

The vehicle in front wasn't moving, and Kett pipped the horn as gently as his mood would let him. He wound down the window, the heat rolling in even though it wasn't even nine yet. The van was bright yellow, a red number five painted on the back, enough exhaust pouring out to catch in his throat. He leaned out as far as his permanently sore spine would let him.

"Hey, can you drive on?"

An IRV pulled up behind him, idling there. Kett pipped the horn again, longer this time. He unclipped his seatbelt and was reaching for the handle when the driver's door of the van opened and a man jumped out.

He was in his early thirties, with a shaggy blond beard and a yellow cap that perfectly matched the colour of the van—worn backwards, forcing himself to lift a hand to his forehead to cut out the sun. He was wearing a green T-shirt and brown shorts that both looked like they belonged to somebody twice as big. He waved at Kett as he walked over, pulling off a pair of Oakley sunglasses.

"Alright?" he said as he reached Kett's car. Even though he'd only spoken a single word, the Australian accent was unmistakeable.

"Hi," said Kett. "You lost?"

"I don't think so, mate. Channel 5?"

"No, this is the police station," said Kett.

"*We're* Channel 5," the man went on, lifting his cap so he could wipe the sweat from his brow. "So this is the police station?"

Kett rubbed his own brow, pinching the bridge of his nose.

"Yeah, this is the police station. And you're in the way."

"No, we're Channel 5," the man said, with absolutely no indication that he was joking. He started walking away, heading past the van towards the main building. "This is the place. You wanna grab the gear, Milo?"

"Hey," Kett called after him. "You can't park there."

The man looked back, one eyebrow raised.

"We're from the TV, mate," he said, as if that explained everything.

Kett's patience was long gone.

"I couldn't care less if you were a Tellytubby, *mate*. Can you move your bloody van so the rest of us can go to work?"

The man looked like he was going to keep arguing, but a quick blast of the siren from the IRV behind Kett's Volvo made him reconsider. The guy rolled his eyes as he clambered back into the van, and a few seconds later it trundled down the road towards the hulking main building. There, it pulled across three disabled parking bays before the driver cut the engine.

"Unbelievable," said Kett, driving past the van and pulling into an empty parking space.

He waited for another monstrous yawn to pass before exiting the car, shuffling with no great enthusiasm across the car park. By the time he'd reached the van, all its doors were open, and the young man had been joined by three other people.

One was another young guy, this one dressed—inexplicably, given the heat—in a brown corduroy suit and a knitted hat. The other was an even younger woman, barely into her twenties, who was wearing what looked like a striped bathing suit from Victorian times. The third was a slim older woman who wore an expensive beige trouser suit, her short hair dyed blonde and immaculately styled. There was something familiar about her. She was studying her phone as Kett approached, oblivious to him until he cleared his throat.

"Morning," he said when she looked up.

She peered at him over a slim pair of glasses in a way that made him feel like he was a kid about to be scolded by a teacher.

"Hello?" she said in a voice that reminded him of Anne Robinson.

"Hi," he said, gesturing to the van with both hands. "Top marks for parking. Any chance I could see your disabled badge?"

The woman went back to her phone like Kett hadn't said a word. The young man he'd spoken to earlier took her place, sweating profusely.

"Just unloading, mate, we won't be a second."

"That's really not—"

"If somebody comes, we'll move up," he went on. "Please, give us a couple of minutes."

He leaned in, nodding towards the older woman and continuing in a whisper.

"I'll get my arse chewed off if we have to move."

"That sounds... painful," said Kett. "Go on then, but make it quick."

The young man grinned.

"I'm Josh, by the way," he said. He spun on his heels and ran towards the back of the van.

"What are you guys doing here, anyway?" Kett called after him.

Things had been pretty quiet across the county since February, and the two accidental deaths and spate of farm burglaries they'd had this week certainly weren't newsworthy.

Nobody answered, the trio of younger people hustling at the back doors and the older woman lost in her phone.

"Just hanging out, taking up the disabled spaces, browsing Facebook," Kett went on.

Still nothing.

"Right," he said. "Lovely chatting to you."

He made his way to the main entrance, pushing through

the doors to see that there was already a small crowd waiting in reception. A couple of people looked up, dismissing him with a glance. He nodded politely as he walked to the desk, greeting Shelley with another yawn that seemed to take about forty minutes to run its course.

"Congratulations," she said. "Your tonsils look fine, you've passed your examination."

"God, sorry," he said, rubbing his mouth. "Bad night."

"Yeah, I heard there were some horrible little oiks causing trouble," said Shelley. "Drunk off their faces, weren't they?"

Kett laughed.

"I don't think they were drunk, but they were definitely causing trouble. One of them threw up in my bed."

Shelley's eyes widened.

"I wasn't on duty last night," he said with a laugh. "Kids are sick."

She laughed too, a noise like a diesel engine coming to life. Kett nodded back to the doors where the yellow van could be seen.

"You know why there's a TV crew here?"

"Yeah," said Shelley. "For your mate."

Kett shook his head.

"Aaron," she said. "They're doing a show about Britain's bravest copper."

"What?" he said. "*Duke*?"

Shelley nodded.

"I thought all that was over," said Kett. "I mean, he's hardly Britain's bravest copper, is he? He was in the back of a lorry, it was sheer luck that the doors blew open when it exploded."

Shelley raised an eyebrow.

"Jealous?"

"No!" he exclaimed, although there was an unpleasant heat creeping up his neck. In all the times he'd almost died on the job, all the cases he'd solved, even after the King Rat nightmare, he'd never once had a TV crew show up to document his life.

"You don't look like him though, do you?" said Shelley, reading his mind. She flashed a wicked smile. "He's got a face for TV. Yours is more for radio."

"I'm not bloody jealous!" he said.

He rapped his knuckles on the desk to end the conversation, making it halfway to the door before Shelley called him back.

"You couldn't show them through, could you?"

He blew out a sigh and rolled his eyes, but stood his ground until the crew made their way through the door. The young man with the cap was first, carrying a metal crate that looked like it weighed a couple of tonnes. He slogged it past the goggle-eyed crowd, beads of sweat pattering onto the floor and marking a trail for the other members of the team to follow.

"Can you..." he wheezed, nodding to the door next to Kett. "Can you... please..."

Kett took pity on him, opening the internal door and letting him through. The other guy followed, carrying a pair of duffel bags, and behind him came the young woman in the bathing suit, who shouldered an assortment of poles and cables. She gave Kett a nervous look as she followed her colleagues.

"So, you're here for Duke?" he asked as he overtook them.

"That's what they tell me," answered Josh, gurning with the weight of the box. "Britain's best-looking copper."

"Best looking?" said Kett. "I thought he was the bravest?"

"Can't it be both?" said the young woman.

"Or neither," muttered Kett as they reached the corridor that led to the Major Investigation Team's offices. "I can't help but think you're going to be disappointed. Most of what goes on here is incredibly boring."

"Yeah, we worked on *Night Cops*," said the woman. "There's a lot more sitting around drinking tea and eating biscuits than you'd think."

"Right," said Kett, frowning. "I mean, it's not *all* drinking tea and eating biscuits. But it's not all drama either."

He reached the door, resting a hand on it and looking at the film crew.

"It's just never as exciting as you think it's going to be."

And with that, he pushed open the door to reveal a scene of pure chaos.

CHAPTER THREE

All hell had broken loose in the middle of the MIT bullpen—a hurricane of noise and panic that Kett couldn't make head nor tail of.

In the middle of the room, DI Peter Porter stood on a desk with his jacket in his hands, his face red with effort and streaked with sweat. He was yelling obscenities at the ceiling like a drunkard. Next to him, and doing her best to hold the desk so that it didn't tip over, was DC Savage.

"Pete, careful!" she screamed. "You're going to break your neck!"

"*I'm* going to break your bloody neck!" roared a voice from the direction of the Superintendent's office.

Colin Clare stood in the open door, glaring out from the shadows like the hunchback of Notre Dame and flapping his hands wildly.

He wasn't wearing any trousers.

"Bloody get it."

"Uh..." said Kett, whose vocabulary had deserted him.

PC Felicity Niven was by the photocopier, literally

ripping up a loaf of bread. She was cackling like a demented goose as she threw fistfuls of crumbs into the air.

Josh pushed his way past Kett, dumping the heavy box on the floor with a thud.

"What the hell is going on?" he asked.

"Uh..." was all Kett could think to say as he tried to make sense of what he was seeing.

His eyes drifted to the other side of the room, where DS Alison Spalding crouched beneath another desk, her eyes wild with panic. She clutched a pencil in one hand, jabbing it wildly like it was a spear.

"Uh..." Kett said for a third time.

Josh had opened the box and was removing an enormous camera. Before Kett could tell him to stop, he heard his name being bellowed by the Super.

"Kett! Don't just stand there tossing yourself off, get in and help!"

"Help with what?" he asked as he jogged into the middle of the room, seeing Porter waving his jacket in the air, Savage shouting warnings, PC Niven hurling chunks of Hovis wholemeal over her head, Spalding jabbing at ghosts. "You've all gone bloody mad."

"With that fucking thing!" Clare roared, and as if he'd summoned it, a gargantuan seagull dropped down from one of the ceiling lights. It dived earthwards, its wingspan making it look more like a pterodactyl than a bird as it flapped towards Porter.

The big DI screamed like a twelve-year-old girl and launched himself from the desk, tipping it over in the process and almost crushing Savage. He hit the floor and fell onto his hands and knees, screaming again as the gull landed on his back.

"Catch it, you tosser, don't mate with it!" Clare bellowed.

The seagull strutted onto Porter's shoulders, pecking at his head and forcing his screams up an octave. It flapped its wings, creating a hurricane of papers. Niven ran over, lobbing slices of bread that all seemed to hit Porter in the face.

"You can't catch it with your arse cheeks, Porter!" Clare shouted. "Turn around!"

"This is amazing," said Josh as he moved forward, the camera on his shoulder.

"You really shouldn't, uh..." Kett started, then he almost screamed himself as the gull launched itself back into the air, wheeling towards him. It screeched loud enough to make his ears ring, swerving at the last minute and careening towards the window.

"It's not open!" yelled Niven, as if the gull might understand her. It didn't, striking the glass hard enough to crack it. It screeched again, propelling itself back towards Porter, who had only just managed to get back to his feet.

"Somebody bloody do something!" Clare screamed, sounding like a seagull himself.

"Out of the way," came a reply from the direction of the kitchen.

All eyes turned to the door as Duke burst through it, a binbag in his hands. He bounded across the room, almost tripping on the upturned desk but somehow managing to keep his balance.

The gull tried to turn around when it saw him, knocking the monitor off another desk and flapping towards the window again. But Duke threw himself at it, wrapping the giant bird in the binbag before collapsing to the floor. It struggled for all of ten seconds before falling still.

There was a pattering of applause as Duke struggled to his feet. Most of it was coming from the camera crew, who had managed to fully assemble their equipment in the time it had taken him to catch the gull. Only now did Duke seem to notice them, and he grinned as he held up the bag.

"Britain's bravest copper," he said.

"Brilliant!" yelled Josh as he lowered the camera. "Bloody TV gold that is, mate."

"What?" said Porter, stomping over. He was still holding his jacket and his hair looked like the gull had made a nest in it. "*He* didn't bloody do anything, *I* was the one who got it down from the ceiling."

"It only came down from the ceiling because it thought you were offering yourself to it," said Clare as he finally emerged from inside his office. "I've never known anyone to bend over for a seagull before."

"I didn't bend over, sir," said Porter. "I fell off the desk. It was *heroic*."

"Since when has falling off things been heroic?" said Clare. "Heroic would have been getting back up and catching it."

"I couldn't get up, sir, Flick was throwing bread in my face."

"Sorry, sir," said PC Niven, still holding the half-empty bag of Hovis. "I was trying to lure it."

"With my tossing lunch?" said Clare, fuming. "In all my days on the job, I've never seen such a bunch of useless toss-biscuits. Call yourself an elite crime-fighting force?"

"To be fair, sir," said Kett, "*you* didn't seem to be helping."

Clare eyeballed him like he was trying to psychically bring on an aneurism.

"I was coordinating," he growled. "Like a good boss. Trust me, if I'd wanted to catch the bloody thing, I'd have caught it. Seagulls and I have history, they don't fuck around with me."

"Right," said Kett. "And where are your trousers, sir?"

Everyone stared at Clare's knobbly knees.

"None of your business, you pervert," he said.

The gull seemed to have renewed its bid for freedom, the binbag trembling in Duke's hands.

"Get rid of the bastard thing, Constable," said Clare. "Now."

"I can do that, sir," Duke replied.

Josh had lifted his camera again, and Kett gently pushed it down. Clare angled his head towards them, narrowing his gaze.

"Why are you lot squirting toss over my bullpen?" he asked.

"Squirting *what*?" said the woman in the bathing suit, horrified.

"They're here for Duke, sir," said Savage, picking up the fallen desk. "The show. Channel 5."

"I have no idea what you're talking about," said Clare.

"Britain's bravest copper," said Duke as he struggled towards the window.

"Britain's *what*?" barked the Super.

"Britain's biggest dickhead," muttered Porter.

"Britain's best-looking copper," said the woman, eyeing Duke. "Right?"

"Britain's worst eyebrows," said Porter.

"It was all agreed to," said Josh. "Weeks ago."

"Oh, it was, was it?" said Clare, pointing a finger at him in a way that made him shrink back. "You know, the last time I saw a video camera, it was being inserted into my arsehole for a rectal examination. Shall we see if we can fit that one up yours?"

Josh paled considerably.

"So if you—"

Clare had to stop speaking because the phone in his office was ringing. He jabbed his finger towards each of the camera crew in turn, then at Kett, before spinning around and heading back.

"Wow, he's... something," said Josh. "He get out of bed on the wrong side this morning?"

"Try every morning," said Kett.

He walked to Savage, helping her lift the desk onto its legs.

"Some homecoming," he said, nodding to Duke, who was trying to open the window with one hand while holding the squirming bag in the other. "How's he doing?"

"Happy to be back, sir," said Savage, collecting the spilled papers. "I don't think he was expecting that, though."

"Bet he bloody was expecting it," said Porter, still fuming. "Bet he brought it with him just so he could catch it in front of the cameras."

"Yes, sir," said Savage, dryly. "He smuggled a seagull in beneath his hat, waited for the TV crew to arrive, then released it into the room."

"Where *did* it come from?" asked Kett.

"Somebody left the window open in the kitchen last night, it was in there when we arrived."

"Ate all the biscuits," said Porter. He ran a hand through his hair then pulled a face, studying his fingers. "I think it shat on my head."

Savage took a look, nodding.

"Yeah, it shat on your head, sir."

"For fuck's sake."

He stormed off towards the kitchen, and Kett turned his attention to Duke. The big PC was struggling with the seagull as it made a renewed bid for freedom. He finally managed to open the window, loosening the top of the bag.

As one, everyone in the room cried out.

"No!"

The seagull launched itself in an explosion of feathers, flying back into the bullpen and making a beeline for Porter. The camera was up again, the film crew chasing the bird across the room.

"Jesus Christ," said Kett. "Grab it!"

"There's no time," yelled Clare as he stormed from the office, buckling up his brown trousers. "Let somebody else do it. We have to move."

Porter *was* moving, screaming towards the main doors as the gull flapped behind him. Savage grabbed her jacket from her chair.

"Extreme crime, sir?" she asked.

"Doesn't get much more extreme than this," said the Super. "One dead, one injured, one missing. Let's go."

CHAPTER FOUR

THEY MOVED OUT IN A CONVOY, SAVAGE DRIVING AN IRV with Duke in the passenger seat and the Australian cameraman in the back. Kett followed in Porter's Mondeo, the DI doing his best to keep up as Savage cut through the heavy morning traffic. There was still a streak of bird shit on the back of his head.

Two members of the camera crew sat in the back of the Mondeo. One was the young woman in the striped bathing suit, who held a smaller camera in her trembling hands. The other was the older woman, who had finally put away her phone. Kett turned to face them, spotting Clare's gurning face through the windshield of the ancient Mercedes further down the road, and past that, the bright yellow van.

"Can you go any faster?" asked the older woman over the wail of the sirens. "You're going to lose them."

"I'm going plenty fast enough," said Porter, edging the speed up a little. "You should film me. I'm one of the best drivers on the Force."

The woman didn't look impressed. She seemed as if she was going to ask again, and Kett intervened.

"I didn't have time to introduce myself before," he said. "My name's DCI Robbie Kett."

"I know," said the older woman. "You're pretty legendary, Robbie."

"Not legendary enough for a TV show, though," he said, with a little more bitterness than he'd intended.

"He's just got the face for it," said the woman, looking through the windscreen to the car in front. "Some people have that star quality, some don't."

"I have it," said Porter.

"You have... *something*," said the woman, and Porter almost smiled before she finished. "In your hair."

"You're familiar too," Kett said to the woman. "You're on the telly, right?"

"Kelly Armstrong," she said. "Yeah, I'm on the telly. You've probably watched me on *Night Cops*."

"I don't tend to watch police stuff," said Kett.

"*Romance Island*?" said Kelly. Kett shook his head. "*Makeover Mums*? *Britain's Ugliest Postmen*?"

"Are you making these up?" said Kett.

"*Cake Wars*?" she said, increasingly desperate.

"Oh, yeah," said Kett. "That's the one where they bake, and then end the show with a food fight, right? My kids watch it."

She looked a little disappointed.

"Fun job," said Kett.

"You'd think so," she replied. "This is Megan, she's B-roll."

Megan smiled nervously.

"Josh, the Aussie, is up front. Milo is driving the van. I don't even know what he does."

"Sound," said Megan. "And coffee."

"Oh, yes, right."

Porter slowed down as they reached a roundabout, waiting for traffic to give way to the IRV in front before pulling out.

"Is this an emergency?" asked Kelly, leaning between the seats.

"Kind of," said Kett. "Why?"

"It's just he's going so *slow*. Can *you* drive?"

"I'm not going slow!" said Porter, accelerating a little harder than he needed to. "It's bloody ridiculous that you're here for him anyway. You know he only has one eyebrow?"

"It's part of his charm," said Kelly. "We want to give the public a hero, let them see how much danger the police face in their day-to-day life."

Porter actually blew a raspberry.

"Well, I'm sure you've already had this conversation with the Super," said Kett, "but there are only some things we can let you show. A lot of it is confidential. When we get there, I'm going to have to ask you all to remain in the cars until we establish what's going on."

"Obviously," said Kelly, pulling out her phone. "It's not my first rodeo, Robert. How long until we get there?"

"We'll get there when we get there," Kett told her, turning to the front and seeing Savage's IRV half a street ahead. "But it wouldn't kill you to go a *little* bit quicker, Pete."

IT TURNED out to be a longer drive than he'd expected, Savage leading them out of the city on the A47 before slowing down on the tangled weave of coastal roads. It felt utterly deserted out here, the fields baking in the sun, the trees crowned with canopies that seemed to touch the sky.

Everything shimmered in a heat haze that made the whole scene feel like a mirage, as if they were caught in the middle of a dream.

A dream that grew even more feverish when they turned a corner and drove into a sea of blue lights.

The quiet country lane was mobbed with emergency vehicles, four IRVs and two ambulances making it impossible to pass. Uniformed constables swarmed between them, shouting orders to each other.

"Wow," said Megan, aiming her camera out of the window.

"Stay here," Kett told them, exiting the car and closing the door behind him with enough force to punctuate his order. Porter slammed his door too.

"Want me to lock them in, sir?"

Kett shook his head, looking back as Clare's Mercedes pulled onto the street. The Super was honking his horn like an ungifted kid blowing a trumpet in a school orchestra, his eyes like pickled eggs through the windscreen. He parked up behind the Mondeo and got out, using his sleeve to wipe the sweat from his brow.

"Where is it?" he asked.

Kett wasn't sure what he was talking about, but fortunately Savage bounded over.

"Local coppers say there's a teenage girl in the ambulance, sir, and a boy somewhere too. There's a body in the woods, over by the church. One other girl missing."

She frowned.

"They were talking about a witch."

"A *what*?" said Clare.

"A witch, sir," said Savage. "This place, I think it's the witch's tree."

"I don't understand a single piece of toss that's coming

out of your mouth, Kate," said Clare. "You and Kett, speak to the witnesses. We'll tackle the body."

"And the witch, sir?" asked Duke.

Clare ignored him, stomping into the dense woods that lined the side of the road. The Australian cameraman, Josh, had left the IRV, his camera mounted on his shoulder as he took in the street.

"Hey," Kett yelled at him. "Back in the car until we say otherwise."

"Just a bit of establishing footage," he said. "You won't even notice me."

Kett gave him a look and he held up his free hand, slinking back to the IRV.

"Watch out for seagulls, yeah?" he called out.

"I'll give *him* a bloody seagull," said Porter.

"Good comeback," Kett told him.

Porter disappeared into the bushes, then Duke, who fired a serious look back in case anyone was filming him.

"He's loving this, isn't he?" said Kett as he and Savage made their way towards the ambulance.

"A bit too much, sir," she replied.

They reached the first ambulance to find that it was empty, making their way past it to see that the doors of the second one were open. Two uniformed constables stood outside, one of whom looked very familiar.

"Malcolm!" said Savage, breaking into an enormous grin. "I wondered if you'd be here."

PC Malcolm Hook, who Kett hadn't seen since the Whip Crack case nearly four years ago, greeted them with a nod and a smile. The young officer hadn't changed, although he was a little broader in the shoulders and chest. The scar still sat on his face, right along the line of his cheekbone. Kett had never found out how he'd got it.

"Kate," he said. "Sorry, I was going to text you, but it's been mad."

"So I hear. One dead? One injured? One missing?"

Hook nodded.

"And one doing okay," he said.

"There's four of them?"

"Yeah."

Hook pointed a finger into the cluster of IRVs, and Kett noticed another car there, a battered Nissan Micra.

"I take it this is the injured one," said Kett, nodding through the back doors of the ambulance to the gurney. He couldn't see who lay in it, just their feet—no shoes, filthy socks. A paramedic stood beside the bed, scrolling through something on his phone.

"Yeah, sir," said Hook, scratching the scar on his face. "She's delirious, I think. Not making any sense. ID in the wallet says she's Charlene Ford, eighteen. Something gave her a nasty cut on the side of her head."

"She say what?" asked Kett.

Hook glanced into the ambulance, breathing out a long sigh.

"She says it was a witch," he said after a moment.

"Right," said Kett.

"This is the witch's tree, though, isn't it?" asked Savage. "I recognise it. Granddad brought me here a couple of times when I was a kid. Never managed to shake the feeling it gave me."

As if to prove the point, she shuddered.

"Oh, sorry," she said. "Didn't mean for that to happen."

"It's got an atmosphere for sure," said Hook, glancing into the woods. "The ruins of St Mary's. Not the kind of place you go for shits and giggles."

"What were they doing here?" asked Kett.

"Judging by the equipment we found up by the church, they were filming," said Hook. "Probably YouTubers. It's a popular spot."

"When did all this happen?"

"999 call came in just after eight-forty," said Hook, taking off his hat to smooth back his hair. "A guy called Matthew Kamau claimed he and his friends found a dead body and were attacked. They split up, he got lost in the woods. By the time he'd got back, one of his friends was unconscious, the other was gone."

"Did he say it was a witch as well?" asked Kett.

"I don't know, sir."

"Let's talk with him first."

Kett popped his lips for a few seconds, bracing himself. He realised Savage was looking at him, her face gaunt.

"Here we go again, sir," she said.

He nodded, waking past the ambulance into the sea of swirling blue.

"Here we go again."

CHAPTER FIVE

"Have I ever mentioned how much I hate the bastarding woods?" said Porter to nobody in particular.

The trees were doing their best to kill him, knotted branches snatching at his clothes, pulling at his hair, roots tangling his feet and making him trip not once, not twice, but *three* times as they walked away from the road. The only thing that made it bearable was that both Duke and the Superintendent seemed to be having the same trouble, both men tripping and slipping and jerking like puppets as the bushes got the better of them.

It was only for a few minutes, though, before the vegetation started to thin, the trees separating to reveal a rough path. It was dark beneath the ceiling of their entwined canopies, the birds quietened by the unbroken flood of obscenities that spewed from Clare's mouth. Something about this place made Porter break out in a sweat that had little to do with the heat of the morning.

He didn't just hate the woods. He was scared of them.

Get it together, you prat, he told himself. And he'd

almost done exactly that when he glanced up and saw something impossible.

It was a church, but only the ghost of one. The building was a ruin that nature had tried to mend, the stone supporting a roof made of branches and leaves. The archway that separated it from the forest was immense, maybe twenty-foot tall, and through it, Porter could make out a shadowy interior that promised nothing good. There were half a dozen coppers inside, clustered in the weak beams of sunlight that cut through the trees, but the sight of them brought little relief.

"What on Earth is this thing doing here?" asked Duke, his expression nervous.

"What do you mean, what is it doing?" spat Clare as he walked up to the archway. "Dancing a jig? Having a shit? It's not doing anything, it's a church."

But even he hesitated for a second before crossing that threshold, his face taut with worry. Porter commanded his legs to follow, but they didn't obey.

"Scared, sir?" asked Duke.

He shot the PC a look.

"*You're* scared, mate."

"I'm Britain's bravest copper," said Duke. "I'm not scared of anything." He frowned. "Except lorries. And explosions."

"I'm scared of your face," said Porter. "That missing eyebrow makes you look like an egg."

"At least I'm not scared of seagulls, sir," said Duke.

"I'm not bloody scared of seagulls," Porter snapped back. "I was screaming to distract it. I—"

"Porter! Duke! Get in here!"

Clare's yell made them both jump, a handful of crows scattering from the trees with chuckling caws. They bustled through the archway together, shoulder to shoulder. The ruin seemed even bigger inside than out, and Porter was surprised to see an enormous tree growing in the middle of it, pushing through the missing roof into the canopy overhead. More crows roosted there, waiting.

It seemed quieter here than it had in the woods, even though there were no windows and no doors to mute the sound from outside. The constables, gathered in the pockets of muted light as if it might provide safety, spoke to each other in whispers. The church felt like it was holding its breath.

Only Clare seemed brave enough to break the quiet.

"Where's the body?" he shouted from where he was standing by the tree. He leaned on its crooked trunk like he was ready to collapse.

A constable appeared from the back of the church, waving them on.

"Over here, sir," she said. "Careful, it's dark."

Clare set off, and Porter broke into a jog to catch them up. Somebody had stretched some tangled ribbons of police tape between the tree and the left-hand wall and he saw a camera lying on the dirt floor, a fuzzy microphone stuck to the top. Past the tree was a doorway that led into a pocket of absolute darkness. But there was life in there, Porter could hear it—the serenade of a thousand flies as they feasted on whatever sat in the shadows. He breathed in slowly, tasting death, feeling his stomach turn.

"Let there be light," said Clare, and it took the constable a moment to work out what he was saying. She pulled out her torch and clicked it on, aiming it through the open doorway.

"Forensics have been called, sir," she said. "They're on their way. They'll have a genny."

Duke retrieved his torch, and Porter pulled his own from his pocket. They stood either side of the Superintendent, peeling away every scrap of darkness to reveal the gift that had been left for them.

"Fuck me," said Porter, his stomach shifting. He put the back of his free hand to his mouth, belching acid.

"Is that a head?" asked Duke.

"No," said Clare. "It's an arse. An arse with a nose and a chin and ears. Of course it's a head, you moron."

The head belonged to a man, and it had been here for a while because there was a green shine on the skin that was almost metallic—the kind you sometimes saw when you opened a pack of bacon. The eyes had been removed, or eaten away by the birds, but there was something resting in the empty sockets.

Stones, Porter realised when he shifted his torch. There were more of them in his open mouth, past the yellow nubbins of his teeth.

"Urgh," he said, the sound rising from the very depths of him. He'd made scrambled eggs for him and Allie and Bobby that morning, and he was regretting every single bite.

The head had been severed with some ferocity, flaps of skin resting on a bed of churned soil. There was no sign of blood on the ground, but the man's scalp was thick with it, his hair clotted upright as if he'd used his own gore as hair gel. The butcher's shop smell of it was overpowered by something else, something that burned into Porter's sinuses.

"Brandy," said Clare, his voice quiet.

It was, Porter realised. It stank like a whole bottle of the stuff had been spilled here. It caught in his throat, made his eyes water so much he had to scrub away tears. He ducked down so that nobody would see him, laying his torch on the ground. He worked on a pair of latex gloves, then fished a pen from his pocket with his free hand. He slid the tip carefully into the dead man's mouth.

"Careful, Pete," said Clare. "I don't want you messing it up before forensics gets here."

The head joggled as Porter worked, the flaps of the empty eyes winking at him. He probed at the collection of pebbles inside until one of them popped free, landing on his outstretched hand. The little black orb wasn't a stone at all, the shape was too round, too perfect.

"I think it's a bean," he said.

"A bean?" said Duke, crowding in too close, almost knocking Porter through the door. His heart seemed to hit the top of his skull like a fairground hammer-ring and he pushed himself to his feet, using a shoulder to shunt the big PC back a little.

He pinched the bean between his thumb and forefinger and held it up. It was hard, uncooked.

"A bean," said Clare, leaning in so close that Porter could smell the coffee on his breath even over the reek of the brandy in the air.

"There's dozens of them in there," said Porter. "Hundreds, maybe. And in his eyes."

"His ears, too," said Duke, staring at the head. The PC shivered like somebody had sprayed him with cold water, dancing a little jig on the spot. "Oh shit, that was a bug. He's got bugs in his ears."

"Britain's bravest copper, eh?" said Porter, giving him a look.

"But they're *bugs*," hissed Duke.

Clare stepped back, rubbing his mouth. In the wavering light from the torches, his bloodshot eyes didn't look human.

"I want everybody out of here until forensics gets here,"

he said. "Jesus Christ. Every time I think it can't get any worse, the universe proves me wrong."

He patted his pockets, then turned to Duke.

"Get an evidence bag for that bean," he said. "Before Porter eats it."

Duke bounded off, crashing past the tree.

"Wasn't planning to eat it, sir," said Porter.

They both turned to the head, to its cap of dried blood, to its gaping sockets, to the millipede that crawled out from between those fat, brandy-drenched lips and into the puckered hole of its nostril. It was all too much, the church spinning around Porter like it had picked itself up from the forest floor and was lumbering away.

"Nope," he said quietly. "I'm going to see if Duke needs help."

"Carrying an evidence bag?" asked Clare.

"Yep."

He trotted past the tree, only taking a breath again when he'd reached the archway.

"We need everyone out of the church," he yelled.

There was a collective sigh of relief from the coppers as they filed past him, all but one looking anxiously over their shoulder before stepping into the relative safety of the woods. Porter chased them out, telling himself that he didn't need to glance back, promising himself that he wouldn't, because at the end of the day, it was just another body, just another dead man.

But as he walked away, the sensation of something following him—the image of that butchered head sprouting insect legs and scuttling across the dirt—was so strong that he literally couldn't stop himself from taking one last look back.

CHAPTER SIX

It took them a while to find the right police car in the swarm of vehicles, but when Kett leaned down and peered through the window of the IRV at the front of the pack, there was no denying this was the man they were looking for.

He was in his late teens, but his face bore a look of terror that belonged to a much younger person. His eyes were wide, his dark skin streaked with sweat. There was a smattering of acne scars hiding beneath his three-day stubble. He was tall, and he'd bent himself almost double in the back seat, his knees touching his chin. When he turned and saw Kett peering through the window, he unfolded like a coiled spring, as if he meant to jettison himself through the top of the car.

"Sorry," said Kett. "We didn't know where you were."

He opened the back door, and the kid scooted away from him. Kett held up his hands.

"You're not in any trouble. You're Matthew?"

The young man stared back like he didn't understand the question. Then, after a handful of seconds, he nodded.

"Matt," he said.

"You're the one who called us?"

He nodded.

"My name's Robbie, I'm a policeman," he said, although he didn't bother to pull out his warrant card. "This is Kate."

"Hey," said Savage, leaning past Kett's shoulder. "How are you doing?"

"Have you found her?" Matt asked. "Aggie? Have you found her?"

"Not yet," said Kett. "We'd just like to have a little chat first. You want to come out, or would you like us to come in? It'll be tight with the three of us."

Matt hesitated again, then eased himself along the seat. Kett offered him a hand and he took it, his palm sweaty. The boy was definitely tall, but it was hard to put a number on his exact height because of the way he stood—stooped, as if he was carrying an invisible man on his back. It was so pronounced that Kett wondered if he'd injured himself.

"Okay, Matt," said Kett. "I'd like you to tell us everything you remember. Start from the beginning, start with some names."

"I'm Matt," he said, looking between Kett and Savage. He was rubbing his hands together, trying to remove the stains on his fingers—what looked like dirt, and maybe blood. "Matt Kamau."

"Who were you here with today, Matt?" asked Kett.

"Agnes Clegg," he said. "Aggie. And Charlie."

"Charlene Ford?"

Matt frowned like he wasn't sure.

"I think so, yeah. I can't remember her surname. Is she okay?"

"You don't know her too well?" said Kett, ignoring his question.

"No, I do," he said. "I go to college with her. Went. We've just finished our exams. City College, in the city. Obviously."

He shook his head.

"Wouldn't be called City College if it wasn't in the city."

"You were all in classes together?" Kett asked.

"Yes, sir."

"Which ones?"

"Oh, uh..." Matt shook his head again, staring into the shivering branches overhead. "Like, media. And art. Charlie's not in the art one, just me and Aggie. And we've all finished now, obviously."

Kett nodded, taking in the young man's loose shirt, the beads around his neck and the friendship bracelet that was in danger of slipping off his skinny wrist. He wore beige combat trousers and battered Converse trainers. Kett had seen a million kids like him walking to and fro from the college.

"So why were you out here today, Matt?"

He looked embarrassed.

"You'll think it's stupid," he said.

"Try me."

"Aggie and I do this... it's like a TV show, but for YouTube. It's all paranormal stuff, all the stories of Norfolk."

He stopped to see if there would be a reaction, but Kett just waited.

"We're called *Paranormal Norfolk*, but it's, like, not just Norfolk. It's all of East Anglia, really."

"So you visit haunted places, do some filming, tell people the legend, that kind of thing?"

Matt nodded.

"Sort of like Norman Balls?"

"You know *Balls Knows It All*?" Matt asked, frowning.

"Oh yes," said Kett. "We know Norman."

"Those two are best friends," said Savage. "Right, sir?"

"Not best friends," said Kett. "But yours is the same kind of thing?"

"Yeah. It's stupid. It's just a bit of fun, and like practice for uni. Aggie's the one who believes it all, she likes all the creepiness, all the horror stuff. I just like..."

"Aggie," said Kett when he didn't finish. "And Charlene, Charlie, she's part of this?"

"No, not until today. We have another guy, Dougie, he usually does the camera stuff but his mum's sick. Aggie thought we could manage without him, but it's impossible. You need somebody to work the camera. I asked Charlie and she said she would help. She knows her stuff when it comes to cameras, and stuff."

He shook his head again like he couldn't believe what was coming out of his mouth.

"Sorry."

"You're doing great," said Kett. "So Charlie stepped in, you asked her this morning?"

"Last night," said Matt. "Afternoon, whatever. She always offers to help, and when Dougie said he couldn't do it I asked her. She said yeah."

Kett glanced past the IRV to the little Micra that had been abandoned by the side of the road.

"You drove out in that?"

"In Donkey, yeah," said Matt. "It's Aggie's car. Doesn't look like much but we've been everywhere in it."

His brow furrowed.

"You haven't found her?"

"We've only just got here," said Kett. "Don't worry, it

hasn't been long. But if we're going to work out where Aggie is, we need to know what happened. What time did you get here?"

"Like, a few minutes before eight?" he said. "Aggie made us leave a little earlier than usual. Light's always creepier in the morning, and you get mist and stuff. Atmosphere."

He took a stuttering breath, staring into the woods, still working compulsively at his hands.

"We parked up, got out, it's only a little walk to the woods. There's a church there, you seen it?"

"St Mary's?" asked Savage. "The ruins?"

"Yeah, it's... You've seen it?" he asked again.

"A long time ago," Savage told him. "There's a legend that goes with this place, isn't there? The witch."

It was like she'd slapped him. Matt recoiled so hard he bumped into the car.

"You know the legend?" asked Kett.

"Yeah," he said when he'd recovered. "There's a tree in the church, and everyone says it grew after a witch was buried alive there. But it's... it isn't *true*, is it?"

"Only if you believe it," said Kett. "You believe it?"

Matt opened his mouth, but only a low groan fell out.

"Tell us what you saw," said Kett. "You got to the church. What happened next?"

"We... uh, we started filming. We'd rehearsed, we knew what we were going to say. Charlie had the camera..."

He stared upwards, swallowing hard.

"We wanted to do the thing everyone says not to do. We wanted to wake her."

A magpie flew down from a tree, landing clumsily on the roof of the next car over. It studied Kett with eyes as black as beetle shells. He flapped his hands at it, but it didn't even flinch.

"It's part of the story," said Matt, eyeing the bird warily. "You walk around the tree three times and the witch wakes up. But it's not... It can't be real. And besides, we didn't even do it, we only went round twice, didn't we?"

He looked at Kett as if he might know the answer.

"You walked around the tree twice?" he asked. "Then what? What stopped you going round again?"

"Charlie," he said. "She saw something. There's a room at the back of the church, it used to be the stairs that led up the tower. No stairs anymore, it's just... just dark. And Charlie said she saw something, but we thought she was too scared to follow us around, until we looked, and..."

He seemed to stoop even lower.

"You see it?" he asked. "The head?"

The magpie made a chuckling sound that seemed far too loud for the quiet street. Matt couldn't take his eyes off it, like he saw something else sitting there, something impossible. Kett clapped his hands at the bird but it still didn't move.

"Fucking thing," he grumbled. "Kate, get rid of it."

Savage ran at it, waving her arms. The magpie hopped onto the roof of the next car, unimpressed.

"Go on!" she yelled as she chased after it. "Get!"

"The dead man," Kett said, bringing Matt back to the conversation. "It's just a head?"

"I don't know," said Matt, still watching Savage. "I couldn't see it. I didn't want to see it. I just..."

"You ran," said Kett.

Matt peeked at him for a second, then let his head drop.

"I thought they were running too," he said. "I thought they were behind me. I was going to the car, I thought they were coming too. I didn't even know they hadn't until I got here."

"You ran back to the road?" said Kett. "How long after you arrived did this happen?"

"Don't know," he said. "Twenty minutes, maybe?"

"You didn't see anything as you were running? Hear anything?"

Matt swallowed hard again.

"I heard *screams*," he said, just a whisper. "I didn't know if it was them."

"What did you do?"

"I went back," he said. "Of course I did. I'm not a... a coward. I went back."

"When?" asked Kett.

Savage was still weaving between the cars, the magpie hopping from roof to roof as it evaded her.

"What?" asked Matt.

"When did you go back?"

He shrugged his lanky shoulders.

"I got lost," he said, no conviction there at all. "I tried to find my way back, it just took me a while. It wasn't long."

"And what did you see when you got there?"

Matt opened his mouth to answer, but was cut off when the magpie landed on the IRV—close enough to touch. It opened its beak and released a long, chattering caw—one that was echoed a dozen times or more from the trees, a legion of invisible birds.

"Bugger off!" Kett yelled, slamming the palm of his hand on the roof and finally chasing it away. It soared gracefully into the canopy overhead, watching from a distance.

"Bloody thing's possessed," said Savage as she rejoined them.

It was the wrong thing to say. Matt's face seemed to wilt

like it was ready to fall off the bone. He shook his head again as if he could will time to reverse, magic himself back to the start of the day.

"What did you see?" asked Kett. "When you got back to the church."

"Just Charlie," he said. "She was unconscious, she had blood on her, like somebody had hit her."

"That's her blood?" asked Kett, nodding to the young man's hands.

He glanced at them like they belonged to somebody else.

"I just checked her," he said, panicking. "That's why it's there. I didn't touch her, just checked her heartbeat, that's all."

"You didn't see Aggie?"

Matt shook his head.

"You didn't see anyone else?"

His head continued to shake.

"Then what?"

"I called you," he said. "But I had to walk a bit; there's no signal here. It took me, like, fifteen minutes? I don't know. I called you, then I ran back. Charlie was awake, but she didn't know what was happening. I think she's... broken. I think that thing broke her."

"That *thing*?" said Kett. "What do you mean?"

Matt struggled, his mouth gaping. Above them, the magpie chuckled, and he turned his wide eyes to it, the expression of horror on his face like nothing Kett had ever seen.

"What do you mean, *thing*?" Kett asked again. "You don't think a person did this?"

"I don't know," said Matt, still staring at the bird. "I

don't know. But Charlie didn't say it was a person. She didn't say a man attacked her."

Kett waited for the inevitable.

"She said it was the witch."

"Charlie said those exact words?" Savage asked.

Matt nodded as his eyes crawled back to them, still not blinking.

"She said something else, too," he whispered. "She said she might have caught it on camera."

CHAPTER SEVEN

"I have no idea what's got into that bloody bird," said Savage after they'd helped Matt Kamau back into the IRV. The magpie was still perched in the branches above them, and she glared at it as they made their way back through the throng of vehicles. "They're fearless, aren't they, sir?"

"Won't be fearless after I've punted it into the woods," muttered Kett. "They're bad news, magpies. One for sorrow and all that. Wherever there's death, you find them. You ever noticed that?"

"Because there's death everywhere, sir," said Savage. "They're psychopomps."

"Psycho *what*?"

"Psychopomps. Magpies, crows, starlings too, I think. They ferry the souls of the dead from this world to the next."

"Christ, Kate. Next you'll be telling me you believe in witches."

She didn't contradict him, and he wasn't sure he blamed her. There was something about the quiet lane, this tunnel of dark light beneath the crest of the trees, the murmuring leaves and the chuckling birds, which made him believe that anything was possible. He felt the goose-bumps break out on his arms, an almost pleasant shiver of cold.

"Could have been worse, though, sir," said Savage, managing a smile.

"Yeah?"

"Yeah. Could have been a seagull."

Kett snorted, the laughter chasing away a little of the tension. They walked down the side of the ambulance to the open doors, looking in to see the paramedic tending to the girl in the bed.

"How's she doing?" asked Kett.

"She'll live," said the man. "But you're not getting anything out of her, I'm afraid. Had to sedate her. Just about to take her in."

"She say anything?"

"Nothing that made any sense," said the man, walking to the doors. "Goblins and ghoulies. Something gave her a nasty bump on the head. She may have a skull fracture, she certainly has a concussion. You mind?"

Kett stood back to let the man pull the door closed.

"Take care of her," he said, and the paramedic nodded.

"It's what we do."

"You want me to go with them?" Savage asked.

"No, not yet," said Kett. "Need you here. You know where the church is?"

"Over there somewhere, sir," she said, nodding into the trees that crowded the side of the road.

The words had barely left her mouth when Duke appeared thirty yards ahead, lumbering out of the vegetation like the famous video of Bigfoot. He brushed a collection of leaves from his beard before spotting them. Even from here, Kett could tell that he was rattled.

"Hey," the PC called out. "Just came for a bag."

"I've got some," said Savage. "You okay?"

"It's not great," he told her.

He waited for them to walk up. By the time they'd reached him, Kett spotted a familiar face among the throng of coppers. Josh was out of the car again, his camera on his shoulder and directed right at them. He was grinning, and when he caught Kett's eye, he actually winked.

"I am starting to really not like that guy," Kett grumbled.

He called out to a nearby constable, pointing at Josh.

"Make sure none of that lot go into the woods, okay?"

The PC nodded, heading off between the cars.

"You remember the way back?" he asked Duke.

"Sure," he said. He frowned. "I mean, *probably*."

It turned out they didn't need directions, because Clare was yelling. They followed his garbled voice through the bushes and around the stunted trunks until, almost like magic, the forest gave way to the ruins of a church. It was every bit something from a fairy tale, the remains of Sleeping Beauty's castle after it had been bound in thorns for a hundred years. Kett half expected to see a dragon stretch its wings from the ruined turret.

Instead, he found himself face-to-face with an ogre.

"Anything?" spat Clare from beneath the enormous archway of stone that led inside. He was literally dripping with sweat.

Porter stood a little further away from the crumbling building, staring miserably at his phone. There was no sign of anyone else, but Kett could hear voices from the trees—a serenade of coppers calling Aggie's name.

"There were three of them here this morning, sir," said

Kett, tripping on a long rope of bramble. "Matthew Kamau, Agnes..."

"Clegg, sir," said Savage.

"Clegg, that's right. And Charlie Ford. Charlie's the one in the ambulance. Matt's in a car. They drove out to make a video about the ruin. Matt told us Charlie found a body. A head, is that right?"

Clare nodded, discharging a monsoon of sweat from his face.

"He panicked, ran, left the two girls. By the time he'd come back, Charlie was unconscious. Paramedic thinks she was struck on the head. Aggie was gone. They got here just before eight, the attack happened about twenty minutes after that."

He checked his watch to see that it had passed ten.

"We're searching the woods," said Clare. "Chopper is inbound. If she's out here, we'll find her."

The Super threw a thumb over his shoulder, gesturing towards a tree that grew right in the middle of the old church. Just visible behind it was a coffin-sized rectangle of darkness.

"Body's over there," said Clare. "There's a lot of blood, so watch your feet."

"It's a head?" asked Kett.

Clare's mouth peeled open into a corpse-like smile.

"Why would I ruin the surprise?" he said.

Kett set off, crossing under the archway and feeling like he'd stepped inside a fridge—which didn't make any sense, he thought, because the building was completely open to the elements. He took a few steps and stopped, looking back.

"You happen to find a camera, sir? Matt said he spoke to Charlie, she said she caught her attacker on camera."

"It's there," said Clare. "By the tree. Wear gloves."

"Duh," said Kett when he moved off again, Savage and Duke by his side. "Obviously. You coming, Pete?"

"No, sir," said Porter. "I'd rather squirt piss into my own eyes than look at that thing again."

"Fair enough."

"That's why you don't get a TV show," said Duke.

"What was that, Aaron?" Porter called after them.

"Didn't say anything, sir," Duke shot back.

Kett crossed the dirt floor of the church, brittle branches snapping like bird bones beneath his feet. It had been an impressive building at one point, that much was clear. It was enormous.

"So, what do you know about this place?" he asked.

"Not much, sir," Savage replied. "It was built in the 1200s, I think. The tower, at least. This bit, the nave, is a couple of hundred years newer. It went to ruin in the seventeenth century."

"You're right, Kate, you barely know a thing."

Savage laughed quietly.

"And the story with the witch?" he said.

"Legend says a woman with a wooden leg was accused of being a witch," said Savage. "The villagers dragged her here and buried her alive."

"Nice," said Kett.

"Happened a lot back then," said Savage. "You just had to be a little different, and they'd call you a witch. Can't imagine it, can you? Being hauled into the woods and thrown into a hole in the ground."

"No," said Kett. "You can't."

Although he *could* imagine it, of course. It made him want to run from the church, from the woods, from the horrors of the past.

And those of the present.

"She had her revenge, though," said Savage, nodding up at the tree. "That thing grew from her wooden leg, pulled the church down around it."

"Yeah?"

"Yeah, sir. Either that, or a squirrel buried a nut there."

They'd reached the tree, and Kett stopped—partly because he'd spotted the little circle of police tape which held a camera, and partly because of the smell. It hit him like a bloodied fist, the butcher's shop stench of rotting meat. Flies landed on his face, on his hands, tasting him, and he did his best to shake them off, to spit them out.

Thousands more waited for him through the door at the end of the church. He could hear them.

"Body first?" he asked Savage. "Or the camera?"

"The camera, sir," she replied without hesitation. "Definitely the camera."

Whoever had tied the police tape to the tree had done such a poor job that most of it lay unspooled on the ground. Kett stepped over it, crouching to get a better look at what had been dropped there. Clare was right, there was a lot of blood. It had soaked into the heat-parched soil as if the ground had tried to drink it.

"You got gloves, Kate?"

"Here, sir," said Savage, handing some over.

He pulled them on, his sweaty fingers feeling four times bigger than the holes in the gloves.

"I bloody hate these things," he muttered.

"Should try putting them on with these, sir," said Duke, holding up his shovel-sized hands. "You should consider yourself lucky you've got child-like fingers."

"Got *what*?" spluttered Kett. "My hands are perfectly normal, thank you very much."

Duke didn't reply. Kett stared at his fingers.

"Aren't they?" he asked.

"The camera, sir," said Savage.

It was a Canon DSLR, not a cheap model. It lay on its back with the zoom lens and the fuzzy microphone both pointing skyward, the strap lying limp beside it. There was a splash of blood on the glass of the lens, more on the body of the camera.

As delicately as he could, Kett used a finger to tip the camera onto its base so that he could see the viewscreen. It was on, showing the wall of the church in remarkable detail, and above that, the shifting canopy of the woods. A message flashed on the screen.

"What does that say?" he said, patting his pockets in search of his glasses.

"Memory card full," said Duke.

"Must have kept filming after the attack," said Savage. "That's good news for us."

"How do we watch it?" said Kett, sliding his glasses on.

"That button, sir," said Savage, pointing past him to the little control panel on the top of the camera. "You have to turn the wheel thing to the play icon."

Kett prodded a button.

"Not that one, sir, the other one."

He tried again, hearing a tut from behind him.

"The wheel, sir."

"Can you do it, Kate?" he said.

She crouched next to him and clicked the dial around until the image on the screen changed. Two people stood maybe five yards away from where Kett was crouching now. He knew one of them, although it was hard to be sure on the tiny monitor, because Matt Kamau looked a lot less like a frightened teenager here. He seemed older, more confident, a big smile on his face.

Next to him was a teenage girl, her pale complexion almost perfectly contrasting Matt's darker skin. She didn't look like she had a hair out of place, but there was no smile on her face. She looked serious, maybe even pissed off.

"How do you make it go?" asked Kett.

"Go, sir?"

"You know, play the bloody thing."

"Oh, right."

Savage gently pressed one of the buttons and the footage played. The girl, it had to be Aggie, was waving her hands at the camera.

"*Back up a bit. I want to try something.*"

It was a ghost's voice, barely audible. Kett leaned in a little more as Charlie—he assumed it was Charlie behind the camera—zoomed out. There was the witch's tree in all its glory, and past that the corner of the door that led up to the bell tower.

"*Five, four, three...*" said Charlie.

A couple of beats of silence, then Aggie started to speak.

"*The legend states that the witch's wooden leg sprouted into a monstrous oak tree, which grew so quickly that it demolished the church.*"

The camera angled up for a moment before returning.

"*Here's where it gets really interesting,*" said Matt. "*And this is what we're here to prove today. The witch lies beneath us, trapped in an eternal sleep. But there is a way to wake her.*"

"*There's a way to bring her back,*" said Aggie.

"*All you have to do to release the witch from her slumber, to set her free,*" said Matt, "*is walk around the tree three times.*"

"*Has anyone ever been brave enough to try it?*" asked Aggie.

"*Not that I know of.*"

"*Are we brave enough to try it?*"

"*I don't know,*" said Matt. "*Are we? What do you think?*"

"Just walk round the bloody tree already," said Duke, loud enough to make Kett jump.

As if they'd heard him, the two presenters set off, hand in hand and skipping like kids. They were chatting to each other as they went. It was too quiet for Kett to make out what they were saying.

They circled the trunk once before stopping, and the footage suddenly dropped to the floor. Aggie was saying something to the camera, but Kett still couldn't hear it over the hum of the flies and the susurrations of the branches overhead.

"Can we turn it up?" he asked.

"Probably not," said Savage. "They're not great speakers."

The muffled chatter continued for a few seconds before Charlie lifted the camera again.

"*Sorry,*" Kett heard her say. He leaned in even closer, the flies crawling over his scalp, making it itch.

Matt and Aggie set off again, and this time the camera followed them. Kett held his breath as the door to the bell tower appeared, that slab of black revealing nothing at all. The three of them circled the tree once, immediately setting off on a second lap. They were moving faster, the footage jerky, frantic—until it suddenly stopped on the far side of the tree.

Kett squinted, seeing the edge of the door.

"That's where the body is?" he asked.

"The head, yeah," said Duke.

Kett heard more talking, Aggie's voice sounding annoyed. Charlie angled the camera so that the doorway filled the screen. She was either walking towards it or zooming in. Either way, it seemed as if the door was bleeding shadows. The sound of the flies on-screen mixed with the real-life hum, making Kett's skin crawl even more. The focus jarred, blurring then unblurring as it fought to find something to lock onto.

And just like that, a head peeled itself from the dark.

"There it is," said Kett.

A light clicked on, and the head was revealed in all of its sickening glory. Seeing it on the screen made it more bearable than the idea of seeing it for real, but only just. The screams of the three teenagers made the whole camera vibrate, the footage swaying from side to side.

Then it settled again, the shot returning to the doorway. Aggie's voice was clearer now.

"*This has never been seen before. This is exclusive to Paranormal Norfolk, guys. A dead body beneath the witch's tree. Look at it.*"

The camera swept around and Charlie appeared, her face full of terror.

"*Even our camera crew are shocked,*" said Aggie. "*They can't believe what they just found.*"

Kett could hear Matt shouting, his voice distant. The camera swung around in time to see him bolting past the tree, heading for the archway without so much as a look back. Charlie was following, colliding with the tree and almost falling. She'd almost caught up with Matt when Aggie turned the camera round again, passing the door to the bell tower. The camera pointed at the wall, moving up and down with the young woman's breaths.

"What's going on?" asked Kett, adjusting his glasses.

He was answered by another scream. The camera wheeled around, revealing the interior of the church again, the archway—only for a second, but long enough to see Charlie standing there, frozen in terror.

Long enough to see the woman who was running towards her.

"Wait," said Kett as the footage shifted again. "You catch that?"

He didn't know how to rewind it, so he kept watching, hearing another shrill scream from Aggie. She must have been wearing the camera around her neck because it was swinging wildly as she moved—revealing the wall, then Charlie, then the other wall, and back again. Kett wasn't sure if it was the pendulum effect of it that was making him nauseous, or the horror of what he was watching, because every time the camera reeled back towards Charlie, the woman was closer.

And there was no denying what she looked like.

She was old, a tangle of grey, unbrushed hair reaching the middle of her back. The clothes she wore looked like rags, like a hessian sack, and her feet were bare. Her arms seemed too long. They seemed to drag along the ground as she ran, as if she'd been stretched on the rack.

But she was moving fast, hurling herself towards Charlie.

The camera swung again, revealing the wall of the church.

"Come on," said Kett.

By the time it had returned, it was over. Charlie was on the ground, the witch—*not a witch*, Kett had to tell himself—standing over her.

"Christ," he said.

Aggie was still retreating, the viewfinder growing dark as she stepped through the door of the bell tower. Past the roar of blood in his ears, Kett could hear the young woman's frantic sobs, a word spoken over and over and over again.

"Please, please, please, please, please."

The camera settled, pointing out through the open door, right at the tree.

"Please, please, please, please, please."

Footsteps, barely audible.

A shape hurled itself through the door, so fast and so hard that Kett flinched. It was there for an instant—an ancient face, slack-jawed, hollow-eyed—then the camera lurched hard, a chaos of movement.

Aggie pushed past the woman, running, making it to the tree before suddenly flying backwards. The camera went black, but not because it was broken—Kett could just about see the cracked dirt floor, beads of light pearling at the edges of the shot.

A cry, one that ended far too abruptly with another sound that could have been a bone breaking.

Kett counted the seconds, eight of them that seemed to span aeons.

The camera jolted as if somebody was tugging on it, eventually tipping onto its back, revealing the frenzied trees overhead.

The woman stepped into view, but only just—that awful face staring at something Kett couldn't see.

She spoke in a voice made of dirt.

"I see you."

And just like that, she vanished off-screen.

"Holy shit," said Duke, leaning in so close that his words tickled Kett's ear.

"Quiet," Kett told him.

He waited, listening to the rustling trees, to the endless song of the flies. But the camera didn't move.

He leaned back on his haunches, his spine aching.

"That was a witch," said Duke, his hands in his hair.

"Don't be daft," Kett replied.

"You saw her, sir," the PC went on. "She looked just like a witch."

"I said pack it in, Aaron," said Kett. "You're a grown man, not a child. Kate, can you rewind it?"

"Sure, sir," said Savage, crouching next to him. "Where to?"

"The bit where we get a look at her," he said.

She gently tapped the wheel, and the footage scrubbed back—too far, because she had to fast-forward it a little before she found the bit she was looking for. She edged the shot forward frame by frame, everyone watching as the woman slid into the shot, as she bounded around the tree and into the bell tower, those too-long arms raised.

Here, she paused it.

The woman's face was blurred with movement, only adding to the horror of it. She had to be in her eighties, her cheeks and her jowls hanging so loose they looked like they might slide right off. Her mouth was an empty bag, her gums red raw and devoid of teeth. Her skin was pale and streaked with grime, as if she'd just crawled out of a grave.

Her eyes, though. They were the worst. They were nothing but black.

A magpie's eyes, thought Kett. They seemed to stare into the very heart of him.

He pulled out his phone and took a photo of the screen.

"That's enough," he said. "Turn it off."

Savage did as he asked. Kett struggled to his feet, Duke

helping him. The pain lanced through his back, into his hips, and he grit his teeth against it.

I am getting too old for this, he thought.

"What was that?" Savage asked as she brushed the dirt from her knees. "*Who* was that, I mean? She looked..."

She struggled for the word, finding one she'd already used that morning, speaking it quietly.

"Possessed."

"It's a witch," said Duke with a shrug.

"It's not a bloody witch," said Kett.

He turned away, looking up at the trees, taking a breath, repeating the same words inside his head in the hope he might believe them.

It's not a bloody witch.

CHAPTER EIGHT

Kett was girding himself to go and look at the dead man's head when he heard an odd grunting sound from outside the church. It was the kind of noise that usually came from Superintendent Clare, so when Kett turned to the archway he was surprised to see Emily Franklin, Norfolk Constabulary's young pathologist, lurch into sight. She was grunting because she was carrying one end of a diesel generator, her cheeks flushed with the effort of it. Holding up the other side was Cara Hay, the head of the forensic team.

"I can't... do it..." said Franklin.

"You guys need a hand?" asked Kett as he jogged over.

"Two... hands..." spluttered Franklin.

She gave up, lowering her side of the genny to the ground and shaking out her fingers. Hay continued to hold on to her end, waiting patiently.

"Bloody hell, that was hard work," Franklin said, throwing a stern glare at Porter, who stood nearby, still lost on his phone. "A dozen big, strong police officers down there and not one of them offered to help. You believe that?"

"We can carry it," said Kett.

"Thanks!"

Franklin jumped back and Kett took her end of the generator, heaving it up. Something crunched in his back and he let out a sound like a hippo falling down a hill, the generator slipping out of his hands.

"Nope," he said, bent almost double. "Duke, can you do it, mate?"

"That sounded bad," said Savage as Kett limped out of the way. It felt like somebody was holding a soldering iron to his spine, his nod sending electric pulses down his back. "You want to sit down, sir?"

"I'll be fine," he croaked. "Just my back."

"Happens when you get old, sir," said Duke.

"Not old," he said.

Duke waved Hay out of the way and hefted the generator up by himself, carrying it like it was an empty cardboard box.

"Where do you want it?" he called out.

"By the dead thing," said Franklin. "Wherever that is."

"I'll show you," said Kett, limping after him. "Haven't seen it yet, not in the flesh anyway."

"I've heard it's a doozy," said Franklin. "I love a jigsaw puzzle."

"Not much of a jigsaw," Kett told her as they passed the tree. "We've only got one piece."

"So far," said Franklin with a grin.

Duke laid the generator between the tree and the entrance to the bell tower. More people were walking through the archway, all of them dressed in white forensic overalls and carrying an assortment of equipment. Two held a rack of halogen lights, and they positioned them by the door. Duke started the genny for them, the stench of exhaust a welcome distraction from the reek of blood.

Kett positioned himself between Franklin and Hay as the field lights snapped on. In the harsh blaze, there was no hiding from what sat at the base of the crumbling tower. The head was so rotten it could have been mistaken for a Halloween prop, if it wasn't for the flies that feasted on it. There were so many of them that it was hard to see the man's features—what features he had left, that was. His eyes were missing, his nose partially eaten away, his lips and gums so withered that his yellow teeth looked enormous.

He stank, there was no doubt about that, but there was another smell too, something alcoholic.

"You beauty," said Franklin, almost in awe.

She ducked down in front of Kett.

"Well, it's certainly a head," she said, as if there was any doubt. "Hacked off with brute force. Look at the skin around the neck, it's been brutally torn. Big blade, probably an axe. Several swings."

Kett belched acid, doing his best not to move so that his back wouldn't twinge again. It was hard, because the flies were crawling on his face, trying to push themselves down the collar of his shirt and up his sleeves, treading the residue of the dead man all over him.

"Eyes have been removed," she went on, using what looked like a plastic spoon to pull away one drooping lid. "Sockets have been filled with something. Looks like..."

She delicately spooned one of the objects out.

"Black beans," she said.

"Beans?" asked Kett.

"Uh-huh. I'd say there's a dozen or so in each eye."

She used the spoon to explore the mouth.

"More in here, packed right back inside his throat."

"Christ," said Kett. "Why?"

"Maybe he really liked beans, sir," suggested Duke.

"I'm going to go out on a limb and say he didn't bean himself to death, Aaron," said Franklin, edging around the side of the corpse's head. "But I might be wrong. There are more beans inside his ears."

"Told you," said Duke, as if he'd solved the case.

"You smell that?" Franklin asked.

"Alcohol," said Savage. "Sweet."

"Brandy," said Franklin. "It's stronger down here. He's doused in it. Take a good whiff."

"No," said Kett. "How long has he been here?"

"That is a very difficult question," she said, positioning herself so she could examine the man's face. "He's been dead a while, I'm guessing between five and seven days. Looks longer because of the heat. The flies have been going nuts, he's full to bursting with eggs."

Kett felt his stomach contract, his back paying the price. He clenched his jaw, wondering where in the woods he'd be able to find some painkillers.

"He's probably in his forties, maybe early fifties. Caucasian. Judging by those teeth I'd guess he was a smoker, certainly didn't put much stock in oral hygiene. I can't see a lot of blood on the ground, so he was beheaded elsewhere and brought here. There is a lot of blood in his hair, though. Makes me think he was upside down when he was killed, or..."

She moved closer, muttering to herself.

"Or what?" asked Kett.

"No, it's something else," she said. "Come here, look at this."

Kett put an arm on the wall and bent as low as his back would let him. His shadow blocked the light, Franklin slapping his leg until he shuffled to the side. The man's hair was light brown, streaked with grey around the temples. There was so much blood that it allowed the hair to defy gravity, standing straight like a Mohican.

"See it?" said Franklin, pointing to his scalp.

"No," said Kett. "What am I looking at?"

"I see it," said Hay, leaning in. "That is very strange."

"Is that writing?" asked Savage, who peeked past Kett's elbow.

"Is what writing?" he said, putting on his glasses, then taking them off again when it didn't help.

"Do you want me to fetch you a magnifying glass, sir?" asked Savage. "And maybe a chair?"

"I'm fine!" he snapped. "I just can't... Oh, right."

He finally saw them, the angry lacerations that criss-crossed the man's head—almost lost in the thick roots of his hair.

"Not words," said Franklin. "But there's definitely a pattern. A shape."

Everyone stayed silent as she probed the man's hair with her spoon.

"Could be a series of circles, but there are crosses too, almost like a crucifix. I don't know. The cuts are as deep as they can be; I can see the skull in places. A very, very sharp blade. Probably a scalpel. Carefully done. I can't see any mistakes."

"How would you know?" asked Kett.

"I mean, there are no careless slips, no rough edges, no double lines. The crosses look identical in size and shape. Whoever did this took their time, and made it as clean as they could."

"But *why*?" said Kett.

"Why chop a man's head off, sir?" said Savage.

"Why fill his orifices with beans?" added Duke.

Kett didn't answer them. He stood straight, both hands rubbing his lower back.

"I'm going to let Cara do her thing," said Franklin. "After that, I'll get him to my table and shave him. Then we'll be able to see the wound for the trees."

"Thanks, Emily. Call us when you find anything."

He walked away, making it as far as the tree, before the pain in his back stopped him. He braced a hand on the cold trunk, sipping air.

"You sure you're okay, sir?" said Savage as she joined him. "You look like a ghost."

"I'm fine," he said again. "It'll pass. It always does."

Savage gave him a sympathetic look.

"Beans," said Duke as he walked over. "It's so weird."

"It is," said Kett. "But it obviously means something to the killer. They take out the eyes and replace them with beans, they put more in the ears and mouth. What does that tell you?"

Duke started to speak, but Kett cut him off.

"If you say he really liked beans again, Aaron, you're going to lose *your* head."

Duke pretended to zip his mouth shut. Savage blew out a long, slow breath.

"Feels like a control thing, sir," she said. "A sensory thing. The killer is using beans to blind their victim, to mute him, to deafen him."

"He's dead," said Duke. "He's already all those things."

"Maybe not in the mind of the killer, though. Maybe they think they're stopping him from seeing and hearing in the afterlife."

"Or from telling anyone who did it," said Kett with a nod. "That's good, Kate."

"Might be way off, sir."

"Or you might be right. Either way, we've got a murderer who doesn't just kill, they desecrate. And I don't think it's a coincidence they do it here, on consecrated ground."

"Almost certainly deconsecrated, sir," said Savage.

"But it's still a church. They picked the site for a reason."

He stood straight, wincing as he waited for the pain to return. But whatever had gone wrong in his back seemed to have righted itself. He took a step, then another, hobbling like an old man.

"You want some help, sir?" asked Duke, offering his arm.

"No," said Kett, but he took it anyway, and they made their way to the archway like they were walking down the aisle.

"You think the woman we saw on the video did this?" asked Savage.

Kett waited until he'd crossed the threshold before answering, feeling an unexpected wave of relief wash over him as soon as he walked back into the sun-drenched forest.

"I don't know," he said. "Feels like too much of a coincidence that she was here, and that she attacked Charlie and Aggie when they found the head. But it doesn't make sense. She kills a man, she—"

"She looked about a hundred years old," said Duke. "How would she kill him?"

"She kills a man," Kett went on, ignoring him. "She cuts off his head, brings it here five, six, seven days ago. Why is she still here? She must have known that eventually somebody would find it, and if she's hanging around picking fights with people, then she's going to get caught."

"Unless it means something to her, sir," said Savage. "This isn't your bog-standard murder. The beans, the marks on the head. It means something, it's... I don't know, special. Sacred."

"Then we figure out why," said Kett. "If we understand what the killer is trying to do, we can find them. Kate, can you head back, see if you can get to the bottom of it?"

"You're sure you don't need me here, sir?" Savage replied.

"We do, but I can spare you. You stand the best shot of figuring it out."

Savage smiled, offering a nod before heading towards the path. Duke waited for his orders, one finger running over the smooth skin where his eyebrow should have been.

"Go with her, Aaron," Kett said. "I'm sure you'll come in useful somehow."

Duke bounded off, calling Savage's name.

"And take that film crew with you!" he yelled after him.

Porter was wandering over, still fixated on his phone.

"You okay, Pete?" Kett asked. "Having a nice rest out here, are you? Enjoying basking in the sun, taking it easy?"

"Sorry, sir," said Porter, sliding his phone into his pocket. "Was trying to get a signal. You find anything?"

"Plenty," said Kett. "Not sure if it will help us, though. Any sign of the Aggie girl yet?"

Porter shook his head.

"You think she's just run, sir?" he said. "Got herself lost? Hiding, maybe?"

"I hope so," said Kett.

Because the alternatives were a lot worse.

"Let's go help with the search," he said, setting off towards the trees. "The sooner we find her, the sooner we can work out what's going on."

CHAPTER NINE

"Can't say I'm sorry to get away from that place," said Duke from the driver's seat of the IRV.

He was attempting a three-point turn in the narrow lane, and was currently on point seven. There weren't many people left to watch them go, most of the uniformed coppers deep in the woods as they searched for Aggie Clegg. There was only Josh, his camera to his shoulder as he filmed them leaving from further down the street.

Judging by the smile on his face, he was enjoying Duke's awful driving a great deal.

Duke finished reversing, then pulled sharply away, the car jolting so hard as it mounted the high verge that Savage's head hit the ceiling.

"Whoops," said Duke, looking in the rear-view mirror. "Hope he didn't get that."

"He definitely got that," said Savage.

She watched the woods fly by the window, her body heavy with guilt as Duke accelerated. Leaving felt like the wrong thing to be doing. They should have been helping look for the missing girl, or the person who had done this to her. She was no good to anyone back at HQ.

"Nice to have some alone time, anyway," Duke went on, and she felt rather than saw the smile he aimed at her.

"Aaron, we've had nothing but alone time for weeks," she said. "Besides, it's not really alone time, is it?"

She glanced over her shoulder at the two women in the back seat. Megan, the assistant camera operator, aimed her camcorder at Savage, her attention firmly on the viewscreen. Next to her, Kelly Armstrong stared at her phone like she was receiving news about the end of the world.

"Oh, just ignore us," said Megan. "Pretend we're not here."

"Easier said than done," Savage muttered, turning to the front.

"But the relationship stuff is good," added Kelly without looking up. "People love a bit of romance. How long have you two been engaged?"

"A while," said Savage, at the same time that Duke replied with, "Five months, two weeks, one day and..."

He glanced at his watch.

"And about fourteen hours."

Savage looked at him with mock horror.

"It's a memorable date," he went on. "The day after Valentine's Day, when I was blown up."

"You weren't blown up," said Savage, wondering how on earth Duke—who struggled to remember which way to put his trousers on some mornings—had calculated the length of their relationship so accurately. "You were... ejected. From a truck."

"As it blew up," said Duke.

"Can you maybe talk about your wedding a little?" said

Kelly. "Like, discuss it, plan it, whatever people do. But just talk between yourselves, like we're not here."

"Uh..." said Savage. "I mean, we haven't really..."

"Probably a barn," said Duke. "For our wedding, yeah?"

"A barn?" Savage replied, turning to look at him. "You want to get married in a *barn*? I'm not a horse, Aaron."

"A big barn," he went on.

"So we can invite all the chickens and sheep?"

Duke's cheeks were starting to mottle beneath his uneven beard.

"No, it will be nice, with like ribbons and baskets and stuff. What were you thinking? A church?"

He pulled a face.

"I mean, yeah," said Savage. "I hadn't really given it much thought."

She hadn't really thought about it at all, even though Duke had taken to leaving clippings from magazines and little doodles around the flat, making practice bouquets of flowers he'd collected walking around the block. While he'd been convalescing at home, he'd even gone as far as crocheting a miniature wedding couple for the top of the cake—her in a white dress, him in uniform.

It was quite sweet, although what he didn't know yet was that Colin the dog had chewed the mini-woollen Duke to shreds. She'd had to bury the evidence in the outside bin.

"Churches are so cold, and dark, and full of severed..." Duke caught himself before he said too much, Kelly's eyes flicking up in interest. "Uh, pews. You know what I mean. Barns are warm and big and welcoming. All the best weddings happen in barns."

"Well, if you want to get married in a barn, I'm happy to get married in a barn," said Savage, eager for the conversation to move on. "A big barn wedding it is."

Duke pumped his fist in the air.

"Can't wait for you to see the tractor I want us to arrive in," he said.

Savage didn't rise to the bait. They'd emerged from the tunnel of trees, the summer sun pouring through the windows, the colour of honey and thick enough to drown in. The woods continued on the left-hand side of the road, but to the right was an enormous field, nothing past that but the promise of the sea.

"Are you allowed to tell us what you found back there?" said Megan. "Somebody's missing, right?"

"Sorry," said Savage. "We can't say anything right now."

"Somebody called Aggie, judging by the shouts."

"Really, when I can tell you something, I will."

"Can you tell us where we're going, at least?"

"HQ," said Savage, to an audible groan of disappointment from Kelly.

Savage was disappointed too. The last thing she felt like doing right now was heading to the office and trying to figure out the meaning behind what they'd discovered at the ruin.

It was hard not to think about it, though.

Why do that to someone? she asked herself. *Why cut off somebody's head and mutilate it like that?*

She was no stranger to extreme crime, but this felt worse than anything she'd seen so far on the job. This felt brutal, and barbaric, and blasphemous.

"The silence isn't really working for us," said Kelly from the back. "You want to be on TV, you need to give us something."

"I *don't* want to be on TV," said Savage.

Duke's mouth opened as he tried to start a conversation. He glanced at Savage, panicking.

"Uh... This weather, eh?"

He pretended to wipe his brow.

"Phew!"

Savage was grateful the cameras were pointed at the back of her head so they couldn't film her rolling her eyes.

Duke slowed the car as they approached a junction, and Savage caught sight of a building in the woods to her left. A cottage. Like the church, it was little more than a ruin, mummified in greenery and almost invisible. The downstairs windows had been smashed, the upstairs ones blinded by a century of filth.

"Hold up, Aaron," she said. "Stop here a second."

Duke brought the car to a halt, keeping the engine running. There was a low brick wall along the side of the road, a wrought-iron gate that drooped under a blanket of ivy, as if the forest had pulled it loose. The path to the house was thick with weeds, and they looked like they'd been recently trampled.

"How far from the church are we?" she asked. "About a mile?"

"About that," said Duke. "You see something?"

Savage opened the door and stepped out, walking to the low wall. Duke switched off the IRV, and in the quiet that followed she realised she could still hear the shouts from the woods. If Aggie had bolted after she'd been attacked, there was every chance she could have run this way. It wasn't like there were many houses around here to take shelter in.

"What're you thinking?" asked Duke as he climbed out of the car.

"Thinking it might be worth a look," she replied.

"I'll come."

"Don't you want to babysit your friends?" she asked.

"I'll come," he repeated, adjusting his equipment belt.

He rested his hand on his Taser to make sure it was still there, walking to her side.

"Hey, can you let us out?" shouted Kelly from the car.

"Sorry," said Savage. "It's for your own safety. We won't be long."

She stepped over the wonky gate, stamping down the brambles that blocked the path. They cut through the thin cotton of her trousers, scratching her legs.

"Ow," she said.

"You want me to go first?" asked Duke.

"You're alright," she replied, ploughing on. "I don't think I need Britain's bravest copper to get me past some weeds."

The path was a short one, just a dozen yards or so to the cottage's front door. It was small, just a two up and two down by the look of it. The front door was still in place so Savage made her way to the nearest window, grabbing hold of the crumbling sash frame to steady herself. It was dark inside, especially after the blindingly bright day, and it stank of neglect.

"Can't see much," said Duke, who was staring through the window on the other side of the front door. "You thinking our killer might be here?"

"I'm thinking our missing girl might be," she said. "Although, I'm not ruling anything out. You—"

Savage stopped at the sound of a thump and a yelp. Her heart had revved into action before she realised it was coming from behind her. Megan was in the process of falling over the front seat of the IRV, her legs in the air.

"Unbelievable," Savage muttered. She turned to the window, clearing her throat. "Aggie? Agnes Clegg, are you in there? It's the police."

She was answered by a soft, insect-like click that made

her skin erupt in goosebumps, her scalp shrivelling. The noise came again, morphing into a low groan.

"You hear that?" she asked, stepping back.

"Yeah," said Duke, one hand on his Taser again.

"Aggie?" Savage called. "If you're here, try to let me know."

The clicks came again, like somebody gently clucking their tongue. It sounded too close, as if somebody was standing right next to her, breathing into her ear. Despite the heat of the day, she was suddenly freezing.

"Aggie?" said Duke.

Savage's eyes had adjusted to the dark a little, and she saw a bare room in front of her, half of the ceiling hanging from the rotten joists. A door sat ajar in the right-hand wall.

She lifted her leg over the sill of the broken window, only to hear a protest from Duke.

"Let me go," he said.

She appreciated the chivalry until she saw him look at the car. Megan was standing by the gate, her camcorder to her face.

"You worried people are going to think less of you if you let me go first?" she asked quietly, straddling the window.

"No," he said. "I mean, yeah, a little. And I don't want you to get hurt, obviously."

She glanced into the house again, into that dark interior where something still clicked and groaned.

"Fair enough," she said. "It's all yours."

He nodded his thanks, unstrapping his Taser. She climbed off the window to let him pass. He threw another look back at the camera, narrowing his eyes like Bruce Willis, then proceeded to squeeze his enormous frame through the gap.

"Police armed with Taser!" he called out, far louder than he needed to. "You have been warned."

Savage rolled her eyes again, then followed him into the house. She hopped down from the window ledge, scrubbing the dirt from her hands. Duke was moving slowly across the room, his Taser out in front of him.

"Surprised you didn't do a combat roll through the window," said Savage, the house turning her voice into a whisper.

"You think I should have?" Duke asked, glancing back. "I can do it again?"

"Just keep moving, you dope."

Duke reached the door, using the toe of his boot to open it. The hinges clicked, groaned, and Savage felt a rush of relief as she realised what she'd heard from outside was just the door moving in a breeze. It was short-lived, though, as she made out the familiar buzz of flies.

"Police," Duke called out again. "If anyone is here, make yourself known."

He lowered the Taser for a moment to pull out his torch, lifting them both together as he walked through the door. Savage used her own torch to search the small room, finding an armchair that had been eviscerated, its steel springs on show. There were ashes in the fireplace, and an empty frame hanging above the hearth, set to a crooked angle. When she looked back, she saw dark curtains drooping on either side of the window like hanged men.

"Cheery," she said to herself, hoping the sound of her voice would take the edge off her panic.

She followed Duke out and into a narrow hallway, peeling apart the dark with her torch to see a staircase to the right and two more doors to the left. Flies hurled themselves drunkenly from side to side, their bloated bodies striking her in the face, in the neck, in the hands. She had to grit her teeth against the fist of panic that pushed up from her stomach.

Duke planted one boot on the bottom stair and the noise it made sounded like the house was about to fall down. Dust rained from the ceiling.

"Careful," she said.

"Careful's my middle name," he replied, climbing slowly.

"Your middle name's Ronald," she replied.

"I told you never to repeat that," he said, his top half sucked into the shadows like the house had taken a bite. "Aggie, you up here? It's the police."

Savage moved towards the other doors, peering into one to see a toilet. It reeked, but not of human waste. It stank like rotting food, and when she angled her torch into the bowl she saw that it was crimson. Flies crawled over the seat, they drowned in the overflowing mess.

"Shit," she said. "Aaron, I've got blood."

"Blood?" he called down.

"Yeah. Stay alert."

She edged past the toilet to the next door, using her foot to open it. Beyond was a small kitchen, brighter than the rest of the house but still dark thanks to the wall of ivy and thorns that had grown over the window. A table occupied most of the space, and a sink and a small oven stood by the door on the far side of the room. Savage took a step inside, feeling her shoe stick to the floor. She thought it was more blood, but when she looked down—her skin crawling—she didn't see any. Something had been spilled here, though, and recently.

She hovered in the door, aiming the torch from wall to

wall and finding nothing but dust. Behind her, Duke was coming down the stairs.

"Two bedrooms," he said, batting at the flies with his torch and making the wild shadows dance. "No sign anyone's been in them. You got anything?"

"I don't know," she said. "I don't want to mess it up. Back door looks like it's blocked by brambles, let's go around."

She hesitated by the toilet again, studying the clotted contents of the bowl.

"That's definitely blood," said Duke, belching uncomfortably. "A lot of blood."

The smell of it was making her stomach churn, and she gave Duke a shove to get him through the living room door. She overtook him, sliding through the window and sucking in fresh, salt-scented air. Through her watering eyes, she saw Megan halfway down the path, still filming.

"Put it away," she told her.

Duke grunted his way out of the house, sliding his Taser back into its holster.

"All clear," he said in a voice that sounded an octave lower than usual. "Any threats have been neutralised."

"Yeah, he swatted a couple of bluebottles," said Savage, heading around the side of the building. The weeds had taken over here as well, a carpet of vegetation stretching from the hedge to the house. She pulled out her phone as she went, calling Kett.

"Yeah," he said when he answered. It sounded like he was speaking through a yawn, and she waited for him to finish before continuing.

"We stopped at a house about a mile away from the church, sir," she said, stamping down the brambles. "Just a hunch, place looked deserted and I thought Aggie might have hidden here."

"You found her?"

"No, sir. But I found blood. Looks fresh."

"You there now?" said Kett.

"Yes, sir. Duke's with me, we're just checking out the back garden."

"I'll see if Cara has somebody who can come take a look," said Kett. "You want backup?"

"Only to keep the bloody camera crew out of the way, sir," she said. "Hang on."

There was a wooden gate separating the path from the garden beyond, but it looked like the gentle breeze would knock it over. Savage slipped her phone into her pocket so she could take it in two hands. When she gave the gate a pull, the dry wood snapped with a puff of rot and she threw it to the ground, pushing past a spider's web of sticky weed into a long, narrow garden.

She pulled her phone out again.

"Sorry, sir," she said. "You there?"

"I am," said Kett. "You see anything?"

"Not much," she replied. "Just a lot of grass."

The lawn had been left to grow, the grass as tall as her waist and topped with seeds. It shivered in a sudden breeze, looking like something was moving through it, something fast. Savage held her ground, turning to the back of the house, seeing the barricaded back door, seeing a little flower patch that had been dug beneath the window, the soil freshly turned over.

Seeing what grew there.

It hit her like a punch, like somebody had physically attacked her. She doubled up, the air crushed from her lungs.

"Kate?" said Kett.

"Kate?" echoed Duke, who was right behind her. "Jesus Christ. Fuck me. Is that… is that real?"

Savage forced herself to stand straight, but she couldn't bear to turn back to the window. There were tears in her eyes, and when she scrubbed them away more followed. She couldn't stop them.

Then Duke was there, wrapping her in a hug. She pushed her face into his chest, into that welcome darkness, breathing in the smell of him until her body had stopped shaking.

Only then did she step back.

Only then did she turn around to that nightmare flower bed.

Four limbs stood upright in the turned earth: two arms and two legs, shed of all clothing and mottled with rot. Flowers grew up each limb; dozens of wispy, white blossoms clinging like spiders to the claws of the fingers, to the outstretched nubbins of the toes.

And right in the middle of the arrangement was a torso, ripe enough to split.

"Kate?" said Kett, and she realised she still held the phone to her ear.

"Sir," she said, just a whisper.

"I said do you need backup?"

The breeze blew again, the grass chattering with laughter, the trees swaying madly. Only those five grotesque plants stayed perfectly still, rooted in the red soil.

"Yeah, sir," she said, heaving a breath. "Yeah, we do."

CHAPTER TEN

Five minutes later, Porter pulled the Mondeo up behind the IRV and killed the engine. Kett got out, scanning the side of the road, taking a second or two to spot the cottage that Savage had told him about. It was almost buried by the surrounding trees, drowning in shifting shadows. She'd done well to spot it from the car, because nature had practically camouflaged it out of existence.

He opened the back door of Porter's car to let Emily Franklin out. She grabbed hold of the sleeve of his jacket to heave herself up, her face drenched in sweat.

"Ever heard of air con, Pete?" she asked.

"What, for that three-minute journey?" he replied, slamming his door.

Kett could hear voices raised in something close to an argument, and he followed them past a broken gate and down a path of brambles that did their best to trip him up. The front door of the cottage was closed, the windows dark, so he cut to the side and passed another mangled gate, entering a sizeable garden.

The four people who occupied it were all speaking at

once. The two members of the film crew, Megan and Kelly, were closest, their backs to him. Standing between them and the house were Savage and Duke. Savage spotted Kett and looked visibly relieved.

"Sir," she said. "I've told them a hundred times, they can't be here."

Both women spun around. Megan held the camera by her side. It didn't look like it was filming.

"As I told your colleague," said Kelly, "anything sensitive or inappropriate is cut out at the editing stage. But we need the full picture if we're going to make a decent show."

Kett held out his hand to Megan, clicking his fingers the same way he did with his kids when they had something they shouldn't.

"Give it," he said.

Megan looked to Kelly for her orders.

"Give it," Kett said again.

"I'll just put it away," she said, tucking the camera behind her back.

"Now," he barked, in a tone which brooked no argument.

Megan reluctantly handed over the camcorder, and Kett slid it into the inside pocket of his jacket. Kelly eyeballed him for a moment.

"He's the one who's missing out," she said, hooking a thumb at Duke. "It's going to be the worst show on TV at this rate."

"It's Channel 5," said Kett. "Nobody will be surprised."

Kelly's mouth fell open and she stormed off down the side of the cottage, almost barging Emily Franklin out of the way. Megan scuttled after her. Duke watched them go with a sad expression.

"The worst show on TV?" he said.

"Thought they were never going to leave," Savage said. She glanced into the trees, where a couple of magpies chattered to each other. "They're almost as annoying as that lot up there."

It took her a moment more to look at Kett, her eyes dark. "Prepare yourself, sir."

She stepped out of the way, and Kett finally saw what sat beneath the cottage's kitchen window. Savage had told him on the phone, of course, but nothing could have prepared him for what he found there, a cultivated nightmare. He put a hand to his mouth before he even knew he was doing it, speaking into his fingers.

"Fuck me."

The limbs had been planted perfectly straight, an arm and a leg on either side of the torso. Flies careened around the display like they couldn't believe their luck, crawling over the filthy skin, clustering around the raw wounds where, presumably, the limbs had been hacked off. The torso was the right way up, everything below the waist buried in the earth. The smell of it overpowered the salt in the air and the sweet aroma of blossom, creating a perfume that made Kett's stomach clench like a fist.

It was, without a doubt, one of the worst things he had ever seen.

"Oh goody!" said Franklin, pushing past him. "The rest of my jigsaw!"

She knelt at the edge of the flowerbed, rocking back and forth like a child at Christmas as she studied the mutilated body. Kett walked up behind her, Savage on one side and Porter on the other.

"Yeah," said Porter, his voice hoarse. "Goody."

"You think it's the same man, Emily?" asked Savage.

"I bloody hope so," Franklin replied. "It would make for

a very worrying coincidence if it wasn't. Identical skin colour, and I'd put money on it being roughly the same time of death. See the slight fungal growth on the skin there, around the belly button?"

"Nope," said Porter.

"And the significant deposit of fly eggs in the wounds there, see it, Pete?"

"No," Porter said.

"Right there in the armpit, and the neck. See how they're clustered around the flaps there, Pete? Are you looking?"

Porter groaned as he turned away.

"Enough, Emily," said Kett.

She laughed quietly.

"Sorry, it's one of my favourite sports. Definitely the same man, though, when you look at the injuries to his neck. Remember the way the skin of the head was almost shredded, like it had been violently ripped away? These wounds correspond almost perfectly."

She lifted a hand and Kett took it, helping her to her feet. She trod carefully around the circumference of the flower bed so she could get a better look at the dead man's trunk.

"We've got several long, deep cuts here. There was no attempt at care or precision, the killer just wanted to get his head off as quickly as possible. I thought it might have been an axe, but the strokes here look too long. Could be a sword."

"A sword?" said Kett.

"Heavy one, too. It went deep. Either that or our murderer is extremely strong."

Kett thought about the video they'd watched, the ancient woman who'd attacked the teenagers in the woods.

She'd barely looked able to lift her own hands, let alone hold a sword.

"Same deal with the limbs," Franklin went on. "All removed with a handful of cuts. It must have been ferocious. I'd almost be tempted to use the word frenzied."

She returned to her original position, careful not to stand on the carefully turned bed of soil.

"He's been dead no longer than a week," she said. "Same as the head. Probably five days, given the heat. But..."

She hesitated, everyone waiting. The magpies clucked overhead, more of them arriving by the second.

"But what?" asked Kett eventually.

"They can't have been here all that time," said Franklin.

"Because something would have eaten them," Savage said. "I was thinking the same thing. Look at all the birds. The magpies were attacking the head over in the church, they'd have feasted on this, right?"

"They would certainly have left a mark," said Franklin. "And there must be foxes around here, maybe cats. If these had been planted fresh, something would have dug them up, gnawed them to the bone."

"So they were placed here more recently?" asked Kett. "The killer hacked them off, left them somewhere for a few days, then brought them here to make their garden?"

"We're assuming it's a killer, sir," said Savage. "But what if they didn't murder this man?"

Kett squinted at her as the sun peeked over the tops of the trees.

"He was already dead?"

"Possibly, sir," said Savage, although she didn't look convinced. "It might explain the delay between his death and when the body parts were left here."

"Not a bad suggestion, Kate," said Franklin. "It could

explain the barbarity of the attack, the lack of hesitation. It's much easier to butcher a cadaver than it is a living person."

Kett nodded.

"Good point. You're thinking the killer might have dug him up?"

"Definitely wasn't formally buried," said Franklin. "Hasn't been embalmed."

"Unlikely, then," said Savage. "Not to mention there's blood inside the house."

"Enough to explain this?" said Kett, nodding at the limbs. Savage shook her head.

"Unless somebody's cleaned it up. Most is in the toilet."

"Cara's on the way," said Kett. "She'll be able to tell us more."

"Kate might have a point," said Franklin, leaning even closer to the limbs. "I don't actually see any bruising around the cuts, not even on the neck. It looks as if the body was dismembered after death, which doesn't rule out the idea that it was dead long before our suspect started working on it."

"Either way," said Kett, "anyone have any ideas why they'd leave the head over by the church and... *plant* the rest of him here?"

For a few seconds, nobody replied. Then Duke cleared his throat.

"Beans, sir?"

Kett gave him a look.

"No, I mean they obviously like gardening," the PC said, holding up his hands in defence. "Beans, plants, they like things that grow. It's... I don't know what word I'm looking for. Natural?"

"This definitely isn't natural," said Kett.

"Nature, then," said Duke. "It's earthy. My mum likes gardening."

"You're saying your mum did this?" said Porter.

"No, sir, but she's... She's part of this club and they're all the same, all women who like getting their fingers dirty. They're like hippies, they like growing stuff. Her house is full of seeds and beans and stuff. They're *earthy*."

He flapped his hands in frustration.

"I don't know what I'm saying," he said.

"That makes all of us," said Porter. "Anyone know what the flowers are?"

"Clematis," said Duke.

"You bloody would know that," muttered Porter.

"He's right," said Franklin. "*Clematis vetalba.* I think it's called Old Man's Beard, because it looks like... well, an old man's beard."

It was more like a spider, thought Kett, each petal long-legged and covered with fine grey hair. They weren't pleasant to look at.

"Plants are mature, no way they've grown up here," said Franklin. "Whoever did this to the limbs added these afterwards. They're hooked over the fingers and between the toes. You seeing this, Pete?"

Kett couldn't work out if Porter was growling or groaning.

"I thought they were called Traveller's Joy," said Savage. "They're native to this part of the world. There's a saying, I think. Uh, Traveller's Joy does the devil's work, or something like that."

"What does that mean?" asked Kett.

Savage shrugged.

"Right," he said.

He heaved out a sigh, closing his eyes for a moment and enjoying the touch of the sun on his face.

"Okay," he went on after a few moments. "Emily, can you put this guy on your table and figure out how he died? Kate, get back to HQ and see if you can figure out why our suspect is... *earthy.*"

"Yes, sir," said Savage.

"What about me, sir?" asked Porter.

Kett took one last look at the macabre garden before heading back to the path.

"I think Kate might be onto something," he said. "We're going to find out where they might have got their hands on a dead man."

CHAPTER ELEVEN

"You want me to *WHAT*, sir?"

DS Spalding's voice was a witch's croak down the line, barely enough signal to hear what she was saying. Kett switched his phone to the other ear like that would make a difference, yelling into it.

"I need you to see if there have been any reports of body snatching. Missing corpses, anything like that."

"You don't have to shout, sir, I can hear you fine. I'm just… dead bodies? Like, from a grave?"

"No, before the grave. Hospitals, morgues, crematoriums. Anything like that. A man in his fifties, maybe late forties. White. Brown hair. We're looking at maybe five to seven days since death."

"Your wish is my command, sir," said Spalding. "Got the details for the cottage you're in, too. Last owned by a woman called Eleanor Gordon. She died in '75, no living relatives. Nobody claimed the property, so it's been sitting empty for almost fifty years."

"Thanks," Kett said. "Call me if you find anything else."

"I appreciate the reminder, sir," said Spalding dryly.

"Disaster averted. My scatty brain might have forgotten to update you on a crucial aspect of the case."

She killed the call before he could reply. Kett slipped his phone into his pocket, looking over the top of Porter's car at the little cottage. He hadn't been inside—there had been enough contamination already, and he wanted to wait for forensics to do their thing—and he wasn't sure he wanted to, either. Whether their victim had been alive or dead when he'd got there, what had happened to him was unspeakable.

"Um, hi?" said a voice from behind him. Kett looked to see Megan there, the young filmmaker rubbing her hands together nervously. Behind her, Kelly leaned against the bonnet of the IRV, scrolling through something on her phone. "Is there any chance I can... uh... have my camera back?"

Kett had completely forgotten about it. He patted his pocket to make sure it was still there, then shook his head.

"Sorry, I'll need to check it. None of this can be released to the public yet."

"I won't," she said. "I promise. I can delete it. I didn't even see the... garden. I was just trying to film Aaron doing his thing."

Kett's reply was cut off by the sound of an engine. Something was coming this way, and they were driving fast. He stepped out from behind the Mondeo in time to see a white van steaming down the narrow road, the shape of the driver barely visible behind the sun-drenched windscreen. Whoever they were, they didn't seem to be paying much attention to the road, the van fifty yards away and still accelerating—even though there was no way it was going to squeeze past the two parked cars.

"Hey!" yelled Kett, waving his hands. "Hey! Slow down!"

The van ploughed towards them, the sound of it deafening. Kett whirled around to the two women.

"Move!"

They scrambled to the gate, Porter alongside them, all taking cover behind the crumbling wall. Kett was about to follow when he heard the crunch of the van finally braking, the screech of its tyres on the hot road. It hit the verge, hard, bouncing to a halt just feet from the front of the IRV.

"Christ," said Kett, marching towards it.

Behind the wheel was a man, and he had his mobile phone to his ear—no attempt to hide it.

Kett grabbed the handle and wrenched the door open. The man was in his forties, almost completely bald on top but boasting an impressive beard that hung almost to his collarbone. His nose was swollen from what had to have been a lifetime of drink, the tip blue. He wore shorts, his legs covered with tattoos. More peeked from the sleeves of his denim shirt. He peered at Kett through bright yellow glasses that were in dire need of a clean, that phone still clamped to his ear.

"What the hell are you doing?" Kett asked him. "You could have flattened us."

"You're police?" the man asked, his voice high-pitched and desperate, with more than a hint of Irish.

"Yeah. Who are you?"

"Kevin," he said. "Kevin Clegg. My daughter's missing. Have you found her? Tell me you've found her."

Kett stepped away from the van, gesturing for Kevin to get out. The man almost fell onto the street, lunging, his eyes wild. He was a good foot shorter than Kett, and he seemed to be having trouble with one of his legs, limping badly.

"You've found her?"

"We haven't found her, but we're looking," Kett told him, backing away. "You got any ID?"

"ID?" said the man. "Who else am I going to be? Fuck your ID."

Kett waited, and eventually the man dug his free hand into his pocket. It seemed to be a struggle to stand up because of his leg. There was a voice coming from the other end of the phone, fast and panicked.

"Left my wallet at home," he said. "Wasn't thinking. Got this."

He pulled out a couple of cards, holding them up. One was a library card with Kevin Clegg written on it in black biro. The other was a Halifax debit card boasting the same name.

"It will do," said Kett.

Kevin looked fearfully at the little cottage, still ignoring the phone.

"It happened here?"

"No," said Kett. "About a mile away. I'll take you in the car, we can talk."

Kevin nodded, still staring at the cottage. Kett didn't think he'd blinked once. He took hold of the man's elbow, steering him away from the van. He was like a stubborn locomotive, moving impossibly slowly because of his limp. He didn't take his eyes off the house.

"You've looked in there?" he asked.

"We have," said Kett. "She's not there. Pete, can you drive?"

Porter nodded, getting into the Mondeo. Kett opened the back door for Kevin, helping him in, then ran around to the other side. Kevin still held onto the phone, that same voice audible.

There was no room to turn around, so Porter slowly reversed.

"You haven't found her?" said Kevin, the whine of the car muting his voice.

"Not yet," said Kett. "But we've got two dozen officers in the woods, so we will. What are you doing out here?

"You lot came to my door, told me what had happened. You expected me to stay at home?"

"We would have brought you, Mr Clegg."

"I wanted to come myself," he said. "Don't trust anyone else to do anything right."

The car weaved left and right as Porter tried to squeeze backwards up the lane, his face gurning between the seats.

"What happened to her? Cops that came to my house said she was attacked. That right? What happened?"

"We don't know," said Kett. "We spoke to a young man, Matt Kamau."

"Fucking creep," said Kevin. "Spends half his life trying to dry hump my girl. He do this?"

"We don't think so, no," said Kett. "They were out here filming, does that sound right?"

"She don't tell me nothing," said Kevin, squeezing his leg and grimacing. "Filming? For that YouTube? Waste of time. Where is Matthew? I'll make him talk."

"He's gone," said Kett, not sure if that was the truth or not. "He and Aggie and a girl called Charlie Ford came out to the woods this morning to record a video."

Kevin frowned.

"Charlie?"

"You know her?"

He shook his head.

"I don't really talk to Aggie anymore. Her choice, not

mine. But I keep tabs on her, same as any da. Don't matter how close you are, you still do anything for 'em."

"There's a place called St Mary's ruins just up the road, you heard of it?"

Kevin shook his head again, still clutching his phone. Whoever had been speaking had fallen quiet.

"It's an old church," said Kett. "According to Matt they were making a film about a local legend. While they were recording, somebody attacked them."

"Matthew told you this?"

"He did, and I've seen the film. They were recording when it happened. The attacker was..."

He hesitated, seeing the woman in his head, her sagging face, those dead eyes.

"Older," he said. "And female, we think. Matt ran—"

"Coward," said Kevin.

"Charlie was knocked out. We don't know what happened to Aggie."

The man's face crumpled.

"But we think she probably bolted," Kett went on. "It's a big stretch of woodland, there's miles of it. It wouldn't take much to get lost in there."

"She wouldn't get lost," said Kevin, turning his red-flecked eyes to Kett. "I took Agnes into the woods all the time when she was young. Taught her how to navigate, how to find food, make shelter. No way she gets lost. Something's happened to her."

He thumped himself on the chest violently enough to make Kett tense up.

"I feel it. I know when my daughter is..."

"Is what?" said Kett.

He didn't finish. Porter had finally reached a passing

place and he set about turning the big car around. It was a painfully slow process.

"Has your daughter ever been in any trouble before?" Kett asked. "Has she ever been scared, ever run away?"

"Don't be fucking daft," said Kevin. "Of course she's been scared. Her ma died when she was born. I nearly went too. Cancer. But she's strong. She has my strength, Tracey's strength, too. She wouldn't run."

Porter accelerated, barely reaching forty miles an hour before slowing down again. Somebody had sealed off the lane that led to the church with police tape, and the stationed constable lifted it over the roof of the car. There were more IRVs here than ever, but one of the ambulances had somehow managed to free itself.

Kevin looked at the sea of rolling lights in horror, the truth of it seeming to dawn in him.

"Agnes," he said quietly.

Porter stopped the car nose to tail with an IRV, and when he switched off the engine Kett heard the distinctive rumble of a helicopter.

"Air support," he said to Kevin. "They'll find her."

The man didn't seem convinced. Kett spotted Clare up ahead, the Super standing in the treeline speaking on his phone. He looked gaunt.

"Mr Clegg, I just need to ask you another difficult question," said Kett. "I don't think it's relevant, but we have to be sure. Has anyone threatened your daughter recently? Has there been anyone new hanging around her? Anything unusual at all?"

Kevin didn't answer, his stare still locked on the army of police vehicles that blocked the road.

"Mr Clegg?"

"No," he said, wiping his face with hands that had been

scored by eczema. He hesitated for a moment, shaking his head. "It's her birthday tomorrow. You know that? Eighteen. Hardly seems a minute since she was born, though. Lost one love of my life that day, gained another."

He sniffed.

"Thought I might make another crack at it, now she's all grown up, you know? Being a da. But what if... what if..."

He didn't seem to have the words. Instead, he opened the door and slid out, struggling on his bad leg.

"Hang on," Kett called after him, escaping the Mondeo and chasing him towards the trees. "Kevin, you can't just go after her."

The man turned back as he limped away, his face twisted into what looked like a corpse's grin.

"And you're going to stop me?" he called back. "Some da you are."

Kett let him go. He turned to the constable at the end of the lane, gesturing for him to follow.

"Just keep him away from the church, yeah?" he said.

"He's got a fair point," said Porter as they watched the constable run into the trees. "If it was one of ours missing in there, we'd burn the whole fucking forest down to find them."

Kett nodded, hearing the familiar clomp of Clare's brogues as the Super marched towards them.

"Who's that cup of spicy toss, and where the fuck does he think he's going?" he shouted.

"It's Aggie Clegg's dad," said Kett.

"And you're just letting him walk into our crime scene?" said Clare, bug-eyed.

"It's his daughter, sir," said Kett. "You think any of us could have stopped him?"

"Yes," said Clare. "Because you're police officers."

He wiped a hand over his dripping face.

"That's it," he said. "I quit. You can toss all over yourselves without me. You can drown in toss for all I care."

"It can't hurt to have him there, sir," said Kett. "There's enough police to supervise him, and he knows his daughter. He knows where she'd go, where she'd try to hide. He can help them find her."

"I don't think he's going to find her in there," said Clare.

"What?" said Kett. "Why?"

Clare lifted his phone like he was going to crack Kett around the head with it.

"I was trying to call you, you greasy bellend. Word's just come in: a witness claims to have seen somebody locked in the boot of a car five miles away."

"Aggie?" said Porter.

"Let's go find out," said Clare.

CHAPTER TWELVE

"Call was to emergency services," said Clare as Porter gunned the Mondeo up the road. An IRV drove in front of them, clearing the way like a minesweeper. "Just over twenty minutes ago, from a garage on the A47."

Kett leaned between the two front seats as the Super continued.

"Why did they call emergency services?" he asked. "Nobody knows Aggie is missing yet."

"Said they saw somebody locked in the boot," said Clare. "That's all I know."

"How would they know she was in the boot?"

"I said that's all I know," said Clare. "Now put your bloody foot down, Pete. The accelerator is the one on the right."

"I'm going plenty fast enough, sir!"

Fortunately for Porter, it was a short journey, the countryside passing in a blur as they cut southwest. The petrol station where the call had come from was on the roundabout where the dual carriageway met the Acle Strait, and there were already two police cars outside by the time they pulled in. Porter parked behind them and they got out together, Kett struggling because of his back. Clare gave him a dirty look.

"Get a bloody move on, Quasimodo!"

A constable held the door open for them and they walked through the deserted shop to the office at the back. Another uniformed officer waited there, alongside a large woman in her early fifties who sat at a desk. A monitor beside her showed the forecourt, an image frozen on the screen.

"Hi," said Kett, offering the woman a nod. "My name's DCI Kett, of the Norfolk Police. You made the 999 call?"

The woman nodded, meeting Clare's scowl with one of her own. If it wasn't for the difference in their size, they could have been siblings.

"Shouldn't I have?" she asked.

"Not at all," said Kett. "You absolutely did the right thing. Mrs..."

"Trunchbull," said the officer in the room. Kett frowned.

"Trunchbull?"

"Turnbull," the woman corrected.

"Oh, right," said the PC. "Sorry. Kids are obsessed with *Matilda* at the moment."

"Right," said Kett. It was impossible to deny how much the woman *did* look like Miss Trunchbull.

"Mrs Turnbull, can you tell us what you saw?" said Kett. "Exactly."

"Of course," she said, bracing her hands on her enormous hips and leaning back so hard in her chair it groaned. "Although, it's a bit of a blur."

She put both hands to her face like she'd written her lines on her palms.

"I was on the tills this morning, because Sandra's off

sick. Again. She's always off sick, although it doesn't stop her going down the Fat Duck every Friday night for the line dancing. And again on Tuesdays. Claims her hips are going so she can't sit at the desk all day. Romesh even got her one of those stools so she don't have to sit down. But my Bill's in the Duck on Fridays and he says she's swinging *her* Bill around like he's a bag of mince, hips sashaying all over the place."

She peered at Kett.

"That's a crime, isn't it? Lying like that?"

"Uh, maybe," said Kett. "We can look into it. After we look into *that*."

He nodded at the screen.

"What happened?"

"So, I was on the tills like I said, and I'm not even looking at the cars, really, because it's quiet. Sandra says I spend half my life doing crosswords, but I wasn't doing one. Just put my head down for the occasional clue between customers. But this woman comes in, and I'm serving her, and I'm thinking, she's odd, but I couldn't put my foot on why. Something about her."

She stopped for a moment, considering something. Kett waited, hearing Clare huff impatiently from the open door.

"Creepy," Mrs Turnbull continued. "Something about her eyes. She's got this hat on, too, down low, and she's got a scarf around her mouth, like she's trying to hide herself."

"You've got her on camera?" asked Kett.

The woman nodded, turning to the screen.

"Lucky we do," she said. "Because Sandra was trying to get Romesh to turn all the cameras off, kept saying it was an invasion of her privacy, like anyone would want to look at her marbled arse, you know? She thinks she's Bridget Bardot when she's actually..."

She seemed to struggle.

"Actually a festering badger shit," she finished with a decisive nod. "I wanted to show you this first, is that okay?"

"Tell me what I'm looking at," said Kett, moving closer.

The camera showed the back of a silver VW parked beside a pump. The picture was fuzzy, but still clear enough to make out the licence plate. Kett put on his glasses so that he could make it out.

"Anyone run this, sir?" he asked.

"Not yet," said Clare. "I'll do it."

He barged Kett out of the way, his phone to his ear. Kett waited until he'd yelled the registration number to Spalding before asking Mrs Turnbull to continue.

She pressed a button on the keyboard and the video started to play. For a few seconds nothing happened, and Kett was about to ask if it was still paused when he noticed something.

"What is that?" he said, leaning in.

Something was wrong with the car's brake light. It looked almost like it was flickering, even though the engine was off. He leaned a little closer, trying to understand what he was seeing, feeling Clare do the same. Porter stepped in on his other side, compressing him.

"Light's been knocked out," said the DI.

"That's what I thought," said Mrs Turnbull, sliding her chair to Porter's side—a little too close. He attempted to shuffle back, but there was nowhere to go with Kett and Clare in the way.

"That car belongs to the woman who came in?" asked Kett. "The one in the hat?"

"The creepy one, yes," she replied, practically resting her head on Porter's arm. "She got thirty pounds of petrol—well, thirty pounds and two pence—and bought a Bounty."

"Good choice," said Clare.

"Paid in cash then walked right out. Didn't say a word. Didn't say thank you. Probably felt me staring daggers into her back."

Kett was still watching the screen. Something was sliding out of the broken brake light, a piece of fabric maybe five or six inches long and bright yellow. It was pulled back up, then let out again.

"Somebody's in there," said Kett.

As if answering him, the fabric rose again, then dropped.

"She's trying to send a message," said Porter.

Somebody walked in front of the car, wearing a coat that was long enough to cover most of their body. A cascade of dirty grey hair spilled down their back, but thanks to the hat and the scarf, it was impossible to see who she was.

She didn't seem to notice the piece of yellow fabric hanging from the brake light, because she climbed into the driver's seat of the VW then, a few seconds later, drove out of sight.

"Like I said, I don't normally look at the cars once they've gone," said Mrs Turnbull. "But something about her gave me the shivers."

"You saw the fabric at the back of the car?" asked Kett.

Mrs Turnbull shook her head.

"I wasn't looking, but I wonder if me noggin had seen it and not told me."

"Huh?" said Kett.

"Because when I came in here for my break a little while ago, something was nagging me to look at the car on the CCTV. You know when you get a feeling that something's not right? And when I did, I saw it right away."

Kett checked the time stamp.

"Happened within half an hour of the attack, sir," he said, looking at Clare. "Hard to pinpoint any details, but this woman isn't a million miles away from the one we saw on Charlie's camera. Can we see her, Mrs Turnbull?"

"I'll get the video up," she said, and she scooted her chair into the back of Porter's legs with enough force to bend his knees. With a yelp, he landed plumb on the woman's lap, then leapt up again like he'd sat on a nail.

"Shit, sorry," he said.

"Don't be," said Mrs Turnbull with a pronounced blink that was almost certainly intended to be a wink. "Just take me out for dinner first, won't you?"

Her laugh was like a sack of cats in a blender.

She closed a window on the monitor, and clicked open another one. It had been taken from a camera mounted above the till, and a woman filled almost the entire frame. Her face was masked by the brim of her hat, and by the mess of grey hair that exploded from beneath it, her nose and mouth were concealed by the scarf. Her coat was buttoned up to her neck and her hands, when they appeared, wore brown gloves.

"Paid in cash, like I told you," said Mrs Turnbull, as the woman on screen did exactly that. "A twenty, a ten, and a pound coin. Didn't wait for her change, so I put it in the charity box."

The woman on-screen turned, limping between the aisles towards the door.

"Although not much point putting it in there, because Sandra empties the bloody thing every Friday and spends it down the Duck. That's something I should report her for n'all."

Kett watched the woman on the screen as she opened the door. She was halfway out before she looked back, her eyes peeking from beneath the brim of the hat—only for a fraction of a second. They seemed to be nothing more than pits, aching with darkness.

Even here, in the warmth and the light of the office, Kett felt his skin crinkle into goosebumps.

"Fuck me," said Porter.

"Told you, young man," said Mrs Turnbull, giving him an almighty slap on the arse. "Only if you buy me dinner first."

She roared another laugh. Porter jumped back, rubbing his rump and looking like he was about to make a break for the door.

"Did you see which way they went?" asked Kett, stepping between the woman and Porter in case she came for him again.

"Right," she said, nodding out of the window. "Took the Norwich road. Wasn't watching, but I saw them on this thing." She slapped the same giant hand on the monitor, making it shake. "Saw them on the A47."

Clare's phone started to ring, the sound of it deafening in the small space.

"Speak," he said as he answered. There was a pause. "You're sure?"

He hung up, holding the phone so tightly it looked like he was about to knock somebody out with it.

"Car's registered to an address in Horning," he said, heading out of the room. "A woman called Bianca Caddel. Move!"

Kett was already moving, following Clare into the shop. The Super used both hands to scoop up every last Bounty from the chocolate rack as he went.

"Evidence!" he roared as he pushed past the constable at the door. "She could have left fingerprints."

"He's going to eat his way to the killer," said Porter, pulling out his phone as he went to the till and picking up a pack of Fruit Pastilles on the way. "I'll get them. You want anything?"

"Lost my appetite a long time ago, Pete," said Kett. "Make it quick."

CHAPTER THIRTEEN

It wasn't a house, it was a caravan, parked in the middle of a field just outside of Horning. Like the church and the cottage, nature was doing its best to hide it, a ten-foot hedge crowding the side of the road and spilling over the gate.

They were late to the party again, an IRV waiting outside, splashing blue light on the hedgerow and the road. One of the constables waited by the gate, fending off the flies with her hat. The other sat in the open front door, speaking on his radio. Overhead, in the flawless sky, a bird of prey wheeled in predatory circles.

"What have we got?" Kett asked the PCs as he stepped out of the Mondeo.

"Nobody here, sir," said the woman, dodging another attack. It wasn't a fly, Kett saw with some relief, it was a wasp. "No building, just a caravan. Big one. Locked. Checked the windows and it's empty, but we didn't go in."

The wasp batted itself against her face and she screamed, ducking.

"Calm down," said Kett.

"Bastard's already stung me once, sir," she said. "Won't leave me alone."

"Get in the car then," Kett told her. "We'll take a look."

She jogged off, the wasp following her all the way to the IRV, then proceeding to throw itself against the window when she'd closed the door.

"She really must have done something to upset it," said Porter as he walked up. "After you, sir."

Kett looked back to the Mondeo, where Clare sat in the passenger seat. He was holding an open Bounty in one hand, staring at it with an unreadable expression. He'd devoured four and a half of them on the way over, and he looked a little green around the gills.

"You coming, sir?" Kett asked.

"I… uh…" Clare belched. "I'm going to stay here."

"Just stop eating them, sir," said Kett.

"I'm either eating them, or inserting them into your tosshole, Detective," he shot back. "What would you rather?"

"That man has an unhealthy obsession with tossholes," said Kett as he made his way to the gate.

He pushed his head through the overgrown hedge, spotting the caravan he'd seen from the road. It was a big one, relatively new, and the way the grass had grown up around it made it pretty obvious it hadn't moved in a while. The field was maybe two acres of untidy scrub, occupied by car-sized bushes and fringed with woodland. The whole thing baked in the unforgiving sun. The bird soared effortlessly, releasing a shrill cry to ward them away.

There was no sign of the silver VW Passat anywhere.

"This is definitely the registered address?" he asked.

"This is where the satnav claims it is, sir," Porter answered. "Didn't see much else on the way out here, did you?"

"A lot of cows," said Kett.

Porter narrowed his eyes.

"Evil bastard cows," he said.

Kett planted a foot on the gate and hefted himself up, only for the entire thing to jolt downwards like it was about to topple over. He jumped back with a yelp, seeing that the rotten post had almost pulled itself free from the earth.

"Fucking thing," he muttered.

Porter stepped up and gave the gate a solid boot, following with one more that sent it crashing to the ground. He looked back almost mournfully.

"Where's the camera crew when I single-handedly kick down a gate?" he asked.

Kett hopped between the rungs, walking into the field. It was in an even worse state than he'd suspected, the tough knots of yellowing grass making every step a hazard. Grasshoppers serenaded him as he went, bouncing out of the way of his boots. The sun was so fierce that he could feel the skin of his forehead burning, and he put a hand up to shield his face.

The caravan watched through dark windows as they neared, as tense as a rabbit about to bolt. He'd almost reached the door when he heard his phone ring, but he left it where it was.

"You got gloves, Pete?" he asked.

"Nope," said Porter, patting his pockets.

Kett rapped his knuckles on the door, standing back.

"Can you open up?" he called out. "It's the police."

He knocked again, then used his elbow to push the door handle down.

It was locked.

"Go that way," he told Porter, nodding to the right.

He set off in the other direction, walking to the back of

the caravan. He had to stand on his tiptoes and cup his hand to the glass to see through the window.

A sizable living space, no sign of life.

"Got a window open here, sir," said Porter.

Kett rounded the corner to see the big DI standing beneath a small window towards the front of the caravan. It was too high off the ground to reach, and looked far too small for anyone to climb through.

"Well done, mate," said Kett, the heat shortening his temper. "What are we going to do with that?"

"We could get through there, sir," said Porter.

"I doubt even Kate could fit through there," Kett said, looking up. It had to be a bathroom window, because the glass was opaque.

"Nah, it's tight, but we can do it. Give me a foot-up, sir, I'll have a look."

Even the thought of it made Kett's back sing with pain. Porter saw the look on his face and linked his hands together, holding them out.

"I'll help you up, then," he said. "Once your top half's through, I'll give you a shunt."

"You'll give me a shunt?"

"Yeah, to push you in."

Porter jiggled his hands.

"Or I can go grab one of the woodentops, sir, if you can't manage it?"

"I can manage it," said Kett.

"Because if you're too old to—"

"I'm not too bloody old!"

He planted a boot in Porter's hands and a hand on the scorching wall of the caravan, then pushed himself up. Porter grunted, obviously struggling.

"Jesus, sir," he said. "You been stealing the kids' chocolate rations?"

Kett didn't answer, focussing on grabbing the open window. It still looked too small for him to fit through, but it wasn't like there was another way in.

"Get your top bit in, sir," said Porter, unhelpfully.

Kett could feel the DI's arms trembling, and it was the fear of being dropped rather than any desire to proceed that made him push his head and arms through the gap. As expected, there was a wet room beneath him, a toilet with a sink built into the cistern, and a microscopic shower unit. It was so tight that his shoulders almost got wedged, but he began to wiggle himself through the window.

"You ready for a push, sir?" Porter said.

"No," he replied, "just give me a sec—"

Porter must have misheard him, because Kett felt his legs shunted upwards, his back almost folding in half. He slid through the window like a package through a letterbox, the weight of his top half dragging him earthwards.

Fortunately, something snagged on the open window before he could hit the lid of the toilet.

Unfortunately, whatever had snagged didn't want to let go.

Kett hung there, literally by the seat of his pants, his legs pointing skyward through the window and everything else dangling like a piñata. His belt cut into his waist, the blood immediately pooling inside his head. He braced a hand on the sink to steady himself.

"You alright, sir?" said Porter from outside, his voice muffled.

"What do you bloody think, Pete?" he replied.

He jiggled his body to try to free himself, his phone and his wallet and his keys dropping to the floor.

"Fuck's sake. I'm stuck!"

"On what?" came the reply.

"The window. Can you see what it is?"

The pain was getting worse by the second. He tried pushing himself up using the top of the toilet, but his arms weren't having it.

"Can't see it," said Porter. "You sure you're stuck?"

"Well I'm not fucking levitating, Pete," he shouted back. His head felt twice as big as it should have been, ready to burst. "I think it's my belt."

He grabbed the sink again, wrenching himself down as hard as he could.

"Oh yeah," said Porter. "It's your belt. You want me to unfasten it?"

"No!" yelled Kett, throwing all his weight towards the floor. The entire caravan seemed to be rocking from side to side. "I can probably get myself—"

The window cracked, Kett falling a couple of inches before snapping to a halt again. The pain was lower, and now infinitely worse.

"Okay, undo it, undo it," he said, almost weeping. He wondered what would happen if he died here, whether the circumstances of his death would appear in his obituary, or on his headstone.

Hero policeman castrated to death by his own belt.

It would be all anyone remembered of him.

"Pete! Un-bloody-do it!"

"I'm trying to find something to stand on, sir," Porter called back. "I can't reach."

"Christ on a bike," groaned Kett, so much blood in his skull that he thought he could hear it sloshing around. It literally couldn't get any worse, he thought, and then he felt Porter fumbling around his crotch.

"Nearly got it, sir."

"Got *what*? That's not my belt!"

"Hang on, just a second..."

It felt like a million years later that the pressure around his middle suddenly vanished. Kett squawked as he fell, his shoulder bouncing off the side of the toilet as he landed in a miserable heap—still upside down.

"You okay, sir?" Porter asked.

"No!" he shot back.

He manoeuvred himself around as best he could in the tiny space, breathing a sigh of relief as the blood began to drain back into the rest of his body. He collected his belongings, seeing that he'd missed another call—from DS Spalding. When he pulled himself back to his feet, his trousers slipped to his knees, and he hoisted them back up, refastening his belt before taking a moment to collect himself.

All in all, it could have been a lot worse.

The camera crew could have been filming the whole thing.

"Right," he said to himself.

There was no point announcing his presence because half of Norfolk must have heard him hit the floor. He opened the folding door and squeezed into a narrow corridor lit only by an algae-ridden skylight. It was hot enough in here to cook chicken, the air dead and heavy. Directly across from him was the main door, and he twisted the latch to open it. Porter was already waiting there.

"Look a bit rosy, sir," said the DI as he followed the breeze inside.

"Next time, *you're* going through the fucking window," growled Kett. "And I'm not even going to open it first. Check the bedroom."

Kett made his way into the living space he'd spotted

earlier, using his knuckles to open the cupboards and the oven. Whoever lived here had kept the place spotless, just a few plates and cups, some cans of tomato soup and packets of croutons. The fridge was switched off and cleaned out, just the faintest of unpleasant aromas.

There was nothing else of note, the carpets were recently vacuumed, the sofas spotless. There were a couple of books on the coffee table, both Miss Marple compendiums creased with age. Kett flicked through them as carefully as he could, but there wasn't so much as a bookmark.

His phone began to ring again, and this time he answered it.

"Oh, so you've got time for me now, sir?" said Spalding.

"Sorry, Alison, I was just... hanging around," he said, disappointed that Porter wasn't here to catch the joke. "What have you got?"

"Bianca Caddel, sir," said Spalding. "She's sixty-three, born in Wales but lived all over the place. Bought the land in 2018, put in planning for a house a few times, latest in 2019, but never got permission. Registered disabled for arthritis. Never married, no children, and no record. She isn't known to us at all. I can't find a single photo of her, other than her driving licence."

"Thanks," said Kett. "The car's definitely hers?"

"It is. Bought four years ago from a dealer in the city. She doesn't own another vehicle. Not one on the system, anyway."

"You found anything to suggest why she'd cut a man's head off and plant his limbs in a garden?" said Kett, leaning against the counter to ease his aching back. "Or attack a group of kids in the woods?"

"No, sir," said Spalding. "I haven't found anything at all.

No family, no friends, no social media, no phone, if you can believe it. She's a ghost."

Or a witch, thought Kett, rubbing his face.

"Thanks, Alison," he said. "Kate back yet?"

"They've just walked in, sir," she said. "Duke's doing push-ups for the camera crew."

Kett laughed quietly as he hung up, stretching his spine while he walked back down the corridor. Porter was on his way out of the master bedroom, shaking his head.

"Nothing," he said. "Some books, some clothes, about a hundred pairs of pants. *Big* pants. Lacy ones."

"I don't need to know about the pants, Pete," said Kett.

"But there's so many of them, sir." He shuddered. "There's a cubby with an extra bed that looks like it's never been slept in. Whole place doesn't have a spot of dust."

Kett retreated towards the door.

"Does this seem like the home of somebody who would kidnap a teenage girl?" he asked. "Something's not adding up."

"Oi!"

Clare's voice rang across the field, the Super approaching with a face like a bull with a bee sting to the bollocks. He was still holding a Bounty.

"Oi!" he said again. "What are you two doing jizzing around in there?"

"Definitely weren't jizzing, sir," said Porter.

Clare pointed the Bounty at Kett like it was a pistol.

"Was that door open when you got here, because according to my constables, it was locked."

"It's open now, sir," said Kett.

Clare glared at him.

"Find anything?"

"No," said Kett. "Clean as a whistle."

"And that helps us how?" said Clare.

Kett didn't know how to answer that. He took a few steps away from the caravan, looking up into the enormous sky as the bird of prey continued to swoop overhead. It called out again, which struck Kett as odd. Why would it draw attention to itself?

It suddenly dived to the ground, maybe fifty yards away, almost too quick to keep track of. It called again as it rose, a long, lonely cry.

"What are you gawping at, Kett?" asked Clare. "Never seen a bird before?"

The kestrel—he was pretty sure that's what it was—screeched again, then plummeted earthwards in the exact same place, disappearing into a copse of low bushes.

"Give me a second, sir," said Kett.

He wasn't sure if it was the exhaustion, or the heat, or the fact that there was still too much blood in his head, but there was definitely something strange about the behaviour of the bird. It flapped into the sky again and swooped overhead, calling out repeatedly. It dived once more. Then, when he had almost reached it, it darted to the side, landing delicately on the branches of a nearby oak tree.

"What is it with birds today?" he said, before realising he was on his own. Porter and Clare watched him from the caravan—which seemed too far away, as if he'd taken giant steps across the field. The shift in perspective gave him a sudden rush of vertigo, the whole world rolling beneath his feet, and he jabbed his hands out to his sides automatically. It was so hot he felt *drunk*.

He walked on, pushing into the bushes, feeling the dark eyes of the kestrel as it watched from its tree.

Then stopping.

A small concrete pillar stood in the middle of the

bushes, maybe three feet high and big enough to hold a metal trapdoor on its shoulders.

"What the hell?"

The kestrel launched itself upwards, vanishing over the trees. Kett stepped back, his heart taking flight alongside the bird. The trapdoor was metal, and sealed with a padlock. He returned through the bushes, yelling.

"Hey! I've found something. Going to need some bolt cutters."

He watched Porter spring into action, running back to the car. Clare was goose-stepping over the long grass towards him. Kett rubbed his face again, the exhaustion almost too much to bear as he returned to the trapdoor.

"What the toss is that doing out here?" said Clare as he walked up beside him, brushing leaves from his hair.

"Nothing good, sir," said Kett. "Looks like a Cold War bunker."

They both waited as Porter shambled through the bushes, almost tripping. He held out the bolt cutters and Kett took them. They made short work of the padlock, and Kett kicked it into the long grass.

"You got any gloves, sir?" asked Kett.

"No," grunted Clare. "Get it open."

Kett grabbed one side of the door and Porter took the other. It weighed a tonne, Kett's spine crunching like there was glass in it as he heaved it up. Eventually, gravity took over, the door crashing against the concrete pillar so hard Kett felt the ground shake.

Inside the pillar was a narrow shaft, a metal ladder fastened into the rough brick walls. It led into a darkness that didn't seem possible on a summer's day like this, as if the entirety of the night had taken shelter in there.

Kett held his breath—*everyone* seemed to hold their

breath—to better hear the aching silence that emanated from whatever lay beneath the ground.

"Nope, fuck this," Porter said, stepping back.

"What is it?" Clare asked, wiping a hand over his chocolate-stained lips.

"What else can it be?" Kett said quietly, his words dropping into the dark like stones. "It's a doorway to hell."

CHAPTER FOURTEEN

"FORTY-TWO, FORTY-THREE, FORTY-FOUR!"

Savage sat at her desk, doing her best to ignore the chant that was taking place in the middle of the bullpen. Duke had stripped to his shirt and was grinning like a circus performer as he showed off his gym skills. He'd already done a hundred push-ups, and now he was on his back doing crunches.

Josh was filming him with his enormous camera, Megan and Kelly perched on chairs as they cheered him on. The fourth member of the crew, Milo, held a mic on a pole, but he was staring at his phone.

A handful of uniformed officers had joined in the vocal support, offering various whoops for the benefit of the show. Only Spalding was unimpressed. She had left the room a few minutes ago, claiming that she was off to find a spoon to gouge her own eyes out with.

"Go on, Aaron!" yelled Megan, who was ogling Duke with a little too much enthusiasm for Savage's liking. "You're nearly there!"

Savage tried to focus on the screen in front of her.

Google's home page waited patiently, but she was struggling to work out where to start. She ran her finger delicately along the keyboard, picking out crumbs and thinking about what they'd found that morning.

It was difficult, because the whole thing felt like a dream. Her memories of the ruins, and of the garden of the cottage, felt fuzzy around the edges, as if her brain was doing its best to erase them.

If you can't remember it, she thought*, it never happened.*

She pulled her phone from her pocket, navigating to the notes she'd made at the crime scene. She'd taken photos too, of course, but she wasn't quite ready to look at them yet.

The first thing she'd written was 'black beans,' so that's where she started.

"Dead man's head, black beans," she said as she typed the words in. "Sorry, Google."

What followed was, rather predictably, a lot of recipes for various dishes that needed black beans. Savage clicked through a few of them, pausing for a moment on the black bean brownies, which looked quite nice. There were a couple of reviews for a book called Dead Man's Head, and plenty of articles about Tex-Mex barbeque, but that was it.

"One hundred!" cheered the crowd.

"Do me!" Megan added. "I mean, do *more*!"

Savage threw a scowl over her shoulder, only to see that Duke *was* doing Megan—in the sense that he had picked up her chair, with her in it, and was proceeding to use her for some arm curls. His audience went wild, especially the young camerawoman, who clung to her chair and squealed like a giddy child. Josh was capturing it all on his camera, zooming in on Duke's biceps which were drenched in sweat and, Savage had to admit, even more impressive than they usually looked.

"Focus," she told herself.

She clicked on the search bar, drumming her fingers on the desk. The head they'd found hadn't been left there randomly, it had been decorated almost like a religious totem. Whatever had been done to it held meaning. It was a ritual, or a rite.

She typed in: *black beans, ritual meaning.*

The first few entries were variations on what she'd found before, but halfway down the page she was surprised to see a Wikipedia entry about an ancient Roman festival.

"The Lemuria," she read, waiting for the page to load and scanning the first paragraph. "'*An annual event where Romans performed rites to exorcise malevolent and fearful ghosts of the restless dead from their homes.*'"

She read quickly, finding the reference to beans in the next section. According to the article, anyone wanting to perform the ritual walked through the house at midnight, washed their hands in spring water, then took a mouthful of black beans.

"Shit," said Savage, pulling out her notepad and patting her pockets for a pen. She couldn't find one, and Duke was now too busy bench pressing his new girlfriend to hear her calling his name. She used her phone instead, starting a text message to DCI Kett.

Black beans have a meaning, they were used by Romans, who spat them out of their mouths for hungry ghosts to gather. Weird coincidence, beans in the mouth?

She didn't send it yet, turning back to Google and scrolling down until she found another entry.

"The spiritual meaning of beans," she read, clicking through to find herself on a flashing neon website that gave her an instant headache.

She read quickly, discovering that beans were a symbol of peace, life and health.

"Not for our victim they're not," she muttered, returning to the home page.

She paused again, wondering whether she should ask for help somewhere. But the only person she could think of who might have had any idea what the crime scene symbolised was Norman Balls, and after the Jack Valentine case they'd been instructed not to contact him for any reason whatsoever because his constant meddling in active cases kept leading to disaster.

"No more," she heard Duke say. "It's too hot. Sorry, sorry."

He limped across the room, his face purple and mottled and slick with sweat. He only managed half a smile before crashing into the seat beside Savage.

"Dying," he groaned. "Was not expecting to have to do that."

"Pretty sure you didn't *have* to do it, Aaron," she replied.

"Hard to say no, though," he said, groaning again. "Can I hide under the desk for a moment?"

It was too late. Kelly had followed him over, Josh beside her, that infernal camera still mounted on his shoulder. Megan came too, her own cheeks flushed.

"Can I get you some water, Aaron?" she said.

"Uh... yeah, that would be lovely, thank you, Meggy," he replied.

Savage would have elbowed him if the camera hadn't been watching.

"Hard to say no, indeed," she muttered instead, closing the browser before anyone could catch what was on it.

"That was fab," said Kelly, giving Duke a smile that

didn't go anywhere near her eyes. "Great B-roll. Everyone loves a bit of skin. But we're here for the action. Any chance we'll be heading out again soon?"

"It's hard to say," Savage answered. "But probably not."

"Can you tell us what you're working on yet?"

"No," said Savage. "Sorry."

Kelly puffed out a sigh.

"What about a little heat between you two?" she went on.

"What?" said Savage. "You're not making *that* sort of film."

"I mean an argument," said Kelly. "The pressures of the job, the strains on your relationship, the perils of devoting yourself to a career to the neglect of everything else. People want to see the downside of being Britain's Bravest Copper and his girlfriend."

"Is that all I am now?" said Savage, a little madder than she had expected to be. "The *girlfriend*?"

"You're a lovely girlfriend," said Duke, completely missing the point. "I mean, *fiancé*."

"You want us to have an argument?" said Savage.

Kelly nodded.

"We don't really do that, sorry."

The woman sucked air through her teeth.

"Of course you don't. Well, we might as well go get our lunch then. If you end up doing anything remotely interesting, please holler."

She strolled off, her phone to her ear. Josh moved in, lowering the camera and speaking quietly.

"Remember, it doesn't have to be real," he said. "Give it a bit of spice. Everyone loves an argument." He wiggled his eyebrows. "Or a bit of passion."

He walked away before Savage could think of a reply.

Megan was crossing the room from the direction of the kitchen, walking painfully slowly so as not to spill anything from the pint glass that she had filled to the brim. She placed it delicately next to the computer, giving Duke an adoring look.

"Thanks, Meggy," he said.

"Thanks, Meggy," Savage mimicked when the girl had run off.

"What?" said Duke after he'd downed half the glass in one go.

"Nothing," said Savage, hating the unpleasant stew of jealousy she felt in her gut.

"I thought we didn't argue."

"We don't. I'm not." She retrieved the browser window. "I'm *working*."

"Cool," said Duke, oblivious. "What are you looking for?"

He leaned in, then laughed.

"Beans! I knew they'd be the key to the case."

Savage laughed too, before she could stop herself.

"You might be right, you dope," she told him. "Found a couple of things about black beans. They've got some kind of supernatural power, especially when you put them in your mouth."

"That's kind of where beans are supposed to go," said Duke. "Isn't it?"

She couldn't argue with that.

"Did witches used to use them?" Duke asked, finishing the drink and using his bare arm to mop his brow. "There must be a connection, given where we found the head."

"The witch's tree," said Savage, nodding. "Good question."

She added 'witches' to the end of the last search. The

top answer this time was an archived magazine article about beans throughout history. She read through it, but Duke beat her to it.

"There," he said, pointing. "If a witch attacks you, put a bean in your mouth then spit it out at her and she'll disappear. That has to be it, right?"

"Makes sense," said Savage. "If somebody believed in the rumour of the witch's tree, and they were worried she might be woken, then planting a dead man's head with a mouth filled with beans kind of fits with this."

"Except dead men can't spit," said Duke with a frown.

"That is very true."

They read on together.

"This ties in more with what I'm thinking," said Savage, tapping the screen. "A ritual of some kind. It says here, beans were used as objects of power by the Ancient Egyptians, and by the Romans—I found something on that already, more beans in mouths."

"Could do with some beans in my mouth," said Duke, rubbing his stomach. "Baked beans, though."

"Focus," Savage told him. "Says here beans were used in arcane rituals as well."

It did, but there were no further details. Savage hopped back to Google and added 'arcane rituals' to her search. There was nothing new until she'd reached the end of the first page, and there she saw something that made her sit forward in her seat.

"The encyclopaedia of darkness," she read.

"Sounds cheery," said Duke as they waited for the page to load. It was littered with so many adverts, all moving at once, that it took Savage a while to find the actual article.

When she did, though, she felt her scalp shrivel.

"'*Method for a demonic summoning*,'" she read, seeing

an illustration of a monstrous creature, its hideous face grinning at her, its eyes burning. "'*From the Grimoirium Verum.*'"

"Shit," said Duke, and she was grateful for the weight of his shoulder against hers as he leaned forward. "Demons?"

Savage read the rest of the piece in her head, not quite willing to speak it aloud. Now that she was aware of it, the bullpen had fallen almost silent, the TV crew nowhere to be seen, the uniformed officers absent and Spalding still not back at her desk. There was only her and Duke, and she pressed herself closer to him as she read.

"'*You must start the ritual before sunrise. Place the head of a dead man in a sacred spot. Put black beans in his mouth, in his eyes, in his ears, then make the mark of the demon upon his head.*'"

There were two illustrations here. The first was a crude sketch of a demon, curved horns meeting over its twisted face. Its eyes burned with fire, its lips pulled back in a growl.

The second was an ornate series of ovals and crosses that Savage had seen before.

"That might be what was cut into the scalp of the victim," she said. "That pattern."

"This is so weird," said Duke. "It says you have to bury the head for nine days, and every morning before the sun comes up you have to water it with brandy."

"That's what we smelled in the ruins," said Savage.

Duke took over, reading quietly.

"'*On the eighth day, you will arrive at the head to find a spirit watching it. The spirit will say three words to you: 'what wilt thou?'*'"

"What wilt thou?" said Duke. "What does that mean?"

"I have no idea," said Savage. "Keep going."

Duke did as he was told.

"'You must tell it that you are there to water your plant, and when the spirit asks if it may water the plant, you must refuse it. After this, the spirit will stretch out its hand and you will see the same mark that you drew upon its head. Only then should you let the spirit water the plant. It will do so, and then depart.'"

He shook his head.

"This is nuts."

Savage took over, whispering the final part.

"'When you return on the ninth and final day, the beans will be germinating. Remove them from the head and put them in your mouth. You will be rendered invisible.'"

"Invisible?" said Duke. "How?"

"I don't think it's real, Aaron," said Savage. She scrolled back to the top of the page, finding the title of the article which she'd missed because of the flashing adverts.

"It says here that the name of the demon is Morail," she said.

Across the room, a window blew open hard enough to shatter the glass. Savage jumped from her seat hard enough to knock it over.

"Fucking Nora," said Duke, a hand to his heart. "I thought I closed that after the whole seagull thing this morning. Sorry."

Duke picked up Savage's chair, and she slumped down again, her pulse like thunder. Static danced in her vision.

"I'll sort it," said Duke. "But it's weird, isn't it? There's no wind today."

"I know," said Savage, looking at the window, then turning once again to the article on-screen.

The image of the demon stared back at her with eyes made of fire, its teeth bared in a lipless grin.

CHAPTER FIFTEEN

"Best two out of three?" said Porter.

Kett stood with Porter and Clare in the middle of Bianca Caddel's field, the sun doing its best to cremate them. In front of them, the shaft of the bunker yawned open, breathing stale, cold air—a dead man's breath if ever Kett had felt one. Porter had tried shining a torch down it, but the light hadn't come close to reaching the bottom. It felt well-deep.

A doorway to hell, he thought again.

"No chance," Kett said to the DI. "You lost. Scissors beat paper."

"That wasn't paper, sir," said Porter, studying his hand as if it had betrayed him. "It was a flat rock."

"A flat rock?"

"Yeah. Like the ones you skim at the beach. They have to be flat or it won't work. That's what I was doing, a flat rock. Scissors don't beat a flat rock."

"I'm going to beat you both with a flat rock in a minute," said Clare. "Kett, get down the bloody hole."

"Why me, sir? Porter lost!"

"Because you're his boss, you should lead by example," said Clare.

"But you're my boss, sir. *You* should lead by example."

Clare wiped his dripping brow, leaning in and speaking dangerously.

"Aggie Clegg might be down there right now. You either climb in, Kett, or I'm going to toss you."

"I'd take the ladder, sir," said Porter, grimacing.

Kett muttered a handful of obscenities beneath his breath as he pulled off his jacket and rolled up his shirt sleeves. He had to climb onto the concrete pillar first, stones digging into the soft flesh beneath his knees. He clung on like he was at the top of a mountain, then reversed slowly over the edge.

It took an age to find the first rung with his foot, and when his boot slipped on the smooth metal he thought his heart had shot right out of his open mouth, soaring above the trees like the bastard kestrel that had led them here.

"Whatever you do, don't fall," said Clare. "I've got enough bloody work to do without filling in your death papers."

"I'll do my best not to inconvenience you, sir," said Kett.

He landed his other foot and took hold of the side of the ladder.

"Just don't look down, sir," said Porter.

He immediately looked down. It seemed even darker than it had before. Porter must have read his mind, because he leaned over to offer Kett his torch.

"Here you go, sir," he said.

"I haven't got any hands, Pete," Kett replied, barely hanging on.

"Open your mouth then."

"What?" Kett said, and in the middle of the word Porter slid the slim torch between his teeth.

"*Pweet, nrgl,*" he told him, but Porter had backed away. "*Jwesus Cwyst.*"

He started down the ladder, the torch doing a feeble job of lighting the way. He counted the rungs as he went, reaching fifteen before the entrance to the shaft was just a pale square of light overhead. It took another twenty before he stretched his foot down and found the base of the shaft. He stepped off carefully, in case the ground wasn't as solid as it looked.

He pulled the torch from his mouth and swept it in a full circle. The only exit was a narrow tunnel opposite the ladder, the walls made from the same bricks as the shaft, the ceiling arched. At the end of that was what looked like a room, the wavering torch making the shadows dance like ghosts.

It was cold down here—freezing, really, compared to the world above—but that wasn't why Kett's entire body seemed to crunch into goosebumps.

"Hello?" he croaked, his voice flitting down the tunnel like a living thing, then bouncing right back.

No reply, but there was something in the swirling currents of cool air that made him feel like he wasn't on his own. He put one hand on the ladder.

"I'm at the bottom," he yelled, his voice echoing upwards. If Clare or Porter had heard him, they didn't reply, and there was no sign of them at the top. "Oi, Pete, you coming down?"

Still nothing, and Kett suddenly pictured the trapdoor slamming shut, burying him alive here while whatever was in the room at the end of the tunnel crawled and whispered towards him.

"Nope," he said, the fear thrashing inside his chest.

He'd set one boot on the bottom rung, ready to start climbing, when a shadow slid into the shaft overhead. It was Porter, the big DI blotting out most of the light as he clattered down. Kett moved into the tunnel to get out of his way, the temperature dropping another few degrees. He turned the torch to the room ahead, the shadows sliding out of the way, darting into hiding.

"God, I hate this fucking place," said Porter as he neared the bottom. "Hate this fucking job, hate every fucking thing."

He stepped off the ladder, ducking to fit inside the tunnel.

"Please tell me there's nothing here, and that we're good to go, sir," he said.

"There's definitely something here," said Kett.

He moved forward, calling out as he went.

"This is the police. If anyone is down here, make yourself known."

The final few words echoed back as if there was a chorus of spirits calling to him. His skin was still armoured with goosebumps, his body so rigid with apprehension that he could barely get a breath in. The cold air stank of the earth, of damp and rot and neglect. As much as he tried not to, he kept thinking of the woman he'd seen on the video in the woods, her dark eyes full of malice.

The witch.

As slowly as he could, and with Porter treading on his heels, he walked to the end of the tunnel. It opened out to the left, the trickle of torchlight revealing a room that was maybe five metres square, the ceiling supported on steel joists. There were no lights, but ten or twelve brackets had been fastened to the wall, each holding a fat, yellow candle.

Sculptures of wax hung from them like stalactites, smoke stains reaching for the ceiling.

The room was largely empty, except for a large wooden table and a metal filing cabinet against the left-hand wall. The floor was tiled with terracotta slabs, most of which were covered by one of the biggest rugs Kett had ever seen.

There were two doors, one directly opposite, and one in the wall to the right.

"Hello?" Kett called out. "Bianca? Aggie? Anyone down here? It's the police."

No sound at all penetrated the silence of the room. Kett walked to the door on the right, opening it to reveal another space, similarly sized. This one was lined with metal shelves that groaned beneath the weight of a supermarket's worth of canned food and bottled water.

"Somebody was worried about the world ending," said Porter.

"Check it out. I'll try the other one."

Kett crept towards the second door, the thick rug muting his footsteps.

"And don't eat anything," he shouted back. "It's evidence."

He tried the handle to find it locked. He ducked down to look through the keyhole, but whatever lay beyond was as black as pitch.

"Hello?" he said. "If anyone's in there, let me know."

He put his ear to the keyhole, holding his breath.

And he heard something tap from deeper inside the room.

It came again, a rhythmic *knock, knock, knock.*

"Shit," he said, standing upright and wincing as a blade of pain slid between his vertebrae.

"Got something, sir?" Porter said, appearing in the first

door. He had his phone in his hand, the weak flashlight powerless.

"Maybe. You?"

"Nothing living," said Porter. "Plenty of biscuits, though."

"Can you yell up to Clare, tell him we need a crowbar?" Kett asked.

Porter nodded to the torch in Kett's hand.

"Can I take that, sir?"

"No."

"But it's dark, and my phone is useless."

"No."

The DI groaned his way out of the room, and Kett heard him hollering up the shaft. He ran back like he had the devil on his tail, taking shelter in the bubble of light from the torch. He brushed both hands down his shirt, shivering.

"Hate it," he said. "Hate it, hate it, hate it."

Kett ignored him, returning to the second door.

"We're about to come in. If you can hear me and can't reply, stand well back."

Nothing answered him.

Kett crossed the rug to the table. It was wooden, and looked like it weighed a tonne. He had no idea how anyone had managed to get it down the shaft. There was nothing on it except for five candles positioned in a rough semi-circle, each one surrounded by a puddle of wax. Deep grooves had been etched into the wood between them, tainted red as if somebody had been let loose with a felt tip.

Porter opened the top drawer of the filing cabinet, rummaging through the paperwork inside.

"Newspaper articles," he said, plucking one out.

Kett held the torch to it, seeing a report from nearly ten years ago—the murder of a child.

"I remember that," Porter said. "Marcy Hudson. Dad killed her and her little brother, over in King's Lynn. Said some kind of spirit made him do it, but he was an addict, off his face."

He pulled out another one, a second death. This was a drowning from four years ago, a woman in her sixties who had wandered into the sea at dawn.

"No idea who that is," said Porter.

He laid several folders on the desk and opened the next drawer down.

"More of them in here, sir."

He tried the bottom drawer, and they both saw that it was empty. Kett pored through the newspaper clippings, seeing death after death after death—from all over the region, and dating back at least thirty years. There were hundreds of them.

"Can you go check on that crowbar, Pete?"

"Do I have to?" Porter asked.

He didn't wait for Kett to answer, making his way back to the tunnel. As he went, something crunched beneath the rug. Porter stopped, looked down, then turned to Kett. They both stepped off the rug, grabbing the end and lifting it. It was heavy, and seemed to resist them with every fabric of its being, but between them, they managed to roll it a quarter of the way across the room.

Far enough to see what was on the floor.

Two triangles had been cut into the tiles, the lines deep enough and straight enough that they could only have been made with an angle grinder. Just like the grooves that had been left in the table, these were stained red. Somebody had drawn symbols along each of the lines, shapes that he could make no sense of. A mound of dry wax sat at the point of each triangle—this was what had crunched beneath Porter's shoe, Kett realised.

"What the hell is it?" Porter said.

"You don't see it?"

The DI frowned, studying the triangles, then the section of floor that was still covered with the rug. Kett saw the moment it dawned on him.

"Holy shit," he said. "It's a pentagon."

"Pentagram," Kett corrected.

"Same thing, sir."

"It's really not," said Kett.

"What's the difference?"

"Did you fail maths at school, Pete?" Kett asked him. "Pentagon is a five-sided shape. A fifty pence coin. A pentagram's used for magic and stuff."

Something rattled across the room, echoing so much that Kett couldn't tell which direction it was coming from. He lifted the torch to the second door, holding his breath as the noise came again.

"What's going on down here?" came a voice from right behind them.

The scream was out of Kett's mouth before he could stop it. Fortunately, it was drowned out by an even louder scream from Porter, who jumped so high his head cracked off one of the steel beams. Kett spun around so fast he almost toppled over, seeing Clare's monstrous face slide from the darkness of the tunnel like some kind of man-eating goblin.

"Jesus Christ," said Kett, choking on his own spit. "You could have bloody warned us you were coming, sir."

"And ruin your little toss-off?" said Clare, blinding Kett with his torch before moving it to Porter. The DI was bent double, rubbing the top of his head with both hands and moaning softly. "What on earth are you two up to?"

Kett spotted the crowbar in Clare's other hand. He pocketed the torch, allowing the shadows to creep back in.

"Can I have that, sir?"

He took the heavy crowbar and carried it to the second door, careful not to trip on the rug. His heart was still going ten to the dozen. He felt like he'd aged about forty years in the last twelve seconds.

"Heard a sound from back here," he said. "A tapping. Might be our missing girl."

"Get it open, then," said Clare. "Stop crying and go help him, Pete."

"Not crying, sir," grumbled Porter as he walked over. "Can I borrow that after you've used it?" he said quietly. "Going to ram it somewhere the sun doesn't shine."

"I heard that," said Clare.

Kett jammed the chisel edge of the crowbar into the door, nodding to Porter to make sure he was ready.

"On three," he said. "One, two..."

He leaned on the crowbar with all his weight, while Porter shoulder-charged the door. It didn't stand a chance, the frame splintering, the door exploding inwards before rebounding off the wall. Porter tumbled into the dark with a yelp, Kett moving in quickly after him, the crowbar raised against the dark.

"Police!" he yelled. "Nobody move!"

It was too dark to see whether there was anything in here capable of moving—other than Porter, who got unsteadily back to his feet. Clare was at the door in a second, holding his torch up to reveal a third room, slightly smaller than the one they'd just left.

Something stared at them through the shifting dark, a grinning, lipless face with insane eyes.

"I said don't move!" Kett yelled, taking a few steps forward, the crowbar heavy in his hand.

Clare moved too, his torch picking out the face in more detail.

It was a painted mask sitting on a metal shelving unit. A pair of ornate horns curled upwards from the leering grin, a long beard that looked as if it was made from real human hair.

The Superintendent swept the light from right to left, picking out a dozen more shelves, each one looking like it belonged inside an art gallery, or a museum. Kett saw blood-red candles, silver chalices, too many taxidermied animals to count and maybe a hundred books. Wooden contraptions and clockwork mechanisms that he couldn't identify teetered in piles. Oil paintings rested against the wall between the shelves, old-fashioned clothes and wicked smiles. In one corner was a stack of poles topped with blades, rusted with age.

In another was an enormous grandfather clock, tick-tocking with solemn precision.

Kett lowered the crowbar and pulled out the torch.

"That's the noise I heard."

"Well done, Robbie," Clare said as he walked into the room. "You've rescued a clock."

Kett shot a look at the back of the Superintendent's head before heading for the nearest shelving unit. It was crammed with stuff, like an antique shop. On the top shelf were seven books that looked ancient, their leather spines cracked and crumbling. He had to put his glasses on to read the words on the spine, but it didn't do much good because they were in French.

"*Grimore de Dragon Rouge*," he said.

"Grimoire of the Red Dragon," Clare translated.

"*The Book of Solomon*," Kett went on, making his way down the shelf. "*The Grand Oracle of Heaven. La Poule Noire.*"

"The Black Chicken?" said Clare.

"Never mind the books," said Porter. "Look at this."

Kett walked to where the DI was standing, following his outstretched finger to a human hand that sat on the shelf. It looked too real to be anything but, the skin waxy, every hair standing out perfectly, the nails partially bitten, blisters on the palm. It had been preserved somehow, then mounted onto a stand, a rusting pole inserted into the flesh of the wrist. The thumb and first two fingers had been bent into the palm, the last two fingers stretched up towards the shelf above.

"Looks like a monkey's paw," said Kett.

"That's definitely not a monkey's paw, sir," Porter replied.

"It's just what they're called. You use them to make a wish. Every time you do, you bend a finger."

He caught Porter looking at him.

"I saw it in a film," he explained. "They're usually monkey hands. And they're not real."

"It looks real," said Porter.

"So does this," said Clare.

Kett and Porter gathered around the Super to see what he was talking about. It was a head, but one that was so old it looked as if it had been mummified. The skin was so warped and leathery that Kett couldn't tell if it was meant to be a man or a woman. He would have argued that it was fake, a Halloween prop, except once again he saw the finer details that made it all too convincing: the top of the tattoo on the skin of the neck, the earring holes, the thin lashes around the closed and sunken eyelids.

"Severed head, that's too much of a coincidence," said Clare. "This is our killer. I want you to turn this shithole upside down. Find out who they are, and where they've taken Aggie."

He beamed his torch at Kett again, detonating a supernova of brightness in his retinas.

"Kett, get up the ladder and call forensics in."

"Yes, sir."

"And leave the torch," Clare added, taking it from him before he could object.

Kett fired up the light on his phone instead, the cowering glow barely penetrating the dark of the first room before being swallowed alive by the tunnel. He had to pocket it to climb the ladder, that pool of black shadow rising beneath him like cold water.

He scaled the last few rungs like a drowning man, clawing his way back onto the pillar, then throwing himself onto the warm grass with such urgency that the waiting officers came running over.

"Are you okay, sir?" asked one. "What happened?"

"I'm fine," he said, rolling onto his back, basking in the glorious day. "I'm fine. Can one of you do me a favour and call a forensic unit? Tell them it's urgent."

Freed from the suffocating tunnel, his phone had come to life. He felt it buzz four times, and when he pulled it out of his pocket, he saw that three of the alerts were missed calls from Savage. The last was a text that she'd sent him a few minutes ago. It was so long it took up the entire screen.

He called her back without reading it.

"Sir?" she said. "Did you get my text? I think I've found something. It's not good."

"What is it, Kate?" he said.

She hesitated, breathing hard.

"Kate?"

"It's going to sound crazy, but I think whoever is doing this is following some kind of black magic ritual," she said. "I think... I think they're trying to summon a demon."

"A demon?"

"It's hard to believe, sir, but..."

She tailed off.

"It's not that hard to believe, Kate," Kett said quietly, closing his eyes and hearing the magpies calling to him from the trees, feeling the stubborn chill of the cellar in his bones. "I think you're right."

CHAPTER SIXTEEN

Climbing back down that ladder was the last thing in the world that Kett wanted to do, but when the forensic vans rolled up half an hour later, he had no choice.

Fortunately, they came equipped, two PCs struggling down the shaft with portable halogens while Cara Hay rigged up the generator. The harsh glow made the cellar a little more bearable, but it also revealed every one of its grotesque contents in exquisite detail.

The rug had been rolled back all the way, discarded on one side of the room, revealing the pentagram in all its glory. It stretched almost from wall to wall, maybe four metres across, and each angle looked perfect. The grooves seemed to pulse red in the halogens, as if the blood that had been spilled there still contained some kind of life.

This place wasn't actually hell, but it wasn't far off.

"I want you in the back room," said Clare, directing the white-suited technicians. "I need a catalogue of everything you find in there. Tell me where it comes from, and what it means."

"Not sure I can do that," said Hay, beads of perspiration on her brow despite the cold air. "But we'll try."

She nodded to the pentagram.

"And that?"

"All I care about is whether it's real blood," said Clare, nodding to the red colouring in the grooves, as bright as a scar. "Same as the stains on the table. If it is, I need to know how old it is, and what it came from."

He turned to the room, his voice filling the space with ease.

"I don't need to remind you that we have a young woman who has been kidnapped. Something here will tell us where she is, I'm sure of it. Find it."

Hay ducked down to open her bag, and Clare turned to Kett.

"What took you so long?" he asked.

"I was speaking with Savage," he said. "She thinks that our killer is trying to—"

He paused because it sounded insane. Then he stared through the open door into the freak show of the cellar's museum and realised there was nothing insane about it at all.

"To summon a demon, sir."

To his surprise, Clare just nodded.

"She's uncovered a ritual online," Kett went on, pulling up her text on his phone. "It's a series of steps that are supposed to awaken a demon called Morail. You basically need a human head, some beans, some brandy, and this spirit will appear and make you invisible."

Clare nodded again.

"Uh..." said Kett, who'd been expecting more of a fight. "Morail's one of hundreds of demons from a book called the... hang on, the..."

"*Grimoirium Verum*," said Clare.

"Yeah, sir. That's right. How did you know?"

Clare headed back to the third room without answering, clicking his fingers until Kett followed. The halogens burned too hot, turning the space into a furnace. The almost subsonic buzz of them made it sound like the walls were crawling with flies. Everything looked too real in the harsh light, the horror of it more apparent than ever.

Kett scanned the objects on display, that macabre collection, seeing a horror film's worth of dull blades, mutated animal embryos in glass tanks, sculptures of wood and metal and bone that looked like they'd been carved by a madman.

From the shelf, the mummified head stared at him with glassy eyes.

His heart rolled over in his chest, his stomach contracting.

"Did you open its eyes, sir?" he asked, nodding to the head.

"What are you talking about, Kett?" barked Clare.

"The head. Its eyes were closed when we found it, weren't they?"

Clare and Porter both looked at the head, then back to Kett.

"You're losing it, Robbie, and I can't have that," said Clare, clicking his fingers again. "Stay awake, stay focussed. Savage say anything else?"

"No, but she's looking into Bianca Caddel for us."

"Good. This is what I wanted to show you."

Clare led Kett to another shelf where a leather-bound book took pride of place. It was enormous, bigger than the Yellow Pages when it had existed, and covered with a soft, pale leather that didn't look like anything Kett had ever seen before. It lay open, revealing pages as yellow as a corpse's teeth, their edges frayed.

The ink was so faded that Kett had to lean in to stand any chance of working out what had been drawn there, and even then he could barely make sense of the tangle of limbs and sinews and teeth and eyes that had been illustrated.

"It's a head, sir," said Porter, leaning over Kett's shoulder.

"Where?" he said, squinting through his glasses.

"Two eyes, a nose, a mouth."

"I know what a head is, Pete, I... Oh, yeah, I see it."

And as soon as he had, he couldn't work out why it had taken him so long. It could have been a sketch of the head they'd found just a few hours ago, resting on a mound of earth, its eyes hollowed out, its mouth gaping.

"It was left open on this page," said Clare. "The text is in Latin and I don't know enough to translate it, but the book is called the *Grimoirium Verum*. That's the True Grimoire."

"Grimoire, sir?" asked Kett.

"A book of spells and invocations," said Clare. "If you want to try to summon a demon, this is what you need. Our killer didn't even try to hide what they were looking at."

"Obviously thought nobody would discover this place, sir," said Porter.

"You found anything else, sir?"

"While you were pissing your boots upstairs?" said Clare.

"Pissing my—"

"We found this," he said, heading back across the room to a shelf that was covered in jars. Judging by the layer of dust on them, they hadn't been touched in a long time.

Clare pointed a finger at one on the second shelf. "Black beans, like the ones we found in our head."

Kett couldn't be sure because the glass was so filthy, but he nodded anyway.

"Oh, and not forgetting this," said Clare, crossing the room diagonally to where the collection of poles and tools and weapons had been propped in the corner.

The Superintendent shone his torch at a brutal sword, the kind a knight might have wielded in battle. There was blood on the dull, rusted blade, more pooling beneath it. It looked dry.

"Feel like maybe you should have led with the sword, sir," said Kett. "Before the beans."

"We've got everything the killer would need right here," said Clare. "This is their workshop, I'm sure of it."

"You think they dissected the body down here, then carried the parts up the ladder?" said Kett. "Drove them to the church, and the cottage, and planted them there?"

He blew out a sigh.

"No joke carrying a human torso up a ladder like that, sir," he said. "That's, what, eight stone at least, once you've taken the head and limbs off? How much does a head weigh?"

"Depends on the head," said Porter. "Yours and mine, five kilograms? Duke, maybe an ounce?"

Kett ignored him.

"From the footage we saw in the garage, Bianca doesn't look like she weighs more than that herself. She'd have struggled."

"She could have winched it, sir," said Porter. "Or tied it to the car, hauled it up that way."

"Or she might not be working alone," said Kett. "I'll head back up, see if Savage has found anything about her."

"I can do that for you, sir," said Porter, heading for the door.

"It's really fine, Pete," said Kett, both of them racing for the exit.

"Bollocks," said Clare, barging past them. "I'm going up. You two keep looking."

Kett followed the Super into the main basement room, watching him vanish into the tunnel. Cara Hay was spraying luminol onto the top of the wooden table while one of her team prepared an ultraviolet light.

"Bet you a fiver it's blood, sir," said Porter.

"You're going to bet that in a creepy bunker, full of dead things and weapons, which possibly belongs to a murderer who enjoys summoning demons, the red stuff we find on a table is blood?" said Kett.

"Yeah."

Cara shut off the nearest bank of lamps while her technician held the light over the table. Kett had been in enough crime scenes to know that when it glowed blue like that, something had been seriously injured.

Or killed.

"Told you, sir," said Porter. "You owe me a fiver."

"It's blood," said Cara, her face eerie in the UV light. "I think some of it is fresher than the rest."

"How do you mean?" asked Kett, walking over.

"I mean blood has been spilled here many times, over a long period. Years, maybe. There has been some effort to clean it up, I think. But the residue has collected in the grooves."

"When do you think it happened last?" asked Kett.

"Hard to say. Recently, though. Days. But..."

She aimed the lamp at the wall behind the table, then onto the floor beneath it.

"But not much. There's no spatter, and no pooling on the ground."

"So nobody carved up a body here?" Kett asked.

"Not unless it had already been drained," said Hay. "There's just not enough blood."

"Not up here there isn't," said Kett.

They turned as one to the pentagram. Dutifully, Cara sprayed luminol on the closest point, turning the lamp towards it. The same blue glow appeared, making it look like somebody had drawn the shape in a fine glow-in-the-dark marker.

"Very strange," said Cara, leaning over. "No spillage at all. Somebody has taken great care either to allow blood to only flow inside the lines, or to clean every drop from the tiles. I am thinking the former, because even a heavy-duty cleaner would leave some trace."

She stood back and switched on the lights again. They were so bright that Kett had to screw his eyes shut for a moment.

"This is not something I've seen before," she said, her brow furrowed. "It is worrying."

"Because they're obsessive," said Kett.

Hay nodded.

"If you take this much care with your work, you are prepared for anything," she said.

"Did you find anything else of note at the ruin, or in the cottage?" Kett asked.

"We're still looking," she said. "But so far, we only found blood in one place in the cottage. The toilet."

"How much?"

"Not enough for a body," she said. "Although last I heard, they've just opened the septic tank in case it was flushed down there. My team did find something interesting, though. Blood clots."

"In the toilet?"

"Yes. Several of them. It suggests to me that the limbs were stored there prior to them being buried. Like..."

She struggled, as if she didn't want to say it.

"Like flowers, stored in a vase to stop them from dying," she finished quietly.

"Shit," said Porter.

"They'd been dead a while before they got to the cottage, then?" Kett asked.

"Before they were put in the toilet, yes," said Hay. "Any more than that, I cannot say."

"Thanks, Cara," said Kett. "Yell if you find anything else."

He left her to go back to work.

"You find anything in the storage room?" he asked Porter.

"Just food, water and medicine, sir," he replied. "No prescription drugs, but a lot of painkillers and antacids. There are enough supplies there to last somebody, I'm guessing, six months. No idea why they'd want to hide, though."

"Because the police are after them for murder?" suggested Kett.

"Yeah, fair point, sir."

In the back room, somebody screamed, followed by a clatter. Kett peeked through the door to see a technician stepping away from a shattered glass container. A dozen or so big-bodied spiders poured from the shards, scuttling beneath the shelves, climbing the dead animals, the mummified limbs. He felt his skin itch beneath his clothes.

"Right," he said, struggling to pull in a breath in the

claustrophobic space. He backtracked to the filing cabinet beside the table. "I'm going to get these files up top. See if I can make any sense of them."

"Why don't you let me do that for you, sir?" said Porter.

"It's fine, Pete. I'd better do it."

"But it's what I'm here for, sir, to make your life easier."

Another scream from the back room.

"Why don't we both go?" said Kett. "Leave forensics to do their thing?"

"We're just getting in the way," said Porter, gathering a pile of folders beneath one arm.

"It'll take two people to carry all these up anyway," said Kett. "It's definitely not because I'm scared."

"I'm definitely not scared either, sir," said Porter, edging towards the tunnel that led to the ladder. He looked back nervously. "But let's get a wiggle on, yeah?"

CHAPTER SEVENTEEN

It was a compendium of death, an encyclopaedia of the very worst of humanity.

With nowhere else to work, Kett started laying the documents from the bunker on the table inside the caravan. But within minutes they'd spilled out over the living room floor, covering the surfaces in the kitchen, and then the beds too. There were hundreds of them, mostly articles cut from local and national papers, the paper so thin that it almost crumbled under Kett's touch. There were printouts from websites, too, as well as countless photographs.

They all had one thing in common.

Murder.

Hundreds of violent deaths had been documented, almost all of them in East Anglia. The oldest that Kett had found was dated 1956: a milkman who was strangled, his body buried in a shallow grave in the woods. The most recent was from earlier this year, when a pair of so-called vigilantes had beaten a man to death for assaulting a teenage boy nearly a decade ago—a crime he'd been found not-guilty of in court.

Kett found some familiar faces in there too, starting with his newspaper girls. There was even a photograph of him at a press conference shortly after they'd found them. By the time every single document had been spread out, he'd spotted almost all of his cases since moving to Norfolk Police.

The Pig Man was there too, of course.

Each article was marked by one of three symbols, written in red pen in the top right corner. The first, on most, was a cross. The second was a question mark. The third, and Kett had only found a handful of these, all of which he'd positioned on the table, was a circle.

"You made any sense of this yet, sir?" said Porter, who was on all fours on the floor as he perused the collection of articles.

"Not yet," said Kett. "But they're obviously obsessed with death. I haven't found anything here that isn't a murder or a kidnapping. Have you?"

"Couple of things," said Porter. "I put them in the bedroom. Oh, wait, here's another circle."

He picked up a newspaper article and dropped it onto the table. Staring up at Kett from a faded black-and-white photograph was a teenage boy. It was the kind of photo they only ever used for an obituary, and sure enough, when he read the headline, he saw that the boy had died.

His name had been James Watton, and he'd fallen prey to a County Lines gang six years ago. The article mentioned that he'd been stabbed to death and dismembered, possibly by a rival group, but it didn't say any more than that.

"You remember this one, Pete?" asked Kett, studying the little red O in the corner.

"It's Lincolnshire, isn't it, sir?" Porter replied. Kett scanned the article again and saw that he was right.

"I remember it happening," Porter went on. "Vaguely. Those cases are hard to forget, right?"

"They put anyone away for it?"

"Not that I can recall, sir," said Porter.

Kett left the article next to the others. They made for a strange selection. Two involved the deaths of pensioners, one who'd been found weeks post-mortem, practically dissolved into his sofa. The other had been discovered by dog walkers in the middle of Foxley Woods, dead from an apparent heart attack.

One didn't involve a human at all. It was a report on missing cats. Six of them had vanished from a town just south of Norwich, and one had been returned with its tail missing—but otherwise in good health. There were five other articles, each detailing a murder, and each more horrific than the last.

"What does that little circle mean?" Kett said. He was talking to himself, but it was Porter who answered.

"You think our killer was responsible for these, sir? They could be detailing their own crimes, making a collection."

"Maybe," said Kett. He leaned back in his chair, sweating through his shirt even though he wasn't wearing his jacket. "But why would they just mix them up with all the others? And why are some labelled with a question mark? Did they forget whether they'd done them or not?"

Porter shrugged.

"Maybe they knew the victims of these cases, sir," he said. "Or there was something else about the crimes that made them think of something, something that got their attention. I don't know."

He coughed, hammering a fist against his chest.

"I'm parched. You think anyone will mind if I make a cuppa in here?"

"I'm thinking if you do, it will have to be added to the 'worst crimes' pile," Kett told him. "Did you say the other stuff was in the bedroom?"

Porter nodded, using a finger to pull the collar of his shirt away from his sweaty neck.

Kett weaved his way carefully around the carpet of documents, entering the bedroom. There were only a handful of papers on the double bed, divided into two piles. Kett sat on the edge of the mattress, examining the smaller of the two.

Like the others, they were mostly cut from newspapers. Here, though, the articles were interviews with various members of the clergy, celebrities and authors. Some passages, anything referencing occult themes, Kett saw, had been outlined. There was another article buried beneath them, the headline screaming '*Witchcraft Alive and Well in Norfolk*'.

Kett read through it. It was a puff piece about various groups across the region who called themselves 'white witches,' and who didn't seem to do much other than hold drunken parties around bonfires and concoct traditional medicines from herbs and flowers. Somebody had underlined a single sentence in the same red pen:

The Sisterhood of Power is one group in Norfolk who claim that witchcraft is a way for us to reconnect with nature and, in the words of their founder, Margaret Bajome, save our souls.

Kett flicked through the rest of the documents in the pile but didn't find anything else of note. He turned to the second stack instead, two folders that were stuffed mostly with things that had been printed from the internet. Dozens of these were historical records for churches, most of which were in Norfolk. Others were seemingly random Right Move pages showing houses for sale.

Kett was close to punching a scream of frustration through the wall of the caravan when he found something else near the bottom of the pile.

It was another website, this one for the same group he'd spotted in the previous pile.

"The Sisterhood of Power," he said, seeing a photograph of an ivy-clad house in the middle of an orchard of stunted apple trees. The only other text on the page was a small introduction, which he read in a whisper. "*Let the sisters guide you on your journey to the heart of white witchery. Trust us.*"

There was nothing else on the printed document, but when he turned the page over he saw that the killer had written something on the back in their signature red pen.

Cunts.

"Wow," said Kett.

"You found something, sir?" Porter called from the other end of the caravan.

"Maybe," said Kett. He rifled through the last of the documents, then stood up. "You ever come across a group called the Sisterhood of Power?"

"Heavy metal band, sir?"

"No, I don't think so." Kett poked his head into the living space. "Witches."

Porter frowned.

"I thought witches weren't real, sir?"

"I might have been wrong," said Kett. "Keep looking, I'm going to follow something up."

"Yes, sir."

Kett hopped out of the oven of the caravan, managing

half a second of relief before the full force of the sun hit him. The field was crawling now, uniformed officers looking like ants as they ferried items from the cellar into the forensic vans.

He glanced skyward, looking for the kestrel that had been making so much noise earlier, seeing only crows. There were dozens of them spiralling overhead, a double helix of darkness.

There was no sign of Clare, so he called Savage.

"Kate," he said when she answered. "Anything happening at HQ?"

"Not enough, sir," she said. "Still no sign of the car we suspect Aggie Clegg was being held in, hasn't pinged off any ANPRs. They've gone into hiding. Did Spalding get hold of you?"

"Not yet," he said.

"She's found something interesting about Bianca Caddel, sir. The land with the caravan has a planning permission application attached to it, made four years ago. Approved but lapsed. A five-bedroom house, positioned right over that bunker. But that's not what's interesting."

"Yeah?" said Kett, moving into the shade of the caravan.

"There's no mention of the bunker on the application, sir. There's no bunker or cellar in the plans at all. It's just ground floor, first floor, loft. They must have been planning to build the house on top of the bunker, to keep it completely hidden."

"But it's a Cold War bunker," said Kett. "There must be records for them. Aren't they listed?"

"I don't think so, sir. I've seen people convert them on TV. But listen to this: Bianca didn't make the application by herself. There was another name attached to it. Robert Flack."

"Shit," said Kett. "You found him?"

"Spalding's looking for him now, sir. You want me to speak to him?"

"I'll go," said Kett. "Send over his details as soon as you have them. Can you do something else for me, though?"

"Sure."

"It might be nothing, but we found a couple of articles about a group of witches."

"Witches, sir?"

"Good witches," he said. "You know, not the ones with pointy hats. The ones who... I don't know what they do, Kate. The group is called the Sisterhood of Power. They're local."

"I'll have a look, sir," she said. "You want me to speak with them?"

"Yeah, thanks. Bianca didn't seem to like them. They might know something we don't."

"No problem, sir."

"And be careful, Kate," said Kett. He looked to the skies again, to that growing cloud of crows. "Something isn't right here."

CHAPTER EIGHTEEN

By the time Savage had managed to locate an address for the Sisterhood of Power, it was well into the afternoon. The day was a furnace, the IRV's air conditioning doing nothing to fend off the heat as they drove away from HQ. She'd stripped off her jacket before she'd left and undone the top button of her shirt—stopping there, because Josh and his camera had taken quite an interest in her at that point—but she felt like she'd been sitting inside a sauna for hours. There surely couldn't be a drop of moisture left inside her.

The same couldn't be said for Duke, who was producing such copious amounts of sweat that he looked like he'd been fished from the ocean. He drove the IRV more slowly than he normally did because he had to keep wiping his hand over his brow. He was lucky his uniform was black, because when he'd hugged Savage back at HQ she'd felt how damp he was. If she'd wrung him out, she could have filled a bucket.

He caught her looking at him, flashing her a nervous smile. Then he turned the same smile to Megan, who sat alone in the back seat staring at Duke through her camera. The rest of the camera crew followed in the yellow van, a little too close to the IRV's back bumper for Savage's liking.

"There's probably something you can do in editing to make me look less... sweaty, right?" said Duke.

"Um, I'm not sure," said Megan. "Maybe. It's not really my department."

"I don't normally sweat this much," he went on. "It's just my body's way of... preparing me for... action."

"Action?" said Savage.

"Yeah. You know, the lighter you are, the faster you can run," Duke went on. "Like ships. You jettison all the excess weight, lighten the load so you can move through the water at a quicker rate of knots."

"Is that right?" said Savage, nodding sagely.

"Basic biology," said Duke. "People who sweat a lot are natural... predators."

"Ew," said Savage.

"Not *that* kind of predator," said Duke. "I mean like a crocodile, or a shark."

"Those famously sweaty creatures," said Savage.

"Yeah."

It was painful to watch, but Megan seemed to be lapping it up. Fortunately for everyone, they were approaching their destination, a microscopic village to the south-east of the city. Savage just about had time to notice the pub and the shop—both closed—before they'd passed through and out the other side. The road continued for another half a mile before a ramshackle house appeared over a thin hedgerow.

"That has to be it," said Savage. "Nothing else round here."

Duke slowed the IRV down, steering it through a break

in the hedge and along a narrow lane towards the cottage. They bounced in the potholes, fat drips of sweat pattering in Duke's lap.

"I mean, they can literally make somebody's face look different in the movies," he said. "They can turn you into, like, a CGI pigeon if they want to. They should be able to make all this disappear."

He gestured to his face.

"Right?"

"Do you think you could actually turn him into a giant pigeon instead?" said Savage. "That's definitely a show I would watch."

Duke pouted, Megan laughed. Savage pointed to the house through the windscreen.

"Aaron, stop here."

He pulled the car to the side of the driveway and switched off the engine. The van trundled up behind them, kissing their back bumper. Savage got out, grateful for the shade of the trees that edged the house's enormous front garden. There was a giant pond too, and she was half tempted to throw off her clothes and jump in.

It would have made for good TV, if nothing else.

Duke slammed his door, stretching his arms over his head. He let Megan out of the back. The other members of the camera crew were approaching from the van, Josh's camera once again mounted on his shoulder. Savage wondered if it had been welded there.

"Right," said Kelly, who was studying the quiet, picturesque garden with a look of profound disappointment. "Can one of you explain why we're here?"

"We can't say too—" Savage began, but Duke had started at the same time.

"The evidence in this extremely dangerous case has led

us to this place." He gestured at the house behind him, glancing at the camera like a kid performing a school play. "So we need to infiltrate the property and conduct a thorough investigation."

He patted his Taser. Savage rolled her eyes.

"We have no idea what's waiting for us in there," said Duke, his voice low and menacing. "It could be a dangerous criminal. It could be a..."

He leaned towards Josh.

"Killer."

"Hello?" called a voice from the direction of the house.

Duke spun around, and Josh stepped forward with his camera. A woman had emerged from a gate down the side of the building, one hand lifted to her brow to shield her eyes from the sun, the other braced on top of a sturdy wooden cane. She was in her seventies, her silver hair cropped short—almost shaved—her body bent under an unseen weight. She would have struggled to hit five-foot-five even if she'd been straightened out.

She couldn't have looked less dangerous if she'd floated out of her garden on a rainbow-coloured cloud.

"Some killer," muttered Kelly.

"Hi," Savage called back as she walked towards the house. "Sorry to disturb you. My name's DC Kate Savage, I'm from the Norfolk Police. Could we have a quick chat?"

The woman squinted through the shadow of her hand.

"You don't look like police," she said when Savage had reached her.

"Oh, that lot? They're filming something, for the telly. I can ask them to stop?"

The woman studied the camera crew as they approached, her eyes as sharp as blades. It seemed to take all her energy to stop herself folding in two, the cane bent beneath the effort of keeping her upright. Her body trembled like there was an old engine running on fumes inside it. She tilted her head towards Savage with what looked like considerable pain.

"For the TV?"

"Yeah," said Savage. "They're making a show about... about Britain's bravest copper."

"You?" said the woman. "Because I can see that in you."

She lowered the arm that was across her face, as quick as a snake, taking Savage's hand in her cool fingers. For the strangest couple of seconds, Savage found that she couldn't pull free—it was as if her body had forgotten how to operate—then she took a breath and slipped out of the woman's grasp.

She clutched her own hand to her chest like she'd been burned, but there was a chill spreading from her fingertips, tingling into her wrists, heading for the very centre of her.

"What?" said Savage, and she wasn't even sure what she was asking.

The woman's face crinkled into a smile, her receding gums making her yellow teeth look too big.

"Courage," she said, and she tapped her cane onto the flagstone path. "Your heart overflows with it."

"Hi," said Duke, who had ambled over like John Wayne. "I'm PC Aaron Duke." He aimed his name at Josh behind him before turning to the woman. "We're police. There's no reason to panic, we just need to have a quick talk."

"Ah, I see," said the woman, throwing a knowing smile at Savage. "*This* must be Britain's bravest copper. Then you'd better come through. We've got some fresh lemonade, we can have it in the garden."

She turned slowly, like a boat, before floating back

through the gate. Duke followed, then the camera crew, and finally Kelly, who grumbled at Savage as she went.

"There better be a fucking cocaine-frenzied bear with knives for hands in that garden."

Savage walked through the gate, closing it behind her. They made their way along the side of the house, which was bigger than it had looked from the driveway, into an orchard. Dozens of apple trees grew from the long grass, each one as gnarled as a dead man's hand. Fruit hung heavy on the crooked branches, and more rotted on the ground, the sweet, sickly aroma making Savage's stomach churn. Flies gorged themselves in the mush.

There were two more women in the garden. One stood unsteadily on a wooden stepladder, a pair of secateurs in one hand as she clipped apples from a tree. She was wearing so many layers of clothing that Savage didn't know how she hadn't roasted to death. She turned as the chatter of the group rose and Savage saw she was the same age, more or less, as the woman who had greeted them.

The third woman was younger by a good two decades, maybe three. She was walking out of a crumbling orangery that leaned against the back of the ivy-drenched house, dressed in the same flowing robes as the others. Her sandy hair hung in long plaits that almost reached her waist. In her hands, she carried a tray of glasses that clinked like a music box as she navigated the long grass. She set it down on a wrought iron table, and Savage counted nine glasses. She had no idea how she'd managed to get it ready so quickly.

The first woman stopped by the table, gesturing to it with her free hand. She looked close to toppling over.

"Drink, my new friends. It's an old recipe. Lemongrass and lavender to cool, peppermint to help you sweat, and a dash of chilli too."

"Um, maybe in a minute," said Savage. "Thank you. Can we start with your names?"

The younger woman collected a chair from the side of the house, placing it next to the table. The older woman practically fell into it, taking an enormous breath of relief. The pain was etched into every line of her face, but that glint hadn't once left her eyes. She reminded Savage a little of her grandmother, a defiant smile in the face of every illness and every disaster, even the death of her husband all those years ago. That word entered her head again.

Courage.

And the woman met her eye like she'd spoken it aloud.

"This is Mother," said the young woman, planting both her hands on the shoulders of the older one.

"Mother?" said Savage.

"Mother Margaret," she went on.

"Bajome," added Margaret. "That was my old name, a long time ago. You do not have to call me Mother, Margaret will suffice."

This earned a disapproving look from her younger friend. The third woman was still pruning the tree with her back to them. The snip and clack of her secateurs was like something snapping its jaw shut over and over again. The heat and the stench of rotting apples was making Savage feel almost delirious.

"Could we ask her to join us?" Savage said.

"You could ask," said the young woman. "But she won't hear you. Deaf as a dead thing."

She laughed, her eyes widening so much that Savage wondered if she was drunk, or maybe high. She still had her hands on Margaret's shoulders, kneading them with some force.

"And you?" asked Savage.

"I lost my name when I came here," she said, another giggle. "I walked out the door one morning and, whoosh, off it went. It fluttered into the trees and it never came calling again."

"Right," said Savage.

"We call her Julia," said Margaret, and the young woman's expression of annoyance returned. "The woman on the ladder is Morag. She won't hear you, and even if she did, she wouldn't talk back. She's taken a vow of silence."

"Silence," whispered Julia with some drama.

"Sounds like something nuns do," said Savage. Her mouth was bone dry, and she kept looking at the glasses on the table. "But you're not nuns, are you?"

"No, we are not," said Margaret.

"You're witches," said Duke.

Margaret and Julia both smiled at him.

"Trust a man to put it so bluntly," said Margaret. "And to say it with such disdain."

She sighed, shrugging her shoulders until Julia let go of her.

"We are a sisterhood," she said. "A trio of wise women. Muses, if you like."

"Like in all the stories," said Savage, and the old woman's smile grew.

"Wise as well as brave," she said. "A true mother goddess."

Savage opened her mouth to reply, but she couldn't think of what to say. The apples continued to drop from the tree as Morag did her work. They weren't falling into a basket, Savage realised, they were dropping to the ground where they rolled into festering piles.

"There were more of us once," said Margaret. "But times are changing. The world forgets."

"Forgets what?" said Duke. He was licking his lips. "You mind if I have some of that?"

"Aaron," warned Savage, but it was too late. Duke picked one of the glasses from the tray and lifted it to his lips. He downed half of it in one go, most of which sluiced into his patchy beard.

"God that's good," he said. "Minty, and..."

He coughed hard, doubling up. Savage's heart was a chainsaw splintering her ribs, and she'd called his name before he stood straight, holding a hand up to show that he was okay.

"Hot," he said. "Hot, hot, hot."

"It's the chillies," said Margaret with a soft laugh. "Did you put too many in again, Julia?"

"Only in his," she replied with a giggle, although she couldn't have known which glass Duke would have picked.

"They help you sweat," said Margaret. "Cool you down. The mint balances it out."

"It really doesn't," said Duke, still coughing. Josh was having a field day, zooming into Duke's bulging eyes, to the scraps of peppermint caught in his beard.

"If you like," said Julia, still laughing, "we could give you something to grow back your eyebrow?"

"Really?" said Duke, but Savage rode over him.

"So you're a sisterhood. You're not related. But you all live here?"

Margaret nodded.

"This is your house, Margaret?"

"It is."

"We found an article online where you talk about being witches," said Savage. "That's what we wanted to speak with you about."

"Nothing illegal about being a witch," said Julia, selecting a glass and taking a delicate sip.

"You're right," said Savage. "But assault, kidnap and murder *are* illegal, and that's why we're here today."

That seemed to shut her up. Savage glanced at Margaret, whose smile had wavered a little.

"I'm not accusing you of anything," Savage said. "I just want to ask some questions. Are any of you familiar with the ruined church in East Somerton? St Mary's?"

"Of course," said Margaret. "The witch's tree."

"You know the legend?"

"I know they did something unspeakable to a woman there," she said. "They punished her for being one of us."

"A witch?"

"A *woman*," she corrected. "A woman who lives her life according to the gospel of nature, who doesn't abide by the law of men."

She shot Duke a look, one that held more than a little anger.

"They buried her alive, and her spirit gave birth to a tree which brought down the church, which forced the men away. Such is our world. The old divinities are around us, inside us. Cut us down, and we will grow new forms, we will live on. We are everywhere, we are nowhere."

"In that case, can you tell me where you were this morning," said Savage. "Between seven and ten? Everywhere and nowhere?"

"Here," said Julia.

"You can find somebody to verify that?"

"I can verify her, she can verify me, and we can all verify the other one, merrily."

Julia laughed again, spinning in a circle and making her

robes fan out from her body. The fermented air seemed to be growing thicker by the second.

"Then..." Savage hesitated, struggling to find her train of thought. "Can I ask you whether you know somebody by the name of..."

It escaped her, fluttering into the trees just like Julia had described.

"Bianca Caddel," said Duke.

The woman on the stepladder stopped cutting. Slowly, she turned her head towards them. Time hadn't shrunk her, like Margaret, it had made her bloat, her cheeks inflated, her eyes puffy. Her nose was swollen as if from a lifetime of drink, the tip purple. She clung to a branch with a hand that was as knotted and gnarled as the tree.

"I thought she was deaf," said Savage.

"As a dead thing," added Julia.

Morag went back to her work, her wheezing breaths the loudest thing in the orchard until Margaret began to speak.

"We know Bianca. She was one of us, before."

"Before what?" said Savage.

"Before she wasn't," said Margaret. "We parted ways."

"Can you tell me why?"

"It is a long story. Decades long. But the gist of it is that Bianca could no longer find herself in harmony with our way of life. In our hearts lies only peace. Peace with ourselves, peace with each other, peace with this."

She gestured to the trees where the flies swarmed.

"Peace must come before all else, and after all else. We renounced the Horned God, but she would not. We prayed to the Mother Goddess, and she would not. Our paths split, and we banished her."

"Hang on," said Savage. "I didn't get any of that. Who's the horned God? The Devil?"

The two women laughed together, the sound of it as intoxicating as the air. Savage's head was pulsing, not an ache as such, but something else, something she'd never felt before. She glanced at Duke to see if he was feeling it too, but he was simply staring at the glass in his hand, licking his lips. The camera crew, too, seemed entranced. Why were they all so quiet?

"Oh, child," said Margaret, leaning forward, speaking to Savage as if they were the last two people on Earth. "If only you knew."

"Then tell me," she said, thinking of the website she'd found, thinking of the images of Morail, picturing the dead man's head they'd found. "The Devil? Demons? This is what you do?"

Margaret held her eye for a moment, then sat back. The anger had returned to her face.

"You know nothing about us. I thought you were different, but you are just another one of *them*."

She thrust her chin towards Duke.

"Forgive me," said Savage, her head reeling. "I asked because we're investigating a missing girl and a possible murder. We found a..."

She glanced at the camera crew, then carried on.

"We found a head this morning, in the ruins of St Mary. It had been set up as some kind of ritual."

"Beans," said Duke, who had finally rejoined the conversation.

"Right, beans," said Savage. "Black beans in the mouth, eyes and ears. Brandy on the head, and something etched into the skull. A sigil of some kind. I did some research and it's part of a ceremony designed to summon a demon called—"

"Morail," said Margaret.

Once again, Morag looked back from her ladder. Her face seemed to have grown puffier even in the few seconds since she'd last revealed it.

"Morail," said Savage. "You know this... *thing*?"

"I know the texts," said Margaret. "Of course I do. I have studied the occult my whole life. Morail, one of the servitors of Syrach, sixteenth in line to the Duke. A demon of invisibility and illusion. Sacrifice to him, and your crimes will remain unseen."

"Right," said Savage. "So you know the ritual to summon him?"

Margaret's smile had vanished, her eyes sharp.

"I know the ritual that is *thought* to summon him," she said. "I also know that no such thing is possible, because demons do not exist. They are a figment of the twisted minds of men, an explanation for their thoughts and an excuse for their sins. Nothing more."

"Of course," said Savage. "I wasn't suggesting they were real. I—"

"But to some people, they are very real," Margaret went on. "To some people, they are everything."

"To Bianca?" asked Savage.

"She was insane," said Julia, looping a finger in front of her ear. "She thought she could—"

"She was misguided," Margaret interrupted. "She lost sight of what matters most. She lost sight of peace. It happens more than you'd think. Our path can lead very close to the place where this world meets others, and some people think they can step through the veil to see what lies there. To perhaps bring something back. Bianca was one of these, and she attempted to steer us towards darker ways. That is why we expelled her."

"That, and the fact she was trying to steal the house," added Julia.

"She was trying to steal the house?" said Savage.

"She petitioned for power of attorney over me, yes," said Margaret. "She claimed I wasn't fit for purpose, and that she should be sole guardian of the estate. She failed to prove it."

She gestured to the garden.

"Obviously."

"Can you tell me when Bianca left the sisterhood?" said Savage.

"A little over four years ago," said Margaret.

"And, just so I'm clear, you expelled her because she believed in demons, she thought they were real, and that they could be summoned?"

"That is correct," said Margaret.

"Did she ever try to summon one here? Did she ever hurt somebody, or perform a ritual like the one we were just talking about?"

"She killed Precious," said Julia.

"Precious?"

"A chicken," said Margaret.

"*My* chicken," said the younger woman. "She cut off her head, she wanted the blood."

"For?"

"We didn't ask," said Margaret, wincing in pain as she tried to adjust her position. "That was the final straw. She moved out the next day. But yes, she killed a chicken—"

"*My* chicken."

"For a ritual. There may have been others. I do not know."

"Cutting the head off a chicken isn't too far removed from cutting the head off a man," said Savage. "When was the last time you saw her? Or heard from her? Heard anything about her?"

"A few letters after she left," said Margaret. "Begging for forgiveness, and for understanding. Burned, I'm afraid. I haven't seen her since the day she walked out."

"Any of you?"

Julia shrugged. Morag had once again frozen on her stepladder. There was another profound silence, broken after a few seconds by the sound of Duke coughing up a lung. He'd downed the last of his drink, and had doubled up again.

"Oh God, so spicy."

"Stop bloody drinking it then," said Savage.

"But I'm so thirsty."

She pulled a business card from her pocket and laid it on the tray where it instantly began to absorb the spilled lemonade.

"Please call me if you think of anything else," she said. "Anything at all."

"I will," said Margaret, tapping her cane on the ground as if to punctuate the conversation. "And keep that courage, child. You're going to need it."

CHAPTER NINETEEN

GIVEN EVERYTHING THAT HAD HAPPENED IN THIS CASE so far, it came as no surprise to Kett that Robert Flack—the man who'd put in a planning application with Bianca Caddel—lived in a church.

It was an old Methodist chapel located just outside of North Walsham, and judging by the state of it, it certainly wasn't used for worship anymore. For one, most of the front garden was taken up by an ancient campervan, on the back of which was a bumper sticker that read: 'If I'm going too slow, suck my gearstick.'

Kett studied the building from the passenger seat of Porter's Mondeo, drumming his fingers on his leg in time to a song that had been stuck inside his skull all afternoon. He couldn't think of the name of it.

"You waiting for him to come out, sir?" asked Porter, who was slapping out a completely different rhythm on the steering wheel. "Because he's going to know we're here."

They hadn't hidden it. Behind the Mondeo were two IRVs, their lights still rolling. A third had driven around to the back of the sizable plot of land that came with the church, just in case Robert Flack turned out to be the kind of man who'd help kidnap a teenage girl, and who'd run.

But if Flack had spotted them, he was keeping it quiet. There hadn't been so much as a curtain twitching.

Kett looked at his phone, reading Spalding's message again.

Robert Graham Flack, 52, served in the army for a while, then had a farm, sold his land three years ago and bought this place. No record, can't see how he knows Caddel.

It wasn't a lot to go on, but they didn't have much else. Bianca's VW hadn't pinged any cameras since the garage that morning, and there had been no more sightings of Aggie, even though the story had hit the news a couple of hours ago and most of the country was looking for her.

"Okay," said Kett. "Let's go knock."

He got out into the late afternoon heat, the world blistering under a grill. His jacket was still in the back seat, and he couldn't face putting it on even though his shirt was plastered to his back and chest, the sleeves rolled up. Porter was still wearing his. Kett didn't know how the DI was managing to stay so cool.

The church was a square of stone topped with a dormer roof, the date 1901 carved into the lintel over the front door. Tombstones had been repurposed as a garden wall, the ground a patchwork of gravel and weeds.

"Stay out here," Kett told the PCs. "I don't think anything's going to happen, but... this is a weird one. Just keep your eyes open."

"In case he tries to escape on his broomstick," said Porter as they opened the gate.

Kett ignored him.

"Or throws us into his cauldron," Porter added.

Kett cupped a hand to the dark glass of the campervan, seeing no sign of life inside.

"Or sets his familiars on us."

"Familiars?"

"You know, pet cat, owl, whatever. Witches have animals. Familiars."

"You're going to be getting a kick to the familiars in a minute, Pete, if you don't stop."

Porter raised his hands in self-defence.

"Sorry," said Kett, scrubbing his sleeve over his brow. "I'm just knackered."

"I hear you," said Porter. "Bobby isn't sleeping. He hates the heat. One's bad enough, don't know how you cope with three."

"Especially when they're sick," said Kett. "Moira was trying to flush the chinchilla down the toilet last night. Said she was giving it a bath. Poor thing was delirious."

"Not surprised. I'd be delirious if somebody tried to flush me down the toilet."

"No, Pete. *Moira* was... never mind."

He thumped a fist on the heavy door, the sound of it echoing deep inside the building. He didn't wait for a reply, making his way along the front of the chapel and taking a peep down the side.

Behind the building were open fields and pockets of woodland, all shimmering in the heat. There were outbuildings a little way off, what could have been stables and an enormous barn at the other end of the meadowed acreage.

Porter knocked again as Kett walked back, calling out.

"Mr Flack, can you open the door, please? It's the police."

"Hang on," came a voice from inside. "Hang on, give me a second."

Kett and Porter stood back as a key turned in the lock. A second later the door swung inwards, but only a little. A face peered out of the dark interior, waist high. It was a man in his early fifties, his hair completely gone, his eyes hidden behind a pair of dark glasses.

"Hang on," he said again, and he retreated into the dark to let the door open fully. Light rushed in like an overeager Labrador, and Kett saw that the man was sitting in a wheelchair, a heavy blanket over his legs and a cat clamped to his lap.

"Told you," whispered Porter. "Familiars."

The man moved forward again, right to the threshold, squinting up at Kett and then Porter.

"Police?" he asked.

Kett showed him his warrant card. The man had to take off his sunglasses and put on a second pair of spectacles, which hung around his neck, in order to study it more closely. After an age, he handed it back. The cat, a tiny black thing, looked like it was trying to get up, but the man's big hand kept it in place. There were scars on his fingers, unlike anything Kett had seen before.

"So you are," said the man. "Can't be too careful these days. Plenty of shits around here that will rob you blind if you're not paying attention."

"My name's DCI Kett. This is DI Porter. You're Robert Flack?"

"What's left of him," said Flack, gesturing to his legs. Kett realised he couldn't see the man's feet even beneath the hem of the blanket. "How can I help?"

"Don't suppose we could come in?" asked Kett, the sun a blowtorch against the back of his head.

Flack seemed to think about it for a moment, running a dry tongue over drier lips. He angled his head back into the house like he was waiting for a silent permission, then he nodded.

"Can't have you passing out on my doorstep," he said. "Careful not to let any of the furry buggers out."

He rolled away to let them through, the cat watching them with enormous yellow eyes. Kett stepped through the door, instantly embraced by the cool touch of the old building. Ahead was a stone-floored hallway with a staircase in the centre of it. Five open doors led into big rooms, the last of these right at the end of the corridor. It was here that Flack gestured.

"Might as well use the kitchen," he said. "I can fix you up a drink. Don't have much. Coke?"

"Water would be appreciated," said Kett. "If it's no trouble."

They followed Flack into a kitchen that looked too big to fit inside the building, maybe eight metres wide and just as long. Sunshine gushed through angled skylights, filling the room like a pool. Two more cats basked on a sofa near the door, a third on the low counter that greeted them with a soft chirrup.

"Nice place," said Porter.

Kett stared out of the French doors, the garden even bigger than he'd first thought. The land had been left to meadow, and past the ocean of grass and flowers, Kett could see the top of the barn.

"This all yours?" he asked.

"The garden, yes," said Flack, following his line of sight. "The equestrian facility, no. I sold them the land after... When I couldn't tend to it anymore. I don't have any dealings with them."

"You were in the military?" asked Kett.

Flack laughed bitterly.

"I was, a long time ago. Came out in one piece, too, if you can believe it."

Kett waited for him to elaborate, but he didn't. He deftly crossed the room in his wheelchair, collecting two glasses from a cupboard and carrying them to the sink. Everything in the kitchen had been lowered so that he could access it. Even the oven looked custom-made. He set the drinks on the island, and Kett picked one up with a grateful nod. He could feel the water crackling down his dry throat, a cool explosion in his belly.

"Thanks," he said, returning the empty glass. "Needed that."

"This weather is a beast," said Flack. "No class."

He backed his chair to the window, gesturing to the sofa and its collection of cats.

"Don't mind them. Sit. Tell me how I can help."

Kett had been planning to stand, but a pang of agony in his back made him reconsider. He didn't trust himself to be able to get up from the sofa itself, so he perched on the arm, gritting his teeth until the worst of the agony had passed. Porter dumped himself into the middle of the sofa with enough force to catapult both cats to the floor. One ran off, the other leapt straight onto his lap. He petted it, the sound of its purr like a diesel generator.

"Have you seen the news today, Mr Flack?" asked Kett.

"Robert, please," he replied, slipping his dark glasses back on. They weren't full tint, the shape of his eyes visible through the dull brown lenses. He had a couple of scars on his face, too, a nasty one that seemed to form a perfect curl around his ear. More disappeared into the collar of his shirt. "And no. I haven't. Trouble?"

"You could say that." Kett took a breath. "This morning a group of teenagers were attacked inside a ruined church in a place called East Somerton, up on the coast. One of the women was kidnapped by the attacker."

Flack's face didn't so much as flinch.

"We also found a dead man inside the same church. He was killed a few days ago, and his head was used as some kind of... totem. It had been defiled."

Still no reaction. Kett wasn't sure if any of it was sinking in.

"Our last sighting of the missing girl was in the boot of a car this morning. The car was a silver VW Passat, registered to a woman called Bianca Caddel."

Flack exhaled slowly, as if he'd been holding his breath. It was almost a sigh of relief.

"You're here because of Bianca," he said.

"You know her?"

"I do. I *did*."

"A friend?" Kett prompted. "Partner? Co-worker? How?"

"All of those things, I suppose, at one point or another," said Flack. "We were engaged to be married, many years ago. Before she lost her mind."

He didn't elaborate, and Kett stared at him until he got the message.

"She's a complicated woman, Bianca. I've known her nearly three decades and I think I only scratched the surface. You ever met somebody who doesn't play by the rules? Doesn't even try? That's her. Free as a bird, and I used to admire her for it, because one day she'd be renting a cottage by the river doing watercolour paintings, the next—literally, the next—she'd be on a plane to Myanmar, or Angola, or wherever, joining in some bloody revolution.

And a few months after that she'd knock on your door like she hadn't been gone a second."

He shook his head, his expression almost wistful.

"Of course, you don't bed down with a woman like that. You don't hang your hopes on her, or your heart. Found that out the hard way."

"When was the last time you saw her, Robert?" asked Kett.

"Going on three years," he said without hesitation. He didn't follow it with anything, even though Kett left the awkward silence going for almost ten seconds.

"You haven't heard from her at all in that time?"

"You'd think she'd send a card or something, wouldn't you? We've been through a lot, she and I. Like I said, Bianca's a free spirit. When she's with you, she'll make you feel like you're the only thing that matters. When she leaves, she'll make you feel worse than death."

"Can you tell us about the land that Bianca owns, near Horning? The field. There was planning permission for a house there, latest application back in 2019. The application was in your name, as well as hers."

Flack's top lip curled up in a snarl, revealing crooked teeth.

"We were going to build a house together," he said. "Build a life. Felt too good to be true, and it was. She never let it happen, even after... even after..."

He stared at the cat on his lap, scratching at the scars on his neck like he was trying to erase them. Kett saw a river of emotion in the man, churning just beneath the surface. He felt like a grenade, the pin pulled, the explosion imminent.

"Tell me about the bunker," Kett said. "It wasn't part of the planning."

"The what?" said Flack.

"The Cold War bunker in the field. Three rooms, accessed by a shaft with a ladder."

"What are you on about?" he said. "There's no house, let alone a fucking bunker."

He didn't seem to be lying.

"Do you mind if I have a quick look around while you're talking, Mr Flack?" asked Porter, trying to push the cat off his lap so that he could get up. A look from the other man knocked him down again.

"You're lucky I let you this far," he said, another snarl. "I'm happy to show you the door."

"There's no need for that," said Kett. "But it would be handy to have a photo of Bianca, if you have one. They're surprisingly hard to find."

"She's surprisingly hard to capture," said Flack. "I may have one or two lying about, I'd need to look for them."

"Even though she meant the world to you?" said Kett.

"You don't keep mementoes of the things you've lost," said Flack. "What purpose do they serve other than a painful reminder of what pissed off and left you?"

"Then let me show you something," he said.

Kett pulled his phone from his pocket and found a photo he'd taken that morning of the image on Aggie Clegg's camera. The woman who'd attacked the teenagers was little more than a blur on the screen, her mouth screaming, her eyes dark pits. Even here, in this floodlit kitchen, Kett felt the chill creeping into his bones, goosebumps ridging his arms again.

He turned the phone to Flack, who had to lean forward in his wheelchair. He slid his glasses up, replacing them with the other set.

"Is this Bianca?" asked Kett.

Flack didn't answer. He was staring at the image with an unnerving intensity—something that bordered on fear.

"This is the thing that attacked those children?" he asked.

"Not *thing*, Robert. It's a woman. Is it Bianca?"

This time, Flack laughed, a brittle, bitter sound. He still didn't take his eyes away from the photograph. His lips were shaping words that Kett couldn't make out, something frantic.

"Robert," he said, pushing the phone closer. "Answer my question."

Flack's whisper grew in volume, filling the kitchen like the susurration of distant birds until, with a sudden snap of his head, he raised the volume of his voice.

"You found a head," he said, spraying flecks. "Defiled? Let me guess, black beans in the orifices, a reek of brandy, the mark of..."

"Morail," said Kett, the word like a bullet in his mouth, louder than he had any intention of making it. The cat leapt off Flack's lap, skittering across the smooth floor. Porter's followed, both of them bolting into the hallway.

Kett's hand was shaking with the effort of holding the phone, but he didn't pull it away.

"Is this her?"

"I can't say," said Flack. "But I'm going to tell you this, and you need to listen. As hard as it is for you to do this, you need to walk away."

"Walk away?" said Kett, almost laughing.

"Walk away," Flack said. "Leave it alone. You can't win."

"Who is she?" asked Kett.

"I don't know."

"Who is she?" he asked again, almost a growl.

"I don't know," he said, and the fear was growing, filling every inch of his face, making those raw scars stand out like they were fresh wounds. "I don't know, but I can tell you this. What's happening here, you're not prepared for it."

Kett met Porter's eye, the pair of them sharing an unspoken thought.

He's mad.

But the fear in Flack's eyes didn't look like madness, it didn't look like paranoia or fantasy. It certainly didn't look like a lie.

"You think you are, but you're not," Flack went on. "This goes beyond anything you've ever experienced, anything you've ever known. You won't find Bianca, not unless she lets you. You can't see her, not now, not after what she's done. And I can promise you this, if she lets you anywhere near her then you're fucked. If..."

He swallowed, almost choking on his words.

"If that *thing* has the girl you're looking for, she's worse than dead. There's no getting her back."

He looked at Kett, his eyes bulging. His fear was contagious. Kett could feel it creep beneath his skin, seep into his bones.

"Walk away," said Flack.

"We don't walk away," said Kett, pushing himself off the arm of the sofa. "Not ever."

"Then I can't help you," said Flack. "Nobody can."

Kett held the man's eye until Flack looked away.

"Let's go, Pete."

Porter followed him out of the kitchen, Kett opening the front door and almost falling into the day. The world gathered them into a hug, chasing away the chill. Kett closed the door, letting a shiver rip through his body before heading back to the road.

"What, the fuck, was that?" said Porter.

"I have no idea," said Kett. "Something scared him, though. He knows more than he's saying."

"Yeah, I agree. We should bring him in."

"Not yet," said Kett.

He reached the nearest IRV, where two young constables sat on the bonnet deep in conversation.

"Comfortable?" Kett asked, and they hopped off together. He didn't think their blushes had much to do with the heat.

"Sorry, sir," said the woman.

"You stay here," he said. "Keep an eye on the place. Let me know if Flack leaves."

"You want us to stop him if he does, sir?" she asked.

"I want him to know we're keeping an eye on him," said Kett. He turned to the other constable. "You, follow us."

He dropped into the Mondeo. Porter was already behind the wheel, brushing cat hair from his trousers.

"Bloody things," he said. "Moult everywhere this time of year."

He paused, pulled a face, then unleashed a sneeze that made the car rock.

"Where now, sir?" he said.

"Did you believe Flack when he said he hadn't seen Bianca for three years?" Kett asked.

"I didn't believe a single word that came out of his mouth," said Porter.

"Me neither." Kett turned back to the chapel. "I don't believe him about the equestrian place, either. So if you lived here, and you had a friend who wanted to hide from the police, who maybe had a kidnapped girl in her car, what would you do?"

Porter sneezed again, wiping his nose.

"I'd probably send them to the bloody great barn out back," he said.

Kett smiled.

"Me too, Pete. Let's go."

CHAPTER TWENTY

Porter kept his speed down, following the narrow lane as it meandered around the land surrounding the chapel. It was idyllic here, the fields bursting with wheat, the trees lining the side of the road shivering with excitement. They crossed a humpback bridge, the stream beneath glittering with sun-jewelled water. There were only a handful of other houses, none as grand as the one that Flack lived in, and Kett didn't see a single other soul for the seven minutes it took them to reach the entrance to the stable yard.

Not that Kett could be sure this was it. There was no sign to let them know that this dirt track led to a facility of some kind, just a metal gate that did a poor job of hiding the barn up ahead. The building was big enough to hold a plane, and Kett wondered if it was an arena of some kind.

"Can you check the gate, Pete?" said Kett as the IRV pulled in behind them.

Porter grumbled his way out of the car, walking to the gate and then shaking his head.

"That's a serious chain," he said when he'd returned to

the car. "And a bigger padlock. Somebody doesn't want visitors."

Kett puffed out a breath and fetched his phone from his pocket, calling Clare.

"Speak," said the Super, his mouth full.

"You know, too many Bounties will kill you, sir," Kett said.

"Actually, Detective," spat Clare, "the toxic chemical in chocolate is theobromine, and in order for me to consume enough of it to kill me, I'd have to eat somewhere in the region of seven hundred Bounties."

"Pretty sure I saw you eat that many this morning, sir."

"Shut your tosshole, Kett, unless you called to actually tell me something."

"We've just paid a visit to Robert Flack, the man who put in the planning application with Bianca on the land with the bunker. He claims he doesn't know where she is. Hasn't spoken to her in years."

"But?" said Clare. "Because I've come to expect it with you. Every single case, you throw your giant, hairy 'but' right in my face, reeking of shit."

"Uh..." There was no way around it. "*But* I think he's lying, sir."

"There you go," muttered Clare. "Kett's festering 'but,' hanging before me. What makes you think that?"

"My gut, sir."

"Your butt?"

"*Gut*. Christ. I think he's lying, I think he knows where Bianca is. There's an equestrian yard right next to his land, good place to hide somebody."

"So you want to waltz in and see if she's there," said Clare.

"It wouldn't hurt," he said.

"It's a public facility?"

"I... I'm not sure, sir. Possibly."

"You can get to it without climbing over a wall?" said the Super.

"Definitely wouldn't need to climb over a *wall*..."

"If I tell you not to look, is it going to make any tossing difference whatsoever?"

Kett thought about Aggie, the young woman not even out of her teens, dragged from the woods by something from a nightmare, thrown in the boot of a car—and yet still smart enough to knock out the brake light and try to alert somebody to her presence. The chances of her being anywhere near here were unfathomably small.

But there *was* still a chance.

"No, sir," he said. "Sorry."

"Stick your apology up your hole," said Clare. "You can pick which one. And we never had this conversation. If you Kett it up, you're going under the bus on your own."

He hung up, Kett's ear ringing.

"What did he say, sir?" asked Porter, leaning through the open door.

"He's cool with it," said Kett.

He cranked open the door, unfolding himself in a series of painful cracks and clicks.

"Getting worse?" asked Porter.

Kett didn't reply, but the answer was written all over his face. They walked to the gate together, the dirt track beyond leading straight towards the barn and hemmed in by woodland so thick that Kett couldn't see anything through it. He held his breath, hearing only the same bastard, chattering magpies in the trees until a gentle, distant whinny relieved the tension.

The PC from the IRV had walked over with them. He didn't have a Taser, but he was a big lad with a baton.

"I can go check it out first, sir?" he asked.

"No, but you can tag along in case we need some backup. What's your name?"

"PC Sales, sir. Alfie."

"You want a hand over, sir?" Porter asked Kett. "I know gates are your greatest nemesis."

"I don't need a hand, Pete," said Kett.

He was determined to prove it, too, scaling the gate with a little more gusto than his aching body was prepared for. He'd just managed to straddle the top when a cramp began in his thigh, and he propelled himself onto the path like an athlete before it could take hold.

"Bloody hell, sir," said Porter, his eyebrows rising. "You've been in training."

"Yep," said Kett, refusing to let the pain show as he limped down the track. "Try to keep up."

Porter vaulted the gate easily, and so did Sales. The woodland was even thicker than Kett had first thought, the trees strangled by the tangled undergrowth, snake-like creepers that choked their way towards the immense weight of the canopy. The magpies clucked and chuckled from where they hid in the shadows. Once again, Kett had the unshakable feeling they were laughing at him.

There were more noises up ahead, a chorus of neighs and the thunder of hooves on dry earth.

"You like horses, Pete?" Kett asked.

"They're half-tonne wild things with devil's eyes and teeth that could take your head off," he said. "*And* they look a bit like cows. What do you think?"

The track widened up ahead, revealing a small car park with a knackered horse trailer on one side and an ancient green Rav 4 on the other. There was a line of smaller brick and flint outbuildings between the car park and the longer edge of the barn. To the right, past a stack of old machine parts, was nothing but woodland, a trail leading into the trees. To the left, the car park led through an open gate into a courtyard.

Kett paused, trying to hear any human sounds past the unseen horses. When he couldn't, he walked quickly and quietly to the gate, peering around the edge. The courtyard was lined with stables, six of them in total. Two horses stared back over their doors, no emotion at all in their dark eyes. The track continued, leading towards a paddock and, just visible over the hedges, the roof of Robert Flack's chapel.

Boxing in the right-hand side of the courtyard was the barn, its huge metal doors shut tight. A chain as big as the one on the main gate had been looped through the handles.

"Sales," said Kett. "See if you can find a way into the barn."

"Yes, sir," said Sales, uncertain.

"Don't enter, just find a way. Pete, with me."

Kett set off across the courtyard, Porter treading on his shadow. Sales was running to the barn doors, his equipment rattling so loud he sounded like a fully laden mule. After a handful of seconds, he was out of sight behind the stables as Kett and Porter reached the paddock. It hadn't been subdivided, seven horses grazing together in the acre or so of grass, their tails whisking at the flies. A path led down the back wall of the stables, vanishing behind a monstrous hedge.

Past the electrified fence at the far side of the paddock was Flack's meadow, the chapel peeking over the top of the grass like it was hiding from them. There was a distinct path mown into it, one that led directly from here to there.

"Doesn't exactly look like a separate property, sir," said Porter.

"It does not."

Kett walked towards the horses, some of them beginning to pay attention. They circled each other, nickering. One reared, causing the others to bolt deeper into the field.

"Easy," called Kett, holding up a hand. "Easy."

But there was something urgent in their skittish movements. They were restless.

He wondered if they were afraid.

"Let's see where that goes," said Kett, heading towards the hedge.

Then freezing when somebody appeared at the other end of the path.

It was a man dressed in jeans and a black T-shirt. The sun was in his face, his squint making him look older than he probably was—maybe Kett's age. He was struggling with a stack of plastic buckets, making such a racket as he walked that he didn't notice he wasn't alone. The horses welcomed him with a serenade of noise.

"Quiet your racket," he barked towards the field, a little Welsh in his accent. "It's coming."

The horses began to trot towards him, their fear overruled by hunger. The man reached the edge of the paddock and set his buckets down, arching his back. He was reaching for the hook that connected the electric wire to the gatepost when Kett spoke.

"Afternoon."

It was as if the man had been electrified by his own fence. His feet literally left the ground, his hand clutching his heart as if to keep it in place.

"Jesus Arsing Christ," he roared. "What the fuck?"

Kett reached into his pocket, pulling out his warrant card.

"Sorry," he said. "We're—"

The man took off, sprinting back the way he'd come, his sudden motion throwing the horses into a stampede of panic.

"Fuck's sake," said Kett, shouting over the thunder of hooves. "Go get him, Pete."

Porter was already running, but the man was fast—already out of sight behind the hedge.

"Sales!" Kett yelled, his voice echoing off the back of the stables. "Incoming!"

He started to jog, every bone in his back feeling like it was close to shattering. He'd made it halfway along the stable block when he caught sight of something in his peripheral vision.

On the far side of the paddock, Robert Flack sat in his wheelchair at the end of the path that led to his house. He was shouting something, but Kett couldn't make any sense of it over the hammer blows of his heart and the drum of the horses in the field. He stopped running, pointing a finger at Flack.

"Don't move!"

Flack didn't show any sign of going anywhere. His voice cut through the hot air, four syllables that Kett still couldn't grasp.

From somewhere behind the stables came a shout of anger, one that might have been Porter.

"Fuck," Kett said.

There was only one way to get to Flack, but he didn't fancy crossing the paddock when the horses were in a frenzy. They hurled themselves from fence to fence, foaming at the mouth, their eyes white with panic.

And still Flack called, his voice rising in pitch.

"Sir?"

Sales ran through the gate from the stables, his baton out. Kett pointed to the hedge.

"That way, one male, my age. DI Porter's gone after him."

The PC ran off, almost tripping on the uneven ground.

Kett turned his attention back to Flack. The man was practically screaming now, his voice driving the horses into an even wilder state of terror. He looked possessed.

Kett ran to the post where the electrified fence was connected, slipping the cables free so that he could step through, then reconnecting them after he'd entered the field. The horses shied away from him, bolting to the far side of the paddock, which edged the dense woodland. There they finally stopped, sheltering in the shadow of the trees.

In the sudden quiet, Kett finally heard what Flack was screaming.

"You brought it here! You brought it here!"

Over and over, his pitch still rising like a kettle.

Even in the relentless heat of the sun, Kett's scalp shrivelled, ice cold.

"You brought it here! You brought it here! You..."

Flack stopped dead, his head twisting slowly to where the horses did their best to hide. His eyes held the lunatic fear of a child who has woken in the night to the sound of something in their room.

"Robert, stay where you are," said Kett, crossing the paddock as quickly as the hoof-churned ground would let him. "Don't move."

Flack wasn't moving. He wasn't doing anything. He was still staring at the horses.

At them, Kett realised, or at the woods beyond.

He wasn't sure why he stopped walking. His body staggered to a halt without his permission, refusing to start up again. Flack was still staring, wild-eyed, at the woods, and Kett turned there too. He tried to peel the trees apart, to see what lay between those crooked branches, in that suffocating blanket of weed, but they refused to give up their secrets.

"Robert?" he said.

His heart was as wild as the horses, refusing to settle. It knew something he didn't, some primal part of him beaming out a warning with every thump of his pulse.

"Robert," he said again. "What's going on?"

The man in the wheelchair turned his head, painfully slowly. His face was so drawn that it could have been a mask.

"I'm sorry," he shouted. "I told you. You should have walked away. You should have—"

It wasn't a sound, it was a *feeling*—a subsonic charge that detonated from the direction of the woods. The horses screamed, there was no other word for it, once again carving up the field in a tsunami of violence.

Heading right for Kett.

"Fuck!" he said, turning, slipping, hurling himself across the paddock towards the fence. It was a race he couldn't win, the horses catching up with him in seconds, the ground shaking beneath the force of them.

Then fading as they wheeled around.

Kett staggered to a halt, looking back to see the animals running away from him now, circling the field. They charged towards Flack, his face a carnival mask of terror as, one by one, they jumped the fence onto the path beyond.

"No!" Kett shouted.

Flack vanished under the hooves of the first horse, the others following, churning up a cloud of dust as they galloped into the meadow. It was over in seconds, the animals subdued by the long grass, beaten into submission by the sudden quiet of the day.

Kett's body came back online and he ran towards where Flack lay in a tangle of metal and flesh. He stopped before he reached him, though, because even from twenty yards away he could see there was no saving him.

"What the fuck?" he said, locking his hands in his hair.

He stared at the woods through the tears that were already gathering.

And he couldn't shake the feeling that the woods were staring back.

CHAPTER TWENTY-ONE

Porter wasn't sure how he'd managed to lose him.

The man had bolted down the path beside the paddock, then vanished into the overgrown hedge like it had swallowed him alive. Porter threw himself in after him, the cool, sharp branches scratching at his face and his neck until it spat him out the other side.

"Fucking twatty hedges," he said, spitting scraps of conifer. He was in a narrow garden, a small pebble-dashed bungalow dead ahead and the barn to his right—so tall that it had thrown almost everything into shade. "Oi! Where are you?"

It was no surprise, really, that the man didn't answer.

Porter ran for the bungalow, making it three strides before he heard footsteps behind him. He whirled around to see PC Sales stagger out of the hedge. He'd lost his hat somewhere, but he held up his baton.

"You found him, sir?" he asked.

"Yeah," said Porter. "Then I gave him a pat on the head and let him go. Course I haven't. Go for the barn. I'll take the house."

Porter jogged across the small garden, reaching the side of the bungalow. There were two windows, both of which had their curtains drawn. He followed the wall to the right, Sales moving the same way as he tried to find the entrance to the barn. They hopped over a neglected flowerbed together and Porter saw the bungalow's front door ahead.

He tried the handle. Locked.

"Gonna lose my job for this," he muttered. Although with everything that had happened today—the severed head, the heat, the bastard hedge—he wasn't sure he cared.

He stepped back, then drove his foot into the door just beneath the handle. It resisted, but only just. He tried again and it wobbled open.

"Police!" he shouted, pushing into a dark corridor. "If you don't let me know you're in here, I'm going to do the same thing to you I just did to the door."

Which wouldn't make much sense, he realised, if nobody had been watching. He ducked into a small living room. The TV was on, a movie paused, a cigarette still burning in the ashtray. Across the hall was a dining room that was being used as an office, the computer off. Both bedrooms at the back were empty.

He was entering the kitchen when he heard a scream from outside.

"Shit," he said, running back into the garden.

The barn was right ahead. It seemed like it had grown even bigger since he'd been in the bungalow. If he'd had any doubts at all that's where the scream had come from, they were dashed when another shriek erupted from the building.

Porter ran around to the back of the barn, finding an open door. By the time he'd reached it, the shouts from inside were coming thick and fast—more than one voice.

He slid into the dark, finding himself in a small storage room. Bags of wood shavings were stacked in one corner, filling the air with the scent of pine. Shelves held an assortment of horse stuff, but there was human food there, too. A lot of it. Pallets of baked beans, canned fruit, and what had to be a hundred bottles of water.

He was halfway across the room when he noticed the shape that had been scored into the floor—another pentagram, gouged into the wooden boards, the trenches crimson.

More shouts poured through a door in the opposite wall, crashes, the unmistakeable soundtrack of a fight.

Porter pushed into the barn's huge interior. Light streamed through slatted windows high in the walls, picking out the two men who rolled on the sawdust-covered floor. Sales was losing the fight, the other man on top of him and throwing punches into the side of his head.

"Oi!" Porter roared, barrelling towards them.

He grabbed the man by the back of his T-shirt, hauling him off Sales. But the guy was stronger than he looked. He thrust his body upwards like a Jack-in-the-box, the top of his head thumping Porter under the chin like a hammer. He staggered away, his head full of fire, the pain so bright it blinded him.

A punch connected with his gut and he fell back, the soft ground breaking his fall. He shook away the panic to see the man pick something up off the floor—Sales' baton—lifting it over his head as he lumbered towards him. Sales was doing his best to get back to his feet, his face bloody. And behind him...

Porter hadn't seen them when he'd entered the barn. He wasn't sure if he was even seeing them now. It felt like a hallucination.

Cages, big ones, lined up against the far wall. Four in total.

Two were occupied.

A teenage boy sat in one cage, his face drawn. A younger girl occupied the other. It was *her* that was screaming, over and over and over.

The man reached Porter, the baton swinging earthwards.

No time to get up. Porter rolled, sawdust filling his mouth. The baton hit the ground, then rose again, ready for another strike.

The man never got the chance.

Kett slammed into him like a train, both of them hitting the floor in a duet of grunts. The DCI grabbed the baton, ripping it out of the man's hand and hurling it across the barn. Then Sales was there, dropping onto the man's arm and pinning it to the floor. The guy was wild, his legs thrashing, his body bucking so hard he almost managed to knock Kett off him.

Porter got to his feet, wheezing from the punch to his stomach. He planted a shoe on the man's other hand while Sales tried to get the cuffs on his wrist. Blood dripped from the PC's nose, from a cut above his eye. He could barely see what he was doing.

"You absolute wanker," said Porter. "Stay still, or you'll be unconscious by the time you get to the station."

The man showed no sign of calming down. He was lost in a frenzy of violence, his body contorting. His face was doing something weird, his jaw bulging, his teeth grinding. It was only when he opened his mouth to take in a breath and a fountain of blood exploded upwards that Porter realised what he was doing.

"His tongue," he said. "He's biting off his fucking tongue."

"Get something!" Kett roared, trying to grab the man's jaw.

He chewed, choking on his own blood, practically convulsing.

Porter scanned the floor, looking for something they could jam between the man's teeth. There was only the baton, and he picked it up, collapsing onto his knees next to the man's head.

"Do it," said Kett, the DCI's face slick with blood as the man continued to choke.

Porter tried to slide the baton into the machine of the man's grinding teeth, but he was whipping his head from side to side. The horror of it was making his skin feel like it was boiling, the girl's screams driving him close to madness.

"Fuck this," he said, and he swung the baton into the man's temple, hard.

It was like a switch had been flicked. The man stopped thrashing, stopped kicking, his desperate breaths rattling wetly. Between them, they rolled the guy onto his side so he wouldn't choke on his own blood. Kett opened the man's mouth, the mess of his tongue drooping. Porter could see the teeth marks, but he hadn't managed to bite it off.

Sales held on for another couple of seconds then scampered towards the main doors, spewing vomit over the sawdust. He doubled over, groaning.

"Christ," said Kett, meeting Porter's eye, mirroring his expression.

The girl's screams were louder now, joined by an angry shout from the boy in the cage beside her.

"You okay?" Kett asked Porter.

"No, sir, I'm not," he replied.

"You okay?" Kett shouted after Sales.

The young PC nodded, wiping the drool from his lips.

"Get the cuffs on him," said Kett. "Then find something we can use to secure his mouth so he doesn't try that again."

"I'll get an ambulance out here," said Porter, going for his phone.

"On its way," said Kett. "Called it on my way to the barn. Backup's coming too."

"Little late for backup, sir," said Porter.

Together, they turned to the cages on the other side of the barn. The girl was almost as frenzied as the man had been, slamming her hand into the bars, her head too. She was maybe sixteen years old, as skinny as a rake and dressed in pink pyjamas. Her hair hung over her face, but it was obvious this wasn't Aggie Clegg.

"Hey," Kett said, holding his hands up. "You're okay. We're police."

It didn't seem to comfort her. Kett walked towards the cages and she tumbled onto her backside, kicking herself into the corner where she continued to scream.

"Find a key," Kett said.

Porter started towards the storage room, then thought better of it, doubling back. He crouched beside the unconscious man and rummaged in the pockets of his greasy jeans, pulling out a phone, a wallet and a sizable collection of keys. He tossed the keys across the barn, missing Kett by a good few feet. Then he opened the wallet.

"David Blethyn," he said, reading the name on the driving licence. "He's thirty-nine."

He wasn't sure if Kett could hear him over the shrieks of the girl. The DCI was trying the keys in the padlock, speaking calmly to her as he did.

Porter walked over, stopping by Sales on the way. The

kid had been beaten up bad, his face already swelling. One eye was almost completely bloodshot. He was shaking so hard his equipment was rattling. Porter knew the feeling well. He could still vividly remember his first scrap on the job, and how desperately he'd wanted to get away from the scene.

"Alfie, wasn't it?" he said. Sales nodded. "Can you do me a favour? Can you head to the road, show the ambulance where we are?"

Sales seemed to breathe out a sigh of relief.

"You're sure, sir?"

"I'm sure. You did good. Go get some air."

Sales managed a weak smile as he jogged back towards the storage room. Porter hesitated for a second, seeing yet another pentagram peeking through the sawdust floor by the main doors—this one much larger. Then he made his way to the cages, where Kett had succeeded in finding the right key. He hadn't pulled the chain out of the door, though, because the girl was still panicking.

"It's okay," said Kett. "My name's Robbie. I'm a policeman. I'm here to help."

He passed the keys to Porter.

"Get the other one open, will you?"

Porter walked past the empty cage to the one that held the young man. He was still in his teens, but only just. Like the girl, he wore pyjamas that looked far too small for him, the striped print faded with age. His hair was jet black, his face covered in a dusting of stubble and acne, a thin moustache barely hanging onto his top lip. The look in his eyes was of somebody who hadn't slept in weeks.

He retreated as far from Porter as he could go, as if he was trying to squeeze himself through the bars of the cage.

"I'm not going to hurt you, mate," Porter said. "I don't

even have to open the door if you don't want me to. My name's Pete. I'm a police officer. Can you tell me your name?"

The boy shook his head, although Kett didn't know if he was refusing, or if he didn't understand the question.

"You're English?" he asked.

Another shake.

The screams were starting to subside from the girl's cage. Kett had dropped to his knees by the door as he continued to comfort her. He had his phone out, showing the girl photos of his daughters. The young man was watching him too, his body beginning to unknot itself. Porter held up the keys.

"You want to come out?"

"Out?" said the guy, his accent strong. "Éxo?"

"Éxo," said Porter, and the young man nodded.

Porter shuffled through the keys, testing seven before the padlock snapped open. He threw it away, removed the chain, and opened the door.

"No hurry, mate," he said, stepping back. "Take your time. There's an ambulance on the way, they're going to make sure you're alright."

He looked past Kett to where the man they'd fought lay on the floor, blood still leaking between his lips. He was groaning in his sleep, his legs kicking like a jackrabbit's.

"He's not going to hurt you," Porter said. "You don't have to worry about him anymore."

The kid didn't understand him, but the girl had calmed herself enough to listen. She spoke from where she crouched at the back of her own cage, her voice so hoarse Porter could barely make sense of it.

"What have you done?"

Unlike the boy, she was English.

"What do you mean?" asked Kett. "We're here to help you, to take you home."

Porter could hear sirens riding the hot air, and he felt that same blissful wave of relief they always carried with them.

The girl sniffed, wiping the back of her hand across her nose. She had her eyes closed like she couldn't bear to look at the man who lay in the middle of the barn.

"You've killed us," she whispered.

"What?" said Kett.

She burrowed her head into her knees, sobbing quietly. "You've killed us. You've killed us both."

CHAPTER TWENTY-TWO

In less than half an hour, the yard was swarming.

Porter had unlocked the chains at the front of the barn, opening the sliding doors. Twenty coppers milled in the building and in the courtyard beyond as Clare coordinated the search, the Superintendent marching between them like a headless chicken.

Nobody had dared to step on the pentagram by the doors, skirting around it like it was a hole in the floor.

Inside the barn, two paramedics had loaded David Blethyn onto a stretcher and were struggling to wheel it across the sawdust floor. Porter must have walloped him with some strength because he still hadn't woken up.

"He's good to go," said one of the paramedics as they passed. "Tongue's mangled, but I don't think he'll lose it."

"He'll be able to speak?" asked Kett.

She shook her head.

It didn't matter, of course. Anyone who tried to chew off their own tongue had made it perfectly clear they weren't ever planning on talking.

"Keep him locked up," said Kett. "And don't leave him alone."

"Suicide watch?"

"Yeah."

"You okay?" she asked, nodding to his face.

Kett touched his cheek with his fingers. He'd managed to wash most of Blethyn's blood away using the hose outside, but he'd obviously missed some.

"Not mine," he said. "I'm fine."

It was a lie, of course, but he didn't think there was anything in the ambulance that could fix what had broken inside him.

The paramedic looked at the cages where the two teenagers still sat. Porter was with them, leaning on the boy's cage and chatting quietly to him even though he showed no sign of talking back. Three other officers, all women, had gathered around the teenage girl, talking freely enough to make her laugh. The cage doors had been open for thirty minutes or so, but neither of them had found the courage to leave. Kett didn't understand it, but he didn't want to force them. They'd been through enough.

"We can come back and have a look at them," said the paramedic. "There's another bus on the way, but they're held up."

"That would be great, thanks," said Kett. "You seen the guy on the field?"

"Seen what's left of him," she said. "No way we're putting that back together, sorry."

They moved off, passing Savage and Duke as they walked into the barn. Savage's face was drawn with worry as she took in the cages and the children. Duke just looked furious, stomping after her like an angry child. Porter walked over, everybody congregating in the puddle of sun that had formed around the open doors.

"Somebody shit in your cereal, Duke?" Porter asked.

"What happened here, sir?" the PC replied. "I saw Alfie by the gate. Somebody beat him into the middle of next week."

"It was that guy," said Kett, nodding to the stretcher as it trundled across the courtyard, the PCs parting like the Red Sea to let it pass. "If it makes you feel any better, he tried to bite off his own tongue, then Porter knocked him out with a baton."

"That's not what he's annoyed about, sir," said Savage. "He's annoyed because he wasn't here."

"Huh?" said Kett.

"The TV crew," said Duke. "You guys get all the action. A chase, a fist fight, blood, you rescue kids in cages, there's a man out there who got trampled to death by horses. It would have been amazing for the show."

Porter laughed.

"Sorry we ruined your big moment, Aaron," he said. "I'm sure they got some good footage of you, too, wherever you've been."

"We literally talked to some old ladies," he said, exasperated. "In a quaint little garden."

"To be fair, you almost died too," Savage told him.

Duke frowned at her.

"He choked on his lemonade," she added.

She hid a laugh behind her hand, but it was short-lived.

"You okay, sirs?" she asked. "What happened?"

"Save this story for me," Clare yelled, finally entering the barn. He looked about as mad as Kett had ever seen him, eyeballing them all in turn, then staring at the kids in their cages on the other side of the barn. "Because I cannot wait to hear your explanation for this, Kett. All I can say is that we're in the right place for a load of bullshit."

"It's technically horse shit, sir," said Porter.

"*You're* horse shit," Clare hissed back. "All of you. Statues of lumpy, stinking horse shit that do nothing but make my life miserable. If it was up to me, I'd ram you all back up the horse's arsehole from whence you came."

Nobody knew what to say to that. Clare took a breath, his eyes bulging.

"Spalding's run David Blethyn through the system. We've never heard of him. No record, no nothing. Thirty-nine years ago he plopped out of his mother in Swansea. Today, we find him here keeping kids in cages. Who is he?"

"I don't know, sir," said Kett. "But he tried to chew off his tongue when we caught him."

"So I heard," said Clare. "Only other time I ever saw that happen was when I was with the NCA investigating a terror cell in Birmingham. We arrested a woman and tried to get her to talk about who she was working with. She bit her tongue clean off."

"Insane," said Kett.

"He can't confess if he can't talk," said Porter.

"Of course he bloody can, Pete," Clare snapped. "Have you never heard of a pen?"

"I don't think this is about confession, sir," said Savage. "You caught him dead to rights. He's not getting off. He bit his tongue so he wouldn't have to give up names."

"Little extreme, don't you think?" said Duke.

"It's fanatical," said Savage. "It's like you were saying, sir, it's almost... I don't know, *religious*."

"He was working with Robert Flack," said Kett. "This place is part of Flack's property, his house is just across the meadow. When we spoke to Flack he… I don't know, sir, he was acting strange, he had this…"

He didn't know how to say it, the words draining from his skull.

"It felt fanatical too," he finished eventually. "He told us to walk away."

"He told you to walk away?" said Clare, one eyebrow arched.

"I saw him in the field, sir, before he…"

"Before you killed him with all the horses?" said Clare.

"I didn't kill him. How could I? He was shouting something at me. '*You brought it here.*'"

"It?"

Kett shrugged.

"He was terrified, sir. It sounded like he thought something had followed us here. He kept looking at the woods, and then…"

He paused again, because he wasn't sure what had happened. Everybody waited.

"It was like a feeling," he said, tapping his chest. "I felt something. The horses bolted, but I sensed it too. I can't explain it."

He waited for the insults, waited for Clare to start screaming at him. But the Super didn't react.

"They jumped the fence on the far side of the paddock," Kett went on. "They went straight for him. But only because he was sitting on the path cut into the meadow, it was the easiest place to make the jump. Still…" He closed his eyes, tried not to see it. "It was weird. A whole acre of field and they pick that place to cross the fence."

"You searched the woods?" Clare said.

"PCs have, didn't find anything. But if somebody had

been there, they'd have had plenty of time to escape while we were in here."

"And what exactly happened in here?"

"I followed Blethyn, sir," Porter said. "Me and PC Sales. Sales attempted to apprehend the suspect. I helped, and so did DCI Kett."

"And then we saw those two," said Kett.

They all turned to look at the cages. The three PCs were doing an amazing job of keeping the two teenagers calm. One was performing what looked like a chicken impression, and the girl was doubled over with laughter.

The boy watched from inside his own cage, clinging to the bars as if worried somebody was going to try and drag him out. He wasn't smiling, but there was less darkness in his expression.

"What's stopping them coming out?" asked Clare.

"They're scared, sir," said Kett. "The girl thinks we somehow put her in more danger by rescuing her. I can't make sense of it. She said we'd killed her."

"What did she mean?" Clare asked.

Nobody knew the answer.

"And there's no sign of Aggie Clegg or Bianca Caddel?" asked Clare.

"No, sir," said Kett. "But Flack knows Caddel. He confirmed it."

Clare considered it for a moment, his jaw flexing like he was eating an invisible Bounty.

"Savage, can you speak with the girl? See if you can coax her out of the cage."

"Yes, sir," said Savage.

Clare walked out of the door, shouting back.

"The rest of you tossjockeys have got about thirty

minutes to figure out what's going on here before you're all fired."

"I dream of being fired," said Kett when the Super was out of earshot. "Can you imagine it? Lie-ins, whole days of pottering around the house, nobody telling you they're going to shove you up a horse's arsehole."

"Sounds like heaven, sir," said Porter. He turned to Savage. "You want some help, Kate?"

"No, sir. I've got it."

"I'm going to have a quick look in those woods," said Kett. "See if I can figure out what happened to the horses."

"I'll come with," said Porter.

"Me too," said Duke. "Might get some action."

"With me and your DCI in the woods?" said Porter. "That's an outrageous thing to say, Aaron."

"Not *that* kind of action, sir," Duke said, frowning.

Kett made his way out of the barn, avoiding the pentagram. He walked through the courtyard, passing the stables to where the paddock lay drenched in sunlight. The path where Robert Flack lay dead was being guarded by a couple of PCs, both of whom kept glancing nervously at the herd of horses who happily grazed on the long grass in the meadow.

He left them to it, walking along the electric fence to where the field met the woods.

"What are you looking for, sir," said Porter, kicking stones into the paddock.

"I honestly don't know," he said, trying to remember exactly what had happened.

One second, the horses had been gathered right here, in the shade of the trees.

Then something had made them bolt. A noise that had been utterly silent, but one Kett had felt right in the marrow of his bones.

He walked to the treeline, the world beyond thrown into darkness by the weight of the canopy, and by the tangled mess of creepers that choked the trees. Snaking limbs of ivy had taken over, their trunks thicker than his leg. It was a wonder they'd left anything else alive. The floor was thick with brambles, a carpet of thorns that was so thick he couldn't see a way to get in.

"There can't have been anyone in there, sir," said Duke. "It's like a jungle."

"Can you both do a circuit of the woods," Kett asked. "See if you can find a path."

"Sir," said Duke, although he didn't look happy about it.

"I'll go this way," said Kett, heading for the road. "Yell if you find anything."

"You'll probably hear Duke screaming if we find something, sir," said Porter.

"Better hope it's not a seagull, eh?" the PC shot back.

Kett walked along the circumference of the woods, the dirt path leading him towards the road. If anything, the trees seemed to get denser, as if the plants were closing ranks against him, wooden limbs pulling tight. The only sign of life from inside was the chatter of the crows—or maybe magpies—but he couldn't see them. He couldn't see anything past the hedgerow that separated the path from the stables, either. Out here, he might have been the last man alive.

It was with some relief, then, that as he approached the road he heard somebody calling to him. It was Megan, the young camera operator. She was climbing over the wooden perimeter fence and using both hands to try to get his attention.

"Hi," said Kett.

"Oh, thank goodness I found you," she said, her face

crimson from the heat. "I'm sorry to be a bother, but you still have my camera. From earlier. I don't suppose I can get it back, can I?"

"Oh, right," said Kett. He patted his pockets. "It's in my jacket, sorry."

"If you tell me where it is, I can grab it," she said, looking back to make sure the coast was clear. "It's just I'll get in so much trouble if I don't have it. With Kelly. I don't want to lose my job."

Kett glanced once more into the woods and nodded.

"We can get it, my jacket's in the car."

She seemed to melt with relief.

"Oh, God, thank you so much." She gestured to the fence. "This way?"

"We'll take the long road," said Kett. "Me and fences don't get on."

He led her back the way he'd walked.

"Did somebody really die?" Megan asked as they passed the paddock. "Is that them? What happened?"

"I can't really say, sorry," said Kett. "I'm sure when we've finished here you can bring the cameras in."

"Not sure there's much point. Kelly's already on the verge of axing the show."

"Yeah?" said Kett. "Why?"

"I don't know. We've missed most of the cool stuff, and even when we're in the right place at the right time we're not allowed in. Be a shame, though. Aaron's... He's really quite..."

She was blushing, so Kett helped her out.

"Taken," he said. "He's really quite taken."

"Oh, God, I know! Sorry, I wasn't..."

Fortunately for the young woman, they'd reached the

main gate. The padlock had been clipped off to let the IRVs and the ambulance through, but Porter's Mondeo was where they'd left it. Kett collected his jacket from the back seat, pulling out Megan's camcorder.

"Just give me a sec," he said. "I need to make sure you didn't capture anything sensitive earlier, at the cottage. How do I turn it on?"

Megan pointed to a button, and Kett pressed it.

"No, the other one."

He tried again.

"It's... hang on."

She leaned over and did it for him, the screen coming to life.

"Some of it's... uh..." the woman said, but whatever she wanted to say, she didn't seem to know how.

Kett scrolled through the clips, seeing the woods and the ruins of St Mary's. He played a couple, most of the shots idling on Duke as he paraded through the crime scene. There were lots of close-ups of his face, a few of his arms, and even a couple of his backside.

"Uh," said Megan, the sweat rolling off her. "They're just... for focus... purposes..."

"Right," said Kett, finally finding what he was looking for.

He pressed play, watching on the screen as Megan filmed herself tumbling over the back seat of the IRV. She stepped out of the car and approached the cottage. Savage and Duke were both at the front door, Duke posing like an action hero.

Megan leaned past Kett's shoulder.

"He's so..."

"Taken," Kett said again.

They both climbed through the window, the camera closing in. Kett could hear the young woman breathing on film as she panned the shot along the front of the cottage, up to the bedroom windows in time to see Duke pass by. He stared out of the right-hand one, then appeared in the second, just for a moment before he was sucked back into the black.

Here, Megan lowered the camera to the window they'd climbed in through. There was nothing in the shot, so it panned up again, almost idly, to where Duke still stood in the bedroom window.

Only, it wasn't Duke.

"Shit," said Kett. The screen was so small he couldn't be sure, so he pulled his glasses from his jacket and put them on.

Somebody stared at him from the upstairs window, a bone-white grin against a blood-red face. They were standing far enough back that just an outline was visible, almost a ghost against the darkness of the room. But there was enough there to see the horns that jutted up from the head, as curved as a ram's.

"What's wrong?" asked Megan, leaning in.

The shot lasted another second or two then the camera dropped back to the downstairs window. Savage and Duke were climbing out, heading around the side of the house towards the garden. Megan followed them as far as the gate, then the shot went dark. There wasn't any more footage.

Kett played the clip again, pausing on the shot of the person in the window. He held it out to Megan.

"Did you see him?"

"Oh, no," she said, leaning in. "I didn't even notice. I didn't have time to watch it back before you took it from me. Who is it?"

"I have no idea," said Kett, heading off in a jog, calling back. "But I'm going to have to hang onto this for a bit longer."

CHAPTER TWENTY-THREE

There was something church-like about the barn, Savage thought as she made her way towards the cages. The high roof could have belonged to a cathedral, and the slatted windows at the top of the walls let light pass almost like stained glass, creating shimmering patterns of sunlight on the sawdust floor. Even with the storm of coppers in the courtyard, the air in here was still and quiet. It felt almost holy.

Except for the pentagrams by the doors, that was.

The PC who'd been doing the chicken impression stopped clucking as Savage reached them, stepping back with a nod of welcome. Savage smiled at the young woman inside the cage. She was in her mid-teens, so slim that it was a wonder she hadn't squeezed between the bars of the cage to make her escape. She'd stopped laughing, and was looking at Savage the way a mouse looks at a cat. It was heartbreaking.

"Hello," Savage said quietly. "Sorry, I didn't mean to ruin the chicken thing. It was pretty good."

"Thanks," said the PC. "I can do a sheep too."

"Well, we can't not hear that now, can we?"

The PC took a deep breath, then bleated out an incredibly realistic sheep noise. The girl in the cage burst out laughing again, clapping her hands together like a much younger child. Savage laughed too, a genuine chuckle.

"Are you sure you're not actually a sheep?" Savage said. "Are you disguised as a police officer? What do you think? Is she a human or a sheep?"

The girl cocked her head, licking her dry lips as she considered the question.

"I think she's a person," she said eventually. "Like me."

"I think so too."

Savage sat down in front of the open door of the cage, cross-legged.

"People have names. I'm Kate. This is..."

"Cilla," said the PC.

"And you are?"

"Freya," the girl said.

"Do you have a second name?"

She didn't answer, and Savage didn't push her luck.

"It's great to meet you, Freya." She looked past the empty cage to the one at the far end. The boy stared back, curious. "Do you know his name too?"

"He's called Dmitri," she said, giving the boy a wave, which he sent right back. "He's from Greece."

"Greece?" said Savage. She wracked her brain, trying to remember the handful of words she'd learned in Crete when her mum had taken her almost a decade ago. "Uh, *kalimera*?"

The boy's face blossomed into a smile.

"*Kalimera!*" he said, followed by a spout of other words she could make no sense of. Savage looked at one of the other constables.

"Can you go see if anyone speaks any Greek?" she said. "If not, try and get a translator out here."

The constable ran off.

"Thank you, Freya," Savage said to the girl. "It doesn't look very comfortable in there, would you like to come out?"

Freya shrank away again, shaking her head. She glanced at the top of the cage, and when Savage angled her head, she saw that there was something fixed to the bars. It looked like a sheet of paper, not much bigger than a business card, hanging from a red ribbon like the tag on a birthday present. She reached through the open door for it, stopping when the girl choked on a scream.

"Don't take it off! Don't take it off!"

"The paper?" said Savage. "What is it?"

"It can't cross it," she said, her words like a machine gun. "It can't cross it and it can't get me."

Savage ducked back down.

"I won't touch it," she said. "Sorry. I don't know what it is."

"It's a... a lock," said Freya, unsure. "A lock, and it doesn't have the key, it doesn't know how to open it, so it can't get me."

"Okay," said Savage. "What do you mean by 'it'?"

Freya clamped her mouth shut so hard Savage heard her teeth clack.

"You don't know?" Savage asked.

The girl didn't reply.

"You can't say?"

She nodded furiously.

"You can't say its name?"

Another nod. Dmitri was nodding too. There was a slip of paper hanging from the top bar of his cage as well.

"So as long as that paper is there, you're safe?" Savage asked, just to make sure. "Is this what that man told you?"

"Dave," said Freya, her face falling. "His name was Dave. They hurt him."

She shot a dirty look towards the open doors, and the coppers who milled there.

"He's going to be okay," said Savage. "We're taking him to the hospital. He'll be just fine, I promise. Listen, do you mind if I ask you some questions about Dave?"

Freya didn't reply.

"Was Dave the person who put you in here?"

A nod, so slight Savage almost missed it.

"Did he say why?"

Nothing.

"And is there ever anyone else here, other than Dave? A man in a wheelchair, maybe? Or a woman, older than me?"

No answer, her mouth forming a tight line.

"Freya, how long have you been here?"

"I don't know," she said.

"Days? Weeks?" No answer. "Longer?"

"We move," she said. "We're not always here."

"But you're always in a cage?" Savage asked, her mind reeling.

Freya nodded.

"How old are you?"

The girl looked at her fingers, as if the answer might be there.

"Seventeen," she said after a moment. If it was true, she was the youngest seventeen-year-old Savage had ever met.

"And how old were you when you first met Dave?"

"Seventeen," she said.

"And how did you meet him?"

She was struggling, her body growing restless.

"How about Dmitri? Has he been here as long as you?"

"I'm hungry," said Freya. "Dave feeds us after the horses, but he never brought us any."

"I can get you something," said Savage. "Or, listen..."

She wasn't sure if a lie would work here, but she tried anyway.

"These cards, the locks, they can work anywhere, you know. Dave told you that, right?"

Freya cocked her head again, making herself look even younger.

"I thought you didn't know what they are," she said.

"I... I don't have my glasses on," Savage told her. "I couldn't see it properly. I'm a police officer, we deal with these things all the time. If you take that card off the bars and put it in your pocket, it works the same way."

"Dave never said that," said Freya.

"He was just being super safe," Savage told her. "But I know how it works. I promise you, if I take the card off and pass it to you, and you put it in the pocket of your PJs—or even hold it, that works too—then you'll be one hundred percent safe. The lock is still locked. Shall we try?"

Freya looked uncertain.

"If we give it a go, I'll drive you to McDonald's," she said. "You like Maccy D's?"

Her face seemed to transform.

"Can I have chicken nuggets?"

"You can have anything you like," said Savage. "Shall we try?"

The girl nodded.

Savage stretched onto her tiptoes, picking at the ribbon. Her fingernails were too short, and the ribbon was too tight, so she gnawed at it with her teeth until it started to fray.

"Be careful," said Freya, who was on her feet. "Please don't break it. If it breaks, it doesn't work."

"Just a sec," said Savage. "It's coming loose."

She teased the knot apart, freeing the card. When she flipped it over, she saw that there was a design on the downward-facing side, a constellation of points and crosses. It wasn't identical to the wounds they'd found on the head in the church, but it was close enough to understand that this wasn't a coincidence.

Freya was reaching for it, her face drawn in terror.

"Please," she said.

Savage offered it through the bars into Freya's trembling fingers, and she hugged it to her chest like it was a flotation device and she was drowning. She looked past Savage to the barn doors, then up to the ceiling, her teeth bared against whatever she expected to appear there.

"You're okay," said Savage. "See? There's nothing to worry about. Nothing is coming. It still works."

It took another minute or so for the girl to relax, the tears rolling down her dirty cheeks. Savage held out a hand to her.

"Come on, Freya, you're good to go."

Freya was clutching the paper too tight to take the hand that had been offered, but she crept to the door and, after another handful of trembling breaths, stepped out of the cage.

Even Savage found herself letting go of a deep breath when nothing bad happened.

"That's brilliant," she said, gathering the girl into a hug. It was like holding onto a bag of bones, every edge sharpened by fear. "Amazing. Well done, Freya."

Dmitri was calling out from his cage, a desperate flurry of Greek.

“Can one of you cut the card loose?” Savage said.

“You have to give it to him,” said Freya, peeling her face away from Savage’s shoulder. “Give it to him or it will be able to get him.”

The constables nodded, picking at the ribbon that held the paper. Dmitri’s voice rose in pitch, those words coming faster and faster until the ribbon came loose and the card dropped into his hands. He stared at it like he’d caught a handful of starlight, then he clamped his hands around his treasure. A laugh exploded out of him, incredulous and insane.

“Come out,” Freya told him, pulling free of Savage’s hug. “It’s fine, look.”

Dmitri emerged from the cage, hunched over with trepidation. Then he whooped again, kicking up clouds of sawdust with his bare feet.

“How did you know?” Freya asked, still holding her card. “How did you know it wouldn’t come?”

“I just did,” Savage replied. “But there are a lot of things I don’t know that I think you do, and I might need some help with that. Do you think you could help me?”

Freya nodded, grinning.

“We can do it at the hospital,” Savage went on. “Because they’ll want to have a look at you, make sure you’re okay. How does that sound?”

“Good,” said Freya. “But only on one condition.”

Savage waited.

“I get a banana milkshake with my nuggets.”

CHAPTER TWENTY-FOUR

"How, in the name of Aunt Linda's monstrous bollocks, did you miss *that*?"

Kett stood in the courtyard outside the barn, caught in a sweaty sandwich between Superintendent Clare, Porter and Duke as they all crowded around the little camcorder in his hand. He'd played the clip twice already, and each time Clare had asked the same question in an increasingly higher pitch.

Duke hadn't said anything at all.

"Play it again," squeaked Clare.

Kett did as he was asked, all of them watching as Duke searched the upstairs of the cottage, as that horned face appeared in the window seconds after he'd moved out of sight.

"How, in the name of Aunt Linda's monstrous—"

"I don't know, sir!" Duke groaned. "It's not... it isn't possible. There was nobody up there."

"There's somebody right there, you mole-sighted pigeon fart," said Clare. The Super jabbed the screen so hard the camcorder nearly fell out of Kett's hand. "That's a face. You must have walked right past him."

"I didn't," said Duke, stepping back. Kett had known the PC for years now, and he'd never seen him this close to tears before—not even when he'd been blown up back in February. "I walked up the stairs, there were two bedrooms, no bathroom. First bedroom..."

He frowned as he tried to remember.

"Just a bed."

"You looked under the bed?" said Clare.

"No need to, sir. There wasn't a mattress, I could see the floor. I checked the curtains, nothing there. Second room was a bed and a wardrobe. I checked under the bed, and..."

"And what?" said Kett. "You checked the wardrobe?"

"Of course, sir. But..."

"But what?" barked Clare.

"There were so many cobwebs, and there was this spider on the handle. It was bigger than my face."

Clare was so red he looked like he was going to pop.

"Duke, if you tell me you didn't open that wardrobe because there was a spider on it, then I'm going to skin you alive right here and use your face as a jockstrap."

"I did open it, sir," he said. "I swear. I used my baton. But it took me a moment because the spider ran at me and I dropped the baton and it rolled under the bed. By the time I'd got it..."

"What?" said Clare.

Duke looked back to where the camera crew were assembled, lowering his voice.

"I took my eye off the wardrobe, sir. That's all I'm saying. But I opened it and checked inside, and there's no way anyone could have got past me, the room was tiny, I would have seen them."

He stared at the screen in horror, at that crimson face and its skeletal grin.

"It's just not possible."

"Un-tossing-believable," said Clare. "He was right there, and we missed him."

He jabbed a finger at Duke.

"I want you back at the cottage now. I want you to search every inch of that place, and the woods. Fix this."

"Sir," said Duke. He beetled off, the camera crew scrambling after him.

"Maybe he didn't see him, sir," said Porter in a rare show of support for the PC. "Didn't Kate tell us the ritual the killer used the head for was to gain the power of invisibility?"

Kett turned to him.

"He wasn't invisible, Pete. We all saw him."

Porter conceded the point with a nod.

"But who was he?"

"Or she," said Kett. "That's a mask, could be the same woman we saw before, or somebody she works with. It's obvious now that Bianca isn't doing this on her own. And the pentagrams here are the same as the ones we saw in the bunker. It's connected."

"You find anything out there?" said Clare.

"No, sir," said Porter. "Woods are too thick."

"Kett?"

"No, sir."

Kett looked past the Super to the barn, where Savage had managed to coax the two teenagers out of their cages. Judging by the tone of their voices, the kids were doing okay.

"But this is a good bust, right?" he went on. "We've found two children that are being kept against their will.

Whoever took them is almost certainly the same person who took Aggie Clegg this morning."

"We don't know that," said Clare.

"No, sir, but everything points that way. Robert Flack, who owns this place, was friends with Bianca Caddel for years. Decades. He's listed on the planning application with her on the site with the bunker. He did his best to keep us away from the barn, certainly didn't want us to find what he had hidden here. Whatever he's part of, I think Bianca's in on it too. But it's good."

"Good?" said Clare.

"Yeah, because they haven't killed these two. Whatever Bianca and these men were doing, they were keeping the kids alive. If we're lucky, Aggie's in the same boat."

Clare chewed on it for a moment, watching Savage as she jogged out of the barn.

"What *were* they doing here?" he asked.

"I don't know," said Savage. "But those two were scared senseless. I think Blethyn told them they were being hunted by something. I'm guessing a demon of some kind, given what we've found so far. There were glyphs on the cages, little cards with a design like the one we found on the dead man's head back at the church. Freya, the girl, told me as long as she stayed in the cage, and as long as that piece of paper was there, she was safe. The thing, whatever it is, can't pass."

"And she believed it?" asked Kett.

"Completely, sir," said Savage. "They were both terrified when I suggested removing it, and overjoyed when I did, but only because I told them it would still work if they kept hold of it. They've been brainwashed, over weeks, maybe months."

"They've been here all this time?" said Kett.

"No, sir," said Savage. "Blethyn and the others were moving them around. I'm hoping the kids will be able to tell us where."

"But why?" said Kett. "You've got two kids in cages in a pretty remote location. Why risk moving them around?"

Nobody answered him.

"She's talking, though," said Clare. "That's something. Can you go with them to the hospital? Keep her chatting?"

Savage pulled a sheepish expression.

"That's what I was coming to see you about, sir," she said. "Freya said she'd tell us everything, but only if I take her to McDonald's first."

"And whose idea was that?" Clare said, his voice like gravel.

"Might have been mine, sir, sorry. We don't have to stop, we can get drive-through, then head straight over. Neither of them has been injured, not physically anyway."

Clare put a big hand to his face, smearing away a shroud of sweat.

"Do it," he said. "But I want uniformed PCs with you. So far, we've got three people working for the same ring. We don't know how many others there are."

"Yes, sir," she said.

"Kett, you go too," said Clare. "I want as many people listening to what they have to say as possible."

"And me, sir?" asked Porter. "Could murder a Big Mac."

"No," said Clare. "I want you to clean up the mess here."

Porter's bottom lip almost hit his chin.

"But—"

"Enough with your buts," Clare snapped. "Or I swear on my Aunt Linda's monstrous bollocks, I'll..."

He seemed to run out of steam, the heat getting to him.

He slouched off towards the parked cars, waving a limp hand back.

"I'm going to ID our kids. Don't Kett this up."

"I really hope I never have to meet his Aunt Linda and her monstrous bollocks," said Porter.

"Those kids ready to go?" Kett asked Savage.

"I'll check, sir," she said, running back.

"You sure you don't need me?" asked Porter. "I'm good with kids, I could help."

"Not my call, Pete," said Kett, patting Porter on the shoulder. "But I'll grab you a burger and fries."

"And an apple pie, sir?"

"Don't push your luck."

CHAPTER TWENTY-FIVE

They could have been a regular family, if it wasn't for the fact that they were riding in a police car.

Savage drove, Kett in the passenger seat and the two kids in the back. Freya was manic with excitement, commenting on everything she saw outside the window, spouting her words so quickly Kett couldn't make out most of what she was saying. She could barely sit still, kicking her bare feet against the back of the seat, and bouncing so much that Savage had to keep telling her to stop rocking the car.

She reminded him of Alice so much that it was painful. He couldn't stop thinking about his eldest daughter locked inside a cage, at the mercy of Blethyn and Flack and whoever else was involved. The anger grew inside him, quiet now, but promising terrible violence.

Dmitri was quieter, his dark eyes staring at the passing world with a frightening intensity. Sometimes he would speak in Greek, but there were English words there too, and when he spoke to Freya, it seemed as if they had their own language. Kett wondered if they'd invented it in captivity.

Both clung to those scraps of paper like their lives depended on it.

They chased the IRV in front and another followed close behind them, four extra coppers split between the two cars. They rode through the winding country lanes, the lights off. It seemed like a ridiculous convoy for two teenage children, but Kett felt happy that they weren't on their own. All he could see in his head was Flack screaming at him from the other side of the paddock. All he could hear were those desperate words.

You brought it here.

All he could feel was that subsonic charge that had rippled across the field, that had sent the horses on their murderous path.

Combined with his exhaustion and the evening heat, the day was a living nightmare. He felt like he was drowning in it.

"Are we nearly there yet?" said Freya, leaning forward as far as her seatbelt would let her. "I'm so hungry. Dave never gave us anything but sandwiches. Ham sandwiches, cheese sandwiches, jam sandwiches. All he knew how to make."

"Crisp," said Dmitri.

"Yeah, crisp sandwiches. Those were Demi's favourite. Salt and vinegar. Not cheese and onion."

Dmitri made a sound like he was throwing up.

"How much longer?"

"Not long," said Savage as the lead car hit the dual carriageway. "There's one just up the road from here."

"So excited," the girl said, practically buzzing. "Haven't had one for so long. Used to go there when I was a kid, but Dave would never take us, not even when we was moving."

Kett glanced at Savage, who met his eye.

"Freya, who did you live with before you met Dave?" asked Savage.

Freya shrugged.

"Loads of people," she said. "Was in foster care, have been for years, ever since Mum left."

"Your dad?"

She shrugged again, throwing herself back in her seat.

"How did you meet Dave?" Kett asked, craning around in his seat so he could talk face to face.

"Do they still give you a toy?" asked Freya, not meeting his eye. "I had a chicken from there once, the one from Moana. Don't know where it is now, though. Feels a bit weird giving you a toy chicken when you're eating chicken nuggies, doesn't it?"

"Freya," Kett insisted. "It's important we know what happened to you."

"We know you don't think Dave was trying to hurt you," said Savage. "If that's true, he's not in trouble. Neither are you. But if we're going to keep you safe, keep *it* away, then we need to know as much as possible."

"Doctor," said Dmitri.

"Doctor?" Kett said.

Dmitri opened his mouth like somebody was looking down his throat.

"Ahhhh."

"Hang on, he was your doctor?" said Kett. "As in, the kind you go see when you're sick?"

Freya looked at Dmitri like she was confused. Dmitri spoke again, but it was all in Greek.

"He wasn't my doctor," she said. "I don't really remember..."

She did. Kett could see in her pained expression that

she remembered everything. But she didn't want to talk about it.

"Were there ever any other children with you?" Savage asked. "In the cages?"

"Sometimes," said Freya, as carefree as if she'd been asked about her friends at school. "They never stay long."

"Do you know where they went after they left?" asked Kett.

"Is that it?" Freya said, leaning forward. "Oh my God, that's it! I see the M!"

Savage followed the IRV off the A47, turning sharply into the car park. It was mobbed with people getting dinner, the queue for the drive-through almost reaching the slip road.

"Looks like we're going in," said Kett. "Park by the doors, Kate."

"Going in?" said Freya, beside herself. "Yay!"

Savage peeled away from the car in front, bypassing the queue and parking outside the main doors. There were three groups of teenagers on the seats there and they all started jeering, one of them throwing a chip at the car's windscreen.

"I mean one of us is going in," said Kett. "Not all of us. You don't even have any shoes on. What do you want?"

"Please," said Freya, jumping in her seat again. "Please let us go. I haven't been out for so long. Just let me have a look."

"Your call, sir," said Savage.

"Please," said Freya, drawing the word out to four, five, six seconds.

"Fine," said Kett. She was too much like Alice for him to say no. "But you stay with us at all times. Understood?"

"Yes!" said Freya. She leaned over and elbowed Dmitri,

almost hard enough to make him drop his slip of paper. He clenched his fist around it, shouting at her in furious Greek.

Kett opened his door, bracing himself for the pain as he got out. The heat was unbearable, the skies dark and low and full of untapped pressure. There was definitely a storm on its way.

Another chip hit the car, and he eyeballed the kid who threw it—the look he usually reserved for the interview rooms. The boy nearly fell off his chair.

"Stay close," he said to Freya as he opened the back door. "You run off, I eat your dinner."

"Deal," said Freya, sliding out. Her eyes were like saucers, and she bounced on the balls of her filthy feet while she waited for Dmitri to exit the car.

Kett took a moment to scan the car park, taking in the line of vehicles spewing poison into the hot air, the two-dozen or so people on foot. One of the IRVs was snared in the line for the drive-through, unable to cut through. The other was parked right behind them, the two constables already out.

"Are we all getting a treat, sir?" asked one.

"Depends if you brought your wallet or not," he replied. "Stay out here, give us a shout if you see anything weird."

"What's weird, sir?" asked the second constable.

"You'll know it if you see it."

Kett opened the door, letting Freya skip through, then a more cautious Dmitri, and finally Savage. They inhaled as one, breathing in the unmistakeable aroma of cheap burgers and fries as they joined the back of the queue.

"This is amazing!" said Freya, running to the tables with the screens, then to the counter, then back again. People watched her, bemused at the sight of a teenage girl in her pyjamas. "I'm going to eat everything!"

Kett's stomach was churning like a cement mixer. He'd barely had a chance to eat all day. He felt guilty being here without his own kids, but that wasn't going to stop him.

"I'll order, sir," said Savage. "You grab a table. What do you want?"

"Whatever you're having," he said.

"Chicken nuggies!" blurted Freya. "And fries, and a banana milkshake if the machine's working, because they never work, but if it's working, I want one. Please."

"Dmitri?" asked Savage.

The boy was too busy watching the crowds of people to hear her, both hands holding the slip of paper so hard his knuckles had blanched. He looked nervous, which wasn't surprising given he'd spent God only knew how long inside a cage.

"Get a selection," said Kett, fishing out his wallet and handing Savage his debit card. "I'll pay."

Savage went to join the queue and Kett scanned the bustling restaurant. He couldn't see an empty table, but he found the next best thing—more teenagers sitting in the corner booth by the window. He walked over, his warrant card out. They fell quiet as he approached.

"Sorry," he told them. "I hate to pull rank, but this is a police emergency."

"Emergency?" said one of the girls. "What kind of emergency?"

"The kind where if I don't sit down soon, I'm going to fall over," said Kett, returning the card to his pocket. "Thanks."

The kids slid out of their seats, chattering to each other as they made for the door. Kett dropped into the booth, Freya plonking herself next to him with such enthusiasm she elbowed him in the ribs. She picked a few chips from the wrappers the teenagers had left behind, stuffing them into her mouth with a groan of satisfaction. Dmitri sat on the other side, still alert.

"Won't be long," Kett told them.

"I'm fine," said Freya, scoffing more chips. "I'm great."

He angled himself around to look out of the window. The third patrol car had finally pulled up next to the first two, the four uniformed coppers perched on the bonnets and laughing about something. The car park was even busier now, a symphony of horns and shouts as people fought for the limited spaces. Even though it was well into the evening, the heat was still unbearable, the world outside shimmering.

"When was the last time you came to a McDonald's then?" Kett asked, turning back to the table.

"Ages," said Freya without hesitation. "Years. I was, like, fifteen? I don't know. Dave didn't like them, said they weren't good for us."

"Not good for you?" said Kett. "I mean, he's not wrong, but I can think of something else that's not good for you. Being locked in a cage."

Freya shrugged like it didn't matter. She found Savage in the queue.

"She's nearly there. My mouth's dribbling. Is yours, Demi?"

Dmitri wasn't listening. He was staring past Kett's head, through the window. His eyes had grown wider still, his mouth muttering quiet words, his fingers kneading the piece of paper in his hands with such urgency that he was in danger of pulling it apart.

"Hey," said Kett. "Dmitri, are you okay?"

The boy was still speaking, the volume of his words growing. His bloodshot eyes were locked on the window, his expression so full of panic that Kett spun in his chair again, every hair on his scalp standing on end.

"What's wrong?" he asked. "What are you seeing?"

Dmitri was loud enough to hear now, but Kett couldn't make any sense of it. He kept his attention on the window, searching the sun-drenched windscreens of the cars, scanning the faces of the pedestrians, seeing nothing.

"Demi, what's wrong?" said Freya, and there was fear in her voice now too. "Stop it. You're scaring me."

"Everything's fine," said Kett, although he didn't believe it. Even with the full force of the sun blasting through the window, he felt cold. It was like he was back there on the field before the horses spooked, that same warning screaming silently inside his head.

He didn't try to ignore it, or rationalise it. He stood up, taking Freya's arm a little harder than he needed to.

"Hey, that—"

"We need to go," he said. "Move. You too, Dmitri."

Dmitri was still staring through the glass, his chant growing louder and louder—enough to draw the attention of other people in the restaurant.

"Dmitri," Kett said. And when he still didn't react, he slapped his hand on the table. "Dmitri!"

The boy finally heard him, those bulging eyes sliding towards Kett, not blinking. He spoke more words in Greek. Kett didn't know what they meant, but he *understood* them.

It's here.

He turned to the window again, still holding onto Freya. He looked.

And this time he saw.

At the other end of the car park, walking slowly towards them, was a figure in black. He wore a long coat, the hood pulled up, the face beneath as dark as old blood and grinning madly. A pair of curved horns jutted upwards like two fingers aimed at the heavens.

The man lifted a gloved hand, extended a finger right at him.

"Shit," said Kett. "Shit, shit, shit."

He ran for the door, almost colliding with Savage as she walked over from the counter, an overladen tray in her hands.

"Let's go," he told her.

He didn't wait for a reply, opening the door and running into the heat, still holding onto Freya's arm. She was screaming at him to let go of her, desperately trying to pull free. Cars crossed in front of them, passing the line of IRVs and the constables who stood there.

"Hey!" he yelled at the PCs. He pointed across the car park to where the man still advanced, maybe thirty yards away now, that finger pointing. "Grab him, *now*."

The four PCs scattered, two almost ending up under the wheels of an SUV that was gunning towards the exit. Freya finally managed to pull free, rubbing her arm where Kett had been holding it. She was sobbing, and he didn't understand why she was so upset until he saw that her hands were empty.

"The lock," she said. "I dropped it, I dropped it!"

Savage exited the door behind her, her face taut with worry.

"It's okay, Freya," she said. "I can make you another one, I—"

"We have to go back," screamed Freya. "It's coming, it's going to take me."

"Get in the car," said Kett. "Let's move."

He tried to take her arm again, but she skittered out of

the way, pushing past Savage in an effort to get back inside McDonald's.

"Hang on," said Savage, struggling with the force of the girl. "You're going to be okay."

"I'm not!" she shrieked, a sound of pure terror. "It's seen me! It's seen me!"

"In the car," Kett said again, a tornado raging in his skull. He took hold of Dmitri instead, the boy too afraid to resist, steering him towards the IRV.

Stopping when he smelled smoke.

The IRV at the back of the line was on fire. A pillar of smoke curled up from beneath the car, growing thicker by the second. There was a soft *whumph*, a tongue of fire licking the tyre, spreading fast.

"Christ," said Kett, backing away as the poisonous air punched into his lungs.

Another soft explosion, flames spreading beneath the IRV in the middle. The air was shimmering with the heat of it, blisteringly hot. People were starting to notice, the teenagers on the tables bolting, a stream of customers running from the restaurant.

"Move," Kett yelled at them, retreating. "Get away!"

He dragged Dmitri into the road, heading for the car park. But the boy fought him, still shouting in Greek. Savage was struggling with Freya, the girl hurling herself towards the door, trying to fight the current of people who were escaping.

"I need it!" she cried. "I need it, I need it."

Kett turned, full of panic, seeing two of the four constables running back, the other two marching deeper into the lines of parked cars.

The masked man had gone.

"Get—" Kett started, then the windows of the middle

IRV exploded, hailing chunks of glass across the street. The car was a pyre, the thunderous roar of it beaten only by the screams as people ran.

"Get back," he finished, still dragging Dmitri away. "Get away, Kate."

He didn't think she'd heard him over Freya's screams. The fire was spreading, the enormous window of the restaurant splitting with a sound like a cannon shot. People fled from the carnage, everyone heading away from the building. The Uniforms were helping evacuate, one holding the door, another two running inside. The fourth was nowhere to be seen.

And neither was the man.

Kett spun in a half-circle, trying to find him in the sea of moving cars, in the stampede of feet.

"He's—"

He was right there, walking towards him from the opposite side of the restaurant, so close to the burning cars that Kett didn't understand how he hadn't burst into flames. The smoke surrounded him like a cloak of crows.

This time, he wasn't pointing a finger.

He was pointing a knife.

It was a long, thin blade, black with dirt and orange with rust but no less lethal for it. It wasn't aimed at him, it was aimed at Freya. The man took another few steps before the smoke swallowed him, but Kett had no doubt he was still moving.

"Knife!" he yelled, although there were no constables left to hear him. He doubled up, coughing, fighting for every breath. "Kate, we need a car!"

It wouldn't do them any good, the panicked traffic was gridlocked all the way to the exit. Kett gave Dmitri's arm a tug, hauling him to the first row of parked vehicles.

"This way!"

He glanced back to make sure Savage had heard him. She'd hefted Freya onto her shoulder, the girl thumping her fists on her back, kicking her, still screaming.

Behind them, the man had once again vanished.

"Come on," he said to Dmitri, squeezing between the cars, heading towards the exit.

Maybe three rows ahead, he could see a young woman trying to unlock her Fiesta, and he upped his speed, calling out.

"Hey, wait. Police!"

If she heard him, she did a good job of pretending she hadn't. She managed to get her door open, climbing in. Kett shoved Dmitri forwards, reaching the woman just as she started her engine.

"Hey," he yelled, slamming a hand on the Fiesta's bonnet. "Police, I said stop."

She crunched the gears, the engine revving.

"I swear to God," he said. "Let us in."

He opened the back door and hurled Dmitri inside. Savage was right behind him, and she dropped Freya as gently as she could. The girl tried to make a break for it again, almost tackling Savage to the ground before Kett got hold of her. Between them, they managed to push her into the back seat of the woman's car.

Savage got in next to her, trying to fend off Freya's punches. Kett opened the passenger door and dived in.

The woman stared at him, gripping the wheel like she meant to rip it off and use it as a weapon.

"Please don't hurt me," she said.

"I'm police," Kett said again, breathless. "I'm sorry, but I need you to drive."

"I'm a single mum, I—"

"Now," said Kett. "Go."

The woman crunched the gears again, putting the car in reverse and pulling sharply out of the space. Her back bumper kissed the car opposite, but she didn't let it stop her. She drove to the end of the aisle and switched on her indicator, trying to join the queue of traffic that had built up around the exit.

"Go round," said Kett. "Just get us—"

One of the IRVs exploded, the shockwave blasting debris across the car park and setting off a keening song of car alarms. The young woman screamed, the Fiesta lurching into the other lane and accelerating hard.

Kett swivelled in the seat, looking back.

No sign of the man.

"He's gone," he said.

"He's *there*," yelled Savage, pointing forward.

Kett faced front, seeing the man by the side of the road, the blade gripped in his fist as he watched them go through the slits of his mask. The car passed him with feet to spare as it bombed past traffic. His head twisted, grinning, the horns pointing towards the heavens like he was the devil himself.

"What the hell?" said Kett. "You seeing this? How did he move so fast?"

The young woman pulled back into the left-hand lane and drove onto the slip road, hitting the A47 so fast she almost lost control.

"Easy," Kett told her, the words barely fitting up his throat. "You did good."

He turned, staring out of the rear window.

The devil watched them go.

CHAPTER TWENTY-SIX

Kett called Superintendent Clare the second McDonald's was out of sight. His fingers felt numb, the phone almost slipping from his hand as the young woman drove them down the dual carriageway. She kept checking her mirror, but Kett didn't think she was worried about somebody following them. She was watching Freya in the back seat. The girl was still fighting Savage with every fibre of her being, her screams loud enough to make Kett's skull vibrate.

"Speak," boomed the Super. "Where... What's all that racket, Kett?"

"It's one of our kids, sir," Kett said. "I'll explain when we get back to the station. I need you to get Gorski onsite."

"Tactical?" said Clare. "At HQ? Why?"

Freya kicked the back of his seat and he grunted in pain.

"You're okay," Savage was saying, over and over. "You're okay, Freya, I promise."

"Somebody followed us to McDonald's," Kett said, not sure if Clare could hear him over the shrieks. "Black clothes, the same red mask we saw on the video, horns. I don't know how he did it, sir, but he set fire to the IRVs. Three of them went up in flames, then he came at us with a knife."

"He tried to kill you?" said Clare.

"I don't think it was us he was after, sir. I think he was gunning for the kids."

"I told you!" roared Freya, a noise of pure fury. "I told you it would find me."

She kicked his chair again, the pain clawing up his spine. He sat forward, his elbows on his knees.

"It will never let me go. Not ever. You've killed me!"

"Where are you now?" said Clare.

"In a car, heading for the city. Driver is..."

He turned to the woman, and it took her a moment to notice him.

"Zoe," she said.

"She's going to take us to HQ. We're on the A47 heading past Postwick if you have any units nearby. Whoever this is, they're not afraid of being caught. And..."

He thought of the man in the mask, the way he'd vanished and then reappeared as if by magic.

"It's more than one person, sir," he said. "It has to be, it's the only way he could have moved like that. Two people, maybe more, all dressed in the same costume."

"I have no idea what you're saying, Kett," said Clare. "What's the reg?"

"Registration," Kett asked. Zoe hesitantly shouted it out. "You get that, sir?"

"I did. Keep moving, you can debrief when you're here. I'll send whoever I can find to escort you back."

"Sir," said Kett, but it was to a dead line.

He pocketed his phone, turning around when Freya kicked his chair again.

"Calm down," he told her. "Freya, you need to stop."

She kicked out again, then smacked Savage in the face with the back of her hand.

"I said calm down," Kett ordered, louder now. "Calm down or we have to stop the car. Understand? We stop right here and we let you out."

His message seemed to cut through her panic. She'd lifted her bare foot for another kick but she held it there, her knee almost touching her chin.

"You can't stop," she said. "It will catch us."

"Then calm down," he said. "Whatever you've lost, we can replace it."

"We can draw you another lock," said Savage, one hand to a bloody lip. "As soon as we get to HQ, I'll make you another one."

"You know how?" said Freya.

Savage nodded, and Freya's violence melted into tears. She curled into Savage, sobbing hard. Savage stroked her hair, staring at Kett with intense shock.

He looked past her, seeing a handful of cars and a couple of lorries behind them. He couldn't tell what sat past the dark windscreens, whether they were faces he was seeing, or masks.

"Can I drop you off here?" asked Zoe, a tremor in her voice. "I don't feel so good."

"Just keep moving," Kett replied, turning to the front again. "It's not much further."

He could hear sirens over the roar of the Ford's engine, but he didn't relax until five minutes later when the first IRV pulled up behind them.

"Oh God," said Zoe.

Another overtook, its siren wailing.

"Oh God!"

"Just keep driving," said Kett.

A third boxed them in on the side, herding them towards the Thickthorn Interchange, then onto the A11. The rest of the journey was mercifully short, just eight minutes until the convoy pulled through the gates of Norfolk Constabulary HQ.

"You can stop," Kett said to Zoe.

She did as she was asked, right in the middle of the road. She let out a breath that she seemed to have held all the way from McDonald's, her hands locked around the steering wheel.

"Zoe," said Kett. She looked at him. "You did good. You saved us, thank you."

She managed a smile, but it didn't last long. In the back, Freya had started up again, her shrill voice like a boiling kettle. Kett got out of the Fiesta, feeling a pressure in the air that was electric, that felt like it was about to split. The uniformed PCs were scrambling out of their cars and waiting for orders.

"Nobody comes in," Kett told them, nodding to the gates. "Unless they've got ID. You see a man in a mask, you take him out."

"A mask, sir?" asked one PC.

"Yeah. Looks like the devil, you can't miss him."

Kett opened the back door of the car, letting Savage slide out. Freya must have hit her with some force because her lip had swollen to twice its size. She leaned back in.

"Come on, Freya. Let's get you safe. Let's get you inside, yeah?"

"Give her a hand," Kett told the PCs who were still loitering. "The boy, too."

"Kett!" called Clare, his voice like thunder as he ran over from the main doors. He watched as Savage pulled Freya from the car, and Dmitri exited from the other side.

Then he turned his attention to the gate. "You were followed?"

"I don't know, sir. I don't think so. But it's not hard to guess where we're going."

"Get them into the bullpen. Tactical's on its way."

"Sir," said Savage, an arm around Freya's shoulders, the girl still sobbing. "I think they're going to feel safer in a cell."

"A cell?" said Clare.

Freya nodded.

"Fine. Do what you have to. Just get them in."

Clare watched as they walked off, then turned to Kett.

"But I want *you* in the Incident Room, you jug of toss. You've got some bloody explaining to do."

HE MADE HIMSELF A CUPPA FIRST, because he didn't think he'd be able to survive another second of this god-awful day without one. He was so tired he was almost delirious. When he closed his eyes, he saw the devil's face against the dark, that finger pointing, the knife glinting through the smoke. The bubbling kettle could have been a voice, whispering to him.

You brought it here.

The devil.

"*Not* the devil," he told himself. "Not the devil, not a witch."

But the exhaustion was doing its best to convince him otherwise. Because how else could he have moved across the car park so quickly?

"Sir?"

He opened his eyes to see Savage in the doorway. She looked like she had been the one locked inside a cage for weeks on end, her face gaunt, her eyes dark. When she touched her fingers to her split lip, they came away red.

"You okay?" Kett asked her.

The kettle reached its crescendo and Kett flicked the switch before it could snap off by itself. It was something Billie did every single time she made tea, and it drove him crazy. Not letting the kettle boil was one of her OCD routines. If she didn't stop it before it clicked automatically, she was inviting disaster into her life.

He wasn't sure what had compelled *him* to do it this time.

"Yeah," said Savage. "I mean, no. Not really." She nodded to the kettle. "You're rattled too, sir. Never seen you do that before."

He took a second mug from the stand and added a teabag to both. He poured in the water, inhaling the fragrant scent of tea as he tried to figure out how to reply. HQ was deathly silent, as if everyone but him and Savage had been spirited away.

"This one's getting to me," he admitted eventually. "Did you see him? The man in the mask, back at McDonald's?"

"Yeah, sir, I did," said Savage.

"You saw the way he moved? The way he was standing by the cars, then by the road as we drove out?"

She nodded.

Kett fished out the teabags and slung them in the bin, adding milk to both cups.

"The kids okay?" he asked.

"I put them in a cell," said Savage. "It's where they wanted to go. They're both in the same one. We stuck Dmitri's lock to the door, and it seems to have done the trick. I just came to get them something to drink."

"Can you talk to them?" Kett asked. "See if they can tell you anything about the person in the mask."

"Yes, sir," she said. She shunted herself off the door frame like her batteries had run out. "Thanks for the brew."

"Make it last," said Kett, carrying his mug out of the room. "We're in for a long night."

He made his way across the bullpen and down the short corridor to the Incident Room. Superintendent Clare and DS Spalding were the only two people there, both of them staring at the evidence wall while Spalding taped up a couple of photographs. Kett spotted Bianca Caddel's driving licence photo, her face as blunt as a spade, her eyes dark. Flack and Blethyn were there too.

Clare did a double take when he spotted the tea in Kett's hand.

"I'm assuming that's for me, Detective?"

"Uh, no, sir," said Kett, stopping in his tracks. "Sorry. Desperate."

"You know the rules as well as I do," said Clare, clomping towards him. "You enter this room with tea, it better be for me. Hand it over."

There was nothing else for it. Kett put the mug to his lips and knocked back two giant gulps. It was like he'd swallowed a hot coal, the fluid searing its way down his gullet and detonating explosions of pain as it went.

"Christ," he grunted, slamming a fist against his chest.

Clare was still advancing. Kett took another long sip, grimacing. He had to choke down the whole mug and turn it upside down before the Super backed off.

"I hope you enjoyed that," Clare said, disgusted.

"Not as much as I'd have liked, sir," croaked Kett, his voice hoarse. "Where is everyone?"

"Duke's on his way from the cottage," said Clare. "Porter's at the stable yard."

"They found anything?"

Clare didn't answer, pointing instead to one of the photographs Spalding had just tacked to the wall. The young woman had such a big smile and bright eyes that it took Kett a moment to recognise her.

"Holy shit, that's Freya."

"Freya Martin," said Spalding. "She's seventeen. Turns eighteen next month. She's been in the system since she was five. Dad was absent, mother in Hellesdon after a suicide attempt. Freya was in too many foster homes to count, last one was a couple of years ago."

"Nobody's been checking on her?" said Kett.

Spalding shrugged.

"She's getting close to the age where nobody cares. Waiting for social to get back to me. Last foster parents are Elaine and Graham Hamilton, can't reach them by phone."

"I can go," said Kett. "What about the boy?"

"No clue, sir," said Spalding. "There's no MP report for somebody of that name. Got the plods scouring the files for a match, though."

"Tell me what happened at McDonald's," said Clare, perching on the edge of a table. "Fire service says three cars were burnt to their shells, and they still might lose the building."

Kett scrubbed his hands over his face, trying to remember.

"We were sitting down to eat, sir. I saw the man through the window. He was wearing a mask, he was pointing at us, at the kids, I think. It's the same guy."

He pointed to the wall, to a pixelated photo of the

masked figure they'd seen through the cottage window on Megan's camera.

"Or the same mask, anyway. I got the kids out, went for the car, but..."

"But the car was on fire," said Clare when Kett didn't finish. "Because only you could make an IRV spontaneously combust, Kett."

"Wasn't me, sir. But... but it *did* seem like it was spontaneous. The man in the mask was nowhere near them, but as soon as he pointed, they just..."

He lifted his hands, then slapped them down again.

"They say how the fire started, sir?"

"Not yet," said Clare. "I'll get the report in the next hour. I'm not expecting it to say witchcraft."

"Was anyone hurt?"

"By some miracle, no," said Clare. "You said you think there's more than one person? That they're wearing the same costume?"

"It's the only way I can explain it, sir," said Kett. "The guy was behind us in the car park as we drove away. Then he was in front of us, by the road. He couldn't have moved that quickly. It had to have been somebody else wearing the same clothes, the same mask."

"We already know this isn't one person," said Clare. "We found two men keeping the kids in cages, and we think they're working with Bianca Caddel, who—as far as I know—still has Aggie Clegg. Your devil makes four, but we could be looking at five, six, a hundred more. We don't know."

"But that's what doesn't make sense, sir," said Kett. "The kids weren't afraid of the men who were holding them prisoner. They were afraid of the guy in the mask."

"They're afraid of demons," said Savage as she walked through the door. "Freya just told me. The cages, the little bits of paper with the strange markings, those things were all designed to hide the children from whatever was looking for them."

"The man in the mask?" said Kett.

"Bullshit," said Clare. "These guys are all in on it together. Whoever the twat at McDonald's was, he was there to get his prisoners back."

"That's just what the kids believe, sir," said Savage. "All of them, according to Freya. Not just her and Dmitri."

"All of them?" said Kett.

"There were others, sir. Freya can't remember how many, but it's a lot. At least four, all kept in the cages before being moved out. None of them were told why they were there, only that it wouldn't be forever."

"That's what she said?" Kett asked. "That they wouldn't be prisoners forever?"

Savage nodded.

"This doesn't make any sense," said Kett, rubbing his face again. He started to speak, but was stopped by a yawn that almost unhinged his jaw.

"Sorry, Robert, are we keeping you up?" said Clare, glaring.

The yawn was still going. Clare checked his watch.

"Any time today, Detective."

"Sorry," said Kett when he'd got control of his face again. "I..."

He'd completely forgotten what he'd been about to say.

It didn't matter, because a thunder of voices rose up in the corridor outside, and a few seconds later Duke walked in, accompanied by Josh, the cameraman, and Kelly, the presenter.

"I'm sorry," Duke was saying. "I can't control it. It's the job, it can't always be exciting."

"Yes, but *some* excitement might be nice," said Kelly.

"Nice of you to join us, Duke," muttered Clare. "Any news from the cottage? Did you walk right past our killer again? Or maybe this time you stopped for a chat? Perhaps you stayed long enough to trade eyebrows?"

Duke rubbed his forehead sadly. Josh lifted his camera, but a glare from Clare made him lower it almost immediately.

"There was nothing in the cottage," said Kelly, before Duke could reply. "We filmed him wandering from room to room for twenty minutes, like some kind of homeless, hungry kitten, and that was it."

Duke slumped onto a chair in the corner, looking, for all his size, like a sad little boy.

"Got lots of humming, though," said Josh.

"Oh please, don't mention the humming," said Kelly. "He never stops. I tell him to be quiet for the shot, and three seconds later he's humming again."

"I don't hum!" said Duke. "And it's not my fault. I bet these guys didn't get to do anything exciting either."

Duke stared hopefully at Kett, then at Savage.

"Right?"

"I mean..." started Kett. "It depends on your definition of exciting."

"It wasn't really *that* exciting," said Savage. "It wasn't an attack, really."

"And the IRVs didn't explode *too* much."

"It wasn't like we were in a *huge* car chase."

"And the knife wasn't *too* big..."

Duke stared at them.

"The point of all this," said Clare, turning to Kelly, "is that you aren't authorised to be in here. So toss off and leave us to it."

"With pleasure," said Kelly, heading for the door. "If you're lucky, we'll be back in the morning."

"If we're lucky, you'll climb into an elephant's tosshole and suffocate in smegma," said Clare, although Kett didn't think anyone heard him over the sound of the door closing. "Nothing to report then, Duke?"

"No, sir," he said, utterly miserable. "I still don't understand how I missed him. It's like he... It's like he had *powers*. Like he was a real demon or something."

"He's not a demon," said Kett. "Just like the woman we saw this morning isn't a real witch."

"That's what I was about to say, sir," said Savage. "I asked the kids if they'd seen the woman who took Aggie, I showed them the photo of her. They told me she *was* a witch, but that she wasn't the thing that scared them the most. There's something worse out there."

"Worse?" said Clare.

Savage seemed to steel herself.

"Yes, sir. They said the thing that scares them the most, the thing that's chasing them, is the devil."

CHAPTER TWENTY-SEVEN

"Sir, you need to see this."

DI Porter looked up from the floor of the cage where Freya Martin had been kept, spotting a PC standing in the open door of the barn. He was beckoning furiously.

"You found something?" Porter called back.

"I'm not sure, sir. Maybe."

"Maybe," Porter echoed quietly. He backed out of the cage and stood up. "Maybe's no good to us, mate."

They'd found fuck all so far in their search of the stables, and even less inside Robert Flack's house. Whatever Flack and Blethyn had been doing here, they'd made sure there was no paper trail. Other than the cages, and their occupants, there was nothing incriminating on site at all.

"What?" Porter barked as he reached the constable, sidestepping the pentagram on the barn floor.

"Over here, sir," the man said. "There's something weird with the stables."

"Weird how?" said Porter.

The man didn't reply, jogging across the courtyard and stopping at the last of the six stables, where another handful of coppers were gathered like restless geese. He gestured at the door with such enthusiasm that Porter was surprised he didn't say, "*Ta-daa!*"

"What am I looking at?" he said once he'd caught up.

"Have a peek, sir."

Porter was in no mood for mysteries. The sun had sunk beneath the trees, but the evening heat was as thick and as hot as soup. If there wasn't a storm later, he'd eat his hat.

"Just in there," the PC hinted, nodding at the stable.

"Fuck's sake," muttered Porter.

He opened the door and squinted into the dark. The stable was maybe twelve feet square, the walls crumbling brick, the cement floor covered in a dusting of straw but otherwise clean. A mahogany wardrobe stood in one corner like it had got lost on the way to a bedroom somewhere.

The PC walked around the outside of the stable block to the back wall, and Porter reluctantly followed.

"Can you just tell me what I'm supposed to be looking at?" he said, dry mud crunching beneath his boots.

"This," said the PC, gesturing again.

Porter sighed as he took in the back wall of the building. Like the rest of the stable block, it was brick and flint and looked close to collapsing. There were no doors, no markings, no anything.

"It's a wall," he said. "What do you want me to say?"

"Yeah, it's a wall to *what*, sir?"

Porter sucked air through his teeth, eyeballing the man.

"Any chance I could borrow your baton, mate?"

"My baton, sir?" said the PC. "Why?"

"Because I'm going to give you an enema with it, unless you tell me what you're on about."

"The wall, sir," said the PC, backing away. "It's too far out. *Look.*"

Porter looked again, and this time he saw it. This section of the stable block jutted out from the rest by about five feet, as if somebody had added a small extension. There were no windows and no doors.

He ran back around to the stable, then checked the one next door. Both were the same size, the rear wall ended at the same spot.

"Shit," he said, walking back into the stable. "There's a room there. You could have just bloody said that."

"Sorry, sir," said the PC.

Porter opened the wardrobe to see that it was empty. It was too close to the wall to make out if there was anything behind it.

"Stand back," he told the PC, grabbing the top of the wardrobe and pulling hard.

It tipped, dirt raining from the top.

"You need a hand, sir?"

"Nope," said Porter, every muscle straining.

The wardrobe was too heavy, crunching back against the wall and almost taking his fingers off.

"Shit," he said. "Little help?"

"I just..."

The PC stopped arguing, squeezing between the wardrobe and the wall.

"On three," said Porter. "One, two, three."

They pulled the top of the wardrobe together and it toppled like a redwood. It hit the floor with an explosion of dust that was so thick it took Porter a moment to see what sat behind it.

A door.

"Holy shit," said Porter. "Good find."

He tried the brass handle, giving it a good tug to no avail. The door was an old one, and it was solid. The keyhole was enormous, but when Porter put his eye to it, he saw only darkness.

"Get some tools," he said. "Get it open."

"Yes, sir," said the PC, practically flying out of the stable.

Porter put an ear to the door but couldn't hear a thing. He rapped his fist on it.

"Police, is anyone in there?"

If there was, they didn't want to talk to him.

He stood back as the PC reappeared, a crowbar in his hand. Two more followed, armed with whatever they'd managed to find inside the yard's outbuildings. One held a mallet and a chisel, the other was struggling with what looked like an old-fashioned hoe. They set to work like the Three Stooges, the guy with the hoe almost taking off the head of the one with the mallet, while the PC with the crowbar wedged it into the wrong side of the door.

"Jesus Christ," muttered Porter as he watched.

But they found their rhythm before he could say anything, and after thirty seconds or so the door splintered out of its frame. The hinges had to have been in worse shape than the door because they gave up completely, the entire thing collapsing on top of the upturned wardrobe. Another storm of dust filled the stables, this one billowing in a wake of foul air from the room beyond the wall.

"Police with Taser!" yelled the PC, dropping his crowbar in order to pull his Taser from its holster. "Make yourself known."

He moved through the door into the darkness beyond, followed by the other two constables—one still armed with his hoe. Porter pulled out his torch as he walked after them.

The room was microscopic, barely enough space for the four of them even standing shoulder to shoulder. In the weak glow of his torch it was painfully obvious it was empty—other than the carpet of ancient manure.

"Fuck's sake," muttered Porter, coughing a decade's worth of powdered horse shit from his lungs. "Good job, lads, you found the toilet."

"There's something here, sir," said one of the men. Porter didn't know what he was talking about until the PC dropped his boot onto the ground.

It rang like an old bell.

"Move," said Porter, pushing the other men out of the way so that he could angle his torch downwards.

A sheet of corrugated iron covered the floor, maybe four-foot square.

"Get it up," he said.

Porter grabbed one end while two constables took the other. Between them, they hefted it up, manure sliding off the sheet as they propped it against the wall.

A circular hole. A wooden ladder, dropping into darkness.

Porter aimed the torch into the opening, but the beam wasn't brave enough to reach the bottom. A draft was still pushing upwards, stale air laced with the smell of death. Unlike the bunker, this shaft wasn't built from bricks. Algae-slicked stones made up the walls. They looked like they'd been there since the dawn of time.

It was a well, he realised.

"Police," he yelled, making one of the PCs grunt in shock. "Anyone down there?"

Only his echo replied.

"Fuck's sake," he said again.

"You want, uh, us to go first, sir?" said the PC, his voice dripping with reluctance.

Porter pulled off his jacket and handed it to one of them.

"No," he said. "I'll go. But you'd better be right behind me."

He didn't wait for a reply, grabbing the ladder and stepping onto a rung. It wobbled, his sphincter clenching so tight it could have cracked a nut. He clamped the torch between his teeth as he made his way down, trying not to gag at the stench that rose to meet him.

"You okay, sir?"

He didn't look up. He didn't want to know how deep he'd gone. He kept moving, the shaft swallowing him up just like the one at the bunker had done until, finally, a shape peeled itself from the dark below.

It was a face, the mouth open in a silent scream, its eyes pitch-black blisters of pure malice.

"Fuck," he said, and the torch fell out of his mouth. It hit the ladder with another clang, spinning for a second or two until it landed on the body at the bottom of the well.

It was definitely a body. It lay on its back, the head twisted up, the arms caught beneath it, the legs propped against the wall as if it had tried to climb its way to freedom. It was wearing clothes that had rotted with age, its skin crawling with insects—so many of them that they teemed over the head of the torch, making the walls of the shaft look like they were crawling. Rot had set in, the air thick with it. Only the face seemed unaffected.

"Sir?" said the PC.

Porter felt the ladder shake as the copper made his way down, and he suddenly pictured the man falling, knocking him off and pinning him against the liquifying remains.

"Hang on," he called up. "Stay there, don't come down."

The ladder stopped shaking. Porter clung to it,

squinting into the bottom of the well. There was no sign of a tunnel leading out of it like there had been in the bunker. There was just the corpse.

"Can somebody call in a forensic team?" he said as he dropped onto the next rung. "Tell them we've got a body."

He kept going before his joints could lock up, reaching the end of the ladder. The smell was so bad here he could barely breathe, could barely see past the tears in his eyes. He didn't want to step off the rung because he couldn't see where the corpse's clothes ended and its limbs began. But he touched the toes of his shoe to the ground until it felt solid enough not to be flesh.

The corpse watched him as he ducked onto his haunches.

"Nope," he said, picking up his torch and shaking away a forest of ants and millipedes. They crawled onto his hand, up his sleeves. More were swarming into his trousers and down his shoes. "Nope, nope, not happening."

"Sir?" came a voice from too far overhead.

"I fucking hate this job," he replied, his gut heaving.

He couldn't make sense of what the corpse was wearing. There was what looked like a black dress, but there was something else covering the legs. Maybe jeans. He pinched the hem of the dress and peeled it back, releasing a fresh wave of rot that made his entire body contract.

"Nope."

They were definitely jeans. He patted the pockets, his fingers sinking into the mush beneath.

"Oh, I fucking hate you," he said, gagging again.

He tried the other side, and this time he felt something harder beneath the damp fabric of the jeans. He worked his hand into the pocket, recoiling when a spider the size of a golf ball bristled up his wrist.

"No!" he screamed, shaking it away. "You can fuck right off!"

"Sir?" asked the PC.

"Hate it, hate it, hate it," Porter said, ripping the wallet out of the corpse's jeans. He didn't have anywhere else to put it, so he slid it into his own pocket.

He started to climb the ladder again, pausing after a couple of rungs.

The corpse was still watching him, dark eyes in a distorted face. There was something wrong with it. He'd seen more than his fair share of the dead and he'd never met one that looked like this before.

Cursing beneath his breath, he dropped back down, aiming the torch at the face and finally understanding what he was seeing.

It was a mask, the torchlight revealing a second face through the gaping mouth. Porter pulled a pen from his pocket, inserting it into an eyehole and tugging gently. The mask lifted with a wet sound, peeling away from the corpse below. It was heavy, a blanket of grey hair spilling out from it. More insects rained from the wig, landing in the ruin of what lay below.

"Fuck me," said Porter.

He turned away so he didn't have to see it, but the imprint of that sunken, insect-ravaged face was seared into his skull. He'd be seeing it for the rest of his life.

He didn't want to put the torch back in his mouth, knowing where it had been. He slid it into his back pocket, holding the mask in one hand as he made his way slowly up the wobbly ladder. It could have been a thousand years later that he reached the top, two pairs of strong arms hauling him from the opening and laying him down on the floor of the hidden room.

"What the hell is *that*?" said one of the coppers, staring at the mask.

Porter sat up with a groan, examining it. In the relative brightness of the room, the mask didn't look anywhere near as real as it had down the shaft. But it wasn't a cheap Halloween prop. It was well made, the latex heavy, every wrinkle created with care. There were wisps of stubble sprouting from the chin, and more than a few moles. The hair looked like it had been taken from a real person, although Porter wasn't willing to touch it to see if that was true.

He'd seen the face before, of course. This was the witch that had attacked the kids in the woods.

He dropped the mask and pulled the wallet from his pocket, holding it in hands that wouldn't stop shaking.

"Need a light," he said, and one of the PCs obliged.

"No offence, sir," he said, "but you reek."

"You try rolling around with a dead person at the bottom of a fucking well," he shot back. "Bet you wouldn't smell like bloody roses either."

He opened the wallet, finding a handful of cards, thirty pounds in notes and a wedge of receipts that the damp had welded together.

There was a driver's licence too.

"Light," Porter barked again as the torch slid away. It snapped back, revealing a man's face—too damaged to make out.

He scanned the name on the licence.

"Oh shit."

He pulled out his phone, trying to ignore the filth that coated his fingers, the scraps of the dead that had gathered beneath his nails, as he called Kett.

CHAPTER TWENTY-EIGHT

"You're sure?" Kett asked.

Porter's voice was faint, and full of static as he replied.

"I'm tired, sir, but I can still read. The dead man's ID says Kevin Clegg."

"But we met Clegg this morning," said Kett. "He showed up looking for his daughter. How old's the body?"

"Weeks," said Porter. "Maybe months. We'll need Franklin to say for sure, but this person carked it a long time ago."

Kett looked up from his desk, but the Super was nowhere to be seen. Savage was watching him like a hawk from across the room, and he waved her over.

"What's he look like?" he asked.

"Like he's been at the bottom of a well," said Porter.

"No, the photo on the licence, Pete."

"That's what I mean. Damp has destroyed it. He looks like the guy we gave a lift to this morning, more or less. Younger, though. Beard, a little chunky. But I don't think it's the same guy."

"You're sure?"

Porter took his time.

"I'm pretty sure, sir."

"So who did we let into the crime scene?" said Kett.

Nobody answered.

"Fuck," said Kett, pushing himself out of his chair. "I checked his ID, he had... he had Clegg's library card, his debit card. I..."

He should have looked harder.

"Kate, can you pull up Clegg's driving licence," Kett called across the room. "What's the address, Pete? Same one we've got for Aggie?"

"No, sir. It's a place in Portsmouth. But I'm looking through the receipts in his wallet. There's a delivery slip for a generator, dated March, and the address is across the city. Looks like an industrial estate in Heartsease. I'll text the details."

"Good work," said Kett. "Let me know if you find anything else."

"The only thing I'm going to find is a shower, sir," Porter said. "I'm covered in dead person."

"That sounds... horrible," said Kett. "Go home, get changed. But I need you back, Pete."

"Yes, sir."

Kett hung up, pulling his jacket from the back of his chair and walking to Savage's desk. Clegg's details were on the computer, a man glowering at them from the screen. There was a definite resemblance to the guy who'd claimed to be Kevin Clegg that morning, but Kett wasn't convinced. He had a full head of hair, for one, and his nose was smaller.

"Fuck," he said.

"It wasn't Aggie's dad in the woods?" said Savage.

"I have no idea," Kett replied, heading for the door. "You coming?"

"I am, sir," she said, running the other way. "Just let me grab Aaron. He wouldn't want to miss out on any more fun."

IT WASN'T AN INDUSTRIAL ESTATE. That much was clear the moment Savage pulled the Audi into an alleyway off Salhouse Road. The narrow track ran between a Co-op store and a gym, both of which were boarded up. It led into a small courtyard ringed by a two-storey office building on two sides and a sad strip of woodland on the other.

A tent had been pitched in one corner, in the shade of the trees, and two women sat on deckchairs beside it, drowning in a cloud of smoke. They watched through red, puffy eyes as Savage steered the car into the middle of the yard and cut the engine.

"Smells like somebody's having a party," said Duke from the back seat.

Kett sniffed the air, finding the unmistakeable aroma of weed.

"That's the place," said Savage, tapping her window to draw attention to the building on the right. The big glass windows had been secured with metal plates, and the rusting chain around the door made it clear it hadn't been used in some time. "Owned by a registered charity that went bankrupt last year. Mr Bumpy Enterprises Ltd."

"Mr Bumpy?" said Kett. "What the hell was it?"

"Some kind of kids' play area, I think," said Savage. "Doesn't seem to be any connection at all to Kevin Clegg or anyone else on the case. I have no idea why he'd order something to be delivered here, given the place has been empty for months."

"Especially a generator," said Kett. "Unless he was squatting."

He opened his door, every joint clicking like an action figure as he got out. He was greeted by a mesmerising chorus of birdsong from the woodland, the sound of it taking a little of the weight from his shoulders. Savage got out, and for a moment they both stood in the honey-coloured evening light, releasing a long, steady breath that was perfectly synchronised.

Then a roll of distant thunder rippled through the sky, killing the mood.

The women passed their spliff between them, unconcerned until Duke emerged from the back of the car in full uniform. Then, with a noise like a chicken being eaten by a fox, one of them popped the entire joint into her mouth. She clamped her lips around it, coughing so much there was smoke emerging from her mouth and her nose—and quite possibly her ears.

"We don't care," Kett called out before she injured herself. "We're not here for you."

The woman doubled up, spitting the mangled spliff into her hand. She was somewhere in her late forties, although her almost complete lack of teeth made her look older than that. Her hair was dyed black, but it hadn't been a good job. Some of it had leaked onto her forehead, looking like melted liquorice.

The other woman was old enough to be her mother, her greying hair matted in some places, missing in others. Her face was etched with a tapestry of deep lines that only hard women who'd lived harder lives seemed to have. She gave the younger woman a hefty pat on the back as she continued to cough up a lung.

"You living here?" Kett asked them, nodding at the tent.

"What's it to you?" asked the older woman. Her accent was local, and strong, her voice heavy with gravel.

"Just curious," said Kett, walking over. "Because if you *don't* want to live here, we can help."

"For a favour?" said the woman. "No thanks."

"No favour needed," he said.

"You're not going to move us on?" asked the younger woman, her voice hoarse. She looked scared, her bare heels scuffing patterns into the dirty concrete ground. "Took us ages to find this place."

"We're not going to do anything," said Kett. "Don't worry. I don't care about the tent, or the weed. But I want you to be safe."

"Safe as houses here," said the older woman. "Nobody knows about it. If they don't see you, they don't touch you."

It wasn't a ringing endorsement of their situation, but there wasn't much more he could do.

"How long have you been here, Miss, uh?"

"Clunge," said the older woman.

"Miss *Clunge*?" said Kett.

"Just Clunge."

"Clunge?"

"What about it?" she said, her face compressing into an even more complex arrangement of creases.

"Nothing. Clunge is... fine. And you are?"

He looked at the younger woman.

"Flaps," she said.

"Clunge and Flaps?"

"You deaf?"

"No, you just sound like some kind of terrible erotic variety act," he said. He nodded at the building on the other side of the courtyard. "You been here since that place closed down?"

"Was shut when we got here," said Flaps. "Everything's shut, *int'it*? City's gone to the dogs."

"You ever seen anyone in there? Anyone locking up, anything like that?"

Flaps looked like she was going to answer, but Clunge covered her mouth with a dirt-caked hand.

"We can tell you, for a price," she said.

"Or you can tell us down at the station," said Savage.

"It's okay," said Kett. He fished out his wallet and opened it up. Yesterday, there had been three twenties in it. He knew that because he'd taken a hundred out of the cash machine and paid forty to the piano teacher.

All of those twenties had gone, and in their place were three slips of paper covered in dozens of sticky gems and crayon drawings of the Queen. Somebody—Evie, he suspected—had written 'this is a real twenty-pound note so don't ask any questions' on each one.

Kett pulled one out and held it up.

"Would you believe me if I said this was legal tender?"

Clunge and Flaps looked deeply unimpressed.

"Kate? Aaron?"

Savage pulled out her wallet, while Duke extracted something from his pocket that looked like a cuddly bumblebee. He opened it up conspiratorially, and Kett heard the jingle of coins.

"Aaron, what the hell is that?" he asked.

"My purse," said the giant PC.

"He crocheted it himself," said Savage, holding up a fiver. "All I've got, sir, sorry."

Duke tipped a handful of change into his hand.

"About two fifty," he said.

Kett turned back to the women. Clunge rolled her eyes.

"You know, back in my day, coppers had proper money for their eyes and ears." She clicked her yellow fingers. "Hand it over."

Savage and Duke made payment. It didn't take Clunge long to count it out, the money vanishing in the well-practiced flick of a hand.

"So," Kett said. "Tell me, who's been here?"

"No idea," said Clunge. "Baked off my face most of the day."

She erupted into a wheezy laugh, slapping her knee so hard she almost fell off her chair.

"Right," said Kett. "Flaps?"

"There aren't many people know about this place," said the younger woman. "Folk drop in, but there ain't much to see, and less to steal. Seen a couple of people inside, though."

"Inside *that* building," said Kett, pointing at the soft play just to be clear. "Who?"

"Couple of fellas," she said. "Little older than me."

"Fifty?" said Kett, and this time it was Flaps' turn to almost fall off her chair.

"I'm thirty-two," she said.

"Really?" blurted Duke, and the two women glared at him. "Because I'd have guessed younger," he added without much conviction.

"They were in their forties," said Flaps with a sad sigh. She wiped a hand over the dye stains on her face. "Hard to see 'cause most of the windows are covered. Saw them going in, though. They don't cause no bother."

"What did they look like?"

"Like most of the folk you see skulking around," she said. "They looked like they were wearing hoods."

"They get in through the door?" Kett asked.

"Nobody getting through that," said Clunge, pulling a metal tin from her pocket and proceeding to roll another joint. "Padlock's rusted shut. But you don't need to unlock the door. There's another way in."

"Where?" said Kett.

The woman let go of her joint to rub her thumb and fingers together.

"You've cleaned us out," said Kett. "All, uh, £7.50 of it."

Clunge looked up at Duke, her leathery face peeling open into a smile.

"You could leave him with us for half an hour," she said. "Tent's big enough. Just."

Duke gulped. Savage was trying not to smile.

"He's alright, even with the eyebrow thing," Clunge went on.

"Tempting," said Kett. "But no. Like my colleague told you, though, we can do this at the station, if you'd rather."

"Fine," said Clunge. She licked the edge of the rolling paper with a yellow tongue. "Board over the basement window's loose, you can get in that way."

"You been in?" Kett asked her.

Clunge didn't answer. Flaps folded her hands over her chest, shaking her head.

"Only once," she said. "Never again."

"Why?" Kett asked her. "What happened?"

"Nothing happened," she said, shrinking into her chair. "Some places are best left alone, that's all. Some places are just... evil."

CHAPTER TWENTY-NINE

Finding the basement window was harder than Kett had expected, mainly because it was tucked away down the narrow side of the building and almost hidden beneath a blanket of weeds and a mammoth buddleia plant. A dozen fat bumblebees, drunk on pollen, guarded the way in, and Kett gently shooed them away with his hand.

He'd take bees over flies any day.

Another roll of distant thunder echoed across the courtyard.

"Storm's a-coming," said Duke, like a wise old man.

Kett used his boot to strip away some of the flora from the ground, revealing a plywood board. It had been bolted to the cracked concrete, but the bolts were rusted almost to nothing, and when he dug his fingers beneath it and lifted one corner, it came up easily. The window beneath held a little bit of broken glass and a whole lot of darkness.

"Here we go again," said Kett. He hefted the board up, the plywood cracking. "Knock the glass out, will you, Aaron?"

Duke flicked out his baton and ran it around the edge of

the frame, causing a hail of shards to fall into the shadows. Kett clicked on his torch and aimed it down, seeing a short drop.

"Wanna toss a coin?" he asked.

"Gave all mine away," said Duke, patting his pockets.

"Rock, paper, scissors?" he tried.

"I'll go, sir," said Savage.

"No way," Duke told her. "I'll go first."

"I can look after myself, Aaron," she told him.

"I'll go," said Kett before they could start arguing. "But can I borrow the baton?"

"You want to borrow Kate, sir?" he asked.

"What?"

Duke looked at the weapon in his hand.

"You called your baton *Kate*?" said Savage.

"Everyone names their baton," he said. "Yours was called Betsy, wasn't it?"

"Yeah, but..." Savage didn't seem to know what to say.

"Give it," said Kett, snapping his fingers until Duke handed it over.

"Bye, Kate," the PC said quietly.

Kett sat on the edge of the window and slid down onto the ledge. His torch picked out a large basement room below, empty metal shelving units standing shoulder to shoulder like armoured knights. He dropped to the floor, one sweaty hand holding the baton by his ear while the other swept the torch from side to side.

"All clear," he said.

He crossed the room, hearing Duke slide down behind him, then Savage. Their own torchlight brought the shelves to life, making the shadows dance. There were two doors in the far wall and Kett pointed the baton at the one on the right.

"Check over there."

"Yes, sir," said Duke.

Kett made his way to the door on the left, opening it into a short corridor. Two more doors waited for him, and past them, a set of stairs led up to the ground floor. There was no sound at all in the building. He couldn't even hear Savage and Duke. It was as if they'd been swallowed alive by the dark.

He beamed the torch up the stairs to make sure there was nothing up there, then opened the closest door. It was a closet, more shelves that had been stripped of everything except a pile of rags and some empty mouse traps. He tried the next door along, but this one was locked.

"Duke," he called back, the volume of his voice surprising him.

There was a pounding of feet, then the big PC appeared.

"Sir?"

"Give me a hand, will you?"

Kett stood back, preparing himself for the pain.

"Now."

He lifted his boot and drove it into the door, feeling it resist. Duke's boot hit a second later, though, and the door crunched out of its frame.

"That was mostly me," said Kett, lifting his torch and taking a step into the room.

A step is as far as he got, though.

"Holy shit."

The room had been a kitchen at one time, but only the sink remained, hanging from the wall like a loose tooth. Everything else had been stripped away, leaving a space about ten-foot square.

Every inch of the floor and walls had been drawn on—

the ceiling too, he noticed when he looked up. There were hundreds of markings, so close together and drawn with such ferocity that Kett couldn't tell if they were words or pictures or some combination of both.

The only thing that seemed painfully clear was that the symbols had been drawn in red paint.

Or maybe blood.

"Oh my God, sir," said Savage, peering past his arm. "This is insane."

"Insane is right," said Kett. "Duke, can you radio for some backup, and get forensics out here too?"

"Yes, sir," said Duke.

The PC didn't move, standing there long enough for Kett to work out what he wanted. He returned the baton, and Duke gave it a gentle kiss before charging up the stairs.

"That's definitely not hygienic," said Savage, grimacing as she watched him go.

"Duke and hygienic have never been two words I'd put together," Kett said. "You make head or tail of this?"

He shuffled to the side so Savage could get in next to him.

"They look like the same kind of markings we found at the church this morning," she said. "On the dead man's head. And the paper locks we took from the cages back at the stables. Those lines and crosses, they're demonic glyphs, or seals, or at least that's what the internet tells me. I don't know about the words."

She leaned through the door, and Kett aimed his torch at the wall she was studying.

"Looks like Latin," she said. "'*Veni, veni, o comitis* something.' Duke would know."

Kett scanned the rest of the text he could see, but none of it made a scrap of sense. It looked like the markings of a madman, the lunatic scrolls of somebody who had long ago lost their mind.

"Can you take some photos, Kate?" he asked. "We need to get this up on the board, see if we can translate it. But it has to be connected."

"It does, sir," said Savage. "This is our killer."

"Or killers."

He backed away from the door, feeling an unpleasant stew of anger inside his gut as he thought about the man who had been posing as Kevin Clegg.

"He was right there," he said. "This morning, in the woods. He just showed up, claiming to be Aggie's dad, and I believed him."

"He had ID, sir," said Savage.

"He had a bloody library card," said Kett. "I should have known better."

"But if he's not Aggie Clegg's father, who is he?"

Kett checked his watch to see that nine had come and gone.

"I don't know, Kate," he said. "I thought the attack on the teens this morning was random. I thought they'd stumbled onto the head inside the ruins, that whoever left it there attacked them before they could call us."

"But it wasn't random, sir," Savage went on. "Aggie's Clegg's dad's been dead at the bottom of a well for days. Maybe weeks."

"And somebody else has been pretending to be him," said Kett. "Because our coppers spoke to Kevin on the phone this morning, before he showed up at the ruins."

"And nobody has reported him missing, sir," said Savage. "If they had, the system would have spat his name out when we were looking for Aggie."

Kett massaged his head with his free hand, a storm

brewing behind his eyes to match the one that grumbled in the distance.

"What the hell is going on, Kate?"

He was answered not by her, but by Duke—the PC's voice booming down the stairs.

"Uh, you guys should probably get up here."

Kett met Savage's eye, his expression mirrored there—*what now?*

Savage bolted, taking the stairs two at a time. Kett went more slowly, hauling himself up using the handrail. By the time he'd reached the corridor above, his back a solid pad of pain, Savage was through the door. Kett followed the sound of her voice as she cried out in alarm, finding himself in the main building.

It was brighter here, beads of amber light squeezing past the edges of the metal window boards, revealing a space that was far bigger than it had looked from outside. Skeletal frameworks covered both walls, stretching high overhead, some still bearing scraps of colourful fabric or plastic sections that had once been ladders and slides. Three bears grinned down at him from a mural on the wall, although he didn't know what they were so happy about. Somebody had scratched away their eyes.

Birds flapped in the shadows overhead, chattering softly.

Magpies, Kett realised. Three of them.

Duke and Savage stood in the middle of the floor, in front of a large sunken area that could only have been a ball pit.

There were no balls here anymore, though.

Kett lifted his torch, the ribbon of faltering light reaching the pit, finding what looked like a nest of branches and leaves that filled the sunken container from corner to corner. Laid carefully on top of the branches, forming a crude circle, were countless strands of red and yellow ribbon. More were stretched across the centre of the circle to make a pentagram.

And lying in the middle of it all was a body.

This one had been dead for a long time. The skeleton was yellow with age, stripped of any last scrap of flesh and polished to a dull shine. It lay on its back, its arms by its side, its legs straight. Its head had been tilted up, the jaw unhinged into a silent scream. A coil of barbed wire had been wrapped around its eyes and the base of its skull.

"Jesus," Kett said, his voice reduced to a whisper. It was still enough to scatter the birds overhead, their wings applauding as they crossed the room.

"Candles, sir," said Duke, nodding to the dozen or so candles that edged the ball pit. They were black, which was why Kett hadn't noticed them. He wondered if that's why the air smelled funny, then he angled his torch to the far end of the container and saw a table there, stalks of incense reaching for the roof like charred fingers.

There was more writing on the floor around the pit and the table, the words neater than they were downstairs. Lines of alien text stretched up the walls, a spiderweb of scrawled symbols.

"Take photos," Kett said, his throat so dry he could barely get the words out. "You called for backup?"

"Yes, sir," said Duke, one hand resting on his Taser. "On their way."

Kett walked to the table, almost tripping on the generator that sat next to it. He followed the wires, finding a set of lights that weren't too different from the ones the forensic team used. He ducked down and gave the generator a shake, hearing the slosh of fuel inside. Then he grabbed the starter cord and pulled hard.

The generator coughed, wheezed, then came to life. The lamps blazed on, filling the space with so much light that Kett felt like he'd looked at the sun. He stood up, shielding his face with a hand until the pain in his retinas had ebbed away.

Only then did he look at the table, which groaned beneath the weight of everything it held. More candles stood next to the incense, jug-sized stalagmites of black wax. On the left side of the table was a large leather pouch. Photographs surrounded it, hacked and shredded into crude circles. There was a woman in every one, but her face had been scratched into oblivion. On the right were two knives, one that looked as if it had been taken from the kitchen downstairs, the other a ten-inch curved monstrosity with a red quartz handle.

Between them were six books, bound in leather, their crumbling pages as yellow as the bones in the pit. One was open, and Kett slid his glasses on to get a better look at what was displayed there.

It was an illustration, sketched in black lines. A body, lying on a bed of branches, a crown of thorns on its head.

The table stood at the head of the ball pit like an altar, and from where he stood Kett could see the body that lay beneath him in its coffin of branches and ribbon—too similar to the image in the book to be anything other than an attempted recreation.

"It doesn't look real," said Savage, who crouched at the edge of the pit.

"You think it's fake?" Kett asked her.

"No, it's not that, sir. I think the bones are genuine. But

they're too clean. It looks like a museum piece or something. It's been treated."

The magpies answered her, perched on the uppermost level of the scaffold and watching with dark eyes. More birds danced inside the scaffold of the soft play, chittering.

"How did they even get in?" asked Duke, who studied them with a nervous expression. His hand still rested on the Taser.

"You found anything, sir?" asked Savage, standing up.

"Yeah," he said. "Books. They're like the ones in the bunker. Old."

She walked to his side, tilting her head to read the titles on the spines.

"Grimoires," she said. "For summoning demons. Who're they trying to summon?"

"Not sure. It's the same words we found downstairs. *Veni, veni, o comitis*."

He looked over at Duke.

"Oh, right," said the PC, his brow wrinkling as he stared at the ceiling. "Uh, basically come, come, my comrade."

"How do you know that?" said Kett.

Duke shrugged.

"What's the name of the demon they're trying to call, sir?" asked Savage. "Morail, again?"

They leaned over the book together, reading the faded print at the top of the page.

"Andra..." Kett started, struggling to make sense of it. "Andramal-something."

"Andramalech," Savage finished. "*Veni, veni, o comitis, Andramalech.*"

Something boomed deeper inside the building, an echoing explosion of sound that punched adrenaline into Kett's veins, that detonated a supernova of light inside his skull. He spun around, staring past the frames into the darkness at the far end of the room.

"What the fuck was that?" he said. "Duke?"

Duke was already moving towards it, the Taser in his hands. Savage chased after him.

"Careful, Aaron."

Kett followed, the adrenaline causing havoc inside his body, slowing everything down. He felt like he was walking through water, like this was all a dream. And that same primal warning he'd felt back at the stables called out to him with every frantic beat of his heart.

Get out. Get out. Get out.

"You get out," he said quietly, hoping that the sound of his voice might chase away some of the dread.

"Sir?" said Savage.

"Nothing," said Kett.

They were approaching the end of the room, a set of double doors up ahead. Duke positioned himself beside them, the Taser still in his hands.

Kett grabbed one of the doors, nodded at Duke, then wrenched it open.

"Police!" shouted Duke, moving through. "Armed with Taser!"

Kett chased after him, entering a space that was only slightly smaller than the one they'd just left. Picnic benches covered the floor, litter everywhere.

Across the room, twenty yards away, a door was slowly swinging shut.

"Go," he said.

Duke didn't need any encouragement, barrelling past the picnic benches, doing his best not to slip on the carpet of crisp wrappers and beer cans. Savage kept up with him, holding open the door while he ran through.

"Police!" he roared again.

Kett struggled after them, following Savage into a smaller room that must have been the lobby at one point. A desk sat in one corner, a door behind it. The main entrance lay to the right.

"There," said Kett, nodding to the door behind the desk.

They converged on it together, more litter crunching beneath their feet. Kett shunted the door, feeling something push back from the darkness beyond.

"Police," he said. "We're coming in, so get on the floor."

He drove his shoulder into the door and it opened, something toppling over on the other side. Savage aimed her torch through the gap, revealing stacks of play equipment. Hundreds of colourful balls rolled away from them like they were panicking.

Other than that, the room was empty.

"Shit," said Kett.

He barged past Savage and Duke, running around the desk to the main doors.

"They're locked, sir," said Duke.

They had been, with one of the biggest chains Kett had ever seen. But when he grabbed the handle and pulled, the door shuddered open.

A man was standing right there, and he reeled back in shock.

"Police!" Kett yelled, stepping through the door. "Don't..."

He stopped, because he recognised him. It was Josh from the TV crew, his camera hanging by his side. He lifted his free hand, still retreating.

"Sorry," he said.

Kett looked past him, seeing the courtyard, the woods,

the back of the supermarket and the gym. There was nobody else in sight.

He turned to Josh.

"What the hell are you doing here?" he said.

"Nothing," squeaked Josh. "Honest."

Kett eyeballed him.

"Okay, I followed you," he said. "Kelly told me to, asked me to get some more footage. I'm sorry, okay? It's my job."

"You were inside?" Kett asked him.

"No," said Josh. "I just got here, I swear. I didn't even know where you'd gone. I heard shouting, was going to come in. Never got the chance."

"Chain's unlocked, sir," said Savage from the door. "Padlock's missing."

"Did you see anyone come out?" Kett said.

Josh shook his head.

"You see anything at all? Think, because it's important."

"No," squeaked Josh. "I just got here. Van's on the street. I walked over, didn't see anyone or anything."

Kett walked past him, heading across the courtyard to where Clunge and Flaps had been sitting. It had been less than twenty minutes since he'd spoken with them, but in that time the sun had dipped behind the trees, a dark tide of shadows flooding the yard. He'd almost reached the spot where their tent had been pitched when he stopped in his tracks.

The tent lay on the ground like a deflated balloon, covered in a tangle of brambles. The same plants wove their way around two upended camping chairs, as thick as giant's fingers.

He stepped over the plants, lifting the flap of the tent, seeing nothing inside but months' worth of dirt and damp, and two small wicker dolls—each no bigger than a toothbrush.

He stepped back, the thorns catching his leg, trying to bring him down.

"Were there two women here when you arrived, Josh?" he asked.

The cameraman shook his head.

"A tent?" said Kett.

"Just that one," he said.

"What happened to it, sir?" asked Savage, walking up. "It looks like it's been there forever, the brambles have grown right *through* it."

Kett grabbed a fistful of his hair, as if he could pull the exhaustion and the confusion and the frustration right out of him. The hot air trembled, a rumble of thunder that sounded much closer than it had before.

"I have no idea, Kate," he said eventually. "I have no idea what's going on."

CHAPTER THIRTY

Night had fallen. Not that anyone would have known it.

The courtyard outside the soft play was illuminated by a dozen pairs of headlights; the IRVs circled like wagons and doing their best to chase away the shadows. In the glow, the white-suited forensic team looked a little too much like ghosts for Kett's liking. Uniformed police beetled around the soft play, burrowing into the rubbish, scouring every inch of the place.

Finding nothing.

The air was heavy, as charged as the chair before an execution. The storm was still gathering force somewhere to the east, probably out over the sea, but it was holding back its attack. Kett's body bristled with the heat, with the electricity, with the promise of violence.

He finished writing his text to Billie—*It's going to be a late one, sorry. Don't wait up*—firing it off just as Superintendent Clare stropped out of the door. He gazed at the sky for a moment, muttering beneath his breath, then directed his angry face at Kett.

"Not sure if I've told you this before, Detective, but I genuinely hate you."

"Again," said Kett, sliding his phone back into his pocket. "*I* didn't do it."

"But you *found* it," said Clare.

He paused as another almost subsonic rumble of thunder shook the air.

"Franklin's examined the skeleton," he said. "It's real. But it's old. Too clean for a grave, unless the killer has cleaned it up. The writing in the room downstairs and on the floor around the ball pit is blood. She's going to let us know whether it's human or not, but it will take a while. You didn't see anyone?"

"No, sir," said Kett.

He nodded across the courtyard to where Josh leaned against a wall. He was a portrait of misery, although Kett didn't know whether that was because he hadn't been allowed to leave, or because his camera had been confiscated.

Maybe it was something else entirely.

"Just him. He was hovering by the door. Says he followed us here."

"You believe him?"

Kett shrugged.

"There was definitely somebody inside with us. We saw a door closing. They're fire doors, a breeze wouldn't have shifted it. By the time we'd got through, there was no sign of them, but he was right outside."

More thunder, louder now, like the sky was howling out a warning.

"There were two women here when we arrived, sitting outside that tent."

Kett nodded at the tattered pile of canvas beneath the brambles.

"*That* tent?" said Clare.

"It was up when we got here, sir. They were sitting on those chairs, but they were gone by the time we got out. I... I don't know what happened."

"*You* happened," muttered Clare.

The Super put both of his hands to his face like he was playing peekaboo.

"There's nothing you can do here, Kett," he said, speaking through his fingers. "Go back to HQ, get anything that's relevant on the board. Then go home."

"Sir?" said Kett. "What about Aggie? We need to—"

"I need detectives who aren't so tired they've started hallucinating," said Clare, his hands slapping to his sides. "The night shift is here. So go back to HQ, get your shit in order, then go home."

Thunder rolled across the sky, gathering courage. The pressure in the air was making Kett's temples pound.

"Okay, sir," he said after a moment. "I'm going."

THE BULLPEN WAS PRACTICALLY EMPTY, just a couple of DCs that had been drafted from different departments and DS Spalding yawning her head off at Kett's old desk. She tried to cover it with a hand as he walked over, but it was still a good ten seconds before she managed to get her mouth closed.

"You look how I feel, Alison," he said through a yawn of his own.

"Thanks, sir," she replied. "Not sure I could ever look

that bad. Wasn't expecting you back. They can't be finished over at the soft play?"

"I got subbed," he said. "Just going to sort a few things out. Anything new?"

"Actually, yeah," she said. "The body we found this morning, the head in the church and the rest planted in the cottage garden. I think I've ID'd him."

She pushed herself out of her chair, pausing as a peal of thunder made the building shake. The lights dimmed for a second, everyone looking up.

"Shit," she said. "It's a big one."

"Big and weird," said Kett. "Thunder, lightning, no rain."

"Devil storms," said Spalding, heading for the Incident Room. "That's what my nan always called them."

"You're making that up," said Kett.

"I'm not. Dry storms, or Devil Storms. Something about the heat burning away all of the rain. Look it up."

Kett entered the Incident Room, holding the door for Spalding before closing it behind them. He was surprised to see Savage and Porter sitting next to each other at a desk.

"How'd you get back here so fast, Kate?" he asked.

"On my broomstick, sir," she replied. "I snuck off, wanted to do some research. Sarge, do you want to start?"

"Not really," said Spalding, walking to the front wall. It was almost completely covered in photographs and documents, the lines of red connecting string—almost an accidental pentagram—making Kett think of the ribbons in the ball pit.

She tapped a photo of a man in his forties, a mug shot, by the look of it. He was instantly recognisable.

"Our head," said Kett, crashing into a chair. "How'd you find him?"

"His name's Albert Stafford," she said. "Forty-nine. Died three weeks ago. Cardiac arrest. Paramedics took him in. He didn't make it."

"Three weeks?" said Kett. "Franklin said it was days."

"He's been refrigerated, sir," said Spalding. "In the King's Lynn hospital morgue. They returned my call an hour ago, they had no idea he was missing."

"What?" said Kett. "Somebody stole a body from the morgue? When?"

Spalding shrugged.

"They're checking security footage, but they're not hopeful. Some of the files were corrupted."

"Could be somebody who works there," said Kett.

"I'm putting together a list," said Spalding. "So are they. Locals are knocking on doors. Stafford had no family. No one claimed the body."

She was answered by more thunder, louder now.

"Good work," said Kett. "So, whoever left the head in the ruins didn't kill him. They needed a body for their ritual, or whatever they were doing. They stole Stafford's corpse and used that."

"Same as the body in the soft play, sir," said Savage. "It's real, but they got it from somewhere else. I don't think they killed it."

"But why?" said Kett. "If they really believe in this stuff, in demons and witchcraft, whatever, then why wouldn't they go all the way and murder somebody? Why keep kids in cages if you're not going to... I don't know, do whatever demons want you to do to them?"

"I don't know, sir," said Savage, tapping the notepad in front of her. "But I found out some more about the demon in the book. Andramalech."

Kett almost repeated the name, then decided not to. He didn't want it inside his mouth.

"Been around since Pagan times," Savage went on, reading her notes. "A god of murder."

"God?" said Kett. "Not demon?"

"Same thing in some people's eyes," she said. "People used to worship him, offered him human sacrifices, especially children."

"Not very nice," said Porter, rocking back in his chair.

"That's a bit of an understatement, sir," said Savage. "He's known as the Massacrer of Innocents and the Chancellor of Hell, amongst other things. Used to be an angel, got kicked out of heaven alongside Lucifer. Uh... everyone seems to advise against summoning him because he's an arsehole, apparently."

"Yeah, I get that impression," said Kett.

"But if you do want to summon him," Savage went on. "You need to make the mark of his seal in blood, and you need black candles, incense, and an offering."

"A sacrifice?" asked Porter.

Savage nodded.

"If you do it correctly, and Andramalech doesn't kill you, then he'll grant your wishes."

"What sort of wishes?"

"You name it, sir. Riches, fame, love, death. He seems to have power over it all. But the more you want, the more you have to give."

"And what he wants is dead kids?" said Kett.

The whole of HQ seemed to shake beneath another barrage of thunder—as loud as artillery fire. The lights flickered again, the room falling dark for a couple of seconds this time. As much as Kett hated to admit it, he was rattled.

"Couldn't make it up, sir," said Savage.

"Enough to make you a believer," added Porter, staring at the ceiling.

"That's exactly what this is," said Kett. "A believer. Somebody believes in all of this enough to try to summon a demon. They're willing to steal bodies and kidnap children. I don't know if they've killed anyone yet, but it feels like they're building up to it, right?"

"I think so too, sir," said Savage. "The bunker was full of research. The books, the sigils, the writing, the pentagram. It's like a... like a rehearsal space. Same with the room beneath the soft play, all of those marks on the walls. It was like somebody was learning how to do it, like they were practising, making it perfect."

She hesitated, deep in thought.

"Maybe the ball pit was a rehearsal too," she said. "That's why they didn't use a real body. I mean, someone they killed. Everything I've read says that if you're going to summon a demon, the ritual has to be perfect. If you make a single mistake, one wrong word, or the smallest of gaps in your protective circle, or a letter out of place, the demon will tear you to pieces."

"Not very nice," said Porter.

"What is it with you and understatements today, Pete?" said Kett.

"So if you believe in this stuff, sir," Savage went on, "then you want to make it perfect. You have to. There can't be any mistakes."

"Okay," said Kett. "This is good. It gives us an insight into their thought process. They're building up to a ritual that will involve a sacrifice, possibly a child."

"Almost certainly more than one," said Porter.

"And that's bad," said Savage. "Because we rescued the two kids they had in cages."

"That's not bad," said Porter, frowning.

"It's bad for Aggie Clegg," said Kett.

"Exactly, sir," said Savage. "If they need a sacrifice, then she's what they've got left."

More thunder, the lights stuttering.

"Okay," said Kett, rubbing his temples to try to ease his headache. "We've got at least four suspects. Bianca Caddel is the main one. It was her car we saw with Aggie in the back, and the bunker was on her property. She was in cahoots with Robert Flack, who owned the stables where the kids were found, and David Blethyn, who was keeping them in cages. Flack was in a wheelchair, although we never confirmed his injuries. But Caddel or Blethyn, or another member of their group, could have attacked the teens this morning in the woods."

"Wearing a witch mask," said Porter, nodding. "Like the one I found on Kevin Clegg's body."

"Exactly," said Kett. "They dressed up like an old woman, like a witch. I have no idea why."

"I do, sir," said Savage. "Witches and devils go hand in hand. In stories, anyway. That's why people always tried to go after witches, because they believed they were in league with Satan."

"Some of these guys are dressed as witches, others as devils," said Porter. "Feels like a cult."

"Right," said Kett. "So they attack the kids, they take Aggie. And there's a reason they take her, and not one of the others. There has to be."

"Because they've been targeting her for a while," said Spalding, nodding. "They killed her dad, replaced him."

"You found out any more about that, Alison?" asked Kett. "Because most people would know if their father was replaced."

"Not if they don't talk," said Spalding. "Aggie lives with her grandmother. Mum died when she was a baby, she hasn't spoken to her dad in years. Clegg's on long-term disability, no job. Neighbours have seen him, but not up close, and nobody's spoken to him."

"The man in the woods knew all this," said Porter. "He's not just pretending to be Kevin Clegg, he's done his research."

"Okay," said Kett. "So they kill Clegg, put in a lookalike so nobody reports him missing. The real Clegg is dumped in the well beneath the stables, wearing a mask just like our witch. Why?"

The only answer came from the heavens, a concussive boom of thunder.

"Why him?" he asked again. "Why Aggie? Why were they targeting her? What's special about her?"

"Nothing, sir," said Spalding. "She's at college, pretty unremarkable in every way. Turns eighteen tomorrow."

"Hang on, Sarge," said Savage. "August first?"

"Yeah," said Spalding.

"That's Freya's birthday too."

"Shit," said Kett, kicking himself for missing it. "You're right. That can't be a coincidence. What about Dmitri?"

"I'll go check," said Savage, getting up and leaving the room.

"What's special about that date?" Kett asked, clicking his fingers at nobody in particular.

Porter pulled out his phone, typing.

"National Girlfriends Day," he said. "Respect Your Parents Day."

"Pretty sure you don't need a demon for either of those, Pete."

"I don't know, sir," he said. "You've met my mother,

right? It's Spider-Man Day as well, apparently. Cycle to Work Day, Homemade Pie Day... Who the hell makes these up? Lammas Day, Lugnuts Day, National Andrew Day."

"Lugnuts?" said Spalding.

"Yeah," said Porter. "Wait, no, it's Lug-hun-asa-dah. I don't know how to say it."

"Lughnasadh," said Spalding. "Harvest Day. It's a pagan thing, I think. My ex was from Ireland, her family were mad on this sort of stuff. They have festivals, storytelling, music, all that jazz."

"People bake a figure of a god and then eat it," Porter said, reading from his phone. "To symbolise the sanctity and the sacrifice of harvest."

"This is something," said Kett. "We've got two kidnap victims who have their birthdays on Lungnadsday."

"Lugnutshday," said Porter.

"Lughnasadh," said Spalding.

"And it's three," said Savage as she ran back into the room, out of breath. "Dmitri's got the same birthday. I'm sorry, I should have checked."

"We know now," said Kett. "This is it. This is the connection. We've got a killer who's preparing a sacrifice, and three kids with the same birthday. It adds up."

He checked his watch, even though he didn't need to.

He knew the date all too well.

"It's the first of August tomorrow," he said. "And unless we figure out who's doing this, something very bad is going to happen."

CHAPTER THIRTY-ONE

Tuesday

It was after midnight by the time he parked the Volvo on the driveway, but nobody had told his house. Every window was lit up, the building a beacon of light on the dark street. As soon as he got out, he heard screams from inside.

If it wasn't the same noise he heard from his children most days, he'd have been alarmed.

He rubbed his eyes, any hope of a quick sleep before returning to the fray dashed. He hadn't been planning to come home at all, but Clare had returned to HQ an hour or so after they'd figured out that the kids had matching birthdays, and he'd given Kett a powerful kick in the rump to get him out of the door.

"Toss! Off! Kett! You! Giant! Cesspool! Of! Toss!" he'd roared.

Kett's right cheek was still smarting.

The storm was still going, although it had softened a little. In the three hours or so it had taken it to cross the city, not one single drop of rain had fallen.

Kett opened the front door, embraced by a chorus of angry squeals from upstairs. He kicked off his shoes and his jacket, resting his head on the wall for a moment. Sleep ambushed him, a rush of vertigo that hit like an uppercut, almost knocking him clean off his feet.

Maybe Clare had a point. He was exhausted.

"Robbie?" came a voice from the kitchen. Billie poked her head around the door, squinting at him. She looked even worse than he did, barely able to keep her eyes open, but the smile she gave him was as bright as ever.

"I take it they're not feeling any better?" he asked.

"What gave you that impression?" she said, and for a few seconds they stood in silence, listening to the hurricane of noise from upstairs.

"Anything I can do?"

"Backup," she said, disappearing again. "I'm trying to give Evie some Calpol, but she won't take it."

Evie never took Calpol because she was always too suspicious of it. According to her, it was made of goblin snot and was poisonous.

"She's burning up," said Billie, appearing once again, this time with a purple plastic syringe in her hand. "39.7. She needs it."

Kett rolled up his sleeves and washed his hands in the bathroom under the stairs. He half thought about grabbing something to defend himself, because Evie was as strong as a bull when they were trying to give her medicine, and more often than not, he got a fist or a foot to the crotch. But Billie was already halfway up the stairs.

"Evie," she called out. "Daddy's home."

He followed her up, reaching the top just as Evie's head popped out of her bedroom door. Only her eyes were visible, because she'd wrapped everything from the neck up in a towel.

"No!" she yelled, her voice muffled. "Stay away!"

She made a break for Moira's room, slamming the door. Both the girls were screaming, and there were shouts coming from Alice's room too.

"Shut up! I'm trying to sleep!"

"You grab her," said Billie. "I'll squirt it in. Be ready to hold her mouth shut."

"Last time I did that, I almost lost a finger," said Kett.

He braced himself outside the door while Billie turned the handle. Evie must have been leaning on the other side, because it was a struggle to get it open.

"Evie, you've got a fever, you have to take it," she said.

"No!" Evie screamed back. "Never! I won't eat your goblin snot poison, you monster!"

"You don't want to have to go to the hospital, do you?" Billie tried, applying more pressure to the door.

"Better there than here with you," Evie yelled back. "You're evil! Daddy, help me, Mummy's evil and she's trying to kill me!"

"She's trying to help you, Evie," said Kett. "It's just Calpol, it won't hurt you."

"She's a monster," roared Evie, sounding a little possessed herself. "Daddy, help me!"

Even though he knew Evie was being ridiculous, her terror still tugged on his heartstrings.

"Don't you dare," said Billie, looking back.

"Dare what?"

"Say she doesn't need it," she said. "I know that look, Robert Kett."

He held his hands up.

"I wasn't thinking anything!"

Billie gave the door another push, and Evie must have let go because she was suddenly falling into Moira's bedroom. Their middle daughter exited like a streak of lightning, slipping past her mum, then trying to pass Kett. He bent down to grab her, his spine full of broken glass.

"Argh," he said.

Evie was almost out of reach, heading for their bedroom, but he managed to grab the trailing end of the towel. He pulled her towards him like he was fishing, reeling her in as she flailed desperately.

"Don't let go!" Billie shouted, right next to him.

He hefted her up, trying to hug her even as she screamed in his face. She was as heavy as a bag of cement.

"You're okay," he said. "Calm down!"

"You're evil too!" she said, almost choking on the words. "You're killing me! You're killing me!"

Her foot smacked him in the groin with the force of a Premier League striker taking a penalty. He doubled over, his stomach trying to crawl up his throat. He didn't know how, but he managed to keep hold of her.

"You're killing me!" Evie went on. "You're—"

Billie jammed the syringe into Evie's open mouth, using her other hand to hold it shut. Evie's eyes bulged as she swallowed noisily.

"It's done," said Billie, resting a hand on Evie's cheek. "It's done, you're okay."

Kett lowered his daughter to the landing, collapsing onto his knees. Evie gagged, and so did he, the pain like somebody was trying to extract his soul through his trousers.

"That wasn't so bad," said Evie, licking her lips.

"Yeah, not bad at all," groaned Kett. "You ready for bed now?"

Evie nodded. He held out his arms and she fell into them, resting her head on his shoulder. It was like carrying a hot water bottle. By the time he laid Evie on her bed, she was almost asleep.

Kett rested a hand on her sweaty forehead, smoothing back her hair, trying to ignore the same unbearable dread he felt every time they were ill—the same terror he'd felt when they'd been at the mercy of the Pig Man. Billie sat next to her, pulling the duvet up to her chest.

"Get to sleep," she said.

"I'm sorry," said Evie.

"You're fine," said Billie. "I love you."

"So do I," said Kett.

Evie's mouth moved like she was replying, but there was no sound. Three breaths later, she was out.

"Now, if she'd done that five hours ago, I wouldn't be so close to losing my mind," said Billie, taking Kett's hand and squeezing it. "Thank you for being the angel to my devil."

Her words cut deeper than she'd meant them to, and she seemed to see it in his face.

"Sorry," he said.

"Don't be," said Billie. "The case?"

He nodded.

"I saw it on the news."

She stood, pulling him up with her and gathering him into a hug. The day seemed to slough from him, the weight tumbling from his shoulders, his head clearing. Like Evie, he almost drifted off right there.

Moira's screams and Alice's shouts were the only thing keeping him awake.

"Please tell me we don't need to give them Calpol too," he said, speaking the words into her hair.

Billie laughed.

"Oh yes," she said. "Yes, we do."

GIVEN the nightmare of the day, the bad dreams were inevitable.

In the ruins of St Mary's, Kett dug into the wet, worm-riddled soil with his fingers, looking for a corpse he knew was there but couldn't see. When he found it, though, it wasn't a corpse at all, it was a living face, caked in dirt and choking on mud. It was Aggie Clegg, and no matter how hard he tried to dig her out, he couldn't—the soil pouring back on top of her, burying her twice as fast as he could shovel it out.

Then the face wasn't Aggie anymore. It was Alice, his oldest daughter, pleading for him to rescue her.

And falling silent as she disappeared into the ground.

He woke like a man on the gallows, kicking the covers off the bed, knocking his glass from the table. He ran to Alice's room, seeing her fast asleep in her nest of duvets. Then he checked on Evie, but she wasn't in her bed.

"Evie?" he called.

He made his way into Moira's room to see that it wasn't her room at all, it was another ruin, and in the middle of it was an open trapdoor. The dark spilled out of it like dirty water, and he knew that his girls were down there, that he had to find them before they drowned.

So he jumped, landing in treacle-thick shadows, pulling himself headfirst down the shaft. No air to breathe, no room to turn around. His lungs were already screaming. He reached for his girls, found them, only for a face to rise from the churning gloom—black eyes burning, a sagging mouth that rose up and clamped its cold lips over his.

You brought me here, it breathed into him, words that tasted of long-dead flesh.

He punched, he kicked. No air, just the reek of the old woman's breath, her wet gums gnawing at his face, the feel of her body rocking with laughter.

All while his children floated beneath him.

"No!"

He woke again, choking on his own spit. The bedroom was dark, except for the weak light that crept in from the landing. Billie lay next to him, murmuring gently as if she, too, was in the middle of a nightmare.

Across the room, in the fraction of space beside the wardrobe, something shifted—a soft thump.

There was somebody standing there, a hunched shadow, a wet breath.

Kett felt as if he'd been crushed in a cold fist of dread. He tried to lift his head, but his muscles weren't working. He was paralysed.

What the fuck? he tried to say.

The shadow took a step towards him, nothing more than an outline. Where its face should have been, there was only darkness.

And yet it spoke.

I see you.

Kett tried to get out of bed, but his body wouldn't listen to him.

I see you.

The outline stepped closer. Kett wanted to open his mouth and scream, but he couldn't do that either. The only thing that worked were his eyes, and he swept them from side to side.

The figure moved closer, close enough to touch. It wore a mask, the horns curling up in front of the brim of a hood. Fire burned through the slits of its eyes, smoke rising, flesh bubbling.

I see you, it whispered.

"No!" Kett shouted. The sound of his voice set off a chain reaction, his head twisting up, his arms breaking free from their invisible manacles.

The figure loomed over him.

"No!" Kett screamed.

He grabbed the man's neck in both hands, squeezing hard. But the devil only laughed, his body shaking with the force of it, those burning eyes full of glee.

Kett twisted harder, just wanting it to end, wanting...

The man choked, hitting him in the head, in the arms.

Calling his name.

"Robbie!"

And that face, it wasn't a mask anymore, it was Billie's—warped by fear, crimson with the effort of trying to draw in a breath.

Kett had his hands around her throat.

He had his hands around his wife's throat.

He let go, and Billie rolled away, coughing hard.

"Billie?"

She threw herself off the bed, switching on the lamp with such urgency that she knocked it over. It rolled back and forth, sending spinning shadows across the room.

"What the fuck, Robbie?" she said, her hands to her neck.

"I'm so sorry," he said. "It was... I was dreaming, it wasn't you. Are you okay?"

She ran her fingers over her throat for a moment more, then nodded.

"I'm okay," she said. "It wasn't hard, it was... you just scared me. Are *you* okay?"

He didn't know how to answer her.

Slowly, as if she wasn't sure who he was, Billie got back into the bed. There was a red mark on her throat from where he'd choked her, but it was already fading. He looked at his hands, then back at her.

"It was so real," he said. "I saw..."

The devil.

"Not the devil," he whispered.

"Not the *what*?"

Kett picked up his phone from his bedside table, seeing that it was just after four. There was a missed call from Savage that had come through half an hour ago, followed by a text.

Charlene Ford's finally awake, sir. Heading to hospital.

He dropped the phone, turning to Billie. He opened his arms and she slid into them, resting her head on his shoulder. He could feel how tense she was, and it broke his heart.

"I'm so sorry," he said again. "It just felt so real."

He could still see the devil there, gliding across the room. He could still hear his voice.

I see you.

Billie pulled free, moving to the other side of the mattress. She'd never seemed so far away.

"I can sleep with Alice for the rest of the night," she said.

"No, it's okay," Kett replied, rubbing his eyes. He girded himself, then swung his legs out of the bed. "I'm awake. I'm going to head back in."

The truth was, he didn't think he'd ever sleep again.

"I'm so sorry," he said. "Are we okay?"

Billie nodded, her lips pressed shut, her fingers touching her throat.

"I love you," he said.

She nodded again, watching him go.

CHAPTER THIRTY-TWO

"Bad night, sir?"

DC Savage was waiting for Kett when he arrived at the hospital forty minutes later. She stood outside the main doors to the East Wing, downing the last of a strawberry milkshake before using the bottle to salute him. The swelling in her lip had gone down, but there was a nasty cut there, and she kept poking it with her tongue. When he reached her, she pinched his arm and gave him a gentle punch.

"First of the month, sir."

It was an August day, for sure. The sun was up, and it was angry. The devil's storm had done nothing to disperse the heat. The day was as dry as kindling, ready to ignite.

"Yeah, a bad night," said Kett. "The worst. Nightmares. I haven't had dreams like that for years, not since Billie was missing. I..."

He hesitated, because he couldn't be sure if it had actually happened, or if it had been part of the same sequence of dreams.

"I tried to strangle her," he said.

"Who, sir? *Billie?*"

Kett nodded.

"I was asleep. I thought she was... I thought she was the man in the mask. The devil."

"She okay?" Savage asked.

"I think so. I don't know. I don't think I hurt her, but... I mean how do you trust somebody after that? I tried to choke my own wife."

"You didn't have to come in, sir," said Savage. "I could have handled this."

Kett opened the door, ushering her through before him.

"I just want to end this bastard case, Kate. I just want to catch whoever's doing this. Only way I can relax again is if they're not out there anymore. Anything happen while I was asleep?"

"In those three and a bit hours, sir?" said Savage as they walked through the lobby. "Not much. But the Greek translator has been chatting to Dmitri and we think we've ID'd him. Dmitri Eliopoulos, he's seventeen. Actually, eighteen, as of today. His family are in Dereham and he's been missing for three weeks. But nobody bothered to report it."

"What?" said Kett. "Why?"

"I don't know, sir. I think they're into some shady stuff. Dmitri claims he was doing a delivery for his uncle, taking a package to the house of a doctor in the town, when he got jumped. Woke up in a van, then he ended up in a warehouse. He said Blethyn was one of the guys, but there was another one. He didn't see his face, but he wasn't in a wheelchair. He was caged in the warehouse for ten days or so, then moved to the stables. That's when he met Freya."

"He remember where the warehouse was?"

"No, sir."

"Did he say anything else about why they were keeping him there?"

"He heard them talking, but he didn't understand much. One thing he heard a few times, though, was demon. Or devil. He said the men kept mentioning it. He said there was a lot of weird stuff on display in the warehouse, the same marks or runes or whatever they are."

They reached the lifts, and Savage pressed the button.

"Blethyn talking yet?" said Kett.

"No, and he tried to jump out of the window in his room last night," said Savage as the doors opened. "Smashed it. Needed to be sedated. They had to amputate his tongue, and even if he still had it, I can't see him talking. Whatever secrets he's carrying, he's planning to take them to his grave."

Kett swore, counting the seconds until the lift doors opened.

"But like I said, Charlene Ford's finally *compos mentis*," said Savage, stepping out. "She's scared, but she wants to talk. It's this way, sir."

Kett had taken the wrong corridor, and he doubled back, following Savage to the entrance of the ward. Kett pressed the bell, both of them peering through the window in the door as a nurse ran to the desk and buzzed them in.

"Ford?" she asked as they walked over. Kett nodded. "Room four, right around the corner."

"She doing okay?" asked Kett.

"Body, yes," said the nurse. "Mind, not so much."

"You want to take the lead on this, sir?" asked Savage.

"No," said Kett. "I think she'll respond better to you."

They stopped at the open door of the private room. Charlie Ford lay in the bed, looking as fragile as a porcelain doll. Her skin was so pale it was almost translucent, her eyes wide and glassy. Somebody had woven her hair into a perfect braid which fell over her left shoulder, resting on the prominent ridge of her clavicle.

A woman in her forties sat in the chair next to the bed. She had her daughter's face, if a little fuller. A man stood at the window behind her, dressed in a black suit and staring into the car park with his hands linked behind his back. He seemed too old to be Charlie's father, his pink scalp hairless and as wrinkled as a walnut.

At the sound of Kett's voice, everyone looked around. The woman started in fright, the man glowering over his shoulder at Kett as if he might be responsible for putting Charlene in hospital. The young woman in the bed didn't react, her expression unchanged, her eyes wide. Whatever they'd given her to calm her down was doing its job.

"Hi," said Kett. "Sorry. My name is DCI Robert Kett. Robbie. I'm with the police. We heard you were awake, Charlene. Do you mind if I come in?"

The woman in the chair lifted a hand like a kid in a classroom.

"It's probably better if you let her—"

"Have you found them yet?" the older man said, cutting across her. He'd turned to the room, his hands still behind his back. He had to be in his seventies, but there was a strength there, and something in his posture that made Kett think he was a military man. "The person who did this to my granddaughter?"

"We're doing everything we can," said Kett as he walked to the bed. The man scoffed at this, his face creasing into a mask of irritation.

"Of course," he said, sneering. "Norfolk plods. World's finest."

The woman in the chair flinched like his words had been fists. Kett ignored the man, facing the girl instead.

"How are you doing, Charlene?"

"It's Charlie," said the woman.

"It's Charl*ene*," the old man snapped, his spit hanging in the light from the window. "She's not a bloody lesbian."

"Hey," said Kett, giving him a look. "That's enough. I'm here to talk to Charlie, not you. If you want, you can leave."

"If you want, you can make me," said the man, and his body tensed like he was gearing up for a fight. Despite the fact he was as thin as a wire, Kett wasn't sure he could take him—especially after the night he'd had, and with the pain that radiated down his spine.

"Then keep quiet," he said. "If you want us to do our jobs, let us work."

The man sneered again as he turned back to the window.

"Work my arse," he muttered.

The woman flinched again, her eye catching Kett's for a fraction of a second—full of apologetic misery.

"Charlie, this is Kate," said Kett, gesturing to Savage. "You mind if we talk to you for a little while?"

Charlie shook her head. Savage perched on the edge of the bed, smoothing down the quilt. She tongued the cut on her lip for a moment before continuing.

"How are you feeling, Charlie?"

Charlie shrugged, her eyes wide.

"Better than yesterday?"

She nodded.

"That's good," said Savage. "Look, I know it's probably the last thing you want to do, but we need to catch the person who did this to you, and we want to find your friend. So we have to—"

"You haven't found her yet?" said Charlie, some emotion breaking through the rubber mask of her features.

"We haven't said anything to her," said the woman. "We thought it was better if..."

She tailed off like a clockwork mouse.

"We haven't found her," said Savage. "Which is why it's really important that we talk to you. Can you run us through what happened yesterday? As much as you can remember."

It was too much for the girl, her mouth opening, but nothing coming out.

"Start with why you were there," Savage said. "This was your first time filming with Aggie and Matt, wasn't it?"

Charlie nodded, licking her dry lips.

"It's usually Dougie," she said. "Dougie Herring. But his mum was ill, so he couldn't do it. Matt asked me."

"Because you go to school together," said Savage. "Media, right?"

"And other stuff."

"Other pointless stuff," growled the old man at the window. "Media, my arse."

"Your granddad?" asked Savage. Charlie nodded. "I think media's an awesome course, did a bit myself at college."

"Really?"

"We made a short film about penguins," she said.

"In Norfolk?" asked Kett. Savage laughed.

"Yeah. It was a little hard finding wild ones. Went to the aquarium in Yarmouth instead, but we got kicked out for trying to climb over the wall. They thought we were going to steal one."

Charlie laughed, putting a hand to her mouth.

"Can you imagine coming home one day with a penguin

tucked under your arm?" said Savage. "My mum would have freaked."

"Your mum would have freaked, too," said the woman in the chair. She wore a smile that didn't sit easily.

Charlie laughed again, while her grandfather steamed up the window with another angry grunt.

"So, anyway. You agreed to help Matt and Aggie. How well do you know them?"

"I know Matt," she said. "I like him. Aggie's not so nice, but she's good at what she does. Their YouTube channel has, like, four thousand subscribers."

"So I hear," said Savage. "So you thought this would be a good experience?"

"Yeah. Like for my university application and stuff. It's good to have a portfolio."

"Do you know whose idea it was to go to the ruins of St Mary?" Savage asked.

Charlie burrowed under her covers a little, retreating from the memory of the church.

"I don't know," she said. "But Aggie was in charge. She's a bit obsessed with all this stuff. Matt just does what she tells him."

"Aggie picks the locations for the shoot?" said Savage. "She does the research, she makes the plans?"

Charlie nodded.

"And she drives."

"Did she say why she'd picked that location for yesterday's shoot?" Savage pressed.

"No." Charlie shrugged. "Just a cool place, I guess, and they've already done most of the haunted stuff in Norfolk."

"Do you know when she decided to go there? Was it planned, or more spontaneous?"

"I don't know. She must have planned a bit, she didn't say. But..."

The girl hesitated, mulling something over in her head. Savage gave her all the time she needed.

"She seemed like she was worried about something yesterday," she said. "Or not worried, exactly. It was like we needed to do it quickly, like somebody else was going to beat us to it."

"Did she say who?"

Charlie shook her head.

"A rival YouTube channel?" asked Savage. "Somebody like that?"

No reply.

"I don't see how this is going to help us," said the old man. "You want me to give you my life story too?"

"Not if you want me to stay awake," said Savage, her reply putting a smile on Kett's face. The man gave her evils, but she ignored him, her attention on the girl. "Think back. Did Aggie say anything about why she was worried?"

"She wasn't *worried*," said Charlie. "I said that wrong, it wasn't what I meant. It's just, originally she told Matt she wanted to get there for nine, then when she found out I was going to be there she decided we should go earlier, for, like, the light or something. Or maybe because she thought I didn't know what I was doing. It was more like... Wait, she did say something, something about the sponsor. I can't remember what."

"The sponsor?" said Savage. "For the channel? You know who that is?"

"No," she said. "They're new, I think? Matt said Aggie went everywhere looking for money for the show, asked pretty much every business in the city. Didn't have much luck, but somebody gave her something. It was to do with the cameras, I think, the kit. They let Aggie have the stuff if she promised to give them a shout. I don't remember, but I think it was something to do with them. That's as clear as mud, sorry."

"Don't be sorry," said Savage. "This is very helpful. Do you remember the name of the sponsor?"

"No."

Savage gave the girl's arm a squeeze beneath the blanket, then passed the baton to Kett.

"Charlie, did you ever meet Aggie's family?" he asked. "Her dad?"

"I don't know her that well," she said. "I don't think she spoke to him, though. She never mentioned him. Matt said she talks about her mum a lot, but she died when she was little."

"You never met her father?"

Charlie shook her head.

"I hardly knew her, sorry. I'm friends with Matt. I don't think she likes me much."

"Why do you say that?" asked Kett.

"Just she didn't seem to want me there yesterday, was annoyed when they picked me up. Think she thought I was muscling in."

"On the show?" said Savage.

She shrugged.

"On Matt?" suggested Kett.

She didn't answer.

"I know you won't want to remember it," said Savage. "But can you tell us about the person who attacked you?"

Charlie shuffled deeper into her blanket, just her head visible.

As if it had been cut off and left there, thought Kett, his skin crawling like he'd carried the creatures of the woods beneath his clothes.

"We saw the footage on the camera," Savage went on. "We saw the woman."

"Woman?" said the girl, peering up with frightened eyes.

"It was a woman, wasn't it?"

Charlie's head slid from side to side. Her whisper was too quiet to hear, but Kett saw the shape of it on her lips.

The witch.

"Why do you say that?" asked Savage.

"You saw her?" Charlie said. "On the camera."

Savage nodded.

"You saw the way she moved? She was... She was too fast to be a..."

Charlie was struggling, her legs kicking the blanket like they were preparing to run.

"She was too strong, she knocked me over like I wasn't even there. Hit me so hard I..."

The words seemed to be choking her. Her mum sat forward in the chair and put a hand to her forehead.

"She picked Aggie up off the ground," Charlie went on. "She picked her up like she didn't weigh anything at all. She hit her, hit her hard, there was so much blood. And then she..."

She turned her enormous eyes to Savage.

"She slid back beneath the ground."

"She went *into* the ground?" asked Savage.

"Like she was burying herself. I *saw* it. One second she was standing there looking at me, the next she dropped right into the dirt, her whole body just, like, slithered in. She just disappeared, and she took Aggie with her."

"You saw Aggie being pulled into the ground?"

Charlie nodded, but there was a frown on her face.

"I saw it," she said, like she was trying to convince herself.

"Charlie, do you think it could have been somebody wearing a mask?" asked Savage. "Because we found a mask that looks like the woman who attacked you."

"A mask?" asked Charlie's mum.

"A witch's face, long, grey hair. It's incredibly realistic."

The frown was still on the girl's face, and after a handful of seconds, she shook her head.

"So she wasn't real?" she said, a breath of relief. "Like the head we found. That wasn't real either?"

Savage glanced at Kett again, only for an instant.

"You don't have to worry about the head," she said. "Just think carefully. See the woman in your mind. Could it have been somebody wearing a mask?"

Charlie closed her eyes, her body twitching like she was caught inside a nightmare.

"I don't know," she said when she'd opened them again. "It's too painful. I can't remember."

"Last thing," said Kett. "You didn't hear Aggie mention anyone who might want to hurt her."

"No."

"And she didn't mention her dad?"

"No, sorry. But I don't always remember. Brain like a sieve, like Granddad always says."

The man at the window nodded sharply in agreement.

"You did great," said Savage, giving her another reassuring squeeze before pushing herself off the bed. "Your brain is perfect. Thank you, Charlie."

Charlie smiled, and so did her mum. But the man at the window turned like a scarecrow in the wind, pointing a hooked finger at Savage.

"Her name is Charlene," he said.

Savage lifted her hands in surrender.

"Alright, sir," she said. "Keep your hair on."

All eyes in the room slid to his bald, pink scalp.

"Oh, sorry, too late," said Savage.

The man's jaw unhinged in shock, but Savage was already out of the room. Kett tried and failed to keep the smile from his face as he pulled out a card and laid it on the bed.

"Thanks for your help," he said. "If you think of anything else, call us."

By the time he'd caught up with Savage in the corridor outside, she was laughing so hard there were tears in her eyes.

"What on earth has got into you?" Kett asked her.

"I'm sorry, sir," she said, wiping her face. "Guess it's all catching up with me."

"Well, some people deserve it," he said.

He pressed the door-release button, and they left the ward, Savage still giggling.

"Where now, sir?" she asked when she'd recovered. "You thinking what I'm thinking?"

"The sponsor?" asked Kett, and she nodded.

"Worth a shot," he said as they reached the lifts. "Let's go."

CHAPTER THIRTY-THREE

THEY STOPPED BY HQ FIRST, BECAUSE IT WAS ONLY A ten-minute drive from the hospital. The Channel 5 van was already there, parked across the same three disabled spaces it had been yesterday.

"Guess they haven't given up on Aaron yet," Kett said once he'd parked the car and caught up to Savage at the main doors.

"No, sir," she said as they walked through the lobby. "But it's close. They sent him an email last night with a list of things they wanted, with a very clear message that if he didn't deliver, the show could be cancelled."

"What was on the list?"

"What *wasn't* on it?" Savage said, counting them off on her fingers. "A car chase, a foot chase, a bike chase."

"*Bike* chase?" said Kett.

"A fistfight with a suspect, a Tasering, an arrest which involves a suspect being thrown over the bonnet of the car."

"Christ."

"An argument with a colleague, a clash with a superior officer that involves some kind of violence, or a kiss."

"A kiss with a superior officer?" said Kett.

"I think the kiss was with me, sir," said Savage. "I hope so, anyway, for Aaron's sake. There was more. Those are the ones I remember."

"No pressure, then," said Kett as he walked into the MIT offices.

He was surprised to see that a small crowd had gathered in the middle of the room. The TV crew were there, Josh with his camera on his shoulder, Megan filming from a lower angle with her little camcorder, Kelly on her phone. He couldn't even remember the name of the fourth guy, who held the boom pole and the microphone.

They were arranged around Duke, who was sitting in a chair by Kett's desk, looking utterly miserable. About ten feet away from him was a bin, and surrounding that were countless balls of screwed up paper. A dozen or so coppers watched with smiles on their faces, including Porter, whose gleeful grin was almost clown-like.

"Come on, mate," the DI said, giving Duke a powerful slap on the shoulder. "Twenty-third time's the charm."

"You're overthinking it," said Josh. "No pressure, just relax and take the shot."

"There *is* pressure," said Kelly, who looked furious. "We need a good finishing shot for the first episode. I thought this would be easy."

"It's my hand-eye coordination," said Duke. "It needs time to wake up."

"That is very true," Savage said to Kett as they joined the crowd. "He's broken about eight of my mugs making coffee in the morning."

"Do it," ordered Kelly. "And this time, don't miss."

Duke looked like he was close to tears. He picked up another sheet of paper and rolled it into a ball. Then he held it to his face, closed one eye, stuck his tongue between his lips, and threw.

The ball missed the waste basket by about three feet, and the crowd burst into a round of disappointed groans. Kelly bit her lip so hard she looked like she was going to draw blood. Porter was holding his sides to stop them from splitting.

"Can't we move it a *little* closer?" said Duke.

"It won't look good if we move it closer," said Kelly. "Just hit the bloody target!"

Duke started to roll up another ball in his giant hands. Josh aimed the camera. Megan ducked even lower beside the bin.

"Duke," said Kett before the PC could take the shot. "Enough messing around, we need you."

Duke looked like a child who had been pulled out of the path of wild dogs. He jumped out of his chair, apologising to Kelly as he squeezed past.

"Oh, God, thank you, sir," he said when he'd run up. "I thought I was going to be there all day. What do you need me for?"

"Nothing," said Kett. "I just felt sorry for you."

He was still holding the ball of paper, and Savage clicked her fingers until he passed it over. She took aim as they walked across the bullpen, then fired from twenty feet.

It went in.

Everybody cheered, the TV crew catching the whole thing on film. Duke, though, did not look impressed.

"Sorry," said Savage. "I couldn't help myself. It's my competitive streak."

"Enough," said Kett. "I want you two on the sponsor. Find out who they are, and why they wanted Aggie at that particular site yesterday morning. We might get lucky."

"Yes, sir," said Savage.

"Where's the boss?"

"In his office, sir," said Duke. "Been in there all night. I think he's asleep."

Kett doubled back to Clare's office. Sure enough, when he put his ear to the door, he heard a sound like an angle grinder in a cement mixer. He knocked gently before turning the handle.

Clare sat in his reclining chair with his feet on the desk. He was still wearing his socks and his awful brown brogues, but he'd taken his trousers off, his knobbly knees reaching for the heavens. His mouth was open so wide that Kett thought he could have fitted his entire head inside, like a lion tamer.

"Sir," he said.

Clare drew in another grating breath, his entire soft palate vibrating.

"Sir," said Kett.

The man's snores were unlike anything Kett had ever heard, loud enough to bring down the entire building. He walked to the desk and rapped his fist on it.

"Sir!"

Clare stopped breathing. He sat there, perfectly still, his chest not rising or falling.

Kett counted to seven before he started to panic.

"Shit," he said, running around the desk. "Colin?"

He still wasn't breathing. Kett put a hand on the Superintendent's chest, then to his neck, feeling for a pulse. It had been twelve seconds and counting now since he'd taken a breath.

"Sir," he said, ready to grab the phone and call an ambulance. "Come on!"

With a sound like a blocked toilet finally clearing, Clare

drew in a wet, ragged lungful of air. His eyes opened, bloodshot and bleary, roving in their sockets. Kett drew his hand back like it had been bitten.

"What in the name of toss are you doing, Kett?" Clare said, spraying the words as much as speaking them.

"Nothing, sir, you were asleep, you weren't breathing."

"Why were you touching me?"

"I wasn't touching you, sir," pleaded Kett. "I mean, I was checking for a pulse. You weren't brea—"

"What have you done with my trousers?"

"I didn't... I haven't touched... *I* didn't take them off, sir."

"Likely bloody story, you pervert!" said Clare.

He dropped his legs to the floor, the chair snapping upright. He wiped a hand over his drooling mouth, taking in the desk, then the computer, and finally the clock on the wall.

"Is it morning or evening?" he said.

"Morning, sir," said Kett. "I didn't mean to wake you. But honestly, you weren't breathing."

"Fiona says it happens all the time," said Clare, clearing his throat. "Nothing to worry about."

"Pretty sure that's something to worry about, sir," said Kett.

"What do you want?" Clare demanded. "Other than to sneak in and molest me in my sleep?"

"I wasn't..." Kett shook his head. "I wanted to check in, see if we'd got anywhere with the man who was posing as Kevin Clegg."

"No," said Clare. "Nobody managed to catch him on camera, not even the bloody film crew—a lot of good they've been. PCs said he accompanied them to the ruins, then into the woods where he joined the search for Aggie. Nobody knows when he left. We've got his van, but it was stolen back in February, and there's nothing in it. Only thing anyone remembers about him is he has a limp."

"That doesn't make any sense, sir," said Kett. "If he has anything to do with this, if he's one of the people who took Aggie, why would he throw himself into the middle of a police investigation?"

"Maybe he doesn't have anything to do with it," said Clare, rubbing his kneecaps.

"But he does. We found the body of the *real* Kevin Clegg at the bottom of a well, in a property owned by Robert Flack. This guy has been pretending to be him for weeks, then he shows up after Aggie Clegg is kidnapped. What's he looking for?"

Clare shrugged, still rubbing his hairy knees. The sight of it was nauseating, and Kett struggled to keep his train of thought.

"Did anything come up in the Clegg house, sir?"

"Nothing," said Clare. "Clegg lived in a shithole of a flat on Mountergate, and from the look of it, our imposter has been staying there too. Barely any possessions, just a bed and some books and a lot of empty vodka bottles. We're checking CCTV in the area, but so far we've got toss all. Aggie's gran told us Aggie and her dad haven't spoken for five or six years. We can't find anyone else who cares enough about him to have paid him a visit. He's a loner with no other family, no friends and a lot of debt."

He was rubbing his knees with even more enthusiasm now, his face gurning. Kett was starting to wonder if he was still trapped inside last night's nightmare.

"Sir, what are you doing?"

"My legs are cold," the Super snapped.

"You could always put your trousers on?"

Clare shot him a look of disgust.

"You'd like that, wouldn't you?" he said.

"Um, yes, sir," he said. "Very much."

"Pervert."

"I—"

"What have *you* found, then?" Clare barked. "Eh? I want an update."

"Kate and I spoke to Charlie Ford. She's lucid. She didn't have a lot to give us, but she did mention a sponsor for Aggie's show. Said Aggie was worried about them, panicked. She didn't know why. Kate's finding out who they are."

"Trying, sir," came a voice from the door. Savage poked her head through, stopping when she saw Clare's legs. "Oh, sorry. I didn't realise you were... What *are* you doing, sir?"

"None of your bee's toss," said Clare, once again rubbing his knees. "Who's the sponsor?"

"Uh..." said Savage, mesmerised by the Super's actions. "There's nothing in any of the paperwork we took from Aggie's house, and nothing in her emails. None of her past videos have had a sponsor, so this is new. Charlie said she thought it was connected to the cameras they were using. I just checked, there was a note for the equipment buried in a bunch of paperwork in the car, got a business name but no address."

"So what are you still doing here?" Clare asked, slapping his hands on his bare knees. "Go find it! Both of you!"

They escaped through the door just in time to avoid the pair of brown trousers that Clare hurled after them.

"NOTE'S from a place called Complete Vision," said Savage as they reached the Incident Room.

She closed the door behind them while Kett walked to the evidence wall. It didn't take him long to spot the slip of paper that had been pinned next to Aggie Clegg's photo. It was the size of a postcard and marked with a mug ring. The name Complete Vision was printed along the top in faded ink, along with a phone number with a local dial code.

Somebody had doodled a handful of little sketches along the circumference of the paper—Kett could make out a bee, an elephant with a long trunk, and what looked like a balloon, plus about six others.

"You've tried the number?"

"Yes, sir. Disconnected."

The only other information on the receipt were two lines of scruffy handwritten text:

Canon 40d, and mic.

9DBL.

There was no name and no address.

"Or should I say it was never connected," Savage went on. "It's a dead line. More to the point, there's no company with that name in the city. Never has been."

She tapped the note.

"What do you think nine means?"

Kett thought about it for all of four seconds.

"The time," he said. "Right? They got to the ruins around then yesterday morning."

"Well, a little earlier, sir. Eight. It was supposed to be nine, but Charlie said Aggie wanted to be there for the light. And DBL?"

That he didn't have an answer for.

"I'm thinking it means Don't Be Late," said Savage, answering her own question.

"So this person made contact with Aggie, offering

equipment in return for a shout-out for a company that doesn't exist," said Kett. "You tried Matt?"

"Yes, sir. Just spoke to him. He didn't know where the cameras came from. He said Aggie showed up with them. She told him they were from the sponsor, but didn't say who. Douglas, the other member of the team, usually used his own kit for the videos, but we haven't managed to get hold of him."

"Where is he, again?"

"Out of town, sick mother. We've spoken to her and she's confirmed he's there, but he's not made himself available yet."

"You like him for this?"

"I would, sir, if he didn't have a firm alibi for yesterday morning. He was caught on a dozen NPRCs on the A47, and we've got footage of him inside a petrol station there."

Kett scratched an itch over his eye.

"Something's not adding up," said Kett. "Somebody has been watching Aggie for weeks, they killed her father, replaced him with a lookalike. We know it's Aggie they've been targeting because her birthday falls on the same day as the kids in the cages. It can't be a coincidence that Douglas is unavailable on the day of the attack, and that the first sponsor they get for their show falls into their laps at the exact same time."

"Right, sir," said Savage.

"So this company that doesn't exist offers kit in exchange for publicity, but what they're really getting in return is..."

"Aggie Clegg," said Savage. "In the middle of nowhere, at precisely nine in the morning."

Kett blew out a long breath.

"There are easier ways to do it, right? To kidnap a young

woman. Why bring her out to the woods with two other people? Why on a Monday morning? I mean, it's quiet there, but it's not deserted. Uniforms talked to half a dozen dog walkers in the area yesterday morning while they were searching the woods. And what about the head? What does that have to do with it?"

Savage shrugged.

"Maybe it's about the ritual of it, sir," she said. "These people seem like they're bound by the laws of whatever belief system they've invented for themselves. The rites, the pentagrams, all that stuff. It's insane, but there's a logic to it. This fits into it, somehow."

Kett looked at her, waiting for her to continue.

"I don't know how, though, sir. Sorry."

"Me neither," he said quietly.

The Incident Room door opened and Duke wandered in, frowning at Savage and Kett like he couldn't remember who they were. Megan was right behind him, the sound guy following.

"Not in here, guys," said Kett. "Sensitive information."

Megan aimed her camcorder at the wall of photographs, soaking it all in.

"Hey," said Kett, clicking his fingers. "Off, or you lose it again."

She dropped the camera to her side with a dramatic sigh.

"Sorry for the inconvenience," Kett muttered. "So we've got nothing? What about the pictures on the sponsor's note? They mean anything?"

Savage blew out a breath.

"I think they're just doodles, sir. The kind you make when you're talking on the phone."

"Beans," said Duke, who had walked to the wall.

"What?" said Kett.

"Some of these look like beans."

"They really don't," said Savage.

"I bet that's what DBL stands for," he said. "Death Beans. I don't know about the L, though."

"Death beans?" said Kett.

Duke shrugged, still perusing the paper.

"You checked for imprints?" he said.

"Fingerprints?" said Kett.

"No, imprints, like if somebody was leaning on this sheet of paper while they were writing something on the sheet above it. I do it all the time, when I'm on the phone."

"He doodles too, sir," said Savage, walking to his side. "Usually rude things."

"They're rocket ships," said Duke. He jabbed a finger on the paper. "Just looks like something here, see it?"

"You're right," said Savage. "How did I miss that?"

She plucked out the drawing pin and carried the paper to Kett's desk.

"Anyone got a pencil?"

"I do," said Megan, pulling one out of the scraggly bun of her hair.

"Are you still here?" Kett scowled at her.

He took the pencil and passed it to Savage. As delicately as she could, she began to rub it on the paper. Everyone crowded in as pale islands appeared in the graphite sea, a single line of numbers.

"I never thought I'd say this, Aaron," said Kett. "But you're a genius."

"Can you say it again, sir?" said Duke, looking at Megan. "But with the cameras rolling?"

"I'm never saying it again for as long as I live. What is it?"

"Looks like a mobile number, sir."

"Let's try it."

He typed the digits into his phone, double-checked them, then pressed call. It connected after seven rings and he put it on speaker.

"Yello?" said a man's voice—older, hoarse, and more than a little breathless.

"Hi, who is this, please?" said Kett.

"Who is *this*, please?" came the reply. There was a slight accent there, possibly Scottish.

"I asked first."

"And I'm no in the habit of talking to scum," said the man, wheezing. "Get a proper job, you spamming piece of shit."

"Wait," said Kett, sensing that the call was about to end. "It's the police. My name's DCI Kett, I'm with Norfolk Constabulary."

"Kett?" said the voice.

"Yes, with the police."

"Oh, sorry." He sounded utterly confused. "Are you calling *about* the spammers?"

"No," said Kett. "I'm calling about an ongoing case. Can I ask your name, please?"

"Alex," said the guy. "Rimple."

"Alex Rimple," Kett echoed. "P-O-L-E?"

"No, like pimple, but with an R."

Savage wrote it down.

"Are you sure you're police? Because these people will do anything to trick you. The last one I spoke to said he was Jesus, and that he needed my bank details in order to get back to heaven."

"Right..." said Kett. "I'm definitely the police, not Jesus."

"I wouldn't fall for it, obviously," said Rimple. "Jesus wouldn't use a phone, he'd write a letter."

Savage lifted an eyebrow.

"Mr Rimple, do you know a young woman called Agnes Clegg?"

"No," came the reply, a little too quickly.

"You sure about that?"

"I don't know an Agnes Clegg. I know an *Aggie* Clegg, if that helps?"

"How do you know her?"

"She does this thing on the telly," he said, still wheezing a little. "But young people telly, not *Songs of Praise* or anything. I can't remember what it's called, the show. You Tubes? I couldn't find it in the Radio Times, alas, but I don't really have the attention for it anymore. Doctors call it fibro something or other, but in my day we just called it getting old."

"How did you make contact with Aggie, Alex?"

"I didn't, *she* did. She popped into my shop one day and asked me if I'd sponsor some kind of charity, I can't remember. I wasn't really listening. She's quite fetching, you know."

"She was also seventeen," said Kett. "Your shop? In the city?"

"Aye."

"What's it called?"

"Specs," he replied.

"Not Complete Vision?" said Kett.

The man spluttered out a wet laugh.

"Well, we were going to be called that, until Vision Bastard Express threatened to sue us. I had all the paperwork printed, I had signs for the bloody place. Can you believe that? How can you trademark the word vision? I told them I was going to trademark the word express, and the word glasses, and the word prick so I could stamp it on every one of their foreheads, then take them to court."

The man cleared his throat.

"Bastards."

"You're a glasses shop?" said Kett. "Why would you want to sponsor a supernatural YouTube show?"

"A what?"

"Aggie's show was about haunted places in Norfolk, Alex. Ghosts and stuff."

"You've lost me. *Goats*? She never mentioned goats. I didn't think there were any charities for goats. They always seem to do quite well for themselves."

Kett rubbed his eyes.

"Like I said, I wasn't listening particularly well. She really is quite fetching. Impossible to say no to a smile like that."

"Did you give Aggie some equipment for her video?" Kett asked, trying to keep the frustration out of his voice.

"Aye," he said. "She asked for money, and we don't have any. But we did happen to have some old shooting stuff from when we made an advertising campaign a couple of years back. Before the whole Vision Wanker Express debacle. A camera and some fuzzy microphone thing. We don't need it anymore, it was just gathering dust in the cupboard, so I said she could have it if she gave us a shout-out on the TV. Nothing beats organic publicity like that, word of mouth."

"When was this?"

"Uh, Saturday morning, I think? She collected it from the shop."

"Have you heard from her since?"

"No, but she said it would take her a while to do what

she needed to do. She said she'd return the equipment, and I told her not to bother."

"Did you give her a slip of paper with the instructions to be there at nine, and not to be late?"

"Aye, probably," said Rimple. "I can't remember."

He cleared his throat again, something nervous in the sound of it.

"Why be so specific with the time, if you didn't even know what she was doing?"

"What?"

He'd heard the question, Kett didn't doubt it. He stayed quiet, waiting.

"Nine?" said Rimple, catching up. "I didn't want her to be late to pick everything up. We open at ten, so I thought nine would give us a chance to, you know, get to know each other..."

He cleared his throat again.

"She really was quite—"

"Fetching," said Kett. "Yes, you mentioned it. So she came in twice? You gave her the paper the first time with a time to come and collect the equipment?"

"Aye, that's right. I needed to run it past the staff."

"Sunday morning?"

"Aye."

Kett puffed out a breath.

"You mind if one of us pops in to speak to you in person, Mr Rimple?"

"Today?" he said, startled. "We're not open yet."

"You're at home?"

"No."

Kett waited.

"I'm at my other place of work," Rimple said after a pause. "Not as much money in glasses as there used to be, thanks to companies like Vision Cunty Express. I manage a storage facility."

"Where?" said Kett.

Rimple wheezed out a long sigh.

"It's on the Hellesdon Park Estate, you know it?"

"Yeah."

"Hellesdon Park Road, last building on the right. We don't have a sign, but you can't miss it. Tiny windows."

"Thanks," said Kett. "Don't go anywhere."

He hung up, tapping the phone gently on the desk.

"I have no idea what to make of that," he said. "He doesn't sound like much of a threat."

"Rimple's not on our radar at all, sir," said Savage, studying her phone. "Specs is a legit business in town. And Charlie told us that Aggie went door to door looking for sponsors. But there's always a chance he could be linked to this."

"Which still doesn't make sense," said Kett, trying to wrap his head around it. "Let's say Rimple loaned Aggie the camera in order to somehow lure her out to the ruins and attack her. A, there's nothing to say he was the one who suggested St Mary's as a location, and B, he's not going to give her a piece of paper with his details on it, is he? He'd know that if the police found it, it would lead right to him."

Kett's back was aching even more in this position, so he pushed himself off the desk.

"We got anything else?" he asked.

Nobody answered him.

"Any leads at all?"

Nothing.

"Then let's go check out Rimple's story, because I have no idea what else to do."

CHAPTER THIRTY-FOUR

THE ROADS WERE DESERTED, EVEN THE BRAVEST OF motorists deterred by the heat. The streets were already shimmering, a heat haze making it look like Savage was driving the Audi through water. Duke rode in the back, along with Megan. She hadn't taken the camera off him since they'd pulled out of HQ, and Kett hadn't missed the daggers Savage was shooting at the young woman in the rear-view mirror.

Two IRVs chased their shadow, mainly because Kett didn't want to take any chances.

He'd seen enough death on this case already.

Behind the IRVs rode the film crew's obnoxious yellow van, Josh an outline through the windscreen.

It took fifteen minutes to reach the industrial estate, and another ten to find the building they were looking for in the tangle of side streets and cul-de-sacs. It was one of the bigger warehouses towards the back, fringed by the tall trees that hid the drab estate from the golf course behind it.

"You sure this is it?" asked Kett as Savage came to a halt outside the gate.

The two-storey building was as ugly as they came, almost completely clad in corrugated iron. The minuscule windows at ground level had been stitched shut by metal bars, and there was no sign anywhere.

"Small windows, sir," Savage replied, looking around. "This has to be it, last building on the street."

"I guess there's only one way to find out."

He exited the car into the hot, heavy air. They were in a sun trap here, the car park baking even though it was still early. Savage and Duke joined him, Megan still filming. The coppers were climbing out of the IRVs and wandering over. The only noise was coming from the yellow van as Kelly yelled something at Josh.

"Aaron, can you go tell your friends to keep it down," said Kett.

Duke jogged off, waving his arms to get their attention. Megan scuttled after him, her camera aimed at his rear end.

Kett turned back to the building. There was absolutely no sign of life here. It looked empty.

"Rimple said he was here, didn't he?" said Savage.

"No car," said Kett. "Maybe he bolted."

"Maybe he walks to work, sir?"

"Maybe. Kate, with me. The rest of you, fan out. I want somebody round the back. There's a chance—a very small chance—this is our guy, so he could be dangerous. Do not intercept. Okay?"

There was a muttering of agreement. Kett wondered if he should call Gorski, then dismissed the thought.

"Just a look," he said.

"Just a look," echoed Savage. "Famous last words, sir."

He took the lead, walking to the double doors at the front of the building. There were no signs anywhere, no indication that this place was in use.

He offered the door to Savage, who pounded on it like a wrecking ball.

"Police," she yelled. "Rimple, are you in there?"

If he was, he wasn't advertising it. Kett turned the handle, the door remaining stubbornly shut.

"Could have seen that coming," he said, heading along the front of the building. A couple of uniforms were ahead of him, one trying a smaller door.

"Locked, sir," she called back. "That's open, though."

She nodded at a small window set at head height, and it wasn't open so much as broken, the textured glass almost completely knocked out of the frame. It had a set of bars, but when the PC pushed them up, Kett saw they were on hinges.

"Nothing over here," called a PC who'd reached the end of the building. "Back doors are locked."

"The window it is, then," said Kett, trying not to think about his experience in the caravan yesterday. "It's pretty small. I'm not sure I..."

He tailed off, looking hopefully at Savage.

"You want me to..." she started.

"I mean, I don't *mind* going in," said Kett, shrugging.

"I'll do it," said Duke, marching up with more than a little swagger. The camera crew was hot on his heels.

"Nice sentiment, Aaron," Kett told him. "But you're a bit big."

"Please, sir," he said, leaning in and whispering. "I'm desperate. All they've got so far is me talking to some old ladies and failing to throw a paper ball into the bin."

Kett looked at the window, then back at Duke.

"You won't fit."

"I'll fit," said Duke, glancing back. "I'll make myself fit. And quick, sir, say something that makes me look brave."

Kett blew out a long breath.

"Fine," he said, speaking a little louder so the TV crew could hear. "We need somebody, uh, brave to make entry. Any volunteers?"

Duke's hand shot up.

"Great," said Kett, speaking through gritted teeth. "Britain's bravest, once again. Can you get inside, Duke, and open the door?"

"Yes, sir!" barked Duke, throwing a salute at Kett.

"Bloody hell," Kett muttered. "You need a foot up?"

"Yes, sir," Duke said, a little more quietly.

Kett braced one shoulder against the wall, cradling his hands and holding them out. Duke planted an enormous boot in one, grabbed the bottom of the window, then heaved himself up. Kett's back screamed, and he nearly did too.

"What the hell, Aaron?" he grunted, the sweat already rolling off him. "What have you been eating?"

"Chicken, sir," said Savage. "A *lot* of chicken."

"For my muscles," said Duke, grinning at the camera.

He pulled out his baton and cleared the glass from the frame, raining chunks into Kett's hair.

"Police! I'm coming in, stay where you are!"

"Less talking, more moving," grunted Kett, his entire body quivering with the effort of holding Duke. He noticed that Megan had her camera trained on his sweaty face, and he did his best to glare at her.

"Ready or not, here I come."

"You're not playing bloody hide and seek, Aaron. Go!"

Duke slipped his arms and his head through the window, then began to worm his way through, painfully slowly. It was far too small for him, and there was a point where his shoulders looked like they were wedged in the gap, but Kett planted both hands on his arse and repeatedly shunted him through the gap until, more than a minute later, he tumbled down the other side, his legs whipping after him. A couple of items from his utility belt clattered to the ground and Savage picked them up.

"You okay?" Kett called.

There was no answer.

"Aaron?" he said.

Still nothing.

The idiot had landed on his head, thought Kett, and he could tell by the look on Savage's face she thought the same thing.

A few seconds later, though, the side door opened and Duke stood there, grinning at Josh's camera.

"You knocked?"

"Good job," said Kett. "So brave."

He poked his head through the door, seeing a small corridor. Duke flicked the switch, the fluorescent bulbs blinking on to reveal a double door up ahead, and a set of stairs leading to a small landing.

Then his eyes trailed down.

"Shit," he said.

Etched into the concrete floor in front of him, and stretching the entire width of the corridor, was a pentagram. Just like the one they'd found in the bunker, it was covered with letters and symbols.

And just like that one, the grooves here were stained red.

"Duke, get off that," said Kett, realising that the PC was standing on it. "Don't step on it."

Nothing to do with the evidence, he thought. He just didn't like it.

Duke retreated into the building.

"Police," Kett yelled, his voice echoing back off the

walls. "We're inside the building. If anyone is here, make yourself known."

Nothing. The air was still. It felt empty.

"I think we should call tactical, sir," said Savage. "This is them."

"Do it," said Kett. "But for all we know, Aggie's inside. There's no time."

He turned to the pack of PCs that had gathered by the open door.

"I need you lot to check the ground floor," he said. "Don't touch anything, and stay with each other. Duke, Savage, you're with me."

He took a run-up, launching himself over the pentagram with such urgency that he almost slipped on the other side. He grabbed the bannister, his heart ready to burst like a water balloon. Savage followed, leaping like a cat, Duke catching her. Josh and the sound guy came next, skirting around the edge, their trainers scuffing the pentagram.

Only Kelly stayed on the other side of it, hovering by the door. She was eyeballing the floor like there were snakes instead of symbols.

"I'll stay here," she said to Josh. "Try to keep up with him."

Duke was already climbing the steps, his Taser in his hand. Kett set off after him only for Josh to barge past, his camera on his shoulder.

"Don't bloody mind me," Kett muttered.

He waited for the sound guy to follow, then hauled himself upwards.

"Need a hand, sir?" asked Savage. "Or a push, maybe?"

"I'll give you a bloody push, Kate," he grumbled. "Over the edge."

Duke kicked his way through the doors at the top of the stairs, his voice like thunder.

"Police armed with Taser, do not mess with me."

Kett chased after him, finding himself in another corridor. Savage turned on the lights, although the fluorescents seemed reluctant to wake, strobing on and off a dozen times before finally settling. There were two doors on the landing, one on the left and one up ahead. Duke tried the first and it opened.

"Police!" he yelled, aiming his Taser into the shadowy interior.

Kett walked up behind him, seeing a room beyond the door. It was dark, but enough light crept through from the corridor to reveal that it was huge—it must have taken up half of the upstairs of the warehouse. Dozens of shelves partitioned the space, each one loaded to the point of collapse.

"Check the other door," Kett told Duke. "I'll take this one."

Duke set off, dragging the TV crew behind him. Kett stepped into the room, slapping the wall until he found some switches. He flicked them all, the lights overhead blinking on one by one. If anything, they made the room seem even bigger.

"Police," he called out, the vast space swallowing his shout.

He was having second thoughts about sending Duke away, but when he turned around to call him back he saw that he wasn't on his own. Savage stood behind him, offering a weak smile.

"Thanks," he said to her.

"No problem, sir."

He made his way into the room, approaching the first of

the dozen or so rows of shelving units. It was groaning under the weight of dozens of cardboard boxes, all of them marked up with black pen. Kett read a few of the labels—*pots, yellow; pots, terracotta; pots, white*—before crossing to the next aisle.

"They're all props, sir," said Savage, taking a closer look. "I'm guessing for theatres, film shoots, that kind of stuff."

There were hundreds of boxes. Thousands, maybe. None of them looked big enough to hide a body in.

Unless it had been dismembered.

"Police!" came Duke's voice from deeper inside the building. He sounded impossibly far away. The air answered with silence, the kind that felt deep enough to drown in.

"Check the far side, will you, Kate?" Kett said, pointing across the room. "It'll take forever unless we split up."

"Sir," she replied, peeling off down the next aisle. This one didn't hold boxes, it held furniture—maybe fifty sofas stacked like street barricades.

Kett kept walking, seeing an aisle full of dining tables and chairs, then another laden with patio furniture. Duke called out again, so far away now that Kett couldn't make out what he was saying. The room felt too big, as if it was stretching itself to fit them in, that far wall moving further away with every step he took.

He passed the next aisle and then stopped, his stomach clenching.

Somebody was staring back at him from the next row of shelves.

Not just one person, he realised. There were dozens, all standing in a neat line, perfectly silent and perfectly still, their emaciated bodies and skeletal faces full of horror.

Masks, he thought, and he had to force his lungs to

exhale, the adrenaline run-off making his vision pulse white and black.

He must have reached the costume section, because there were too many to count, all hanging from rails that ran the length of the aisle. It looked like a Halloween store, with vampires and aliens shoulder to shoulder with werewolves and wizards. Empty eye sockets watched him as he started walking again, talons bared and fangs slick with blood.

"Anything, sir?" Savage called.

"Not yet," he shouted back. "You?"

"So many garden gnomes."

He made his way down the aisle, past a posse of hanged clowns whose painted grins made his blood run cold.

Then he stopped again, because another face stared at him, this one horribly familiar.

"You again," he said.

It was a witch, her face lined with wrinkles, her mouth sagging, cords of greying hair falling over her eyes. Another identical costume hung next to her, and a third, and a fourth.

He walked over to them, unhooking the nearest from the rail and holding it up. There was no doubt at all that this was the same face that had stared at him from the camera footage yesterday morning. The same face that had greeted Porter at the bottom of the well.

"I think I've got something, Kate," he called out. "Where—"

Something clinked behind him, the softest of sounds. He twisted his head around so fast that something twanged inside his neck.

One of the witch costumes was swinging gently on its hanger, its sagging face aimed right at Kett.

The machete in its gloved hand didn't look like it was made of rubber.

"Kate?" he called out again.

No reply, and the witch kept on staring. It was just the way the mask was hanging, it was just the illusion of life in the dark eyeholes of its face.

Right?

And he'd almost managed to convince himself of this when the witch exploded from the aisle and started running towards him.

"Kate!" he screamed.

He dropped the costume he still held and lurched away —making it just three steps before the lights snapped off.

CHAPTER THIRTY-FIVE

THE DARKNESS WAS ABSOLUTE, LIKE SOMEBODY HAD hollowed his eyes from their sockets.

Kett stumbled in the churning void, no idea which way was up or down.

There was only the slap of feet as the witch ran towards him.

He opened his mouth to call Kate's name, then snapped it shut again. He scrabbled backwards, aware—even without seeing—of the shape that rose up right in front of him. The smell of her engulfed him, filthy skin, unwashed clothes.

Something sliced through the air beside his head, clanging off a metal shelf. He fell, landing on his backside, vertigo making the room spin. The witch was breathing hard, grunting like a pig as she moved closer.

"Where are you?" she said, just a whisper.

Kett kicked back, the machete cutting the air in front of his face. He rolled away, trying to hold his breath, trying not to give his attacker any clue about where he was.

His boot hit a shelf and knocked something over, the metallic sound of it louder than a church bell.

The machete swished, sparking as it struck the concrete floor—a flash of light that revealed the grotesque face of the witch just inches away.

"Fuck," grunted Kett.

He rolled again, reaching out, finding the leg of a shelf.

"You fucked up," growled the witch. "You fucked up."

He heard the sound of the blade as it dropped, as it thwacked into the floor by his foot.

"Stop," he said, choking on his own spit, hacking out a cough.

He started to pull himself up only to feel a hand grab his ankle, hauling him back. He kicked out with his other foot, hitting air, trying again, finding something solid.

A grunt of pain, and the witch let go.

Kett rolled for a third time, making it onto his hands and knees and crawling. He couldn't see where he was going, couldn't see *anything*, and after a handful of seconds his head rammed into one of the metal units.

He swore again, grabbing the shelf, heaving himself onto his feet. He didn't stop moving, feeling his way down the shelf.

"Where are you?" said the witch, too close.

Kett didn't answer, but Savage did—a scream that seemed to fill the whole room.

"Kate?" said Kett. He took a breath, bellowing. "Help! We need help in here!"

Footsteps, running fast. He pressed himself into the costumes that hung behind him, finding a gap, squeezing through it. The stench of the masks was overpowering, rubber and hair pushing into his mouth, suffocating him.

"You in there?" said the witch, too close.

Kett heard the machete tear its way through the costume beside him.

"You hiding?"

He pushed backwards, the blade punching into fabric, searching for him. Across the room, Savage screamed again.

Then, thank God, more voices.

"Sir?"

It was Duke, his footsteps echoing as he ran into the room.

"Where are you?"

"Here!" answered Savage.

Kett couldn't reply. The witch was right there, hacking at the costumes around him. The smell of her was enough to make him gag. He retreated, the metal bars of the shelving unit stopping him from going any further.

"You're stuck, aren't you?" said the witch. "Like a pig."

The blade slid in, and this time Kett felt it—the razor-sharp point pushing against his chest, threatening to slide into the tender flesh between his ribs.

Fuck this.

He reached through the forest of fabric, finding the other end of the machete, grabbing the wrist of whoever held it. He pushed himself out of the rail of costumes, keeping hold of the hand, using his elbow to trap the blade against his side. He kept moving, driving the witch backwards.

"No," she grunted.

The witch hit the shelf on the other side of the aisle, hard enough to loosen her hold on the machete. Kett wrenched it free, lobbing it into the dark.

"Sir?" Duke called.

"Over here!" he roared back.

He threw a punch at where the witch's head should have been, but it rang off the shelf instead—the pain so bright it made the room light up.

"I won't let you," the witch grunted again, hands reaching for his hair, his throat, his eyes.

He threw a punch again, glancing off the soft flesh of the mask. Then he drove his knee between her legs.

The witch let out a cry of pain and Kett grabbed fistfuls of her costume, throwing her onto the floor. He straddled her, his knees pinning her arms.

"Stop moving," he spat, breathless. "Stop fucking moving, or I knock you out."

Not that he had the strength to do anything. He could barely get a breath in, his lungs locked tight, not enough air.

Fortunately, there was a light growing at the end of the aisle.

"Sir?" said a voice.

It wasn't Duke, it was another constable. He aimed his torch at Kett, a supernova exploding in his retinas. The shape beneath him bucked hard and he almost fell, hanging on like a rodeo rider until the PC slid down beside them.

"Enough," he shouted. "Stay still or I'll Taser you."

The witch couldn't have cared less, heaving and bucking.

"Careful," Kett said, trying to hang on. "She had a—"

She bucked hard and he slid off, hitting the shelf again. He pulled himself back to his feet just so he could find some air, the entire building swaying like it had been mounted onto a seesaw.

The PC had taken Kett's place on top of the witch, doing his best to cuff her while she fought him. Kett dropped down again, holding her arm as she threw punch after punch. She was making a noise like she was choking, and Kett remembered David Blethyn, the way he'd chewed off his tongue.

"Shit," he said.

He grabbed the mask, ripping it away, revealing Bianca Caddel. Her eyes were demonic, her mouth foaming, the spittle red. The smell of her was unreal.

"Don't you fucking dare," he said.

He reached into his pocket, pulling out his warrant card in its leather wallet. The woman had her tongue between her teeth, blood dripping down her throat, making her gargle.

"Help me," said Kett, grabbing the woman's jaw with one hand.

The PC saw what was happening, his fingers in her mouth, both of them wrenching the jaw until it was wide enough for Kett to ram the warrant card in. He pressed hard, feeling the woman's jaw tense, feeling her body rock from side to side in an effort to dislodge him.

"Calm down," he said, all his weight on her head as he tried to stop her from spitting out the warrant card. "Stop fighting."

The PC had managed to cuff her, but she was still as strong as a bear.

"You're going to have to Taser her," said Kett. "We have to knock her out."

The woman bucked, and he almost fell off her.

"Now, Constable!"

"I'll do it," said Duke.

The PC loomed from the dark, a couple of torches picking him out like he was on stage. He aimed the Taser at the woman, his finger tense on the trigger.

"Wait until I'm—" Kett started.

Duke fired, the barbs hitting the woman in her chest. Kett dived away, the charge tingling up his arms from where he'd been holding her. She tensed, her back arched, the warrant card clenched in her jaw.

Then she slumped back to the ground, groaning.

"I said wait till I'm bloody off her, Aaron," Kett said.

He scrabbled to the woman's side, pulling the warrant card out of her mouth so that she could breathe. She wasn't out, but she was done—her body twitching and spasming from the shock.

"Find me something to put in her mouth," he said. "A tube, a cord, wooden spoon, anything to stop her getting to her tongue."

The PC who'd arrived first ran off. Kett realised that the TV crew was there, filming from the shadows, but he didn't have the energy to start shouting at them.

"Is Kate okay?" he said instead, looking up at Duke. "I heard her screaming."

"She's fine," Duke replied. "Wasn't her."

"Who was it?"

Duke shrugged.

"Some woman."

It seemed to take every ounce of strength he had left to get back on his feet. He braced a hand on the nearest shelf until the vertigo passed, then he pushed past Duke and the crew.

"Where is she?"

"Far side, sir," said Duke, gesturing with his Taser.

Kett followed the pale haze of the torches, making it halfway across the enormous space before the overhead lights started to come back on. The sudden light blinded him as much as the dark had, and he had to screw his eyes shut, feeling his way along the shelf until the pain ebbed away enough for him to look.

Ahead of him, at the end of another aisle of high shelves, was Savage. She was kneeling next to a metal cage, identical to the ones they'd found at the stable yard.

Inside the cage, her legs curled up, her head buried in her knees, was a young woman.

She was wearing a filthy grey tracksuit, the hood up. Her hair spilled out of it, hiding her face. Judging by the way her shoulders jerked up and down, she was sobbing.

A handful of coppers explored the rest of the warehouse, their shouts filling the enormous space.

"Check everywhere," Kett told them. "Every piece of furniture, every costume. There might be more of them."

He jogged the last few feet to where Savage was.

"You okay?"

She nodded, although her face said otherwise.

"You, sir?"

"I'm alive," he told her. "Bloody miracle, though. Got jumped by a witch."

"A *witch*?"

"With a machete. What happened to you?"

"Lights went out," said Savage, nodding to the other woman. "I heard her scream."

"Who is she?" said Kett.

But he already knew.

"Aggie?" he asked.

The woman lifted her head, that cascade of hair spilling away from her face. Agnes Clegg looked up at him with tear-swollen eyes, still sobbing. Her face was a ruin of cuts and bruises, one side swollen up so much it looked like she, too, was wearing a mask.

But it was her. There was no doubt about it.

"Holy shit," said Kett. "You found her."

"*We* found her."

Kett crouched down beside the cage. It was bolted, and secured with a heavy-duty padlock.

"You okay, Aggie?"

It was a stupid question. Her nostrils were clogged with old blood. It had crusted on her lips and her chin, like a beard. The capillaries in one eye had burst, making it crimson.

Everything about her made it clear she wasn't okay.

But she was *alive*.

"You're safe," he told her. "Kate, call an ambulance."

"Already have, sir," she said. "It's on its way."

"We need to find the key."

He stood up, bracing a hand on the cage to stop himself from falling. Just like the others, this one had a scrap of paper secured to the bars with ribbon, a pattern of crosses and lines drawn on it.

"Who attacked you, sir?" asked Savage, her knees cracking as she stood up.

"Bianca Caddel," he said. "But somebody must have switched off the lights for her."

"Maybe not, sir," said Duke as he crossed the aisle. "Lights are on a timer. That Aggie Clegg?"

"Yeah," said Savage.

"Thank God for that," said Duke with a grin.

They all looked down at Aggie, then over to where the uniformed police crowded around Bianca Caddel in her witch costume.

"It's over, then," Duke went on. "It's finished."

Kett heaved in a breath.

"No," he said after a moment. "It's not."

CHAPTER THIRTY-SIX

Kett stepped out of the side door into the oven of the day. He'd taken off his jacket and rolled up his shirt sleeves, but the heat was still unbearable, made worse by the fact he'd spent the last half an hour scouring every last inch of the stifling warehouse.

The place was a hoarder's dream, a collection of anything and everything in towering piles. If the first floor had been bad, downstairs was even worse. Dozens of vehicles occupied one-half of the ground floor—including Bianca Caddel's VW Passat—the rest dominated by actual buildings: sheds and portaloos and children's playhouses, all fully erected.

A small section had been dedicated to electrical equipment, generators and projectors and giant speakers, plus a handful of lighting rigs in the corner next to the kitchen.

The same ornate pentagram had been carved into the floor in front of every door, and into the wall beside every window—each design etched with symbols and stained with old blood.

There was nobody else in the building, but it didn't

matter. They had their missing girl, and the woman who had taken her.

An ambulance sat like an island in the ocean of IRVs that filled the car park and the street beyond. They'd called it for Agnes, but it was Bianca Caddel who lay there. It had taken six coppers to get her down the stairs, the woman fighting them with every inch of her being, screaming into the rubber tube that Kett had tied around her head to stop her from biting off her own tongue. Even after the paramedics had rushed over and given her a shot, she'd resisted with monstrous strength before finally falling still.

It had taken some effort to get Aggie out as well. Her legs had been too weak to hold her, so Uniforms had carried her down the stairs and out of the door—everyone nervously skirting the pentagrams.

She now rested in the back of an IRV, a foil blanket on her lap and an untouched bottle of water in her hands. Savage sat next to her, chatting quietly. She'd checked the girl to make sure she wasn't injured, but other than the nasty wound to her face, and a few bruises on her wrists where she'd been tied, she was unharmed.

The way she flinched when Kett appeared, though, and the look of terror that sat on her face until she recognised him as a policeman, made it clear that her mind was broken.

"Sorry," he said, holding up his hands. "I didn't mean to scare you. My name is Robbie. It's Aggie, right?"

The young woman nodded, shuffling a few inches away from him and sliding into Savage. She jumped again, every part of her wound tight with anxiety.

"You're okay, Aggie," said Savage. "Remember what we talked about. Deep breaths. You're safe."

"I can come back?" said Kett, dropping uncomfortably

onto his haunches outside the door. "It would just be good to have a quick chat, if you're up for it?"

She didn't look up for it at all, but she nodded.

"It's her birthday," said Savage. "Right, Aggie? Eighteen?"

"Happy Birthday," said Kett. "Although I imagine you've had better. Your grandmother's on the way to the hospital, she's going to meet you there so they can check you over. Did Kate tell you?"

Aggie nodded, her eyes locked on the seat in front.

"Can you go over what happened?" Kett asked. His quads were burning from the effort of squatting, but he didn't want to risk startling her again. "As much as you can remember."

She'd clamped up, her clenched jaw bulging.

"Start with what you were just telling me," said Savage. "Start with the masks."

Aggie looked at Savage, then turned to Kett.

"They were masks?" she said, and he wasn't sure if it was a question or not until she fell silent.

"Yeah," he said. "The witch? It was a mask."

The girl nodded, her eyes glazing over like she was being pulled into a memory.

"It looked so real," she said. "I thought she was real. She was so strong."

"She attacked you in the ruins, right?" said Kett. "We saw it on the camera."

Aggie looked confused for a moment, as if she couldn't remember what camera he was talking about.

"Oh, yeah," she said. "The camera. Is it... did we break it?"

"It's fine," said Kett.

"That's good," said Aggie—quietly, as if she was in some kind of dream. "I was worried, it's not mine."

"Let's start there, then," said Kett. "The equipment you were using. You got it from the same man who owns this place, didn't you? Complete Vision?"

She frowned, shaking her head.

"This place?" she said.

"His name's Alex Rimple," said Kett. "We spoke to him, he said he was sponsoring your show, lending you equipment."

"Right," she said, still shaking her head. "Feels like a million years ago. Alex? He gave us the kit, yeah. What do you mean, he owns this place?"

"Hang on," said Kett. "When did you get the equipment from him?"

"Like, Saturday?" she said. "We usually use a guy, Dougie, but his stuff's old, crap lenses. They used to be his brother's and he never looked after them."

"And Alex offered you new stuff?" asked Kett. "You went to him?"

"No," she said. "He messaged me."

"That's not what he told us."

"You spoke to him?" Aggie said, looking up. "Did he do this to me? Why didn't you arrest him?"

"We will," said Kett. "He led us here. He invited us here. Why?"

Aggie's brow furrowed. She stared at the bottle in her hands as if it might help her make sense of it.

"Did you see him in the warehouse?" Kett asked.

"No, it was just *her*," she spat.

"But you met with Rimple when you collected the gear? In his shop?"

"Yeah, I guess," she said.

"Can you describe him?"

"No. He was just a guy."

"Old? Young? Tall? Short?"

"I can't remember. I wasn't really looking. I just wanted the kit."

"Did you speak to him? Did he say anything unusual?"

"No. He was just... like I said, I just wanted the kit."

"Did he say anything else at all?"

Nothing.

"Okay," said Kett. His legs were threatening to cramp so he shifted onto his knees. "So you drove out to East Somerton yesterday morning. You, Matt and Charlie, right?"

"We don't usually have Charlie," said Aggie, a flash of irritation crossing her filthy face. "But Dougie couldn't do it, he had to go see his mum or something."

"The three of you drive out in your car, you get there just before eight."

"Yeah," she said. "We were running late. We found the church, set up."

"And there was no sign of anyone else there? No other cars?"

"No," she said, although the colour was draining from her fast. "We started filming, doing our thing, then... then Charlie said she'd seen something. She..."

She turned to Kett, her eyes dark.

"You found the head?"

"We did," said Kett.

"It was real?"

He didn't answer, but she found the truth in his silence. She put a hand to her mouth, shaking her head.

"I thought it was him," she said, speaking through her fingers.

"Alex?"

"Yeah, I thought he'd set it up to make the episode look good, like to give us a boost or something. All the good stuff on YouTube has shocks and surprises like that, you know? But it... it was real? Who was it?"

"What happened after you found the head?" said Kett, dodging the question.

Aggie's face twisted into a mask of misery.

"*She* did. *She* happened. She came out of nowhere, she hit Charlie and then..." She swallowed, her eyes bulging. "I tried to help, I wanted to... But she was so fast, and so strong. She grabbed me, she..."

Her hands flexed around the water bottle like she was choking it. The wounds on her face looked worse than ever in the half-light of the car.

"She was so strong, I couldn't fight her. She pushed me down and hit me, she hit me, over and over, in the face. I... I didn't know what was going to happen. It was so fast, she tied me up, she..."

Aggie made a noise like she was going to vomit, and Savage rested a hand on top of hers until she'd recovered.

"Just a little longer," he said. "She tied you up?"

"She tied me up, my hands, my feet. Then she lifted me like I was nothing, she picked me up and carried me... I was screaming for Matt, he wasn't there, he fucking ran. And she carried me to the road. There was this car there, and she put me in the boot. In the *boot*. I couldn't breathe, I..."

She gagged again.

"You want to come out of there?" Kett asked. "Get some fresh air?"

Her head swayed from side to side, but all she vomited out were words.

"I couldn't breathe, and she was going so fast I kept

sliding around, cracking my head. But I remembered this TV show I'd watched. Somebody was kidnapped and they were in the boot and they kicked out the light, managed to signal to the police. So I... I kept my head, pulled up the cloth bit, found the light and I managed to pop it loose. There was some ribbon in there, I used that."

"We saw it," said Kett. "You did good."

"You saw it?" she echoed, her face twisting into an expression of abject misery. "Then why didn't you get me out?"

"We saw it on a camera," said Savage. "We didn't know where you were. But it's how we found out about Bianca, and how we got to you here. I'm sorry it wasn't sooner."

Aggie was still shaking her head.

"You should have found me," she said. "You took too long. It's not fair."

"Did the woman bring you straight here?" asked Kett.

Aggie looked through the windscreen as if she couldn't remember where she was.

"I don't think so," she said. "We stopped twice, and both times she got out. I heard her walking off and I tried to get out, tried to kick the boot open. But she wasn't gone long enough, was she? She came back and heard me, told me to shut up or I'd lose my tongue."

She broke down, a sob exploding from her.

"Then we were driving again," she said, scrubbing her face. "When she opened the boot we were inside, in there, and she had a knife, a big one. She said... I can't remember what she said, she still had the mask on, she..."

"You're sure it was the same woman we found with you upstairs?" said Kett. "It wasn't somebody else wearing the mask?"

"It was her," said Aggie, still speaking through tears, her

voice hitching. "I could smell her. Same stink, same voice, too. She said if I did what she said she'd let me go, I remember now. She said if I stayed with her for forty-eight hours, if I didn't try to escape, she'd let me go and she wouldn't hurt me."

"You believed her?"

"Fucking choice did I have?" she spat. "She had a knife, she was so strong. I got out of the boot and she made me go up the stairs. Put me in a cage. A fucking *cage*. Gave me water, and some clothes—these clothes—because I'd..."

She didn't finish, but she didn't need to.

"She said forty-eight hours?" asked Kett. "So she needed you there until after your birthday was over?"

Aggie shrugged, staring at the bottle again.

"Did she say why? Did she say anything at all?"

"No. But I heard her on the phone, heard her saying stuff. Saying all this shit about the devil."

"The devil," said Kett when she didn't go on.

"I didn't listen. *Couldn't* listen. I was too scared. She said nobody would find me here. She kept talking about the devil, and evil. That's what she kept saying: evil."

"Evil?" said Kett, and he found himself thinking about what had happened when he'd arrived home last night, Evie running away down the corridor.

Daddy, help me, Mummy's evil and she's trying to kill me.

"Yeah," Aggie said, bringing him back. "All she said to me was to be quiet, so I was. Didn't dare make a noise, not even when you lot came in, in case it was a trick. Didn't know how long I was in there, because there were no windows. Felt like forever, but it can't have been, if today's my birthday."

"Was the woman in there with you all this time?" asked Kett.

"I don't know. She came and went. Sometimes she was wearing the mask, other times she wasn't. Don't know which was worse."

"And you've never seen her before?"

"Never. Never want to see her again." She twisted in her seat to look out of the back window. "Where is she?"

"She's gone," said Savage.

"Nothing can happen to you now, Aggie," said Kett. "I promise."

His back was throbbing, and his legs had gone numb. He stood up, every single joint cracking.

"Thank you," he said. "You have no idea how helpful that is. Kate can take you to meet your grandmother now, if you like?"

"I can go?" she asked, nodding as if to answer herself. "What time is it?"

"Just after ten thirty," said Kett, checking his watch.

He tapped the roof of the car a couple of times, then turned away.

"There's something else," said Aggie before he could leave. "But I can't remember if it's real, or just a dream."

He leaned over so he could see her through the open door.

"I was sleeping. Don't even know how, but I must have drifted off. No idea what the time was, but I woke up because of the screaming."

"Screaming?" said Kett.

"I thought it was somebody else like me, you know? In one of the cages. Then I saw it was that woman. She was on the other side of the room, she was running from one side to the other and she was screaming like she was... like she'd lost her mind. I've never heard anything like it, made me want to just curl up and die."

"Do you have any idea why she was screaming?" asked Kett.

"No. But it went on forever. Running back and forth, back and forth. She didn't have the mask on but she looked just like her, you know? Like the witch. Her mouth was too big, her eyes were these awful, gaping holes. She didn't look real."

Aggie's head dropped, the tears raining onto her lap.

"A dream," she said. "Had to be a dream."

"I'm sorry," said Kett. He looked at Savage. "Get her out of here, she's been through enough."

"Yes, sir."

Savage got out of the car, opening the driver's door.

"And Kate, take some backup, yeah?"

She nodded.

Kett crossed the car park, heading for the ambulance. He spotted Duke on the way, the big PC sitting on the bonnet of an IRV looking as forlorn as a lost child. The TV crew were skulking by the open front doors of the warehouse, and for once all of the cameras were down.

"You okay, Aaron?" asked Kett as he passed. "Thought you'd be happy. Tasering a suspect was on the list, wasn't it?"

"Yeah, sir," said Duke. "But it was too dark to see anything. I look like some big old gorilla shambling around, you can't tell it's me."

"To be fair, if I saw a big, shambling gorilla, I'd think it was you," said Kett.

Duke's face fell.

"Sorry, mate," said Kett, clapping him on the shoulder.

"Savage is taking Aggie Clegg to the hospital if you want to escort her? Might get some good footage."

"Of me babysitting, sir?" said Duke. "No thanks."

"You could always order a coffee and a pastry at the café too. Good TV, that."

Duke glowered at him.

"Then go back to HQ, help Porter out."

Duke groaned like a bored donkey.

"Or stay here," said Kett, his patience waning. "Whatever floats your boat, *Constable*."

He reached the ambulance, four officers parting to let him through. There were two more PCs in the back, making it difficult for the paramedic to move around. She didn't look like she was complaining, though, her cheek swollen and a bruise forming around her eye.

"Shit," said Kett as he grabbed the handle and hauled himself up. "You okay?"

"All part of the job," said the woman. "She's an ox, came round. Had to give her another shot to put her back to sleep, and even that's not really working."

She stood to one side to reveal Bianca Caddel on the stretcher. She'd been masked during the fight, and in the struggle to get her down the stairs, Kett hadn't had a chance to really look at her. Only now did he see how striking she was—a wide, flat Germanic face with prominent cheekbones and a nose that looked like it had been broken more than once.

Her hair was more grey than blonde, as knotted and dreaded as the mask that she'd been wearing. Her neck was thick with muscle, and Kett could see a number of tattoos peeking over the top of her jumper—the unmistakeable point of a pentagram. She was wearing an identical tracksuit to the one she'd given Aggie, and it stank like she hadn't washed it in years.

"Yeah," said the paramedic as she watched Kett's nose wrinkle. "It's bad."

Bianca's eyes were closed, but her body writhed like she was caught in a fever dream, sweat pouring from her face, collecting in the hollow of her throat. She was secured to both sides of the stretcher, the cuffs rattling as she struggled. The tube in her mouth had been removed, and thankfully her tongue was still attached.

"She say anything?" he asked.

"Plenty," said one of the constables from where he stood in the corner of the ambulance, his head ducked beneath the low ceiling. "But I couldn't make out much of it. She was screaming."

"Yeah, I remember," said Kett. His ears were still ringing from trying to get her down the stairs.

"Said something about us messing up, sir," said the second constable by the door. "She didn't say messing, though."

"Fucking up," said the first. "Said we'd fucked up, that somebody was going to pay."

"Yeah, that was it."

"Did she say who?" asked Kett.

"No, sir," said the second PC, nodding into the car park. "But she was looking at the girl."

"Aggie?"

They both nodded.

Bianca groaned, her body thrashing as if she was trying to wake herself from a dream. Her arms tensed, straining against the handcuffs, the skin of her wrists bleeding.

"Can you give her another shot?" asked Kett.

"Not without killing her," said the paramedic. "I don't know how she's still going."

One of Bianca's eyes peeled open, red and raw. It roved madly in its socket, a blister of hatred that found the paramedic, then the PCs, then Kett. He'd taken a step back before he knew it, almost tumbling out of the ambulance. Aggie was right, he didn't know which sight scared him more: Bianca in her mask, or out of it.

The woman's mouth opened, slick with saliva. Her teeth were big and yellow, they reminded Kett of a horse's teeth. Her tongue was a slab of meat that pushed itself out, her throat gargling. Her body tensed, her back arching, her feet kicking out like she was being electrified. But that one, mad eye still held Kett.

"You should get out," said the paramedic, her hand on Bianca's chest to try to calm her. "No good getting her riled up again."

It was advice he was happy to take, but he couldn't seem to pull his gaze away from her. His body had locked, as if she'd taken control of every string. Bianca's tongue flexed, her jaw twisted, the guttural noises in her throat finally forming words.

"You... killed..."

"Go," said the paramedic, moving towards Kett. "She's going to hurt herself."

He couldn't move, as if an invisible wire had been threaded between Bianca's eye and his own.

"You... killed... them," she said, spitting the words from wet lips. "You killed them. You killed them."

"Who?" said Kett. "Robert Flack? David Blethyn? David's still alive, Bianca."

"Now," said the paramedic. She stepped between Kett and Bianca, breaking their eye contact. Kett's body came back online with such force that his back started to cramp. He dropped onto the step, one of the constables helping him onto the ground.

"You killed them!"

Bianca was screaming now, her body flailing, the stretcher threatening to overturn. The paramedic gave Kett a frightened look as she closed the doors. The other paramedic must have been ready to go because the ambulance trundled away, weaving a path between the IRVs before gunning up the road.

Even from back here, Kett could still hear the woman inside, her words turning the hot air to ice.

"You killed them! You killed them! You killed them!"

CHAPTER THIRTY-SEVEN

"You okay back there?" asked Savage. "You can sit in the front if you like?"

She glanced into the rear-view mirror in time to see Aggie shake her head. The young woman looked exhausted, which wasn't exactly surprising. Savage couldn't imagine what she'd been through—attacked, injured, kidnapped and kept in a cage by a madwoman.

"Well, it's not a long drive," she said, starting the engine of the IRV. "Just sit back, relax. I'm going to take you right to your granny."

She put the car in gear, reversing out of the space. The car park was mobbed, but she took her time, weaving through the forest of IRVs towards the exit. Another car followed, two uniformed officers in the front. Neither of them was Duke, which annoyed her a little. Yes, he'd come to the rescue when Kett was being attacked. But the whole TV thing had changed him, he was distracted—even more distracted than usual, that was. She couldn't wait until it was over.

Part of her was even hoping they'd give up and go home.

She stuck her hand out of the window to acknowledge the car behind, earning a bleep from their siren in return. Then she picked up speed, the BMW accelerating effortlessly. It wasn't an emergency, but she flicked on the blues anyway. The sooner Aggie got to the hospital and was reunited with her grandmother, the better.

Of course the bad news wasn't over. Nobody had told her about her father yet.

"You want some music?" Savage asked as she reached the end of the estate. "I can put the radio on."

"No," said Aggie.

She was looking through the window, her expression full of fear.

"I promise you," Savage said. "that woman can't hurt you anymore. She's handcuffed, and they sedated her. She's out cold."

It didn't seem to help. Aggie strained in her seat, staring through the back window.

"They're going to put her in prison, Aggie, for a long time."

Traffic had stopped to let her out, so she pulled onto the main road, heading towards the city. The second car followed, staying close. Aggie was still looking behind them, as if she expected to see Bianca soaring overhead on her broomstick.

"Are you worried that she wasn't doing this alone?" Savage asked. "Because we know there were others working with her. Two men. We found them, Aggie. One's dead, the other one is in hospital, under police supervision. They can't hurt you."

Aggie sniffed, wiping her eyes. She was crying again, but Savage wasn't sure if it was because she was afraid or relieved.

"Bianca didn't talk to you about any other children?" she asked.

"No," said Aggie. "Why?"

"No reason," said Savage. She didn't want to worry her.

"There were other people like me?" Aggie asked. "Who? Where are they?"

"We found them too," said Savage. "Everything's fine, I promise."

"But what if it's not?" said Aggie.

"What do you mean?"

There was a set of red lights ahead where Drayton Road met the ring road, the traffic at a standstill. It was busy here, and Savage switched off the lights so people wouldn't start driving out of her way like headless chickens. She joined the queue, the engine idling.

Aggie was silent in the back seat, other than the soft sniff of her sobs.

"What do you mean, Aggie?" Savage asked again.

"I mean what if it isn't okay?" she said. "What if there are more people doing this?"

"You're safe," said Savage. "If there are others, we'll get them too. That woman was... she was insane, Aggie. She did something terrible, I'm not even sure we'll ever know why. Not really. But she can't hurt you anymore. None of them can."

Savage could hear the growl of an engine, something big approaching behind them. She checked her side mirror but she couldn't see past the second IRV. Aggie could hear it too, because she turned in her seat again, looking back.

"What if you *can't* keep me safe?" she said.

The engine was growing louder, as if it was picking up speed. Savage's heart began to rev, her pulse clattering as she kept her eyes on the mirror. She touched the accelerator

—not that there was anywhere to go. The lights were still red, the cars lined up like bricks in a wall.

"What if nobody can keep me safe?" said Aggie, looking forward, her eyes like saucers.

Savage didn't reply. Somebody was honking their horn, furiously. The sound of the engine was like thunder.

"Kate?" said Aggie.

Something rose over the top of the second IRV—*a bus*, thought Savage, and that was all she had time to think before it collided with the car behind.

"Shit," she said, spinning the wheel and flooring it.

Too slow.

The bus shunted the second IRV into the back of their car, the rear window exploding. Savage's head hit the steering wheel, the world detonating into noise and light as their car lifted off the ground and slammed into the one in front. Aggie was screaming, and Savage would have been too if she could breathe.

The bus was reversing for another hit. Its windscreen had shattered, Savage couldn't see who was driving.

"Hang on," she said, as much to herself as to Aggie.

The car had slipped out of gear and she fought to get it back in, driving her foot down as soon as it caught. The car in front was still too close, the driver scrabbling out with a look of terror on his face. Savage drove into the back of it, shunting it out of the way, her tyres smoking as they fought to get purchase.

The bus hurtled forward again, a battering ram that knocked the second IRV into the other side of the road. It kept going, piling into the back of Savage's car.

Knocking it free of the vehicle in front.

She floored it, almost losing control as she gunned up the wrong side of the street. The bumper must have been hanging off, a shower of sparks chasing them. There was no room to move, the IRV scraping between the two lines of cars with the sound of shearing metal.

In the mirror, she saw the bus pull out after them. It was a small one, a white minibus, but it ploughed through the cars like an icebreaker, ripping off doors like they were chicken wings.

Aggie was still screaming, doubled up in her seat with her hands over her head.

"It's okay," said Savage, just a grunt. "Stay down."

She had to slow as she reached the junction because the traffic was still moving, cars and lorries barrelling past at forty miles an hour. She flicked on the lights again, and the siren, pulling out so sharply that a speeding Porsche had to stamp on the brakes, spinning out.

The bus was gaining, filling her rear-view mirror.

She floored it again, crossing both lanes onto the road that led into the city. She grabbed the radio set as she went.

"Control, this is DC Savage, I need emergency backup."

A hiss of static, then a woman's voice.

"We know, the unit behind you called it in."

"They okay?" she asked.

She was gaining ground, the BMW's big engine pulling them away effortlessly.

"They're bruised, but they'll live," said the operator. "I've got units on the way from the south, and from the east. Tactical's been alerted. Are you clear?"

Savage checked the mirror again, the bus still there but getting smaller. It slipped out of view as they turned a corner.

"I'm—"

There was a skip lorry ahead, taking up both sides of the road as it backed into somebody's drive. Savage slammed her foot on the brake, the back of the car starting to slide. She lifted her foot, fighting the wheel.

A road to the right. She didn't have a choice, momentum making the turn for her. She saw the wide-open park ahead of her, realised her mistake too late.

A dead end.

"Shit," she said again.

"DC Savage, what's going on?" said the voice on the radio.

No time to reply. She braked hard, spun the wheel, the IRV punching between two stone pillars and down a footpath. Pedestrians scattered, lifting their kids and their dogs as they leapt off the path. There was a car park to the left, no exit that way. A barrier blocked the road ahead.

No choice. The bus had made the turn and was catching up, fast.

"Hang on to something," she told Aggie.

She pushed her foot down, gritting her teeth so hard they could have shattered.

The BMW hit the metal barrier, tearing it free. It slipped under the car, catapulting them upwards, and for a second they were airborne. They landed hard, something exploding beneath the car. Savage fought to keep control, the BMW resisting her in a way that could only mean one thing.

One of the tyres had popped.

"Who is it?" Aggie's screams had choked themselves into words. "What do they want? What do they want?"

It wasn't hard to guess. The IRV was limping, the bus closing in, still no clue who was driving it past the cobweb of cracks that spread across the windscreen.

Savage kept her foot down, her hands locked on the wheel. They passed a stone pavilion, the operator's voice still blasting from the radio, barely audible over the rattle of something underneath them—the exhaust, Savage guessed. The car was hanging on by a thread, it couldn't last much longer.

The bus roared up, ripping the injured bumper clean away. Savage locked the scream in her throat, trying not to let the car spin out. The road continued, but not for much longer, dead-ended by a hedge a hundred yards away. To the right was a BMX track, half a dozen bikers watching them pass. To the left was a playpark full of kids, their parents basking in the sun.

"Come on," Savage said, trying to force her panic-stricken brain into gear.

The bus hit them again, harder this time. The IRV's windscreen cracked in two, the engine sounding like a spanner inside a washing mashing.

"What do we do?" shouted Aggie, her hands still over her head. "We're going to die."

Savage kept moving, as fast as the battered car would let her.

And then she saw it, a break in the hedge, a footpath that was barely wider than the car.

"Come on," she said again, willing the IRV to keep going. Her foot was on the floor, but despite that they were moving at less than thirty. The bus slammed into them again and this time their back end fishtailed.

Savage held onto the wheel, straightening them out. Just fifty yards now. It wasn't just a footpath, she saw, it was a bridge. There had to be a gulley there.

Thirty yards. There was smoke pouring from the bonnet, and according to the temperature gauge on the dash, they should have been on fire.

"Don't quit on me," Savage said.

Ten yards. The bus hit them again, shunting them past two metal poles and onto the wooden footbridge. It was out of her hands, the IRV shrieking as it hurtled through the gap, scraping along the handrails.

The bus crunched into the posts behind them, bucking like a horse before rolling onto its side.

Savage hit the brake but nothing happened. The IRV bounced down a small slope and onto another footpath, chunks of glass raining from the windscreen. Only when it hit the rise on the other side of the track did it come to a stop.

She looked back, the bus hidden by the hedge.

"DC Savage?" came the voice from the radio.

She picked up the handset, keeping the engine running.

"I'm okay," she said. "We're okay. I think we're on Marriot's Way, heading, uh, east. The bus didn't make it."

"Are you still mobile?"

"Yeah," she said. She gave the dash a couple of gentle taps. "Just. The old girl saved us. We can make it."

"I'll have units meet you at the junction with Mile Cross, it's half a mile ahead."

"Thanks," said Savage.

She threw the radio onto the passenger seat, looking back. Wind blasted through the broken windscreen and out the shattered back window. Aggie lay on the seat, her hair sparkling with glass, her battered face streaked with blood.

"You okay?" asked Savage.

Aggie shook her head.

"Me neither," said Savage.

She checked the mirror, half expecting to see the bus tear through the hedge and thump down onto the track. If it caught up to them again, they were dead.

But there was just the sky, and a storm of crows that had been shaken loose from the trees.

She hauled in a breath to try to calm her trembling body. Then she wrestled the IRV into gear and started moving.

“Me neither.”

CHAPTER THIRTY-EIGHT

"It's all about the temperature ratios," said Porter.

He was standing in the MIT's small kitchen, the kettle rumbling on the countertop as it came to the boil. Milo, the fourth member of the TV crew, and the one whose role Porter hadn't quite figured out, stood beside him. The young man was pointing a small camera at Porter, but he looked bored out of his skull.

Which was a little rude, Porter thought, because what he was sharing was the sort of stuff that TV legends were made from.

"Most people think you put the hot water straight in with the teabag," he went on, opening the cupboard to retrieve a couple of mugs. "But that's insane, because boiling water is really hot."

"You don't say?" said Milo.

"Well think about it," Porter went on. "What would happen if you poured boiling water on a house plant, eh? It would die. What would happen if you stood in a shower and the water was boiling?"

He waited.

"You'd die," said Milo after a moment. "Look, I'm sorry, but who are you again?"

"Detective Inspector Peter Porter," said Porter.

"Is that a real name?"

"Obviously," said Porter.

"Because we're only really supposed to film Duke," said Milo.

"Well, Duke's not here, is he? And I am. So focus on this."

He gestured to his face with both hands.

"And listen closely."

Milo blew out a long sigh of frustration. Porter ignored it, taking the milk from the fridge. The carton was almost completely empty, and when he unscrewed the cap he got the distinct impression that it was past its sell-by date.

"Doesn't matter," he said. "Milk's like cheese. The older it is, the more flavour it has."

"I don't think anyone in the history of the world has wanted their milk to have flavour," said Milo.

"You'd be surprised," said Porter.

He dropped a teabag into both cups, then added a glug of milk. Then he used a spoon to mash the teabags around a little. A haze of brown escaped, staining the milk. Milo leaned over to get a closer look with the camera.

"You want to caress the tea," said Porter. "Not cook it. A little milk lets the taste seep out. See that?"

"What?"

"The seepage, right there."

"Please never say seepage again," said Milo.

"It's a technical term. I wouldn't expect you to get it." He squeezed the teabags around a little, then lifted the kettle just as it boiled. "Got to get the water in when it's a hundred degrees exactly," he said, swishing the kettle a little.

"I mean, technically that would be steam," said Milo.

"No, it's *wa-ter*," Porter told him, sounding the word out.

He filled both cups, the milk hissing angrily as the water flowed in. The teabags spasmed like living things.

"Oh my God," said Milo.

He sounded impressed, Porter thought.

"Exactly. Temperature ratios, just like I said. You want to trick the tea by caressing it, embracing its seepage."

"Please don't say—"

"Then shocking it into submission," Porter said, thumping the counter hard enough to jolt the mugs. "Boom, the perfect cuppa."

The teabags had given up the fight, floating at the top of the mug like corpses in a canal. Porter jabbed them both with his spoon then fished them out, tossing them into the sink. Milo was still filming, which had to count for something. Porter added another glug of milk to both cups.

"*More* milk?" said Milo.

"Yup," said Porter, using the last of the carton. One of the mugs was so full it was overflowing, forming a puddle on the counter. "The best kind of tea is the colour of marble, like all those Greek statues. Royal tea." He laughed, impressed by his own wit. "Royalty, ha, get it?"

Milo obviously didn't. He was still filming the tea, which was a little annoying because Porter wanted to get his face on the telly. It would be an amazing thing to show Allie, and Bobby too, when he was older. It could be the start of a brand-new adventure. He might even be offered his own show, like Jamie Oliver and his Naked Chef, or whatever it was called.

"Peter Porter's Perfect *Puh*," he thought aloud. "What food thing starts with P?"

"What?" asked Milo, a worried look on his face.

"P?"

"*What?*"

"Puddings," said Porter. "Peter Porter's Perfect Puddings. No, Peter Porter, the Police Pastry... Person."

"I'm so confused," said Milo.

"Forget it. Anyway, there you go. Help yourself."

Milo kept the camera rolling, still focussing on the tea.

"What are those little white bits floating around?" he asked.

"Flavour," said Porter.

"And the oily dark bits?"

"More flavour."

"I..." Milo finally lowered his camera. "I can't drink that, sorry. I think it, uh, goes against my religion?"

"Porter? Where are you?"

Superintendent Clare popped his head around the door, pulling an expression of distaste when he saw Porter—one that grew more disgusted when he saw the tea on the counter.

"I've just had a memory," he said. "More of a flashback, really."

"Sir?" said Porter.

"When I was sixteen or so, I did some work on the farm up the road from our house. They were wanking the pigs."

"They were *what*, sir?"

"Wanking the pigs," said Clare. "How do you think baby pigs are born, you muppet?"

"I, uh..."

"Anyway, they collected all the pig toss in a bucket."

Porter waited for the end of the story, but it didn't come.

"And?" he asked.

Clare looked at Porter's tea again.

"Nothing, you just made me think of it. Spalding's looking for you."

"Oh, right, sir," Porter said. He walked to the door, only for Milo to call out.

"You don't want your tea?"

"Not now," he said, squeezing past Clare. "Not sure I ever want to drink tea again. Thanks for that, sir."

"You're welcome."

Porter made his way back into the bullpen, but Spalding was nowhere to be found. He tried the Investigation Room, seeing her sitting at one of the tables, a laptop open in front of her. She didn't look up.

"How's it going?" he asked, pulling up a chair. "Boss said you might have something."

"I do," she said. "I was—"

"Alison, you don't think my tea looks like a bucket of pig toss, do you?"

Spalding looked up, her eyebrows reaching for the sky. She opened her mouth to answer, then must have thought better of it. Porter spluttered out a sigh.

"Peter Porter's Perfect Puddings isn't bloody happening then, is it?"

"What, sir?"

"Nothing, carry on."

"Two things," she said. "The body we found at the stables is on Franklin's table. She's working on it as we speak. First impression is that Kevin Clegg sustained a blow to the head, probably a sledgehammer."

"Ouch."

"It demolished his face but didn't kill him outright.

Based on what Hay found in the well, he was thrown in afterwards and bled out down there."

"Fuck," said Porter, trying not to imagine it. "What's the other thing?"

"I was looking into Alex Rimple, sir," she said. "Rimple owns the glasses shop in town, Specs, but there's no connection at all between Rimple and the warehouse we raided today. That's owned by a shell corporation that runs out of Bermuda, if you can believe it."

"What?"

"It gets weirder, sir," Spalding went on. "I checked the records. Alex Rimple isn't a man, it's a woman. Alex is short for Alexina."

"*What?*" said Porter. "So who did Kett speak to?"

Before Spalding could answer, the Incident Room door crashed open and the Superintendent flew in. He looked wild. More than that, he looked *scared*.

"Sir?" said Porter.

"Savage is under attack," Clare said, a bullet of adrenaline hitting Porter in the gut. "She was driving Aggie to the hospital and somebody tried to run her off the road."

"She okay?" Porter said, moving to the door. "Where is she?"

Clare was jogging back to the bullpen, and Porter followed.

"I don't know," said the Super. "I've dispatched tactical, but it's a fucking mess."

"I'll go, sir," said Porter.

Clare spun around, his jabbing finger almost taking Porter's eye out.

"No, you won't. I need you here. I need you on the case. I want to know who these tossers are, all of them. Nobody does this to one of our own."

Clare ran for the doors, uniformed PCs chasing after him. The silence they left behind was almost overwhelming.

"Shit," Porter said, pulling out his phone. He called Savage, counting nine rings before it went to voicemail. He tried Kett instead, but the DCI wasn't answering. Neither was Duke.

"She'll be okay," said Spalding, who stood in the open door that led to the Incident Room. "It's Kate."

"Who the fuck are these people?" Porter said. "They're like rats in the woodwork. You take one out, another two appear."

He tried Savage again, forcing himself not to hurl his phone into the wall when she didn't answer.

"Fuck!"

"The boss is right, sir," said Spalding. "We're not going to do any good out there. We need to find—"

She stopped as a claxon ripped through the quiet room, the station's fire alarm blaring like an air-raid siren. Porter's adrenaline spiked again, his nervous system shredded.

"What now?" he said.

"I'll check it out," said Spalding, but Porter waved her back.

"Keep working the case, Alison, I'll go see what's happening."

He ran into the corridor. The alarm was louder here, a handful of coppers making their way towards the exit.

"Drill?" he shouted, answered only by shrugged shoulders.

"Fuck's sake."

He pushed past them, following the maze of HQ towards the lobby. Shelley the receptionist stood by the main doors, ushering police and civilians into the car park.

"What's going on?" Porter asked, yelling over the alarm. "Drill?"

"What's your nose telling you?" said Shelley.

Porter sniffed, the acrid scent of smoke crawling into his sinuses.

"Shit," he said. "Where?"

Shelley shrugged.

Porter doubled back, pushing against the current of people. He called Spalding as he went.

"Sir?" she answered.

"Fire's real, Alison. I'd get out until they work out where it is."

He hung up before she could reply, trying Kett again. This time, the DCI answered, his voice thin.

"Pete? You on your way?"

"No, sir," said Porter. "Clare told me to stay here. Kate okay?"

"They're looking for her now," he said, out of breath, like he was running. "Somebody came at them with a bus."

"A bus?" said Porter.

"What's going on?" Kett went on. "Is that the fire alarm?"

"Yeah. No idea where, but there's smoke."

More of it now, hanging in the air like gauze. Porter put his sleeve to his face, coughing.

"Pete, where are you?" said Kett.

"Heading to the bullpen, sir," he said. "Spalding's still in there."

"This isn't a coincidence," said Kett. "This is them, Pete."

"The fire?" said Porter, coughing again. "There's no way, sir. Who would set fire to a police station, you'd have to be out of your mind."

"You'd have to be out of your mind to drive a bus into a convoy of police cars," Kett said. "These people are insane, Pete. They're desperate. They knew we'd rescued Aggie Clegg and they were trying to get her back. They..."

Kett fell quiet.

"Shit, Pete. They were trying to get Aggie back, what if..."

"What if they're trying to get the other kids as well?" Porter finished for him. "Freya and Dmitri?"

"If the fire's real, they'll be taken out of their cells, evacuated like everyone else. Easy pickings."

Porter set off again, heading for the holding cells.

"Be careful, Pete," said Kett. "These guys aren't messing about."

Porter didn't answer, shouldering his way through the double doors. The hallways were empty, this side of HQ deserted. The smoke was thick enough to drown in here, Porter struggling for breath. He kept moving, his eyes streaming as he opened the last set of doors and staggered into holding.

The desk sergeant lay on the floor, a crown of blood circling his head.

Further down, almost erased by the smoke, a man was unlocking one of the cells. Porter wasn't sure, because of the blaring alarm, but he thought he could hear screams from inside.

"Hey!" he yelled, coughing the word out. "Get away from there."

The man turned. He was wearing a crimson mask with slits for eyes, two stubby horns curving over his head. He stared at Porter for a second, then went back to his work.

"I said stop," Porter shouted, running at him. As he cleared the desk he saw another uniformed copper on the ground, a third further down. Neither was moving. "Get away from there."

The man unlocked the cell and wrenched open the door, releasing a wave of screams from inside. He dropped the key, reached into his pocket.

Pulled out a knife.

Porter skidded to a halt, ten yards away.

"Put that down, now," he said, struggling for air. "You're in a fucking police station, mate, you're surrounded. Where are you going to go?"

The man didn't answer, staring at Porter through the holes in his mask.

"Put it down, get on the floor," Porter told him. "You're on your own, you're outnumbered, and there's no way out of here."

Even past the mask, Porter could see the smile in the man's eyes. He was grinning at him.

Not *at* him, he realised, too late.

Grinning *past* him.

He turned, seeing a second man standing right behind him. He, too, was wearing a devil's mask. But he didn't hold a knife in his hands.

He held a shotgun.

Porter lifted the phone, hearing Kett's voice.

"Two men," he said. "Horned masks, one has a gun. Tell Bobby I—"

The man lifted the gun. An explosion ripped the world in two.

And there was only darkness.

CHAPTER THIRTY-NINE

"PETE? PETE!"

Kett screamed Porter's name into the phone, his free hand locked in his hair. He'd been running up the road towards the park but he'd stopped when Porter had spoken —"*Tell Bobby I...*"—doubling up with the horror of it.

Because he thought he'd heard a gunshot too.

"Pete?"

Somebody breathed into the line, a rattling wheeze that could barely be heard over the howl of the fire alarm.

"Pete? Talk to me."

Another breath, then a voice—just a whisper.

"Pete's gone," it said. "Stop looking for us."

"Who is this?" said Kett. "I swear to God, if you've hurt him, you—"

"Leave us alone, and we'll kill one of them. Come looking for us, they all die."

"What? Who—"

The line went dead.

Kett stood straight, clenching the phone hard enough to break it. The street was crawling with police cars and officers on foot, a helicopter cleaving through the sky right overhead. He stepped into the road, hailing one of the IRVs. It pulled over, the constable winding down the window.

"I need to get back to HQ," he said. "Now."

"Then get in, sir," the woman said, leaning over to open the passenger side. He dropped in, the car taking off before he could close the door. His phone was ringing, Clare's name on the screen.

"Sir, where are you?" Kett said as he answered. "Something's happened at the station."

"I'm heading back now," said Clare.

"Porter's in trouble, sir," he said, his stomach turning in loops as the car accelerated. "I think the bus was a distraction, they didn't care about Aggie, they just wanted as many of us out of the station as possible."

The car skidded through a junction, gunning it down the ring road.

"They're going for the other two kids we found, sir. Porter said there were two men in holding, one of them has a gun. Pete's down, sir."

The emotion hit him like a fist, the tears gathering in his eyes.

"I've got officers heading to holding now," said Clare, his voice full of rage. "Tactical's on its way back. We'll get them."

"How could we be so fucking *stupid*?" Kett said. "These guys are monsters, they're..."

He fell quiet, something nagging at the back of his head. Once again he saw Evie running down the landing, screaming at him to help her.

She's a monster! Daddy, save me!

"Where are you, Kett?" Clare said, knocking the thought away.

"On my way, sir," he said. "Twenty minutes."

"Make it quicker."

The call ended.

"Hurry," he said to the constable.

"What happened, sir?" she asked, flooring it as the traffic parted in front of them.

He didn't know, so he didn't reply. He called Porter instead, but it went straight to his voicemail. Then he tried Savage.

"Bloody hell, sir," she said when she'd answered. "That was close."

"You're okay?" he asked.

"I'm in pieces, sir," she said, and he could hear it in her voice. "But we're good, me and Aggie. They've checked the bus, no sign of the driver. You here?"

"I'm on my way back to HQ," he said. "They hit it. They were going for the kids. Porter's..."

"He's what, sir?" said Savage.

"I don't know," he said. "They started a fire, cleared out the building. They were armed, Kate. Two of them. They knew exactly what they were doing."

"That's impossible," she said. "They can't..."

Another call was coming through, this one Spalding.

"I've got to go, Kate," he said.

He ended the call, answering Spalding's.

"Alison? You alright? You found Pete?"

"He's in holding, sir," said Spalding. "I can't get in, the whole place is up in flames. Fire service are here, they're working on it, but..."

Don't say it, thought Kett. *Don't you dare say it.*

"Did you see the kids?" he said. "Freya and Dmitri. It sounded like the men were getting them out of their cell."

"It's chaos here, sir," said Spalding. "We've got

Uniforms on the main gate and the back road but there are people everywhere."

"Search the car park," he said. "Every car, even ours. Check the neighbouring houses. Find them."

"Sir," she said, hanging up.

"Fuck," Kett growled, rubbing his face.

They were on the dual carriageway now, the constable doing ninety up the fast lane. More IRVs followed, a convoy that wouldn't do the least bit of good.

The kids were gone. Kett knew that much. The plan had been meticulous, they would have known exactly where they were taking their hostages once they were out of their cells. They'd have vanished in seconds.

It was too late for Freya and Dmitri.

It was too late for Porter, too.

The car slowed, pulling into the left-hand lane, then thumping onto the exit road. The constable took the roundabout so fast that Kett's head rang off the window. When they pulled out of the underpass he saw HQ ahead. A pillar of smoke rose into the summer sky. He could smell it from here.

"Pull over," he said.

There was nowhere to go, the gates jammed with police cars. The constable slowed to a halt and he got out, ignoring the broken glass in his spine as he limped through the crowd. He ran towards the far side of the building, choking on the smoke-drenched air.

Two fire engines blocked the road, their hoses filling the sky with rainbows. There was no fire anymore, but smoke roiled from the broken windows like an upturned waterfall. The burned-out shell of a car sat on the pavement.

Superintendent Clare stood next to the fire chief, both watching with grim eyes.

"Hey!" Kett called out as he ran over. "You found him?"

"They're inside now," said Clare, moving to intercept Kett before he could run past. He planted a big hand on Kett's chest. "They'll find him."

"What the fuck happened?" said Kett.

"The car," said the fire chief. "They turned it into a petrol bomb. Parked it next to the door, set fire to it. Made their move as the building was being evacuated."

"Two of them," said Clare. "Probably another waiting outside in a second vehicle. Spalding's reviewing the security footage."

Kett didn't think it would help. The camera outside the door had melted, and the ones inside would have been blinded by the smoke.

"It was a professional strike," said Clare, shaking his head. "I haven't seen anything like this for years, not since I was in the NCA and we saw organised crime outfits conducting military raids."

"It doesn't make any sense, sir," said Kett. "It's two kids, why are they so important?"

He didn't get a chance to answer. There was a shout from inside the building, and a second later two firefighters emerged from the door, encrusted with smoke and soot. They were holding a third man between them, his feet dragging on the ground.

"Little help," one of the firefighters yelled.

Kett ran forward, Clare by his side. They were beaten to it by another couple of firefighters, who laid the man on the ground at their feet.

"He's alive," said one of the men who'd got him out, and Kett had time to feel a sliver of relief before he noticed that the man was wearing a uniform, sergeant's stripes on his sleeve. "There's another couple in there, they didn't make it."

No.

Kett ran for the door, ignoring the firefighters as they told him to stop, ignoring Clare's protests. He pushed into a wall of smoke, his hand over his mouth as he choked his way into the custody suite. The processing area was empty, but there was a puddle of blood on the floor by the desk.

"Hey," came a voice behind him. One of the firefighters had caught up, speaking through his mask. "You can't be here, mate. The smoke'll fuck you up."

Kett ignored him, heading down the corridor towards the cells. The doors were open, the prisoners already evacuated. Another firefighter crouched there, doing CPR on a man who lay on the floor.

"Shit, Pete," said Kett, running towards them.

The firefighter looked up, and even beneath the gleam of light on her visor Kett saw the resignation there. She shook her head.

"No," said Kett.

He skidded down beside the body, only to see that this one, too, was wearing a uniform. The face belonged to a young PC that he'd seen around the station, and the rage ignited inside him.

The desperation, too.

"There's another body?" he said, resting a hand on the dead man's cooling face—just for a moment, before he got back to his feet. The room swayed, not enough air.

"Down there," said the woman, nodding to the corridor that split off to the right.

Kett ducked low, seeing the body right at the end, making it halfway before he saw the uniform he was wearing. He lay on a raft of blood, like he was sailing away on a river of smoke.

He couldn't get any closer, the smoke was too thick. He struggled back, checking the open doors of the cells, his lungs too empty to call Porter's name.

"Go," said the firefighter who'd been doing CPR. She took his arm hard enough to hurt, dragging him towards the door. They passed the second firefighter, who took Kett's other arm. He didn't fight them, letting them guide him out of the door into the hot, fresh summer air.

"You didn't see anyone else in there?" he asked.

She shook her head before running back in.

"Robbie?" said Clare. His eyes were big and wet, a streak of dirt running across his cheek.

"He's not there, sir," said Kett.

"What do you mean he's not there?"

"He's not there," he said again, staring across the car park, trying to make sense of it. "Porter's gone."

CHAPTER FORTY

THEY ASSEMBLED IN THE INCIDENT ROOM, KETT holding the door open for Clare and then Spalding. More coppers followed, the detectives taking the desks, the uniforms standing around the room like wallflowers at a school dance.

The air still smelled of smoke, but nowhere near as bad as it had been in the custody suite on the far side of the building. The air conditioning rumbled as it worked to clear the room. It could have been a fridge in here.

"Anything on the CCTV?" Clare barked as he walked to the front wall. He stood there, framed by case files and blank-faced photographs.

"They arrived in a Nissan Almera, 54 plate," Spalding said, joining him.

She had a laptop under her arm and she opened it, turning it to the room. Kett had to squint to make out what was on the screen.

"Parked it right outside processing, but far enough from the door to let them out. Two men, both wearing black, with horned devil masks on their faces. Watch."

On-screen, one of the men sparked up a lighter, leaning through the open door of the car. It must have been primed because it went up like a paraffin-soaked bonfire, the fire almost too bright to make out what happened next. The men ran through the doors like they were robbing a bank, one of them holding a shotgun. In seconds, the fire had spread to the camera.

Spalding spun the laptop, pressed a couple of keys, then turned it back. The new footage was taken inside the custody suite. The man holding the gun ran right for the processing desk. The sergeant—a man called Murphy—didn't even look up before the butt of the gun smashed into his nose.

"Bastards," said Clare, his expression dark.

The masked man grabbed the sergeant by the scruff of his neck and dragged him over the desk. It was clear Murphy was out cold, but it didn't stop the guy from delivering a powerful kick to his head. Even from halfway across the room, Kett could see the spray of blood that hit the wall.

The man looked at the camera through the slits in his mask, then he jabbed the gun upwards. The screen went dark.

Spalding changed to a different shot, but within a few seconds it had been smashed as well.

"They took them all out," she said. "That's all we've got. The plates on the Almera were switched, it's a dead end. The bus that battered Kate was registered SORN, it was taken from a scrapyard in Taverham this morning."

"There were four people in holding," said Clare. "Two are accounted for. We were keeping Freya and Dmitri there for their own safety, for all the good it did them. Both kids are missing, along with Porter."

"He's missing, sir?" came a voice from the door. Savage

ran into the room, out of breath. She looked exhausted, a nasty cut on her chin. Duke was right behind her, the TV crew nowhere to be seen.

"Yeah," said Kett. "Where's Aggie?"

"She's in the bullpen, sir. There are six uniforms with her, including Flick. Tactical just walked through the door. They're not going to let her out of their sight. What happened to Porter, sir?"

"Pete called me as he was running to the cells," said Kett. "I heard him shouting at somebody, then..."

He had to stop, the words too painful to fit up his throat. Everybody waited.

"He told me there were two men, one armed with a gun. He told me to say goodbye to Bobby for him."

A ripple of panic spread across the room.

"Did you hear a gunshot, sir?" asked Savage.

"I'm not sure," he said. "I heard a bang. It could have been anything."

It could have been Porter dying.

"We don't give up until we know for sure," said Clare, his face gaunt. "They killed two coppers and left their bodies behind. We have to hope that Porter's missing because he's still alive, because they took him with them. Did you hear anything else on the phone, Kett?"

"Yeah, one of them spoke to me, sir," he said.

The Incident Room fell deathly silent.

"It was a low voice. A man's voice. Just a whisper. He said..." He had to close his eyes, to think back into the chaos of the call. "He said Pete was gone, and that we needed to stop looking for them. He said that if we leave them alone, they'll only kill one. If we keep going after them, they all die."

"All?" said Savage.

Kett nodded.

"Why didn't he say both, sir?"

He turned to her, frowning.

"Two people, Freya and Dmitri. If there are two people, you say both, you don't say all. Right?"

"You think Porter's alive?" asked Kett.

"Either that, or they have more victims," said Clare. "Freya, Dmitri and Aggie might be the tip of the iceberg. We know they have more than one location, we don't know who else they have there. We don't fucking know *anything*."

Clare braced both hands on the desk, looking at Spalding, then Savage, then Kett.

"These tossers murdered PCs Yassin and Evans," he said. "They left Murphy for dead. They tried to run Savage off the road, they might have shot Porter. They waltzed into our fucking house and took two children that were under our care. We need to find them, now. Tell me you've got a lead."

Kett looked past Clare to the wall of photos, rubbing his dry lips with smoke-scented fingers as he scanned the display. The exhaustion was almost too much, mixing with the run-off of adrenaline, making him feel like he was standing outside of his own body, like he might just float away.

But this was *Porter*.

"This is a massive operation, sir," said Spalding, stepping up. "We've got five people that we know about. Bianca Caddel, Robert Flack and David Blethyn are accounted for; we've taken them out of the game. Then there are the two that broke in today."

"Six, Sarge," said Savage. "Because somebody tried to run me off the road, and it can't have been the men who came here."

"Six," said Spalding, nodding.

"We know they're planning some kind of ritual," said Kett, studying the pictures of demons that Savage had pinned to the wall. "They've been practicing, rehearsing for God knows how long. They've had Freya and Dmitri for weeks. And we know today's important, right? All three kids have their birthday today. Whoever these guys are, August first has some kind of meaning. It's sacred. Whatever they're doing, it has to happen today."

He checked his watch.

"That gives us twelve hours at most, and I'm guessing it's going to be sooner rather than later."

"Then we need to scour every single contact linked to Caddel, Blethyn and Flack," said Clare. "Work colleagues, relatives. I don't care if they gave somebody a clumsy tug behind the school hall after prom twenty years ago, I want to know the name of every single person they're connected to."

"We worked out the link between Caddel and the two men at the stables, sir," said Spalding. "We'll find them."

She didn't look confident.

"But it's going to take time," she went on. "I was in the process of going through their online activities before the attack. All three of them were part of numerous occult groups on Facebook and Twitter, and that's a problem. There are hundreds of people in these groups. Thousands. It will take weeks to go through them all."

"We don't have weeks, Alison," said Clare. "We barely have hours. Think."

"What else have we found out about Rimple?" asked Kett.

"Rimple's a woman," said Spalding. "She runs the

glasses shop, Specs, but has no link to the warehouse. Whoever you spoke to earlier, it wasn't her."

"That doesn't make any sense," said Kett. "You've spoken to Rimple? The real one?"

Spalding gestured to the room.

"Got interrupted."

"Find her," said Clare. "Find all of them. Pick your prime suspects. I've got every officer ready to go. These arseholes won't be safe anywhere, I promise you that."

Safe.

Kett closed his eyes, perching on the edge of a desk to stop himself from falling over. Once again he saw Evie in his mind's eye, his middle daughter running away from Billie, screaming her head off.

She's a monster! Daddy, save me!

"Kett! Am I boring you?"

Kett snapped his eyes open to see Clare gurning at him, his eyeballs like peeled grapes.

"No, sir," he said. "I..."

Clare was growling, his foot tapping impatiently on the floor like a metronome. It was almost enough to extinguish the flicker of understanding that had ignited inside Kett's head, and he pushed himself off the desk, desperately trying to keep it alight.

"We're assuming everyone is working together, sir," he said. "We've got a group of people obsessed with the occult, showing every sign that they're trying to summon a demon. They're targeting children. Three teens are attacked at the ruins of St Mary's yesterday morning by Bianca Caddel. She kidnaps Aggie, who has a birthday the following day. We know they've been watching Aggie because we found her father dead inside a well, and we know that the date is important because the two other kids we find have the same birthday."

He studied the photos, finding the two men they'd met at the stables.

"We know Bianca is working with Flack and Blethyn," he said. "Because we linked her to the stables. And it fits, because the two kids we find there are in cages, the same kind of cage that Bianca put Aggie in at the warehouse."

He paused, his thoughts scattering.

"Why cages, sir?" asked Savage, helping him out. "Why not a locked room, a car boot? Why not just kill them?"

"We know they can't kill them," said Kett. "Because this is about something more than murder. It's a ritual, a ceremony. They need to do it on the right date, at the right time, and maybe in the right place. You said it yourself, Kate, if you're going to summon a demon, everything has to be perfect. One mistake and the demon kills you instead."

"Wait, demons are real?" said Duke.

"No, but *they* think they're real," said Kett. "Everything we've seen so far makes it clear that whoever these people are, they're believers. This is real to them. This is everything to them."

She's a monster! Daddy, save me!

Why couldn't he get Evie's words out of his head?

"The kids we rescued, they told us Blethyn and Flack never hurt them," he said. "They seemed to think they put them in those cages to protect them."

"Right," said Savage. "Blethyn and the others convinced them the paper seals on their cages would keep demons out."

"They told them that to keep them quiet," Clare said. "They scared them into doing whatever they were told. It's right out of the kidnapper's playbook."

"But what if Caddel and the others *weren't* lying, sir?" Kett went on.

"You're dribbling toss out of your flesh courgette, Kett."

"Out of my *what?*" he said.

"Carry on, sir," said Savage. "What's going through your head?"

"I don't know. I can't think straight. It's something that happened last night, when we were trying to give the kids Calpol."

"What?" said Clare, aghast.

"Evie wanted me to keep her safe, to keep her hidden from her mum, so she didn't have to take her medicine. She wanted me to protect her. What if Caddel and Flack and Blethyn were telling the truth? They know about the ceremony that's going to take place, they know somebody is going to try to kill the kids, they're going to sacrifice them today, on August first. The only way they can stop it from happening..."

It seemed too ludicrous to be true, and he suddenly doubted himself.

"Is by keeping them prisoner," Savage finished. "Until their birthday is over. Keeping them safe, hiding them from the people who are trying to hurt them. Freya said the same thing. They told her it wasn't forever. It's something, sir."

"It's pig toss," said Clare. "A big bucket of pig toss, like Porter's tea. You're saying Bianca and her cronies are the *good guys*? Blethyn bit off his own tongue so he wouldn't have to talk. That isn't something the good guys do."

"But it is, sir," Kett replied, the pinpoint of light inside his head brightening. "These people were willing to do anything to keep the kids safe, right? They literally kidnap them to keep them away from whoever wants to kill them. If they get caught, if they get arrested, if they talk, it puts the kids in danger."

"You're saying Blethyn chewed off his tongue to keep Dmitri and Freya safe?" said Clare, shaking his head. "That would make them as mad as you, Kett. Bianca's bunker was literally crammed with occult paraphernalia. She had books about summoning demons. Same thing at her warehouse, there were pentagrams everywhere. Why would she have all that if she wasn't planning to use it?"

"To be fair, sir," said Savage, "if anyone ever broke into my flat, they'd find a lot of stuff about serial killers."

"What?" said Clare.

"I've pretty much got a library in there, sir. Books, case files, podcasts."

"Because it's your job," said Kett. "It's your job to catch these people. If you want to stop them, you need to know everything about them. Bianca and the others are the same. This is their job, this is their... their purpose. All that matters is keeping the kids out of harm's way."

"I've just thought of something else, sir," said Savage. "The person we spoke to earlier, the one we thought was Alex Rimple, he's obviously part of this. Why else would he lie about who he is? But why would he make it so easy for us to find the warehouse. It doesn't make sense, because he must have known we'd find Aggie there."

Everyone waited as she gathered her thoughts.

"But it wasn't *his* warehouse, it was Bianca's, right?"

Clare turned to her, his face contorting.

"So? They're working together, what does it matter?"

"What if Kett's right, sir," said Savage. "Rimple invited us there. He told us to come, because he *wanted* us to raid the warehouse. Rimple, or whoever it was we spoke to, knew about the place. He knew that if Bianca got hold of one of the kids, she'd take them there to keep them safe."

"So why wouldn't he get her himself?" said Clare. "These camel vaginas shot their way into a police station, Kate, they wouldn't have had any trouble at all breaking into a warehouse and taking Aggie."

"The seals," said Kett.

"Seals?" said Duke, frowning. "I didn't see any seals."

"Not the kind you find in the sea, Aaron," said Savage. "The seals on the floor, the sigils, whatever they are. The pentagrams. It's all part of their belief system. The warehouse was covered in them, it was protected. Even if the bad guys knew where Aggie was being held, they couldn't get to her."

"But magic pentagrams aren't real, are they?" said Duke, who was struggling.

"Aaron, please be quiet," said Kett.

"Not real to us, because we don't believe it," said Savage. "But if you *do* believe it, if every fabric of your being is invested in the occult, in magic and ritual and whatever, then if you enter that building and cross the seal, something bad is going to happen to you."

"Pig toss," muttered Clare.

"It's a religion," said Kett. "You said it yourself, Kate. It's fanatical. They'll die for it."

"And kill for it, sir," said Savage. "The guy who called himself Rimple was never at the warehouse. But he knew if he told us about it, we'd go check it out and find Aggie. He couldn't reach her there, we could. Once we freed Aggie, he could come after her."

"And he did," said Kett.

"Hang on," said Clare. "Aggie had a letterhead with Rimple's company on it. How?"

"Aggie told us she spoke to a man in the shop, about sponsorship," said Savage. "He gave her the letterhead, and the camera. But the number imprinted on the paper was separate. I don't know who we spoke to on the phone, but he played us, spun some story about giving Aggie a time to come back to the shop. But I think we were right before, it was the time he wanted her to get to the ruins. Nine, yesterday morning, and don't be late."

"No," said Clare. "You're talking a load of pig squirt, all of you. How would he know her birthday? How would he have time to plan a kidnapping?"

"That's what I can't get my head around, sir," said Savage. "But I don't think Rimple got the chance to attack them, because they were early. They got there at eight. They wanted to set up for the morning light or whatever. If Bianca knew Aggie was vulnerable, she might have been waiting there for her. She could have snatched her before Rimple even showed up."

"That's a big might, Kate," said Clare, shaking his head. "How would she know she was going there?"

Savage didn't answer.

"That explains why Kevin Clegg's imposter showed up," said Kett, another piece clicking into place. "We couldn't understand why he'd throw himself into the middle of a police investigation if he was behind Aggie's kidnapping, but he had to be there, because he needed to find Aggie. He didn't know what had happened to her. The imposter is probably the same guy we spoke to on the phone."

"He was desperate," said Savage, nodding. "He had to find Aggie, even if it meant risking being caught. Same as the man in the bus, same as the men who attacked us here. If they don't get a victim by today, it's all over."

Clare rubbed his face, deep in thought.

"This is it," said Kett, massaging the base of his spine. "We don't have one group here, we've got two. They're at war with each other. One group is trying to sacrifice a child for whatever sick ritual they've planned, the other is trying to save the kids before they're killed. Forget about accomplices, acquaintances, internet chat friends, anything like that. We're looking for *conflict*, anyone that Bianca and the others have had run-ins or arguments or fights with."

"That's going to be hard, sir," said Spalding. "They've all got clean records, there's nothing..."

She paused, clacking a pen against her teeth.

"Give me a second," she said, running out of the room.

"Did we find any occult groups capable of this?" Kett asked.

"No," said Clare. "But they don't exactly advertise themselves."

"And we didn't get any leads from the soft play?"

"The building was abandoned," said Clare. "Owner's overseas. Whoever set up the altar broke in and did it without permission."

Everybody turned as Spalding ran back into the room. She was holding a sheet of paper.

"It's a bit of a long shot," she said. "But when I was looking into David Blethyn, I found something. He has no criminal record, but back in 2012 he was involved in an altercation, over in Wales."

"What kind of altercation?" said Kett.

"I was about to tell you, sir," she said, giving him a look. "Obviously. He was detained by the Welsh Police after a fight. Witnesses claimed he stabbed a man in the leg."

"And he has no record?" said Clare.

"Because the victim never pressed charges," said Spalding. "In fact, the victim never showed up at all. It happened late at night on a quiet street, the witnesses were drunk, they retracted their statements. No victim, no witnesses, no crime, or at least that's what the CPS decided."

"Hang on," said Kett. "He stabbed somebody in the leg?"

"Allegedly, sir," said Spalding.

"The man posing as Kevin Clegg walked with a limp, a bad one."

"That's a huge leap, Kett," said Clare.

"It's a link, sir, not a leap," he said. "We're pretty sure the imposter is working with the bad guys, and Blethyn's on the other team. What if they had a confrontation back in 2012? Blethyn stabs our imposter."

"The victim wouldn't have reported it, sir," said Savage. "Would he? He wouldn't have risked the exposure."

"Right," said Kett.

It wasn't much to go on, but it was all they had.

"There might be hospital records," he said. "This could be how we ID our imposter. A stab wound in the leg's no joke, especially if you're still limping a decade later. Can we check that far back?"

"We might not need to, sir," said Spalding. She was studying the papers in her hand, her face creased into a frown. "Didn't I see somewhere that Kevin Clegg—the *real* Kevin Clegg—lived in Swansea for a while?"

"He didn't work, either," added Savage. "He was on long-term disability."

"What does that matter?" said Clare. "The real Clegg's been down a hole for three weeks."

"Or so we're assuming," said Kett.

Everyone turned to him.

"Clegg shows up at the ruins, looking for his daughter.

At least, we assume it's him, because he's got ID. He vanishes, and we later find the body of another man in the well at the stable. He's been there for weeks, his face is destroyed. He has ID too, but proper ID—Clegg's driving licence. The photo doesn't look like the man who came to the woods, but it isn't a million miles off."

"So we assume the man in the well is the real Clegg," said Clare. "Which he is."

"Right. But what if he isn't? What if the *imposter* was down the hole, and the man we spoke to really was Aggie's father?"

"You're out of your mind!" said Clare, aghast. "You're just making shit up now."

"And if that's true, sir," said Savage, looking at Kett. "If Kevin Clegg is alive and well and looking for Aggie in the woods, doesn't that mean he's working with the people who are trying to *kill* his daughter?"

"I don't know," said Kett. The thoughts were made of sand, his exhaustion a rising tide. "But I think that's our best shot. Have we looked into Clegg?"

"Only a little," said Spalding. "He was never a suspect."

"Then look deeper. We need to scour Kevin Clegg's history, find anywhere he might be hiding. There's a chance that if we find him, we find Aggie."

"And we find Porter too," said Clare with a nod.

If it's not too late, thought Kett.

CHAPTER FORTY-ONE

THE CITY WAS A BLAST FURNACE, THE MIDDAY SUN SO bright that the streets could have been on fire. Tempers burned just as fiercely, two men fighting at the end of Mountergate as Savage steered the Audi around the corner. The men stopped when they saw the two IRVs that followed, throwing their arms around each other's shoulders like old friends and grinning drunkenly until the convoy had passed.

"It's in that block, sir," said Savage, pulling the car up to the kerb and nodding to the building on the left.

"We've searched it already, right?" Kett asked, opening the door and climbing out, greeted by a fist of hot air. Savage and Duke joined him on the pavement.

"Uniforms did, yeah. But they were looking for Aggie, I don't know how thorough they were."

He nodded, looking down the street to where the two drunk men were once again throwing clumsy haymakers at each other.

"This bloody heat," he said, shouting to the constables

who were getting out of the IRV. "Can you go and stop that?"

Two of them ran off, the other two following Kett as he made his way to the block of flats that dominated this side of the road. It was barely standing, held together by ivy and graffiti, half the windows blinded by plyboard. The door was boarded too, daubed with a crude illustration that Kett couldn't quite figure out.

"Is that a dick?" said Duke, tilting his head.

"Rocket ship," said Savage.

The door had a card reader, but when Kett gave the handle a tug it opened anyway. He let Duke go first, the big PC entering the cramped lobby. There were no light switches and the sensor was broken, the dark thick enough to drown in until Savage pulled out her torch. She pointed the shaft of weak light towards the lift.

"We going to risk it, sir?"

"No chance," he said. "Where are the stairs?"

They found them behind a stack of old mattresses in the corner of the lobby, the smell of piss and shit so bad that Duke started to gag. The PC kicked open the door, retching as he started up the steps.

"Sorry, *urg*, sir," he said. "It's so... *hrgn*, bad."

"He's not good with smells, sir," Savage explained.

"That makes two of us."

They reached the third floor, Duke going first, then Savage. Kett held the door open for the two PCs who'd followed them up.

"Be alert," he told them. "These guys are dangerous."

When they reached Kevin Clegg's flat, though, the police tape over the door was undisturbed. Savage peeled it away, using the locksmith's key to open the temporary door that had been installed after the last one had been kicked down.

The flat that greeted them was so small that Kett felt instantly claustrophobic, as if the walls were shrinking around him. There wasn't even a hallway, just a nine-foot square space that housed a sink, a cooker, a sofa and a TV. There were no curtains, just a dirty sheet thrown over the pole. Fingers of light probed through it, searching for something amongst the littered vodka bottles and overflowing ashtrays.

Kett crossed the room in three strides, his boots crunching on broken glass. He grabbed the sheet and pulled it away, letting the day flood in. If anything, the light made the room seem even smaller.

"Makes my place look like a palace," said Savage, pocketing her torch.

"Turn it over," said Kett. "Every corner, every crevice."

But his heart was sinking, because there wasn't enough room here to hide anything.

He left Savage and Duke in the living space, making his way through one of two other doors to find himself in the bedroom. It was smaller than a prison cell, and just as stark. A single bed took up three-quarters of the space, nothing beneath it but dust. The wardrobe on the opposite wall nearly collapsed when Kett opened the door. He rifled through a pile of musty clothes, finding a collection of damp, dog-eared horror novels and yet more empty bottles.

He dropped onto his hands and knees to look under the bed, greeted by a wave of damp air so foul that he felt the acid climb his throat.

"Nope," he said. "Nope, nope, nope."

"Got something, sir?" asked Savage from the door.

"Got the distinct feeling I want a new job," he replied,

still staring into the darkness under the bed. "Smells like something died down here."

He pulled out his torch and aimed it beneath the frame. The floor was empty, the walls black with mould.

"Can't see anything," he said, getting back to his feet. "Help me flip the mattress, will you?"

Savage, already gloved up, pulled the sheets off the bed. She took one end and Kett took the other, hauling the heavy mattress onto its back. Spores filled the air, burrowing into his lungs, seeding there. He coughed hard, one arm over his mouth, his eyes watering.

It had been worth it, though. There was a hole in the bottom of the mattress, maybe twelve inches wide and neat enough that it could only have been made by a knife. The stench of death was even worse.

"I'm not putting my hand in there," he said.

"Me neither, sir," said Savage.

They turned to the door together.

"Duke," said Kett. "We need you."

The PC shuffled in, his nose wrinkling. He looked past Kett and Savage to the bed, then shook his head.

"No way, sir."

"We play rock, paper, scissors for it," said Kett.

"But I always lose!" said Duke.

"It's literally chance," said Savage. "You can't always lose."

Duke groaned. Kett counted down, and on three they all thrust a hand out. Duke and Savage both had a rock.

Kett's was scissors.

"I didn't lose!" Duke said, beaming.

"Sorry mate," said Kett. "Not scissors, it's a... an angle grinder. Grinder beats rock."

Duke's face fell.

"I don't make the rules, Aaron, sorry."

Duke muttered darkly as he approached the bed. He peeled open the gap in the mattress with one gloved hand, extending the other through the gap.

"Careful," said Kett. "Could be anything in there."

"Could be a blade," said Savage.

"Or a needle," Kett added.

"Or a mousetrap."

"Or a mouse."

Duke glared at them.

"Could be a body," said Savage.

Duke had found something, because he tugged his hand free. He held onto it long enough for Kett to see the glistening red skin, the lumps of sinew, the covering of green fur, then he tossed it onto the mattress with a squeak.

"What the hell is that?" said Kett, leaning in.

It had been meat once upon a time, of that much he was certain. It looked like something that had been bought at a butcher shop, a large bone running through the middle of it, the flesh rotted to mulch. Somebody had wrapped it in a blanket of twigs and leaves, maybe conifer, binding the bundle in twine to keep it all together. The stench of it was unbearable, Kett's throat closing up so tight he could barely breathe. Duke was gagging like he was choking on a grape.

"That it?" Kett asked.

The big PC shook his head, tears rolling down his cheeks as he continued to retch. As reluctantly as a man walking to the gallows, he pushed his hand into the hole again. Kett held his breath as he watched Duke wrestle a book from inside. He dropped it onto the floor before running from the room.

Kett bent down to get a better look.

Not a book, he realised, a photo album.

Savage crouched next to him, using a finger to delicately open the cover. The pages were spotted with mould and encrusted with dust, and they carried the stench of whatever the album had been hidden with. The photograph on the first page had been mutilated, just a ribbon of paper around an enormous hole. The pictures on the following pages had met the same fate, the subject of each one removed, just the backgrounds remaining.

"Weird," said Savage. "But we've seen these before, sir."

Kett nodded.

"I was thinking the same thing," he said. "At the soft play, right? We found photos of a woman on the altar, the same twigs and leaves, the same rotting meat. We never ID'd her, did we?"

"No, sir. They'd been drawn on, and cut up, the eyes scratched out. It was impossible to see who it was. You think it's Kevin Clegg's wife? Aggie's mum?"

"Makes sense," said Kett. "She died, right?"

"Yes, sir, a long time ago, I think. Aggie was young, I don't remember how old."

"We don't know anything else about her?"

Savage shook her head.

"Can you look into it for me?" said Kett. "Because this is weird. Kevin Clegg lives here, nothing in his apartment but an album of mutilated photos of his dead wife, and *that*."

He nodded at the trophy of meat and ribbon.

"This is our killer. It has to be. He's trying to do something, some kind of ritual related to his wife. I think he needs Aggie for it, and that's why he was in the woods looking for her."

Savage was only half listening to him, her phone to her ear.

"Do you think he's trying to..." she started. "Oh, hey

Sarge, it's Kate. Did we ever learn anything about Aggie Clegg's mum?"

She waited, tapping her toe on the floor.

"Yeah, if you could, thank you."

She kept the phone to her ear.

"She's going to look, sir. Do you think Clegg's trying to make contact with her somehow? His wife. All the demonology stuff we've found, it was about asking demons for help to do something. Fame, fortune, that kind of stuff. But there were other things too. Maybe Clegg's trying to speak with his wife somehow. I found a couple of demons in the grimoires who could do that. They could open a window to the other side and let you communicate with a loved one."

"What?" said Duke. He was standing in the door, wiping his mouth with his sleeve. "For real?"

"No, Aaron, it's not real," said Savage. "We talked about this."

"But it's real to Clegg," said Kett. "He lost his wife years ago. If he's involved in this it means he's been studying the occult for a while. So maybe you're right, he thinks he's found a way to speak with her again or..."

He looked at the album of photographs, at the images of his wife that had been removed, defaced and left on the altar inside the soft play.

"Or bring her back," he finished. "Maybe that's what he's trying to do. That's a bigger job, right? It's not just twigs and candles and animal blood. If you want to bring somebody back from the dead, it's going to take something extreme."

"Like a sacrifice," said Savage, nodding.

"It's personal," said Kett. "That's why he was so

desperate to get hold of the kids. Today's his one shot at bringing his wife back. Nothing else matters."

"But why was he so desperate to take Aggie, sir?" asked Savage. "Surely he wouldn't hurt his own child."

"Clegg and Aggie aren't close," said Kett. "They barely saw each other, it's been that way for years. Clegg's insane. Maybe he doesn't care if Aggie dies, if it means he gets to see his wife again. Aggie's safe, right?"

"Yeah," said Savage. "She's in HQ, there are a hundred coppers around her, she... Oh, hi, Sarge, sorry."

Kett could hear Spalding's voice on the other end of the line.

"Shit," said Savage. "You're... shit, *really*?"

She dropped the phone to her side, locking eyes with Kett.

"Tracey Clegg died eighteen years ago, sir, during childbirth. Aggie never knew her mum."

"Hang on," said Kett. "You're saying she died *today*? What time?"

"Just after seven in the evening, sir."

"That's why he needs the kids," said Kett. "That's why the date matters to him. He's going to sacrifice them to bring her back."

He clasped his hands in his hair.

"Where did she die, Kate?"

"In the hospital, sir. Maternity department. But surely he's not going to try anything there?"

"If he's desperate enough to attack a police station, then he's desperate enough to do anything."

He checked his watch.

"We've got nothing else to go on, and we've got less than two hours to find him. Let's move."

CHAPTER FORTY-TWO

The Norfolk and Norwich University Hospital was mobbed, the crowds heat-punched and hot-tempered. Savage pulled the IRV to the kerb outside the main building, the overworked air con blowing little more than warm dust. There were two police cars already there, four PCs huddled in the sparse shade of the bus shelter. They stood to attention as Kett climbed out of the car.

"Anything?" he called.

"No sign of Clegg, sir," returned one. "Or any, like, witches or anything."

He glanced to the sky as if he might see them arriving on broomsticks.

"Spread out," Kett told them. "We know Clegg's wife died here eighteen years ago at just after seven, up in maternity. This is personal to him, so he might come back. He'll have one or two kids with him, maybe DI Porter too. Look in cars, in cupboards, look everywhere."

He set off without waiting for a reply, running through the blistering air to the main doors. Savage and Duke followed, Duke still looking a little green around the gills. The lobby was packed, the heat pushing everyone to breaking point. Two people were arguing with the woman behind the desk, more shouts spilling out of the waiting area.

Kett didn't stop to help, following the wide corridor around to the stairs and taking them two at a time until they'd reached the maternity ward. He flashed his warrant card, and a sister buzzed them through the door, holding up a hand to stop them.

"It's a hot day, and there are a lot of very angry babies and even angrier mums," she said. "What do you want?"

"Have you seen a man in his forties, no hair, big beard, big nose, walks with a limp?" said Kett.

"You got a photo?"

"No. But you'd remember him. Intimidating, lots of tattoos. He might have been here alone, or with a teenage girl and boy."

The sister looked unimpressed. She held out both her arms, gesturing to the world.

"Man, kids, no photo. You want me to work miracles? I can barely remember my own name today."

"Then do you mind if we look around?"

"She can," the woman replied, nodding to Savage. "You two look like bulls in a pottery shop. You can wait outside."

Savage headed into the ward. Kett doubled back, Duke by his side.

"Aaron, stay close, and stay sharp. If you see Clegg, or anyone that looks anything like him, call me."

"Where are you going, sir?"

Kett got his bearings, heading down the corridor.

"I'm going to get some answers," he shouted.

He ran back to the car park, opening the boot of the IRV and retrieving the totem of meat and ribbons that they'd removed from Clegg's flat. It had been sealed in a transparent evidence bag—three, in fact—but the smell still seeped through, catching in the back of his throat.

He took the stairs to the top floor, finding the ward where Bianca Caddel was being held. An older constable sat on a chair outside her room, reading the newspaper. He folded it and laid it on his lap as Kett jogged up, running a hand over his grey stubble.

"Everything okay, sir?" he asked, studying the sweat that rolled down Kett's face.

"Bianca in there?"

"She is. Still sedated and restrained. The Super told me to call as soon as she woke up, which hasn't happened yet."

"Wait out here," Kett told him.

He pushed through the door, closing it behind him. Bianca was a hulking shape on the solitary bed, her breaths wet and ragged. The curtains had been pulled, the lights switched off—as if she had been left in a mortuary, not a ward.

Kett walked to the window, tugging on the stubborn curtains until they opened. The light seemed reluctant to enter, probing Bianca softly, afraid she might jump up and throttle it.

"Hey," Kett said, walking to the bed.

Bianca had been hooked up to a heart monitor, her pulse fast but steady. A thick rubber strip had been buckled to her mouth, a depressor securing her tongue. Both of her hands had been cuffed to the sides of the bed, and he saw more restraints on her legs beneath the thin blanket.

Kett clicked his fingers in front of her face.

"Hey, Bianca, wake up."

She didn't even stir, the mask turning every breath into a desperate, grasping snort. He used his free hand to give her a gentle slap on the cheek.

"I said wake the fuck up, Bianca."

He hit her again, harder. The sound of it must have carried because the constable appeared in the window of the door. Kett glared at him until he scurried away.

"Bianca, wake up."

He slapped her a third time, and it was like he'd used a defibrillator. She sat up as far as the cuffs would let her, the force of it nearly pulling the metal railings off the bed. She unleashed a groan that became a hacking cough as she choked on her own spit. Her eyes were so wide it looked as if the lids had been peeled away, broken capillaries turning them into devil's eyes. They roved madly for a moment before landing on Kett.

She snapped her arms up again, but this time he was pretty sure she was trying to grab him. He stepped back, the bed rocking as she fought against her restraints. She wouldn't listen to reason, he knew, so he held up the bag of meat instead.

It took her a moment to see it, but when she did, she fell deathly still. Her eyes didn't shift from the bag he held in his hand, full now not of anger, but of fear.

"You know what this is?" he asked.

She couldn't have answered him even if she'd wanted to.

"Nod if I'm right," he said.

She swallowed noisily, then nodded.

"It's dangerous, isn't it?" he asked.

A long pause, then another nod.

"Did you make it?"

She shook her head.

"But you know who did?"

Bianca finally managed to look away from the bag. She stared at Kett instead. He wasn't sure, but it looked like she was trembling.

"If I take off that mask, are you going to do something stupid?"

No response. He stepped closer, lifting the totem over the bed. The meat shifted inside, brown juices pooling. Bianca's body jolted again.

"I couldn't care less if you bite off your own tongue, Bianca," he told her, leaning closer. "Except I need you to be able to talk. I need to know what the fuck is going on. Because I don't think you're the bad guy in all this. I think that somewhere in that head of yours, you think you're doing the right thing."

Still nothing.

"You took those kids because you wanted to keep them safe. Right?"

No reply, until Kett lifted the bag of meat closer to Bianca's face. She nodded furiously.

"I don't think you wanted to hurt them. I think it's the opposite of that. You knew they were being targeted, and you wanted to keep them out of harm's way. Dmitri, Freya, Aggie, and all the others. You wanted to keep them away from whoever was looking for them."

Bianca's eyes swam out of focus. Her head collapsed onto the pillow, her breaths gasping as she fought to pull air through the mask, her heart rate increasing. Kett clicked his fingers until she came back.

"I can take it off," he said. "The mask. But listen to me, Bianca. Listen closely. I know you believe in all this, the demons, the rituals. You know it's real. Maybe you're right, I don't know anymore. I don't know *anything* anymore, not after this. I'm going to take your mask off now. I'm going to ask you some questions. If you so much as clack your teeth together, I'm going to take this thing, whatever the fuck it is—"

He held the bag up to her face, the smell of it filling the room.

"I'm going to make sure it goes everywhere with you. I'm going to make sure it follows you to every prison cell, every secure ward, and when you shuffle off this mortal coil, I'm going to make sure you're buried with it, is that clear?"

Bianca's eyes looked like blisters in her sweat-streaked face, ready to burst. She nodded again, and kept nodding, right up until he reached up to unfasten the mask. He popped the clasps and pulled it free, throwing it to the floor. The woman heaved in a spit-drenched breath, retching hard. The machine by the side of her bed was going wild.

"Bianca," said Kett, clicking his fingers again until she recovered. The stench of rotting flesh and the woman's unwashed body was overpowering, no oxygen in the room. "I need you to tell me who you were keeping the kids safe from. I need to know where I can find them. And I need to know right now."

Bianca tugged her hands, the cuffs snapping against the railings.

"Don't," he said, and this time he rested the totem of meat on her chest.

She recoiled as much as she could, her eyes rolling up like she was close to fitting. She made a gargling sound that was more animal than human, one that slowly morphed into a word.

"No, no, no, no."

Kett lifted the bag, pulling it away from her.

"That was your last warning," he said. "Talk."

"You have no idea," she said, her voice low. "You have no idea what you're dealing with."

"Names," he told her. "Kevin Clegg, right?"

Bianca spat out a laugh, her eyes still swivelling in their sockets.

"He's dead," she said. "He can't hurt anyone, and nobody is bringing him back."

"Clegg's alive. You killed the wrong man."

Bianca stared at him for a moment, her throat gulping. It had been a guess, but the look on her face made it clear he'd got it right.

"Clegg knew you were hunting him, that you were going to try to stop him. He must have hired somebody to be a decoy, a lookalike. We found the body of the man you killed, at the stable. It's not Clegg."

"Morail," said Bianca, the fury almost visible inside her. "He passed right in front of us. Invisible."

"This has nothing to do with demons," he said, and Bianca spat out a laugh.

"You're fucked, you know that, right?" she said. "That thing in your hand, it's going to drag you to hell. It's going to drag all of you to hell."

"Why?" said Kett.

"It's an icon," she said. "A demonic totem. I won't speak *his* name, but that is *his* sigil, created by his servant. Flesh wrapped in forest, death bound in life. It weakens the barriers between this life and the other world, slowly but surely."

She spoke like a fire and brimstone preacher, her voice a growl.

"Left with the dead, it calls them back. They cannot resist it. Left with the living, it pushes them into the dirt and the fire, it sends them to the other place. You think you know pain? Suffering? It's a joke compared to what they have in store for you. He knows your name now, Robert Kett, and he will torture you for an eternity."

"You and me both," said Kett, losing patience. "The demon? Andramalech, right?"

Bianca struggled against her restraints, her mouth open in a silent scream.

"But you didn't call him. You didn't summon this thing, did you? You're trying to keep the kids away from him. We're on the same side, Bianca. All we want to do is keep them safe."

"You can't keep them safe," she spat. "Only we know how to hide them, how to blind the eyes of the other side. You found us, and through you, *he* found *them*. There is no saving them now. They, too, will rot in the pit of hell."

"There's still time," said Kett. "It's not over. We think Kevin Clegg wants to sacrifice the children to bring his wife back from the dead. We think he's going to do it today, at the exact time his wife died eighteen years ago. Where is he, Bianca? Where's he going to do it?"

The door to the room crashed open, and a nurse ran in. The old PC was right behind her, his face creased with worry.

"What's going on in here?" the nurse asked. "What are you doing?"

"Where are they, Bianca?" Kett said, ignoring the question.

"You need to go," said the nurse, moving around the bed.

Kett lifted the totem, hoping to scare Bianca into talking again. It was the nurse who hesitated, though, taking a couple of steps back with her hand to her mouth.

"What is that?" she said. "What have you done?"

"Where?" Kett said again, his own voice close to demonic. He gave the bag a shake. "I swear to God, I'll drop it into your coffin."

Bianca fell still, closing her eyes. After a few moments, her breath settled so much that Kett thought she was going to sleep.

"I don't know," she said, just a whisper. "But you're right. It will happen today. The children we were looking after, they were born on the same day and at the same hour that the woman died. The same with her own daughter. As she died, they were granted life, and as they die, she will be reborn. But it won't be her. Demons do not return the dead, they only give back a shadow of what was taken. A worm-bag. It's a trick, nothing more. The children will die, only sorrow will be birthed. Kevin Clegg's soul will be forever damned, but so will they."

She broke into tears, her face wretched.

"So will they. So will they."

"What?" said the nurse, her hand still clamped to her mouth.

"I have studied the other side all my life," said Bianca. "Not to call them, not to serve them, but to *stop* them from being summoned. We are the guardians who seal the gates, who guard the towers. We know everything they do, but we use it to keep the worlds apart, not to bring them together."

She's mad, Kett thought, seeing the way her eyes still rolled beneath the closed lids, the way her foam-flecked lips worked silent words between the ones she spoke.

"If you know everything they do, then you know where he is," said Kett. "Think. If you were Clegg, if you wanted to bring back your wife, if you wanted to make a sacrifice to Andramalech, where would you do it?"

"Somewhere with power," she said. "A holy place where the living and the dead are already in communion."

"A church?" said Kett. "The ruins of St Mary's, where you took Aggie?"

She shook her head.

"Here?" said Kett. "A hospital. Life and death, hand in hand, right?"

"This place isn't strong enough," she said. "Resurrection needs to rip a hole in our world, so you find the place where the fabric is stretched thin already."

"You're going to need to be more specific, Bianca," said Kett, the impatience gnawing at him. "Tell me where."

"Look to the lines," she said.

"You really need to stop," said the nurse, finding her courage. "Please."

"The lines?" Kett said.

Bianca nodded.

"Sir," said the PC by the door. "I think they need us to leave."

"I'll leave when I'm finished," he shot back. "You know they took one of our own, right?"

The constable reeled like he'd been struck. Kett wiped his face. He didn't think he was getting much more from Bianca anyway. She lay there with her eyes closed, her body vibrating, her teeth chattering.

"Fine," he said. "I'm going. But put that mask back on her, and watch your fingers. She bites."

He walked to the door, only to stop when he heard Bianca speak again.

"Clegg is not the one you're looking for, Robert," she said quietly. "A man like him doesn't know how to open the gates."

"Yeah?" he said. "Then who does?"

"I don't know," she said. "But I meant it, what I said earlier."

"Meant what?"

"It's too late for you. They know your name, the creatures on the other side, they're screaming it now. Can't you hear them?"

She finally peeled her eyes open again, staring at him.

"You're all going to hell."

CHAPTER FORTY-THREE

It was safe to say he was rattled by the time he walked out of the ward and back into the corridor. Bianca's words echoed around his skull like a chant—*you're all going to hell*—while the festering bag of rot and decay in his hands filled the air with the aroma of death. It had seared its stench into his sinuses. He would smell it for the rest of his life, he knew.

He'd have hurled it into the nearest bin if he didn't think they needed it.

"Sir," said a voice from behind him. Savage was walking up, and the sight of her, of somebody familiar, made his next few breaths a little lighter. "She say anything?"

"Not much," he replied. "She confirmed it's Clegg, and that he's not working alone. What's happening downstairs?"

"I did the rounds. Nobody remembers seeing anyone who matches the description of Kevin Clegg, or the kids. Security's checking the feed, but even if he's been here, he's long gone."

Kett swore beneath his breath. He could hear the nurse inside the ward, the grumble of the old PC.

"How did you get her to talk, sir?" said Savage.

"This helped," he replied, holding up the bag of meat. "She was terrified of it."

"That makes two of us," said Savage.

Kett made his way down the corridor, holding the bag as far away from his face as possible.

"She as much as confirmed they killed the man at the stable because they thought it was Clegg. Clegg must have hired him, recruited him somehow, given him his ID. I don't know. They killed him because they thought he was coming after the children. She believes in it all, Kate, the demons, the sacrifices, all of it."

He held open the door for Savage and they walked into the cool stairwell.

"It's insane," he said. "She's studied demonology and the occult all her life, she knows as much as Clegg does, maybe more. I asked her where she'd do the ritual, if it was her. She said somewhere sacred, somewhere powerful. She mentioned the lines, whatever the hell that is."

Savage's brow furrowed as she chewed it over.

"But we were right, Kate," he went on, pushing through the door to the lower level. "It's happening imminently. We're out of time."

He felt his pocket vibrate and pulled out his phone to see Clare's name on the screen.

"Sir, we're hitting dead ends here. Tell me you've got something?"

"I've got a raging headache, Kett, and a haemorrhoid that's almost touching the back of my knee. That's all. I don't want to hear about dead ends, I want to hear that you've done your tossing job."

Kett switched the call to speaker.

"I spoke with Bianca Caddel, sir. She thinks Clegg's going to conduct his ceremony somewhere sacred."

"I've still got coppers at the ruins," Clare said. "As well as the stables, and Bianca's bunker."

"I don't think it's any of those places, sir. She mentioned lines."

"Lines?" said Clare. "Like cocaine?"

"Uh, I don't think so, sir."

"Is it a name?" said Clare. "A pub? Train lines? Ferry lines? Lines on a map? Lines in a theatre? Phone lines."

"Railways, maybe," said Kett. "There are some old railway lines that aren't in use anymore, aren't there? Good place to take somebody if you don't want to be seen."

"There's one near me, sir, in Lakenham," said Savage. "But what do they have to do with churches? They're not holy places, they're..."

She stopped, deep in thought.

"What?" said Kett.

"What?" added Clare.

"Ley lines, sir," she said. "They're sacred, right? Earth energies, that sort of thing."

Kett shrugged.

"I'm almost positive there's one in Norfolk, sir," she went on. "Maybe Suffolk. Definitely East Anglia. Granddad used to talk about it, I think he even took me to some of the places on it when I was a kid. Uh..."

She mopped the sweat from her forehead.

"This heat, sir, can't think straight."

"Then take your clothes off, chug some ice water and stand in a tossing fridge," said Clare. "Just tell me what you're getting at."

"Um, not going to do that, sir," said Savage, giving the phone a weird look. "It might be nothing, I'll have to check."

"Do it," said Kett. "Sir, maybe Aggie can help us. I know she didn't talk to her dad, but maybe he told her something. Maybe it's connected to something they did when she was little. Is she there?"

"Yeah," said Clare. "Spalding's been interviewing her. I'll go get her, call you back. But you need to stop pissing about, Kett. This is Porter. If we don't find out where he is, we've lost him."

"I know, sir," he said, but Clare had gone.

He chased after Savage, finding her outside the main doors. Duke was already there, hot and bothered in his uniform. The heat of the afternoon sun was Biblical. Kett thought he could feel his blood beginning to boil.

Savage looked up from her phone when she heard him approach.

"I've found it, sir. There's a ley line that stretches across South Norfolk. It's probably the most famous one in the world, goes from Yarmouth all the way to Penzance in Cornwall. Takes in the Hurlers, Glastonbury, Avebury, a few other holy sites. It's called St Michael's Alignment."

"But that's, what, a few hundred miles?"

Savage nodded, staring at her phone.

"The line starts in Hopton, sir," she said. "That's where the sun rises on May Day. May first. Exactly three months ago to the day. May Day marks the beginning of summer, halfway between the spring equinox and solstice. Today's Lughnasadh, the exact midpoint between the solstice and the autumn equinox. That has to mean something to these people, right?"

"Best we've got," he said. "You know anything about Hopton?"

"Been a couple of times, sir," she said. "It's just down

from where I grew up. Nothing much there, other than Potters, the holiday place."

"I think that's where the World Indoor Bowls Championships are held," said Duke, scratching his missing eyebrow.

"What?" said Kett and Savage together.

He shrugged.

"Might be connected."

"He's not playing bowls, Aaron," said Kett.

He made his way to the car, slinging the bag of meat in the boot then scrubbing his sweaty hands down his trousers. The skies had darkened even further in the time they'd been inside the hospital, the day a pressure cooker.

"Going to be another storm," he said, climbing into the passenger seat.

"Probably all the demons, sir," said Duke, compressing himself into the back. "You always see storms in horror films."

"Yeah, that'll be it," said Kett. "The demons."

But the skin on his arms crinkled, his scalp shrinking.

You're all going to hell.

"Just bloody drive," he told Savage. He switched on the air con, getting a face full of warm breath, then pulled out his phone to text Clare.

Hopton village our best shot, heading there now, send units just in case.

Savage accelerated out of the car park, heading for the main road. She was halfway over the roundabout when her phone started to ring.

"Sorry, sir, can you grab that?"

He fished the phone from her pocket, seeing an unknown number.

"No idea," she said, glancing at it.

He answered.

"This is DCI Kett on DC Savage's phone."

"Hello?" came the reply, fizzing with static. "I didn't get any of that, sorry. Is this the police officer's phone, the one who left a card at my house?"

"DC Savage, yeah," said Kett. "Who's this?"

"Oh, right, my name's Douglas."

"Herring?" said Kett. He switched the phone to speaker. "Dougie, right?"

"Yeah," came the reply. "You said you wanted to talk to me, about yesterday. Something happened to Aggie?"

"Hi, Dougie," said Savage. "This is Kate. I left the card, you weren't in."

"I was at my mum's," he said. "She's in King's Lynn, long drive. Just got home. Is Aggie okay?"

"She wasn't," said Savage. "But she is now. How's your mum?"

"She's, uh… she's fine," he said, confusion in his voice.

"Because Aggie told us she was sick."

"She's been sick for a while," he said. "Some immune thing, they don't know what. I stay with her a little more during the holidays, help out. Although I was out with some mates last night, which is why I didn't hear about Aggie. Sorry, why are you asking about Mum?"

Savage hit the dual carriageway, her attention on the road for a moment. Kett took over.

"We're asking because Aggie said that's why you couldn't do the shoot yesterday morning," said Kett. "At St Mary's. Is that right?"

"Oh, yeah," he said, his voice fading for a moment. "It's harder to get to places from King's Lynn, middle of nowhere. But that's not why I wasn't there. Aggie said she didn't need me."

"For the video?" said Kett. "Yesterday?"

"Yeah, she said she and Matt had it covered. No idea how, because they're both in front of the camera, so who's going to hold it? But honestly, I was glad. Drag myself all over the shop for Aggie, and it's not like she pays me."

"Hang on," said Kett, sitting forward in his seat. "Aggie told you she didn't need you?"

"Yeah."

"But they took another person with them yesterday, to work the camera."

"Shit," said Dougie. "Seriously? Who?"

"A girl called Charlie Ford."

"Charlie?" came the reply. "Why? She has no gear, does she? Fuck's sake."

He sounded genuinely aggrieved.

"Aggie doesn't even know Charlie," he went on. "Not really. It's not like they're friends. Why would she ask her?"

"I don't know," said Kett. "There must have been a reason."

"Matt," he said. "It'll've been Matt. He has classes with Charlie. I think he likes her. *Likes* likes, you know? Which is funny, because everyone thinks he's into Aggie. Fuck 'em. Like I said, they don't pay me."

"Wait," said Savage. "Matt told us you were with your mum too. Can I just clarify, did you tell Aggie you couldn't do the job?"

"No," said Dougie. "I said I *could* do it, just I'd need a little longer because I was coming from King's Lynn. Aggie told me she didn't need me."

He laughed.

"Then she invites Charlie. You couldn't make this shit up."

"Aggie told you not to come?" asked Savage.

"Yeah."

"Did she say anything else?" asked Kett.

"No," came the reply. "Not really. But I got the impression the whole thing was coming to an end anyway."

"The videos?" said Savage. "Why?"

"Aggie just said she wasn't going to be around much after this," said Dougie. "Figured she meant leaving school, university. Everything ends eventually, right?"

"Thank you, Dougie," said Kett. "That's really helpful."

"No problem. You sure she's okay?"

Kett hung up without answering, his head reeling. Savage must have been thinking the same thing, because she threw him a panicked look.

"Call the Super, sir," she said.

He was already doing it, using Savage's phone. It rang five times before Clare picked up. His voice grated down the line, sounding out of breath.

"Speak, Kate. I haven't got time for this."

"It's me, sir," said Kett. "Can you put Aggie on the line? We really need to speak with her."

"What do you think I'm trying to do, you egg-stained toss-crumpet? I'm trying to find her."

The temperature in the car felt like it had plummeted.

"You can't find her, sir?"

"I know I can't, I just told you that. She was with a bunch of PCs in the bullpen, Gorski and Niven were all over her. They said she needed a bathroom break and Niven took her, but they're not in any of the toilets. How far do you need to walk for a piss? Fucking Waitrose?"

"She's not there," Kett told Savage.

"I fucking know she's not here, Kett," screeched Clare. "I told you a thousand fucking times!"

"When was the last time anyone saw her, sir?"

"Thirty minutes at least," he replied.

"It's her, isn't it?" said Savage.

"It's who?" said Clare.

"It's Aggie, sir," said Kett. "I think she's behind the whole thing. We just spoke to Dougie. Aggie told him not to go to the shoot yesterday, she just wanted it to be her and Matt. *Matt* invited Charlie. But Aggie wanted him there alone."

"Why?" said Clare.

"I think she was planning to murder him, sir," said Kett.

"Bullshit."

"No, it's not," he went on. "Aggie's obsessed with the occult. She always has been. It's why she makes videos on YouTube, right? But it's deeper than that. She believes it. She thinks she can use it to bring her mum back."

"It's bullshit, Kett. Stop talking."

"She tells Dougie to stay away, she invites Matt to the shoot alone, in the ruins. Her Dad's waiting there, they've already begun some kind of ceremony, the severed head. They're planning to knock Matt out, tie him up—I don't know, exactly—ready for the ceremony today. But they never got the chance, because Bianca's been watching Clegg, she thinks he's the one who's planning to do something. She attacks the group, she takes Aggie because of her birthday, she thinks she's saving her."

"I'm not listening," said Clare. "Lalalalalalaaaaa."

"That's why Clegg turned up at the woods," said Savage, speaking over the Super. "He was looking for her, he needed her back."

"Right," said Kett. "Bianca told me Clegg couldn't have done this alone, that he was working with somebody else. But she has no idea that Aggie's in on it, that she was trying to escape from the cage to get back to her dad, to get back for the ritual."

"Matt Kamau's birthday is in January," said Clare. "We checked. Why would she murder him if he didn't fit the criteria for the sacrifice?"

"Because she was desperate, sir," said Savage. "They'd planned to murder Dmitri and Freya, right? But Bianca had taken them."

"Right," said Kett. "She said they'd been born on the same day, at the same hour."

"She didn't know where they were, so maybe she was going to use Matt instead. Better a sacrifice with the wrong birthday than no sacrifice at all."

"But we led them right to the kids," said Kett. "Just like we did with Aggie. We found where they were being held, then offered them to Clegg on a fucking platter."

This time, Clare didn't argue.

"This is what we focus on, sir," said Kett. "Aggie Clegg. She's gone to find her father, she's gone to complete the ritual. They're working together, and they're doing it right now."

"In Hopton?" said Clare, defeated.

"I don't know, sir," said Savage. "It's likely, but we need to know exactly where."

"Leave it with me."

Clare hung up. Savage floored it, the car tearing down the fast lane of the A47, thumping past cars towards the glowering horizon.

"We're close, sir," she said, her face serious, her eyes sharp. "We've still got time."

Kett checked his watch, thinking of Porter, thinking of Allie and baby Bobby.

Thinking they were already too late.

CHAPTER FORTY-FOUR

He woke like he was clawing his way from the grave, pulling himself from a sleep that felt eternal, from a darkness that could have been death.

It was the pain that dragged him into consciousness, his brain thumping so hard somebody could have been striking it with a hammer. He groaned, reaching for his head only to feel something tighten around his wrist. Something was wrong, his skull felt too heavy, full of cement. Every beat of his pulse echoed like gunshots in a cathedral.

He tried to move his legs, but they were completely numb. So was his back, all sensation switched off. The panic hit hard, the terror of paralysis forcing his eyes open.

Flames, the top of the room was full of them, the smoke almost concealing the figures who danced on the ceiling like bats. Their skin was awash with firelight, their devil faces grinning, their horns almost touching the floor.

It's a dream, he screamed silently to himself, the pain in his face too great to form words. *It's a dream, it's a dream.*

But it wasn't a dream. His thoughts were returning like

treacle, impossibly slowly. He saw the police station, the custody suite. He saw the man lift his shotgun.

Bang.

Had he shot him?

Was this *hell*?

He tried to lift his arms again, willing his body to move, only to feel it resist. There were manacles on his wrists, he saw, and above them a metal bucket swilling with blood. Droplets *rose* from his body, hitting the bucket overhead, and he had time to wonder what kind of magic it took to defy gravity before he realised he was upside down.

He hung from the ceiling like a butcher's trophy, more chains around his ankles secured with a padlock. He had been stripped of everything except his underwear, his body daubed with crimson markings that looked like runes. His skin had been wrapped in fronds of ivy. Runnels of blood wound down his neck, filling his eyes, dripping from his hairline. He couldn't see where they were coming from.

The dancing figures stood around a fire in the middle of the room, one that had been lit on the concrete floor and was barely contained by stones. There were two of them, Porter saw, both wearing long black robes that trailed behind them as they moved. Their masks were the colour of blood, the horns like a ram's. They were chanting in a language that might have been Latin, oblivious to the fact that he'd woken up. The taller of the two figures moved with a limp, and he held an old book.

The shorter held a knife.

"Fuck," he said, feeling the word on his lips. He tried to move again, his body swaying, the chains rattling. The sensation was coming back into his feet like they were filling with ice-cold needles, pain lancing down his spine.

He heard more rattling from his side, and he twisted his head as much as his stiff neck would let him.

Two more people hung by their feet from the ceiling beside him. The first was Dmitri. He was unconscious, his body stripped to his underwear and marked with the same symbols Porter had seen on himself. He, too, was wrapped tight in ivy and ribbons. Porter couldn't see the person who struggled next to him, but he didn't need to. He could hear Freya's frantic cries, her choked sobs.

"Please, please, please, please, please, please."

Blood dripped slowly and steadily from both of them, pattering like rain into the buckets below. He could see a nasty wound on Dmitri's back, a gash that formed the centre of a pentagram.

"Please, please, please, please, please, please," Freya went on, a chant of her own.

The two people in the centre of the room showed no sign of hearing her. They continued to sing, their eyes slits of deeper darkness against the coal-black masks.

There were other things here, Porter saw, ribbons and tree branches and dozens of black candles on a table against the far wall, all positioned around a large, framed photograph—the kind you often saw at funerals. It looked like there was a woman in the photo, but her head had been cut out, leaving a perfect circle of absence.

Every inch of wall space had been covered with letters and symbols and pictures, the incantations of a madman.

He couldn't make sense of the room he was in, either. It was maybe eight metres long and six deep, the walls bare stone, the ceiling crumbling concrete. Four windows had been set into the far wall, as slim as letterboxes. All but one had been boarded up, the last doing its best to suck the smoke into a sky that was almost dark.

"Fuck," he said again, the word echoing around the cavern of his head. He wondered how long he'd been hanging here, and how long he had before the pooling blood inside his head made him pass out again.

If that happened, he knew, he was as good as dead.

"Hey," he said, trying to kick his legs to free himself, trying to wrench his arms out of the manacles. The effort caused a wave of dizziness to wash over him, darkness creeping into the corners of his vision. "Hey, you fucks. Let me down."

His words had exactly the effect he thought they'd have. Neither of the two figures acknowledged him, their chants filling the room with sound the same way the fire filled it with smoke.

"Please, please, please, please, please, please," said Freya. "I don't want to die, please let me go."

"Hey, Freya," said Porter, chewing on the words like they were toffee. "It's me, Pete. The policeman. It's going to be okay, yeah?"

He heard the sobs tear out of her, heard the percussive rattle of her chains as she struggled.

"You're not going to die. I won't let them hurt you."

But he had no idea how to stop them.

He kicked again, but it was hopeless. The ceiling was concrete, the hook embedded deeply, the links of the chains as thick as his thumb and sealed with a heavy-duty padlock. The manacles had been screwed into the ground, he couldn't move his hands more than a couple of inches.

And the bucket was still filling, his body emptying drop by drop by drop. Now that the numbness was ebbing away, he could feel the pain that lanced into his back. There was a wound between his shoulder blades, he knew.

"Hey," he growled again. He angled his head as best he could. "Hey, dickheads."

The taller figure glanced over, but only for a fraction of a second. He continued to read from the book, slowly circling the fire—limping heavily. The drone of his words was almost hypnotic, and for a second Porter sank back into the dark—another artillery blast of adrenaline hauling him back out.

"Whatever you're doing, you don't need the kids," he said, his words slurred. "Let them go and you can keep me. Yeah? You can do whatever you want to me, but they don't deserve this."

The first person kept reading. The other one stood still, fixated on the fire, the knife clasped in both gloved hands.

"You listening to me?" Porter yelled. "You going to answer me?"

Nothing, and he wrestled the chains again, his body bucking furiously.

"Fuck!"

"I don't want to die," said Freya. "I don't want to go to hell. Please don't do this, please let me go."

The man with the limp reached into the pocket of his robe and hurled something into the fire. The flames exploded upwards, sparks hitting the ceiling. A fist of heat rolled across the room, singeing Porter's skin.

"It isn't real," he yelled, fear and fury punching the words from his throat. "You have to know that, right? You have to know it's all bullshit. You're murderers. You're delusional, you're pathetic."

Neither of the masked figures responded, the man throwing another fistful of something into the fire. The flames reared like a living thing, roaring in anger. He was still chanting, but Porter realised it was in English now.

"What is the name of the beast that we summon?"

"Andramalech," said the other figure, lifting the knife overhead. Their voice was softer, higher. It was a woman, Porter realised.

"What is the name of the beast that we summon?" the man shouted again.

"Andramalech."

"Lord of Murder, Chancellor of Hell, Andramalech, we call on you."

They both chanted together.

"Hear us, Andramalech. We summon you. *Veni, veni, o comitis* Andramalech!"

Another fistful of powder, this one causing an explosion powerful enough to knock both people back a few steps. It was so bright that Porter had to screw his eyes shut against it, but in the split second before he did, he thought he saw a shape in the flames—a writhing shadow of smoke that seemed to tilt its horned head to the ceiling.

It's not real.

Freya was screaming now, the sound of it drowning out the roar of the fire and the endless chants. Porter's brain felt like it was fizzing, like it was detaching itself from the circumference of his skull. He fought the encroaching dark, forcing himself to keep his eyes open, to search the room. He couldn't die like this. He *wouldn't*.

"We call on you, Andramalech," said the man, coughing the words out, struggling with the smoke. "We call on you to answer our prayers. We offer these three souls, drained of blood, then burned in your fire. We offer these as payment."

The flames writhed, that same figure of smoke coiling in the inferno—*an illusion*, Porter told himself. *Just an illusion.* But there was nothing artificial about the peal of thunder which rocked the room, vibrating through the chains into his bones.

The two masked figures looked at each other, almost in shock.

"Return her to us," they spoke together, their voices united. "*Veni, veni, o comitis* Andramalech, fetch her from the other side, return her."

Porter's vision was swimming, his head so full of blood that it felt close to splitting. He looked again at the photo on the other side of the room, the woman with her face cut away.

"We call on you to open the gate and bring her back. A wife. A mother. Tracey Clegg. We demand it."

Tracey Clegg?

And suddenly it made sense. The limping man from the woods. Not an imposter after all, but Aggie's father.

"Kevin?" he said, the smoke reducing his voice to a witch's croak. "This won't bring her back, this won't save her."

"*Veni, veni, o comitis* Andramalech," the man shouted. "Honour our sacrifice."

"Obey our command," added the woman, holding the knife to the flames. "Return her."

Another crash of thunder overhead, and the woman laughed—a sound full of insane glee. She stared at the wall, at that faceless photo. Then she turned to Porter, staring at him through the holes in her mask.

He knew who she was.

"Aggie," he said.

She didn't reply, she just took a step towards him. The knife caught the fire, glinting.

"This won't bring your mother back," said Porter, struggling in his chains. "This won't do anything, you know that."

Kevin Clegg hurled more powder into the flames, the room exploding with light and heat. Aggie moved closer, her eyes full of a different kind of fire—wild and determined and insane.

And full of belief.

"You're only going to send her to hell, Aggie," said Porter, changing his tack. "Your mum's at peace, she's in a good place. If you do this... you're going to kill her all over again. Don't you see? Nothing good comes from this, nothing good comes from him, from uh..."

He fought the hurricane of his thoughts, found the name.

"Andramalech. He's a demon, Aggie, he won't give you your mum back, he'll... he'll rip her soul away from wherever it is now and he'll take her to hell. You too, and your dad. You're all going to end up there. It can't be what you want."

Aggie was still moving, her voice audible from behind her mask as she continued her dirge. She jutted the blade of the knife towards Porter's chest.

More thunder, the room trembling beneath the force of it.

"Aggie, for fuck's sake," said Porter, his voice rising, his body thrashing against the chains. "He's going to trick you, he's going to take you all to hell."

It was no use. Aggie crossed the room in a handful of steps, looming over him.

"Accept this sacrifice, as we accept your gift," she said. "Bring her—"

"Wait," came a voice from the middle of the room. "Wait, Aggie, what if he's right?"

Aggie stopped talking, turned.

Kevin Clegg stood by the fire. He'd lifted his mask, his face drenched in sweat and wrinkled with concern.

"What if he's right?" he said again. "How do we know?"

"I just know, Dad," said Aggie, her words laced with fury. "Put it back on. We need to finish it."

"I don't want to lose her again, Agnes," said Clegg. "I don't want to lose her forever."

"Then go," spat Aggie, her words shaking more thunder from the heavens. "But I've waited too long for this, Dad. It's too late to stop now."

She whirled back around, the knife dropping towards Porter's throat, her words a growl of defiance.

"Whatever happens, we finish this today."

CHAPTER FORTY-FIVE

The storm had hit like the hammer of God.

And this time, it brought the rain.

Kett felt like they'd driven through a portal, the afternoon sun giving way almost instantly to darkness, the rain drumming against the windscreen so ferociously that the road ahead became a blur. Savage had to slow to a crawl, the traffic on both sides gridlocked in a wash of red light.

"Come on!" she yelled, leaning on the horn. "Move!"

They were on the Acle Straight, nothing on either side of the road but a steep drop into open fields. She kept the car at a steady five miles an hour, blasting the horn again.

"We're not going to get there in time, sir," she said, her face full of misery.

Kett checked his watch. It had just gone half six. If they were right, and the ceremony was due to take place at the exact moment Tracey Clegg had died, then they had a little over half an hour to get to Hopton and work out where Porter and the kids were being held.

And that was only if they were right, of course. Aggie and her father could have already finished their ritual.

They might be driving towards three corpses.

"No," he growled, the word lost beneath the thump of the rain and a sudden peal of thunder.

"Right," said Duke from the back. He was looking at his phone. "There's another ruined church in Hopton, St Margaret's. According to Google, it sits bang on the ley line."

"That has to be it, right?" said Kett. He lifted his phone, calling Clare. The Super answered after a single ring.

"Speak."

"We're thinking it's the church, sir," he said, putting it on speaker. "St Margaret's."

"Plenty of videos on YouTube about how it's spiritually connected," said Duke from the back. "People leave crystals there."

"You've got units in the town, right?" asked Kett.

"Three," said Clare. "More on their way."

"Send them to the church first," said Kett. "It's on..."

It took Duke a moment to catch on.

"Oh, uh... Coast Road, sir. Next to the school."

"Did you find anything, sir?" Kett asked.

"Toss all," said Clare, and he hung up.

The storm still raged, but the traffic had picked up speed on the straighter part of the road. Every time lightning flashed, Kett could see the land ahead, the wind shaking the cars, the rain almost horizontal. The sulphurous light across the open marsh was unreal, it looked like the world was ending.

"This is nuts," he said. "You got Matt Kamau's number, Kate?"

"In my phone, sir," she said.

He found it, calling him from Savage's mobile and putting it on speaker. It rang for so long that he was sure nobody was going to answer, but as he prepared to leave a message, a breathless voice picked up.

"Hey, hi, sorry."

"Matt?" said Kett, thunder rocking the car.

"Yeah. Who's this?"

"DCI Kett, from the police. We spoke yesterday. Can I ask you a very quick question?"

"Only if I can ask you one first," he replied. "You found Aggie?"

"Yeah," he said, and he left it at that.

"Thank God for that," said Matt. "Hang on, got pasta on."

Kett heard him running down the stairs, then the clank of a pan.

"She's okay?" he asked.

"I need to know if Aggie ever mentioned a place in Hopton, on the coast. A house she had there, a place she stayed, relatives, a site she wanted to record a video at. Anything."

"Hopton?" he said, and it was obvious by the tone of his voice that he didn't know anything. "I don't think so. I don't even know where that is."

"Yarmouth," said Kett.

"She hated Yarmouth. We filmed there once, the old tower. Supposed to be haunted. Wasn't much to see. Don't think I've ever been back."

"It would be to do with ley lines," Savage said, her eyes on the road. "St Michael's Alignment, goes from Penzance to Hopton."

"No, sorry," he said. "Like I said before, I don't really believe in it all like she does. I just go along because it's Aggie, you know?"

"Please, think," said Kett. "She never mentioned

Hopton at all, a future location, a place to meet? Somebody's life could depend on it, Matt."

"Shit, seriously?" he said. "Uh, no. I'm really sorry. Aggie didn't really tell us much when she picked a site. If we were going on research trips, she'd give us a location and tell us to meet her there, or we'd drive out together if it was a way out of the city."

"She never gave you a location near Hopton?" said Kett, the hope draining.

"I wouldn't know," said Matt. "She used What3Words most of the time."

"What three words?" said Kett.

"I know it, sir," said Savage. "It's a mapping thing. Every place on the planet has a three-word tag, you can navigate anywhere."

"You've got some of these tags?" Kett asked.

"I mean, somewhere," said Matt. "But she hasn't sent any new ones for a while, and none of the old ones were anywhere near Hopton. Last one we got was for the ruins, and I can't remember what it was. One was elephant, I think."

"Shit," said Kett. "I need you to hang up and look through every message she sent you, you hear me? Every single one. I need those tags."

"But my pasta—"

"Do it," said Kett. "Call me back."

He hung up, pinching the bridge of his nose to calm the storm that raged at the front of his skull. They were approaching the end of the Acle Straight, the lights of Yarmouth a dull haze against the overcast horizon.

"Have we seen anything of Aggie's that might be a location?" he said. "Any notes, any texts, anything at all?"

"Not notes, sir," said Savage. "But we found the paper

in her car, remember? The note from the sponsor. It had pictures on it. I'm certain one was an elephant."

"We don't need pictures," said Kett. "We need words."

"But we know she likes to draw, sir," said Savage. "The illustrations on the walls, the runes, I think that was all Aggie. I took a photo of the note. It's on my phone."

He scrolled through her pictures, finding it and using his fingers to zoom in. There were nine doodles on the paper, none of them done with any care. The one nearest the top left corner could feasibly be an elephant.

"You're right," he said. "Well remembered."

"There's an arrow though, sir," said Duke, leaning over. "Pointing to its penis."

"That's its trunk, Duke," said Savage, glancing over.

"Oh, right," he said, squinting. "I guess so. The next one is a bulb."

There were three lightbulbs, no mistake. The third picture was a bee.

"Trunk, bulb, bee," said Kett. "Hang on."

He Googled What3Words on his own phone, almost losing his grip as Savage broke free of traffic and accelerated around the roundabout.

"We're five minutes from Hopton, sir."

Kett typed the words into the search bar, but nothing happened.

"Try bulbs, sir," said Savage. "Plural."

He did. Still no luck.

"Maybe it *is* a penis," said Duke. "Try that."

"Or buzz, sir," said Savage. "For the bee."

He did, and this time the map zoomed in to a place he recognised.

"Holy shit," he said. "That's the ruins of St Mary. You were right."

"Try the next one," said Duke. "That's a medal, isn't it? With a three on it."

"Bronze?" said Kett.

"Or third," said Savage.

He looked at the next illustration, two black circles with dotted lines spiralling out from it. "But what the hell is that?"

The sky lit up, the dark clouds vomiting thunder almost immediately. The storm was right on top of them. Yarmouth was a blur through the rain-lashed window as Savage took the main road south. Kett glanced at the time on the phone.

18:47.

"The last one, it's just a line," said Savage, looking over. "Dash, maybe?"

"Could be a penis," said Duke.

"Not everything's a fucking penis, Duke," said Kett. "A stick? A ruler?"

"Take away?" said Duke.

"You cannot be hungry," said Savage.

"No, like, subtraction. The little line thing."

"Yeah, it could be," said Kett. "Or a minus? But what's the middle one?"

"Beans?" said Duke.

"Hat?" said Savage. "Shit."

She had to slow down, the traffic ahead at a standstill again. She pulled around the stationary cars, the Audi plunging into a puddle of water that reached the bottom of the doors. The car shook as it ploughed through it, the engine grumbling.

"Come on," said Savage. "Don't quit on me."

"It's a bomb," said Duke, prodding the phone so hard Kett almost dropped it. "An old-fashioned one. See?"

"A bomb," said Kett, nodding. "Good job."

He switched to his phone, typing *third.bomb.dash* into the What3Words search bar.

"Nothing," he said.

"Try minus, sir," said Savage, pulling them out of the flooded street.

"Still nothing," he said. He tried bronze for the first word, and the result remained stubbornly blank. "Fuck's sake."

"Maybe it's explosion," said Duke. "Blast. Uh, boom?"

Kett started typing, stopping when the browser vanished, replaced by an incoming call. It was Clare.

"Not a good time, sir," he said as he answered.

"Church in Hopton is empty," said Clare, his voice almost hysterical. "Nobody there, and nobody's seen anything. They're searching the surrounding houses now, but there's fuck all, Kett. What else do we have?"

"I'm just looking now, sir, we—"

"I don't want you to look, you tosswashing shitbird, I want you to *know*. Find him, now, or I swear to God I'll be flossing my teeth with your foreskin in the morning!"

Clare hung up.

"That's..." said Kett. "*What*?"

"Oh, wait, sir," said Savage. "Fuse. Maybe it's a fuse. Fuses, though. There's more than one."

"Fuses?" said Kett, navigating back to the page.

"Clare made me think of it, sir. Short fuse."

He typed *third.fuses.minus* into the bar.

The map zoomed in to a street by the beach—less than a mile from where they were driving.

"Holy shit, Kate, I could kiss you," he said, the relief flooding into him like cold water. "That's it. Hopton, it's..."

He looked out of the window.

"Take the next left, at the roundabout. Head for the beach."

He called Clare back.

"Speak, Kett."

"I think we've found them, sir," he said. "Beach Road, the very end of it."

"You're sure?"

"No, sir. But it's as good as we're going to get."

He hung up, looking at his watch.

18:54.

"Floor it, Kate," he said, leaning forward as if that might make them move a little faster. "We're out of time."

CHAPTER FORTY-SIX

"What time is it, Dad?"

Aggie Clegg drew the point of her knife down Porter's chest, probing the hollow of his throat. He felt the sting of it as it pierced his flesh, a trickle of blood running over his chin, into his mouth. He spat it at her, struggling against the chains that held him upside down.

Behind Aggie, the fire burned inside its shallow pit, the room so full of smoke that all the hard edges had been erased. Kevin Clegg was a silhouette against the raging flames, his mask back over his face. His chants were lost in the rumble of thunder from the world outside, and in Freya's screams.

Aggie looked at her father.

"I said what time is it?"

"We've got seven minutes," said Clegg. His voice held none of the conviction that his daughter's did. "Agnes, please, maybe we should—"

More thunder, the room shaking.

"You hear that, right?" said Aggie, turning back to

Porter. She pressed the knife harder, working it between the tendons of his neck. "You know who's coming for you?"

"I know it's bullshit," he said, wrenching his legs to try to free them, feeling dust rain onto his skin. "I know they were talking about this storm on the weather forecast last week. I know it had more to do with hot air than some demon."

The blood dripped into his eyes, but he couldn't free his hands to wipe it away.

"You're wrong," said Aggie. "This isn't a normal storm. This is *him*. He's on his way, and he's going to bring my mother home."

"You're mad," said Porter. "You're not getting her back, and the pair of you are going to spend the rest of your life in prison. You think *your* demon is bad? Wait till you get face to face with some of the guys they lock up in there. Then you'll know evil. You especially, Kevin. You're a kidnapper, a child molester. They are going to fuck you up in there."

"I'm none of those things," Kevin snapped, stepping closer. "This wasn't... Agnes, please. I know you want to help her, but this has gone too far. It's not too late to stop."

"It's far too late," said Aggie. "Time?"

The man dropped his head sadly.

"Six minutes."

"Start the final rites," said Aggie. "No hesitation, no mistakes. Just like we practised, Dad."

"Let the kids go," said Porter. "You've got me, you don't need them."

"To call on Andramalech you need a sacrifice of children," said Aggie. "You're just a bonus."

She pulled the knife away, letting Porter haul in a smoke-filled breath. She was moving towards Dmitri, the boy still out cold.

"Just let them go," said Porter, using every ounce of his body weight to pull on the chains. The manacles had cut into his ankles, more blood dripping onto him, pattering into the bucket. The pain was unreal, threatening to push him into a sleep he knew he'd never wake up from. "Let them go, or I swear to God, I—"

"God left the party a long time ago," said Aggie. "Time, Dad?"

"Five minutes, Agnes."

Thunder folded the sky in two. Aggie shot her father a look through her mask, her eyes bright with excitement. Clegg lifted his book and started to speak, his low drone unintelligible and punctuated by coughs. The fire blazed, smoke churning upwards, pooling along the ceiling. The gap in the window was too small, it had nowhere to go.

"*Veni, veni, o comitis* Andramalech," said Aggie. "*Veni, veni, o comitis* Andramalech, honour our first sacrifice."

She held the knife in both hands and pressed the tip of the blade against Dmitri's throat. It was a small mercy that the boy was still unconscious.

"Demi!" howled Freya, rocking in her chains. "Leave him alone! Leave him alone!"

"*Veni, veni, o comitis* Andramalech," chanted Aggie. "*Veni, veni, o comitis* Andramalech!"

The storm answered her, the building trembling.

"Fuck this," said Porter.

He thrashed against the manacles, kicking his legs. A hail of blood hit the floor, but there was something else, too.

Dust.

It fell onto his body, onto his face, blinding him. Bigger chunks hit the floor, splashing into the bucket. He didn't stop moving.

"*Veni, veni, o comitis* Andramalech," Aggie yelled, her

voice blending with her father's chants. "Accept this gift, and answer me."

She drew her hands back, the knife a scorpion's tail.

"No!"

Porter grabbed the chains that held his hands, tensing his body and wrenching his legs down as hard as he could. The bolt in the ceiling groaned, then ripped free in an explosion of concrete. He landed hard, cracking his knees, the bucket of his blood spilling over the floor, hissing into the fire pit.

"Stop!" screamed Aggie. "What are you doing?"

Porter looked up through the blood, through the dust, through the smoke. Aggie was lumbering towards him, the knife still gripped in her hand. Clegg was running over too, almost tripping on his robes. They reached him together.

Porter tried to roll onto his back, but his hands were still manacled to the floor. He kicked out instead, his bare foot connecting with Aggie's shin. She tripped over him into the wall behind.

"Enough of that," said Clegg, grabbing a fistful of Porter's hair, pushing his face into the concrete floor. "Stay still."

No fucking chance.

Porter snapped his head back, hitting something. He managed to flip himself, driving his legs out again, both of them this time, his bare feet hitting Clegg's chest like a sledgehammer. The man was off balance, his robes tangled under his shoes. He staggered back, the book tumbling out of his hand as his arms wheeled.

He dropped into the fire pit without a sound, his robes igniting like they'd been primed with petrol.

"Dad!" shouted Aggie.

She dropped the knife as she ran to help him, but whatever had been in Kevin Clegg's pockets detonated with a concussive blast, filling the room with heat and noise.

The inferno rolled up to the ceiling, an inverse lake of fire that was so bright Porter had to close his eyes, had to turn his face away. All he could hear were screams—maybe from Freya, maybe from Aggie or her father, maybe even his own. He couldn't be sure anymore.

When he looked again, Kevin Clegg was a creature of flame that staggered across the room. Fire dripped from his robes like napalm, crawling up the legs of the table, catching on the dry strands of ivy and the bundled ribbons, on the photograph of the faceless woman. Aggie chased after him, her own robes smouldering.

"Fuck," said Porter.

He got to his knees, grabbing the chains that bound his hands and trying to rip them from the floor.

"Come on!"

They were bolted tight, the concrete strong.

"Come on, you fucks!"

Another scream from behind him, this one burning with rage. He glanced over his shoulder to see that Kevin Clegg had vanished through the door. Aggie was moving towards him. She'd taken off her mask, but the face beneath didn't look real either. She looked possessed, she looked *demonic*.

"What have you done?" she shrieked.

Porter rolled onto his back, trying to kick the knife away, managing somehow to slide it right towards her. She snatched it up, gripping it in one hand as she advanced.

"You have no idea how long I've waited for this," she said. "My whole life, all I wanted to do was meet her, have her hold me, have her love me. You've ruined it, you've ruined it!"

"It isn't real!" Porter cried out, trying to drive himself away from her. "Aggie, it's not fucking real!"

"Then it doesn't matter, does it?" she replied, her eyes flashing like quicksilver. "Nothing matters anymore."

She ran the last few steps, towering over him.

Then she drove the knife home.

CHAPTER FORTY-SEVEN

"LEFT, LEFT, LEFT," YELLED KETT.

Savage pumped the brakes, the car skidding on the rain-slick tarmac. She kept control, barrelling down a smaller road that was lined with houses. The streetlights had been shocked into action by the dark sky, but it was only when another flash of lightning boiled through the clouds that Kett saw the turning.

"Right," he yelled, pointing. "That one."

Savage twisted the wheel and the car thumped into a road that almost wasn't wide enough to hold it. Trees and bushes grew up on either side, making the world even darker. Kett's stomach contracted as she gunned it, the IRV reaching fifty in seconds.

"Should be right there," he said.

They burst from the trees, the road dropping onto the beach a little further ahead. Savage slowed down, the car shuddering to a halt on the wet gravel.

There was nothing here, just the beach, the waves churned into a frenzy by the wind and the rain. Sandy meadows pocked with bushes and stunted trees stretched as far as Kett could see in either direction, a dirt track to the right, heading south. He couldn't see a single building.

An explosion of thunder rolled overhead. It felt like the world was ending.

And in a way, it was.

"What if he's not here, sir?" said Savage, the engine still running.

"Could be a boat?" said Duke, leaning between the seats and staring out at the swollen, angry sea.

"In this?" said Kett. "You'd have to be mad."

"I think it goes without saying that these guys are mad, sir," said Savage.

He opened his door, climbing into the frenzied evening. The wind tried to pick him up, the rain lashing his face. The air was still hot, and it reeked of something acrid, something sulphuric.

The devil's breath, he thought.

"Smoke," said Savage, joining him in the street. "You smell it, sir? Can't see a fire."

The clouds were too dark and too low to see anything at all. Duke got out of the back, adjusting his equipment.

"Is this the exact spot on the map, sir?" he asked.

"Yeah. Down to the metre. I can't see anything, can you?"

"Just that," said Savage, nodding towards the track. "Maybe that's what the coordinates were for? Not a building, but a path? It must lead somewhere."

Kett wiped the rain from his face, staring into the meadow. It rosc towards a low hill, then dropped out of sight. He couldn't see where the track ended. He could barely see where it began, the path was so overgrown.

He checked his watch.

19:02.

Another few minutes and it was over.

"Let's go," he said, dropping into the car. "Quick as you can, Kate."

She got in, setting off before Duke was fully inside. The PC rolled across the back seat, the door slamming behind him. Savage eased them through a gap in the hedge and over an embankment that almost beached them. Then she floored it, the car bucking like a mule on the bumpy terrain.

"What if we're wrong, sir?" said Duke.

"We can't be," said Kett, leaning forward in his seat, his eyes fixed on the view ahead.

The land rose, the tyres slipping in the muck. Savage dropped a gear, spinning the wheel expertly as she navigated between the bushes and trees. The glowering sky lit up again, the edge of a low cliff just feet away, the hungry sea waiting on the other side of it like a predator.

"Careful, Kate," said Kett as he felt the back of the car slide out.

She ploughed on, the car reaching the top of the hill, the meadow opening up in front of them.

"There," said Kett.

A smudge of smoke against the dark horizon.

Savage had already spotted it, the car gunning down the other side of the slope. She almost lost control as she rounded a bush, but once they'd passed it, Kett saw what looked like a building site up ahead. Tall metal fences boxed off an area of the meadow close to the cliff, signs warning people to stay away. Three skips blocked the path like golems, and parked beside them were two cars. The air here was thick with smoke, Kett could smell it from inside the car.

"Duke, radio it in," Kett said. "This is it."

Please let this be it.

The car skidded, sliding, the bumper kissing the closest skip with a dull thud. Kett opened the door, ignoring the pain in his back as he climbed out. The rain hammered against his face, the hot wind driving him towards the edge of the cliff. He pushed against it, reaching the solid fences—too high to look over—and working his way around the corner.

The site was bigger than it had looked. Even over the roll of thunder and the gleeful shrieks of the wind through the steel fences, Kett could hear the crack and pop of fire from inside.

And the screams.

"Hey!" he yelled, running along the fence, trying to find a way in. "Police!"

He was almost at the far corner when he heard Savage crying his name. He doubled back, his rain-drenched clothes so heavy he felt like he was being pulled into the ground.

"Over here!" Savage called.

He squeezed past a skip to see her standing by a gate. She was trying to haul it open, dragging it over the rough ground. Duke grabbed the top and Kett took the middle, the three of them wrenching it inch by inch until the gap was wide enough to squeeze through.

In front of them was a low concrete building, and it took him a moment to recognise it as a pillbox left over from the war. A single door sat in the back wall, no windows. Smoke churned upwards from the far side, tongues of fire reaching for the sky. The heat coming off it was unreal, but it wasn't a pyre just yet—somebody inside was still screaming.

Kett charged towards the building, just feet away when the door crashed open.

A man ran out, entirely wreathed in flames.

"Fuck!" Kett said, trying to dive out of the way.

He wasn't quick enough.

The burning man collided with him, the flames reaching for his clothes, trying to catch in his hair—stopped only by the rain. Kett reeled backwards, landing hard.

"Shit," he said, breathless.

The burning man was still going, staggering through the open gate. There wasn't a single part of him that wasn't lost to the inferno, the rain hissing as it struck him. Kett didn't know how he could be alive.

"Duke, Taser him!" screamed Savage. "It's the only way we're going to put it out."

Duke had hesitated, his eyes full of reflected fire. He was back inside the lorry, Kett knew, inside the fire that had almost killed him six months ago.

"Aaron!" Savage called.

He came around, ripping out his Taser. He was too close to miss, the barbs hitting the man in the back as he struggled towards the skips. He collapsed to the dirt, his body fitting, his clothes and his skin crackling as the fire ate through him. Steam rose from the bonfire of his body.

Savage ripped off her jacket, throwing herself onto the ground next to him and doing her best to smother the flames. Duke joined in, kicking puddle water over the guy, his face still hollow with shock.

There was no time to watch.

Kett covered his mouth with his sleeve and ducked through the open door of the building. The smoke gathered in his eyes, filled his lungs, but he crouched low as he made his way down the narrow corridor towards the sound of screams. There were voices too, he realised, raised in anger.

The corridor opened into a room that must have taken up the full width of the building. Slit windows sat in the wall that faced the sea, all covered by boards except for one where a river of smoke poured out into the evening.

A fire raged in the middle of the room, engulfing a table beneath the window and spitting sparks at the low ceiling. It was so bright that it took Kett a moment to see the figures on the other side of it.

Two people hung upside down from the ceiling. The teenagers, he realised as he closed in, both stripped to their underwear. Freya was struggling, her chains rattling, but Dmitri was still. Buckets sat beneath them, as if they were pigs hung up for slaughter.

A woman was moving past them, her hood down, her face a mask of horror—wide eyes, bared teeth, streaked with smoke—so alien that at first Kett didn't recognise her.

When he did, though, he called her name.

"Aggie!"

She didn't respond, moving fast.

There was a knife in her hand.

Kett ran around the fire, his breath reduced to hacking coughs, the air almost too hot to breathe. He cleared the smoke just as Aggie reached a person sprawled on the floor at her feet.

Porter.

He was alive, thank God, but whatever relief Kett felt didn't last. Porter lay on his back, wearing nothing but his boxers and a sash of ivy and ribbon, his hands manacled to the ground. He kicked out at his attacker, but he wasn't strong enough.

Aggie dropped to her knees next to him, speaking words that were lost to the roar of the fire.

She didn't hesitate, plunging the knife into Porter's flesh.

Kett ran, almost tripping. By some miracle, he stayed on

his feet, reaching Aggie and grabbing her by the hood of her robes. He wrenched her away and she rolled back, leaving her knife embedded in Porter's shoulder.

"Enough, Aggie," said Kett, coughing hard. "It's over."

"You've ruined it!" she screamed, dragging herself onto her hands and knees. "You've ruined it!"

She pushed herself into a sprinter's start, her body tense, her eyes still full of murder. Her hand was inside the pocket of her robes. For all Kett knew, she had another weapon in there.

"Don't," he told Aggie.

She looked at Porter, at the blade embedded in his shoulder. He had curled himself into a ball, his hand on the knife that still jutted from his skin.

"Don't," said Kett. "I won't let you. You go now, I won't stop you. Just leave him alone."

She stared at Porter again, licking her lips.

"This isn't over," she said.

She pushed herself up, bolting for the door.

Kett dropped down next to Porter. He was alive, and he was awake, his face knotted into a fist of pain and worry. The blade hadn't gone deep, wedged into the muscle and releasing a steady flow of blood.

"Is it bad?" he croaked.

"You've got a knife in your bloody shoulder, Pete," said Kett, glancing back to make sure Aggie was gone. "Of course it's bad."

He checked the chains around Porter's wrists. They were secured with a padlock. It was small, but it would take a saw to get through it. There was no time. The whole building was going up in flames, smoke filling the room like water, his suit almost bone dry now, doing nothing to protect him from the blistering heat.

"You see a key?"

"No, sir," said Porter, resting his head on the floor. "Can you get the kids out?"

"I'm getting you all out," said Kett.

But he had no idea how.

"Wait here," he said. "Don't die."

"I'll try, sir," said Porter.

Kett staggered to his feet, moving to where Dmitri hung. He pushed his fingers against the boy's throat, feeling a pulse.

"Please," screamed Freya. "Get me down, get me down."

"I'm going to," said Kett, giving her chains a tug. They were bolted into the ceiling.

"Sir!"

Savage crashed through the door on the other side of the room, taking in the scene with wide eyes. She held up her hand.

"Keys, sir. The guy on fire had them in his pocket."

She ran around the sprawling flames, coughing so hard she almost dropped them. Kett took them from her, flicking through the heavy ring. Eight of the keys were identical, and he tried the first in the padlock that secured Freya's legs.

"Hold her, Kate," he said. "So she doesn't fall. You see Aggie? She ran."

"Got past us, sir," she said. "Duke's in pursuit."

The key didn't work, so he tried the next one. Freya wouldn't stop moving, making it almost impossible.

"I've almost got it," he told her, trying the third. "Calm down, it's—"

The padlock snapped open and Freya plummeted. Savage wasn't ready, both of them tumbling to the floor in a tangle of limbs.

Kett ducked down, trying the keys on the padlock that secured Freya's hands until he found the right one. The girl screamed her relief into the ceiling, Savage gathering her into a hug.

"Go," said Kett, the word just a growl in his smoke-ravaged throat.

He used Dmitri's hanging body to haul himself up, trying the keys until the chains around his ankles loosened. He managed to wrap a hand around the boy's waist, lowering him gently to the floor.

"Don't want to worry you, sir," said Porter, his voice lost behind the fury of the fire. "But we're going to be toast in a minute."

Kett didn't look back. He kept his eyes on the keys, inserting each one in turn into the padlock that secured Dmitri's wrists. It felt like a million years before it opened, and by the time he'd freed him, the fire was scorching the skin on his back, curling the hairs on his head.

He glanced behind him to see that Savage had gone, one side of the building almost lost to the flames.

"Get him out..." said Porter, his words reduced to hacking coughs.

"Not leaving you, Pete," said Kett, scooching over to Porter.

He had no idea which keys he'd tried, so he started again.

"Tell Bobby I..." Porter started. "I love him."

"I'm going to tell him you're an arsehole," said Kett. "Stay still, for fuck's sake."

"I can't stay still," he said. "I've got a bloody knife in me."

The smoke was too thick. Kett couldn't see what he was doing, he couldn't breathe.

Then, a click. The most amazing sound in the world.

The padlock opened.

Kett got to his feet, grabbing Porter's hands and hauling him up. His ankles were still manacled, the chains trailing.

"Can you make it?" he asked.

"You got the kid?"

Kett nodded, even though he didn't think Porter could see him. He squatted, feeling for Dmitri's still body in the smouldering haze, finding him. He didn't think he had the strength to lift him, so he took hold of his wrists and pulled, sliding the boy across the debris-strewn floor.

When he looked across the room, though, he couldn't see the way out. The fire had spread too far, the smoke a wall.

Shit.

He kept moving, dragging Dmitri around the edge of the flames. The heat was unbearable, boiling his blood. The smoke was a solid thing inside his sinuses, it filled his lungs like burning coals.

It was too much. He was going to die in here.

A shape in the chaos, moving towards him. A hand grabbed his sleeve, tugging. He let it guide him as he dragged Dmitri over the wreckage of the room and through the door.

"You still with me, Pete?" he called, seeing Porter's shadow bunny-hopping behind him.

The corridor seemed a hundred times as long as it had when he'd first walked it, but eventually he tumbled out into the glorious rain.

He collapsed to his knees, retching so hard he thought he was going to turn himself inside out. Dmitri lay beside him, finally stirring.

Porter stumbled out, his entire body black from the

smoke. He collapsed, the knife still protruding from his shoulder. Savage sat on the wet ground by the open gate, Freya wrapped in her arms.

"You okay, sir?" she asked him.

"No," said Porter, studying the knife. "Do I take it out? It really hurts."

"*Don't* take it out," Savage told him.

They all turned to the gate at the sound of footsteps. Duke appeared, drenched, his face warped with effort.

"Aggie?" asked Kett.

Duke shook his head.

"She got into one of the cars," he said. "I couldn't stop her. Then Kate said you needed help, I came back."

The PC looked up the hill.

"We can still catch her, sir. She's heading for the road."

Past the ringing in his ears, Kett could hear the sound of an engine. He wasn't sure he could get up again, but somehow he managed it, staggering after Duke through the open gate. He almost tripped on the body that lay there, its robes smoking.

A silver car was struggling up the hill, its back end slipping. Kett started towards the IRV, finding his phone and calling Clare.

"Speak," boomed the Super.

"I'm trying, sir," croaked Kett. "Where the hell are you?"

"You found Porter?"

"He's fine," said Kett. "He's safe. So are the kids. But Aggie's doing a runner, heading back into Hopton."

"Units are on their way," said Clare. "They should be with you. Can you stop her?"

"I'll try," said Kett. He reached the car, saw that there were no keys in the ignition. "Kate! I need you!"

The silver car was approaching the top of the slope, but there was another sound over the whine of its engine. Kett scrubbed the rain from his eyes, watching as a yellow van crested the hill at thirty miles an hour. It was going too fast to stop, the bonnet ploughing through the silver car and knocking it onto its side.

"Shit," said Kett, sliding the phone into his pocket.

He broke into a jog, his broken body barely able to hold him up.

The silver car groaned as gravity pulled it over onto its roof, the windscreen shattering. The van had skidded to a halt, the doors opening. A man hopped out of the driver's seat, his hands in his hair, his face wrinkled in shock. Even through the rain, Kett saw that it was Josh, the young cameraman. Megan had dropped out of the other side, one hand over her mouth, the other holding a camcorder.

Duke overtook Kett, charging up the hill. He reached the upturned car in half a minute, his baton out as he crouched down beside the driver's window. It took Kett twice that long, and he was wheezing like an accordion by the time he got there.

"She's alive, sir," said Duke. "You want me to get her out."

"Yeah," said Kett. "But be careful, she might still be armed."

"I didn't see her," said Josh, his eyes wide. "I swear, I didn't see her, she came out of nowhere. Is she okay? I didn't see her. You have to believe me."

Kett ignored him, watching as Duke tried to open the door of the silver car. When he couldn't, he thwacked his baton into the window. It disintegrated on the second try, screams pouring out from inside.

"You coming out, or am I dragging you?" he said.

Aggie must have given the wrong answer, because Duke reached in. A few seconds later, he hauled the girl out of the vehicle, dragging her kicking and screaming onto the grass. Her face was wracked with emotion, her teeth stained with blood. She struggled for as long as it took Duke to plant a knee on her stomach, then the fight drained out of her.

Kett walked over, bracing his hands on his knees to get his breath back. Aggie glared at him like she could stop his heart with just a thought.

"You said I could go," she hissed. "You said you wouldn't stop me."

"I lied," he replied. "You're not the only devil here, Aggie."

"You want me to do the honours, sir?" said Duke, slipping a set of cuffs around the young woman's wrists.

"I will," said Kett. "Agnes Clegg, you are under—"

"I'm doing it," came Porter's voice.

The DI was staggering up the hill, one hand still clasping the knife in his shoulder. He was still wearing nothing except his underpants.

"Pete, you can't do it, you're basically naked," said Kett.

"And there's *that*," added Duke, nodding to the knife. "How are you even walking?"

"Because it's in my arm, you idiot," said Porter, glaring at him. "Not my leg. I'm doing it."

He stopped beside Aggie, taking a deep breath and reeling like a drunk.

"Agnes Clegg," he said. "You are..."

He doubled up, groaning.

"Actually, can you do it, sir?"

Kett stood over the young woman. She met his eye and held it.

"Agnes Clegg, you're under arrest on charges of kidnapping, attempted murder, and murder. You do not have to say anything, but it may harm your defence if you do not mention when questioned something which you later rely on in court. Anything you do say may be taken in evidence. You understand what's happening here?"

She glared at him, the defiance falling away after a few seconds.

"Dad?" she asked.

Kett didn't know the answer to her question, so he didn't reply. The sky answered for him, the thunder more distant now. The storm was passing, dragging the rain and the wind with it. To the south, past the burning building, the last of the sun was beginning to creep from the glowering clouds, and the birds of the meadow had started to sing. There was an even better sound, too, the call of sirens from over the hill.

"It's over," he said, more to himself than anyone else.

It was Aggie who heard him, though.

"It's not over," she said, licking her dry lips.

Kett nodded. Because that was the way of the world, wasn't it? He'd been here before, he'd be here again. Good against evil. Nobody ever won.

Nothing ever changed.

"Any chance you could all get in the same shot?" said a voice from the direction of the van. Megan stood there, her camcorder to her face. "Maybe repeat that last bit again? Aaron, can we get you in the middle, maybe with your Taser? The light's pretty spectacular right now."

Duke studied the young woman, then shook his head.

"I've got a better idea," he said. "Can I borrow that?"

"The camera?" said Megan, frowning. "You're going to do a selfie?"

"Something like that," said Duke.

He took the camera, then staggered through the tangled undergrowth towards the edge of the cliff. The sea still churned, the gulls wheeling ecstatically as the rain thinned.

"Um, maybe better over here?" shouted Megan. "Aaron?"

With a mighty swing of his enormous arm, Duke lobbed the camera over the cliff. It seemed to soar forever before it dipped out of sight. He turned back, brushing his hands together.

"And cut," he said with a grin.

Kett laughed, watching as the first of the IRVs crested the hill, almost hitting the back of the van.

"Come on," he said, setting off towards the pillbox. "Let's sort this mess out before the boss arrives and starts tossing everywhere."

Too late he remembered the phone in his pocket, the call still active. He pulled it out, hearing Superintendent Clare's tinny voice on the other end.

"I bloody heard that, Kett!"

CHAPTER FORTY-EIGHT

They stood together on the other side of hell.

Kett couldn't quite believe they'd made it out alive.

He leaned against the tail end of an IRV near the top of the hill. The door was open, Porter lying on the back seat, one hand still holding the knife in his shoulder. His back had been sliced open, the cut shallow and wrapped in a bandage. They'd called for an ambulance, of course, but nothing had arrived so far.

The storm had rolled away, dissipating over the North Sea. In its wake, the evening seemed to glow, fingers of golden light pushing through the thinning clouds to the west, bringing every stalk of grass, every branch, every flower to life. To the east, over the calming water, darkness gathered, carried on a cool breeze. Night was on its way, and Kett was more than happy to let it erase the day.

The sooner they were allowed to forget about this week, the better.

He yawned, looking down the hill to where the pillbox burned behind its metal fencing. The fire service was on their way, but Kett didn't think they'd get it out. Maybe it was better they didn't. There was nothing good in there, only evil. The books, the butchered photographs, the candles and incense and unholy markings.

All of it should burn.

But they'd made it. They'd survived. Dmitri and Freya sat in the back of the TV crew's van, wrapped in blankets and watching cartoons on the monitor. Savage had treated the cuts on their backs, and she'd washed off most of the markings on their skin. They were covered in bruises, and the scars on the inside would probably never heal, but even as Kett watched them through the open doors he heard Freya laugh at something on the screen.

Maybe, given enough time, they'd be okay.

The other good thing was that the TV crew seemed to have given up on the show after Duke had lobbed the camcorder into the sea.

"We're off, sir."

Kett looked over the roof of the IRV to see Sergeant Julia Gorski standing by the open door of a police van. Agnes Clegg was secured in the cell at the back—out of sight but very much not out of mind. She hadn't stopped thumping the door since she'd been put in there half an hour ago, and her howls of fury were the loudest thing in the evening. Several tactical officers milled around the van, their weapons secure but their faces alert.

"Straight to HQ," Kett told Gorski. "We don't know who else was working with the Cleggs, and how desperate they are to get her back. They're armed and dangerous, they've already killed two officers."

Gorski nodded, her expression dark.

"Be careful, Julia," he added.

She climbed into the van and started the engine, the rest of the tactical team heading back to their vehicle. Slowly, the two vans pulled away, vanishing over the crest of the hill and pulling a tail of IRVs behind them.

"You worried they're going to come after her again, sir?" said Porter from the darkness of the car.

"I don't know, Pete," he said. "I have no idea who these people are. This case is..."

He didn't have the words, and there was no time to finish anyway because Savage was jogging up the hill. She looked as exhausted as he felt, and she paused when she reached him to claw in some breaths. Duke was heading this way too, taking his time and enjoying the scenery.

"Sorry, sir," said Savage. "The smoke. Lungs have barely recovered from the last fire."

"Take your time," said Kett. "Is Kevin Clegg dead?"

Savage nodded.

"Burned alive, sir," she said when she'd recovered. "He must have had something explosive in his robe because there's whole chunks of him missing."

"Gross," said Porter from the car.

"I'm guessing gunpowder," Savage went on. "Some of the ceremonies I read about online talked about making the fire as strong as possible. The hotter the flame, the easier it is for the demons to pass through. I don't know how he managed to make it as far as he did."

She shuddered at the memory, her eyes dark.

"Doesn't feel real," she added, looking back down the hill. "Aggie gone, sir?"

"Yeah," said Kett.

"Shame we couldn't hurl *her* off the cliff," said Porter.

"We don't do that, Detective," came a reply from the other side of the hill.

Everyone turned to see Clare struggling over the bushy peak, so much sweat on his face and neck that he looked as if he'd been swimming in the sea. It was no wonder he was hot, his awful brown suit looked like it was made from camel hide.

"But rest assured, Aggie will be behind bars for a long time. She thinks she knows what hell is, but she doesn't. Not yet."

The Super slipped down the wet grass until he was standing next to them. He eyeballed Kett, then Savage, then Duke, and finally Porter.

"You really are a bunch of horrible twats, you know that?" he said.

"Nice way of saying well done for solving the case, sir," said Kett.

"Fuck the case," said Clare, spraying spit and sweat. "Why do you lot always insist on being beaten halfway to death? Or burned? Or chased at gunpoint? Or shagged to death by seagulls?"

He leaned down to look through the open door.

"What delicacy did you choose this time, Porter? Oh look, a knife in your shoulder. How original."

"I didn't stab *myself*, sir," Porter objected.

"What about you, Duke?" said Clare, feigning curiosity as he studied the PC. "Did you decide to get blown up again? Did you lose your other eyebrow?"

Duke's hand shot up to check, and he breathed out a sigh of relief.

"It's still there, sir," he said, missing the point entirely.

Clare shook his head in disbelief, staring at the pillbox in its nest of fire.

"What a clusterfuck," he said. "So this was all Aggie and her dad?"

Kett nodded.

"But they had help, sir."

"I know," Clare said. "We caught the man driving the bus. He's a minor player, an addict. Claims he was offered a lot of money to run you off the road, Kate. He has no idea why, and he said the person who paid him was wearing a mask."

"They didn't want Aggie, sir," said Savage. "The whole thing was a distraction. They knew she would be able to sneak out later. They just needed as many of us as possible away from HQ. Is Flick okay, by the way?"

"She's fine. She just took her eye off the ball."

"Any leads on the other man who raided holding, sir?" said Kett.

Clare shook his head.

"We'll find him. Aggie or her dad will talk. I can't see either of them chewing off their tongue."

"Kevin Clegg's dead, sir," said Kett.

"I knocked him into the fire," Porter said, his face pale. "I didn't mean to kill him. He was starting to see sense. I think he might have been able to get Aggie to stop."

"She was trying to bring her mother back?" asked Clare.

Porter shuffled up in the seat, wincing as he tried to get comfortable.

"Yeah," he said. "Aggie believed it. I think they both did. They were going to murder those kids, and me, drain our blood then burn us in the fire. The demon they were calling, that was his price. That was the cost of bringing Tracey Clegg back from the dead."

He blinked, lost in the memory.

"I thought..."

Everybody waited as he struggled for the words.

"They were chanting, calling its name, and for a second, in the fire, I thought I saw it."

"Saw what?" said Clare.

"A shape," said Porter. "This thing, with horns, and eyes, and..."

He faltered, swallowing hard.

"It wasn't real," said Kett, but there was no conviction in his voice.

"What is it, sir?" Savage asked him, the breeze toying with her hair.

"I don't know," he said. "It's... Pete's right, there are some things in this case I can't explain. They don't make sense."

"Like what?" scoffed Clare. "Porter's tea?"

Inside the car, Porter gasped.

"No, sir." Kett thought back. "The kestrel, back on Bianca Caddel's land. It kept diving. It showed me where the bunker was."

"Bullshit," said Clare. "It was diving for prey, you just happened to see it. We'd have found the bunker, for Christ's sake. It's a giant fucking concrete bunker."

"What about the devil in the cottage?" said Duke, frowning as best he could with a single eyebrow. "He was invisible."

"He wasn't invisible," said almost everyone at once.

"You just weren't paying attention, Duke," said Clare. "You haven't been able to focus at all because of this stupid TV thing, you're all over the place. You were probably staring at your reflection or pumping your bloody biceps, and he slipped past you."

"He's not wrong," said Savage, giving Duke a look. "The TV stuff didn't do you any favours, Aaron."

"Well, it's over now," he said, staring mournfully at the van.

"For the best," said Clare. "You're police, Aaron, and you're bloody good at it. The world doesn't need to see it."

Duke's face blossomed into a smile.

"And the world doesn't need to see *that*," added Porter, pointing through the door to Duke's forehead. "You'll be giving kids nightmares."

"What about the two women at the soft play, sir?" said Kett. "They vanished."

"Cameras spotted them walking down Plumstead Road minutes after you spoke with them, Kett," said Clare. "They probably bolted because you were police, and they were smoking weed. They were carrying their tent, the one they left behind was an older one. Stop looking for mysteries where there aren't any."

"But what about the patrol cars that caught fire at McDonald's, sir?" asked Savage.

"Petrol bomb," said Clare. "Thrown from a vehicle that was driving out of the car park."

He looked down the hill to the solitary car that remained outside the pillbox, his eyes like a hawk's.

"*That* car, in fact. Spalding found the footage from the restaurant's cameras. They lobbed it under the last IRV and the fire spread from there."

"Okay," said Kett. "But what about the horses? What spooked them? Something drove them across the field, something made them jump onto Robert Flack." He thumped his chest. "I felt it, sir. This... this sensation, this warning."

Clare's smile was almost as terrifying as the masks that Aggie and her father had worn.

"You know, that one almost got me too, Kett," he said. "But I figured it out while you lot were farting around out here by the sea."

"While we were solving the case, sir?" said Kett. Clare ignored him.

"We found audio equipment when we were searching Bianca Caddel's warehouse," he said. "Speakers and generators. Did you know horses don't hear the same frequencies we do? Blast them with a higher rate of hertz and they freak out. We can sense it, but we can't hear it. Somebody must have been in those woods, they must have rigged up a speaker. The horses bolted. Could have trampled you, but as luck would have it, they went the other way and killed Flack. End of story."

Kett puffed out a breath, shaking his head.

"That sounds a little far-fetched, sir."

"Oh, you're right," Clare said, his voice high-pitched with sarcasm. "It must have been the demons. Grow up, you wank-flavoured cock sock. For these guys, it's all about the theatrics. If they can make you believe it, they've won. It's all an illusion. There's no such thing as magic."

He wiped the sweat from his face, then spun around, clanking up the hill.

"I'm taking the kids to the hospital," he yelled. "Since there's no bloody ambulances. Why don't you tossers make yourself useful for a change?"

They watched him disappear into the yellow van.

"If anything could make me believe in demons," said Kett, "it's him."

Savage laughed quietly, rubbing her smoke-swollen eyes.

"What do you need us to do, sir?" she asked.

"Nothing," he said. "Go home. You've done enough."

He looked from her to Duke.

"Both of you. You saved those kids. And you saved Porter."

"Kate did," Porter yelled from inside the IRV. "Duke didn't do anything."

"And you saved me, too," he went on. "I forgot to ask, who was it who pulled me out of there?"

"Out of where, sir?" said Savage.

"The pillbox. The fire. Somebody took my arm, led me out through the smoke."

Savage and Duke frowned at each other, then at Kett.

"You came out by yourself, sir," said Savage. "You and Porter, with Dmitri."

Kett shook his head. He could still feel the hand on his sleeve, the gentle tug.

"Are you okay, sir?" asked Savage.

"Yeah," said Kett, his skin knotting into goosebumps. "It's just... This bloody case. Go home. We can debrief tomorrow."

"Okay," said Savage. She took Duke's hand, holding it tight. "Are you sure you're alright, sir?"

He didn't know the answer to that, of course, but he answered the only way he could.

"I'm fine, Kate. It's the job."

"The job is the job is the job," she said, nodding.

The pair of them slogged up the hill, hand in hand.

"Any chance you could drive me to the hospital, sir?" said Porter, holding his arm. "By the time the ambulance arrives, I'm going to be dead. Of old age."

"Sure, Pete," Kett replied.

He stared out to sea, taking a deep breath of salt-drenched air. Only when he turned back to the IRV did he hear the chuckling calls from a scraggly bush to his left. It took him a while to see the silhouettes in the hollow of shadowy branches, and when he did, he wasn't sure whether to believe it or not.

Three magpies studied him with dark eyes, warbling to each other.

"What do you want?" he asked them.

They watched for a moment more, then they exploded from the bush with such urgency that Kett's heart almost stopped, soaring out over the cliff with a chattering song of delight, vanishing into the gathering dark.

CHAPTER FORTY-NINE

Saturday

"I WANT TO DO THE BELL!"

Kett followed his kids up the short path that led to DI Porter's house, enjoying the touch of the August sun on his face. Evie and Moira had raced each other out of the car and across the driveway, shoulder to shoulder. Alice slouched after them, annoyed as always that she'd been forced to leave the comfort of her bedroom.

They were all feeling better, which in one way was a good thing, because for the last few nights he and Billie had both managed to get some sleep.

The downside was that they were all back to normal.

"I'm doing the bell," growled Moira, her little fists bunched.

"I am!" said Evie, almost sobbing as she looked at Kett. "Dadda, I am, I always do it."

"We should have given them Calpol anyway," said Billie, giving Kett's hand a squeeze. "Just to sedate them."

He laughed, scooping Evie up in one arm and then Moira in the other. The pain in his back as he straightened was like somebody had stitched cheese graters between his vertebrae. He wondered, as he did more and more these days, how much longer he'd be able to carry them.

"You can play rock, paper, scissors for it," he said. "On three."

He counted down. Evie lifted a flat hand for paper.

Moira held up a middle finger.

"I win," she said.

"Moira!" said Kett. "Who taught you that?"

She glanced at Alice, but said nothing.

"Both of you can press it," he said, exasperated. "Do it together, that way nobody gets upset."

He shuffled towards the door so they could reach the bell, but Alice beat him to it. She threw a smug look at her sisters before jabbing her finger on the button. The sound of chimes was drowned out by the stereophonic screams from Evie and Moira.

Kett crouched, letting go of the girls so that he could insert his fingers into his ears. Billie was saying something, but he couldn't hear her over the ringing.

"What?" he said.

The door opened before she could repeat herself. Allie Porter stood there in a pink-spotted summer dress, her bleach-blonde hair scraped into a ponytail. Baby Bobby was slung on her hip—although he wasn't a baby anymore. He was eighteen months old now, and thanks to his round, red-cheeked face and his bulging double chin, he looked more like his dad than ever.

The poor thing.

"Oh," said Allie, staring in horror at Evie and Moira, who were both still screaming. "They are better, aren't they?"

"Yeah," said Kett, letting Billie walk in ahead of him. "They're sad because they didn't get to press the doorbell."

"Right," said Allie, one eyebrow arching up. "Well, we've got biscuits if that helps?"

It did, kind of, the girls barging past Allie into the house, their screams fading. Kett walked in, pushing the door shut behind him.

"Sorry we're late," he said. "Everyone here?"

"Yeah," she said. "Can you take this one for a second?"

She passed Bobby to Kett and he hugged him to his chest, marvelling at the weight of the boy.

"Never stops eating," said Allie, seeing the look on his face. "Like his dad. Speaking of which, just got to grab some stuff out of the oven. They're in the lounge."

Kett made his way down the hall, peeking through the living room door to see Porter sitting on the enormous sofa, his feet on a pouffe. He was wearing shorts and a T-shirt, a blanket over his lap. There was a thick bandage around his shoulder, more plasters on his arms and face. He'd got some colour back since the last time Kett had seen him, but he looked older, and the deep worry lines etched into his face would be there forever.

Some wounds never healed.

He broke into a grin when he saw Kett, one that grew even bigger at the sight of his son. Bobby reached out to his dad with chubby hands, speaking half-words and laughing hysterically.

Savage sat next to Porter, Duke perched on the arm of

the sofa beside her. Both were wearing matching black Nike tracksuits, Duke's about five sizes bigger than Savage's. The PC looked like he had something smeared on his face over his eye, a smudge of white cream.

"Come in, sir," said Duke. "Take a seat. We're going to be starting soon."

"Oi," said Porter. "This is my house, Aaron, I tell him to come in."

"Sorry, sir," said Duke. "Wasn't sure if you were up to it."

"I'm fine," snapped Porter. "I'm stronger than I ever was. Stronger than you, anyway."

Kett collapsed onto the sofa, Bobby crawling onto Porter's lap. The baby lifted a hand and slapped the DI on his bandaged wound. Porter sucked in a breath, wincing.

"Remember, Bobby, Daddy's injured," said Allie as she walked through the door. She was holding a tray laden with cans, and she set it down on the coffee table, collecting her son as soon as her hands were free. "Sorry, I was going to make lemonade, but, you know..."

She threw a look at Porter, and it wasn't entirely sympathetic.

"We're short-staffed," she finished.

"Luckily I'm here," said Superintendent Clare.

He entered the room holding a second tray, this one stacked with packets of biscuits. He was wearing an apron, which wouldn't have looked so weird if he still had his trousers on.

"Good lord, sir," said Kett, pulling a face. "Why are you undressed?"

"Trust you to notice that, Kett," said Clare as he dumped the tray. "You pervert."

"How can I *not* notice?" he said, looking to the rest of the room for support. "Why?"

"Because it's *hot*, you sweaty mule rectum," said Clare.

"What's a mule rectum, Dadda?" asked Evie as she wandered into the room, her hands full of custard creams.

"You're looking at one," Clare answered.

He sniffed the air, his nose crinkling.

"Speaking of rectums, why can I smell one?"

"It's Duke, sir," said Savage.

She pointed a finger at the smudge of cream over Duke's eye. The PC shot her a look, making hushing noises.

"They have to know, Aaron," said Savage, grinning. "It's too funny not to share."

"Share what?" said Porter.

Savage took a breath, already laughing.

"You remember those witches we went to see? The good ones, the ones who called themselves the Sisterhood of Power?"

Everyone nodded. Duke burrowed his face in his hands.

"Aaron went back to see them," she said. "He thought they might be able to solve his eyebrow problem."

"It's not true," said Duke, speaking through his fingers. "Don't listen to her."

"They gave him a salve," Savage finished, resting a hand on Duke's shoulder to show she meant no ill will. "He has to put it on three times a day. It's made from—"

"Stop," said Duke.

"Lavender, rosemary, lemongrass—"

"Stop!"

"Mayonnaise, and—"

"For the love of God, Kate, stop!"

"Pigeon poo," she finished.

Duke groaned, slumping back into the sofa. Porter burst into howls of laughter that only lasted a few seconds before he had to stop, his hand on his shoulder, his face lined with pain.

"Oh my God," said the DI. "You're rubbing pigeon shit on your face?"

"Language," snapped Allie before Kett could say it himself.

"Pigeon *poo*?" Porter corrected. "You muppet."

"The weird thing is, it's working," said Savage. "It's growing back. Show them."

Duke reluctantly removed his hands. Kett leaned past Porter to see that Savage was telling the truth. There was a smattering of hair on Duke's smooth brow, like a teenage boy growing his first moustache.

"Almost enough to make you believe in magic," said Savage, although her words were a little too close to the bone for Kett to smile.

Clare peeled a bourbon from the packet, snapping it in half so aggressively that crumbs exploded everywhere.

"Before we start this thing," he said, "I should let you know that Aggie Clegg broke under pressure this morning. She's talking. She confessed to the whole thing, said it was her idea. She's obsessed with..."

He glanced at Evie, who was listening intently from the far side of the room.

"With spooky stuff," he went on. "The head, the ruins, the body in the cottage, that was all Aggie and her dad. They thought the ritual would hide them, make them invisible."

"It did," said Duke, quietly.

"Everything else was Bianca and her people, who seem to have been telling the truth about wanting to keep the kids safe. They're theatre folk originally, hence the warehouse full of props. Aggie said they dressed as witches because apparently witches are one of the few things demons are afraid of. It was all part of this world they'd concocted. They seem to have devoted themselves to stopping people who are trying to summon demons. All those files we found in Bianca's caravan were part of their research, they were looking for crimes that fit the profile."

"Did we ID the imposter in the well?" asked Kett.

"No," Clare replied. "We don't think he's a player, though. There's a missing unhoused man who loosely matches his description, looks a lot like Clegg. Clegg was worried Bianca was onto him, he gave them the imposter knowing they'd think it was him, knowing they'd kill him."

He shook his head.

"They're mad, all of them."

"Is it over, though, sir?" said Kett. "Because by my count, we're still a man down. The other guy who attacked HQ alongside Clegg."

Clare sighed.

"Aggie gave us some information about the second guy, but she doesn't know much. She has a name, that's all. Jasper Homandy. We don't know him. He sourced the body for the ritual in the ruins, although we haven't figured out how he got it from the morgue. There's a connection to the glasses shop, though. Specs is managed by a woman called Alex Rimple—she knows nothing about any of this—but the building is owned by somebody else. A man with the same name that Aggie gave us."

"That's something," said Kett.

"It would be, if the name was real," Clare went on. "The person doesn't exist. The letterhead we found in the car wasn't a note from the sponsor at all. It was Aggie's handwriting. We think it might have been instructions from her to her father. She wanted him at St Mary's ruins at nine, and she wanted him to bring the camera kit to make it look like they'd been filming. She didn't know Charlie was going to be there. As soon as she heard Charlie was coming she changed the time, left early. Her plan was to film the episode then get rid of Charlie so she and her father could take Matt."

He devoured his biscuit, spraying crumbs as he continued.

"It was sheer luck we found the phone number on there. *Bad* luck. We fell right into their hands."

"So the man I spoke to," said Kett, "the person posing as Rimple. This was the other guy? Homandy?"

Clare shrugged.

"Makes sense."

"But why did they want Matt, sir?" asked Savage. "He didn't have the right birthday."

"They were going to use him for a secondary ritual, like the head, but she wouldn't say what."

"Did she say *why*?" asked Kett.

"Why she was trying to summon a demon to bring her mother back?" said Clare. He took another biscuit, staring at it like the explanation might be written there. "She was closer to her father than we thought. They reconnected a few years ago, kept it secret. He talked about Tracey all the time. I think he made Aggie fall in love with her mother all over again. She was already obsessed with the occult, and the two things just formed an unholy idea."

The biscuit disappeared into his mouth, then instantly reappeared as a hail of crumbs.

"According to Aggie, though, it only started to get dangerous when Homandy got involved. She doesn't know how it happened. Kevin was the person who made contact with him. Spalding's looking into it. She's going to let me know if we ID the guy. But you're right, Kett. Whoever he is, he's still out there, he—"

He stopped as Billie appeared in the doorway, Moira in her arms. Alice skulked behind them, her cheeks bulging like a hamster's as she devoured biscuits.

"Sorry," said Billie, giving Clare a wary glance. "Poo emergency. You need some time? We can wait in the kitchen."

"No," said Clare. "We're done."

He fell silent for a moment, contemplating.

"I wanted to gather you all here unofficially, before the memorial service next week. A chance to lift a glass to fallen friends."

Kett nodded, thinking of PC Yassin and PC Evans, committing their names to his memory.

"But before we get to that," Clare went on, eyeballing Duke, "shall we give Slugbollocks his fifteen minutes of fame?"

"What are slug bollocks?" asked Moira as Billie lowered her to the carpet.

"Finally," said Duke, leaning forward. He was holding a remote control, Kett saw. "I mean, it's pretty pointless now, because they're not doing the show. But it might be fun, right? See how close we all came to being celebrities?"

He pressed play and the DVD player beneath the TV whirred. On-screen, footage began to roll—the bullpen, a rogue seagull, everyone losing their minds.

"That bloody seagull!" roared Clare, actually lobbing a biscuit at the TV.

"Oi!" squeaked Porter.

Kett leaned back, watching the events play out. It was

comedy gold, and in seconds everyone was laughing, his two younger girls rolling on the floor in hysterics. More footage followed, shots of them working the case. It didn't feel real. It felt like something that had happened to somebody else.

When the woods appeared on the screen, the ruined church in the distance, Kett almost screamed for Duke to turn it off.

Then the shot changed again, more video of Duke as he walked through the corridors of HQ. He kept looking back nervously at the camera.

"Are you sure you need to see this, Meggy?" he asked.

"Yes," came a reply, Megan's voice. "Sorry, Aaron, it's just part of the show."

Duke stopped outside the bathroom door.

"You need to see me pee?" he asked.

"Just a little bit," said Megan.

"Aaron!" said Savage, shocked. "Please tell me you didn't let her film you in the toilet."

Duke covered his face again. Fortunately, on-screen, somebody interrupted the shot. The clip ended.

"Lucky escape," said Porter. "For us. Oh wait, it's me!"

The DI appeared on-screen, in the kitchen.

"Oh Christ," said Clare. "They filmed you making *tea*?"

"Yeah, sir."

"Now we know why they cancelled it," said Clare.

Porter's face fell.

"I was going to get my own show, sir," he said. "Porter's Perfect Puddings."

"Porter's Poisonous Piss," muttered Clare.

"*What*, sir?"

Clare was saved from having to answer when his phone rang. He pulled it out of the pocket of his apron, everyone getting a perfect view of the back of his sagging Y-fronts as he left the room.

"See," said Porter, as a cup of bone-white, oil-flecked fluid filled the TV. "Bloody perfect, that is."

Everyone laughed again, Kett giving the DI's good shoulder a gentle squeeze. The shot changed to one outside Bianca Caddel's warehouse, and Kett was grateful when Clare appeared in the door again, beckoning him out of the room.

He heaved himself from the sofa, following the Super into the open-plan kitchen-diner. Clare leaned against the counter, turning his phone in his hands as if he'd forgotten how to work it.

The sudden quiet was enough to prepare Kett for bad news.

"What is it, sir?"

Clare wiped his nose, staring at the floor for a moment more before lifting his head. He, too, looked older.

"I wasn't sure," he said. "I didn't want to say anything, not until I knew."

He breathed out a sigh, shaking his head.

"What, sir?" said Kett, his pulse quickening. He had to lean against the counter himself, because it felt like the room was tilting.

"That was Spalding. As I said, Aggie gave us the name of the second man, it's all she knows about him."

"Jasper Homandy," said Kett. "Right. Who is he?"

"It's an anagram, Robbie," said Clare. "Spalding worked it out. It's an anagram of Joseph Maynard."

Even here, in the wedge of sun that spilled through the window, in the fierce August heat, Kett grew cold. Because he knew the name. He had done for over two years now, ever since the King Rat case.

Ever since Hollenbeck had fallen.

"No, sir," he said, hearing his voice as if from a mile away. "I don't believe it."

"We always knew there was a chance," said Clare. "And with an operation like this, something as sophisticated and professional and deadly as what we've seen this week, it was only a matter of time."

"We destroyed Hollenbeck," said Kett. "They're all rotting behind bars, or dead."

But he knew that was a lie. They hadn't caught them all.

"Two members weren't there the night we brought down Hollenbeck," said Clare. "Two got away. Maynard was one of them. You've listened to the interviews as much as I have. Everyone knows Maynard is obsessed with the occult. You saw it yourself, your own children were almost sacrificed to the flames of the Pig Man two years ago. Maynard's stench is all over this."

"He's the other man?" said Kett.

"Bianca told you Clegg couldn't have done this by himself," said Clare. "Not even with Aggie's help. They needed an expert, somebody who's spent his life studying demons, who knows how they work. Aggie says her father recruited Homandy because they thought he could make it all real. He showed them how to do the ritual, he taught them how it would work, and he gave them the tools they needed to make it happen. It's Maynard."

The room was spinning faster now, a carnival ride Kett desperately wanted to get off.

"There's no indication he's here for you, Robbie," said Clare. "Kevin Clegg found him, he approached him. Maynard was a consultant, nothing more."

"You believe that, sir?" said Kett.

He could see by the way Clare let his eyes drop that he didn't.

"I thought we'd broken them," said Kett. "I thought we'd won. They as much as said it, sir. They weren't going to come after me anymore."

"And I don't think they will," said Clare. "Hollenbeck are gone, they don't exist. This is something else, I think. You're safe."

It was another lie, and it seemed to clatter around the kitchen like a trapped bird. Kett put his hands in his hair, closing his eyes. For so long now, for over two years, he'd built up the ground beneath him piece by piece so that it felt strong enough to hold him again.

And just like that, it had crumbled away.

Just like that, he was falling.

"No," he said quietly. "This is my fault, sir. We never should have let them go. We should have kept hunting."

"We tried," said Clare. "God only knows, we tried. These are monsters, Robbie. They know how to hide."

"Not monsters, sir," said Kett. "They're devils."

He opened his eyes, some instinct telling him to look back. Billie stood in the doorway, wreathed in shadows, watching them.

Listening.

He couldn't read her expression, but he could see her scars, the ones the Pig Man had given her.

The ones *Hollenbeck* had given her.

They seemed to glow in the half-light.

I'm sorry, he thought, sending the message to her.

"We should have taken them all out while we had the chance, sir," he said, turning back to Clare. "We thought they were going to disappear, but they're back."

He pushed himself off the counter, his entire body

made of broken glass. He didn't know how much he had left in him, how much he had left to give.

But he had *enough*.

"I'm going to end them, sir," he said. "For good, this time. Every single one of them."

He made his way to Billie, calling back as he went.

"Every last fucking devil."

PAPER GIRLS
ALEX SMITH
BAD DOG
ALEX SMITH
THREE LITTLE PIGS
ALEX SMITH
WHIP CRACK
ALEX SMITH
RUN RABBIT RUN
ALEX SMITH
STONE COLD DEAD
ALEX SMITH
EVERY MOTHER'S SON
ALEX SMITH
SWEET BRIAR ROSE
ALEX SMITH
JAW BREAKER
ALEX SMITH
KNOCK KNOCK
ALEX SMITH
KING RAT
ALEX SMITH
KNUCKLE BONES
ALEX SMITH
LUCKY NUMBER SEVEN
ALEX SMITH
UNHOLY SAINTS
ALEX SMITH
TRULY MADLY DEADLY
ALEX SMITH
EVERY LAST DEVIL
ALEX SMITH
READ THE FIRST SIXTEEN BOOKS NOW!

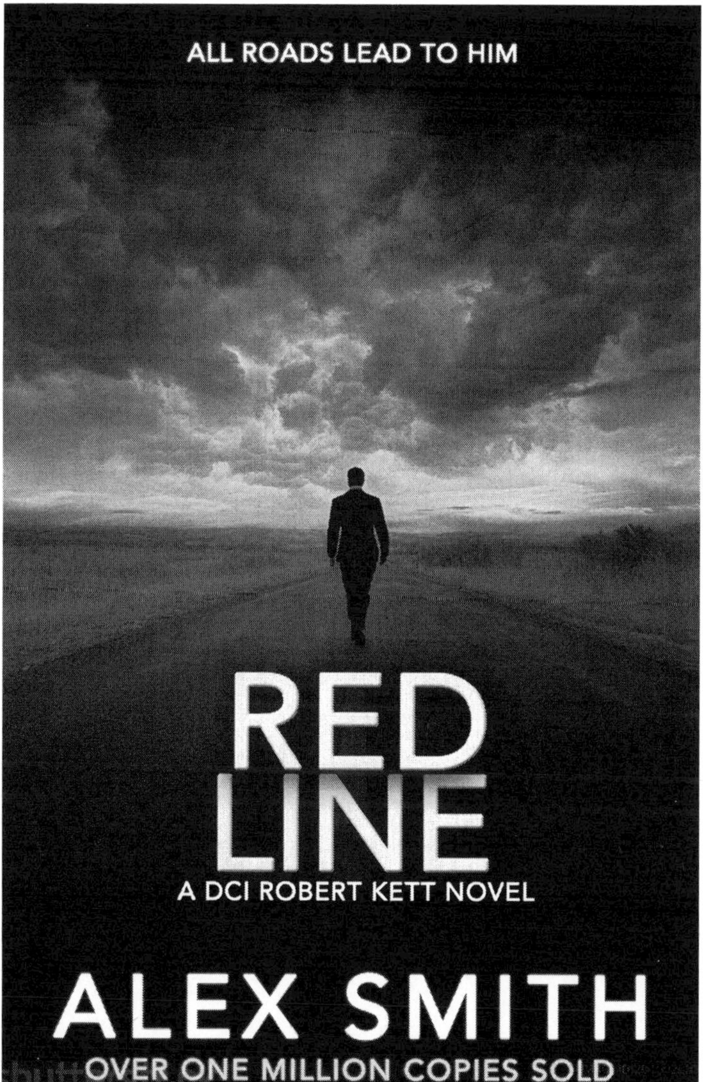
ALL ROADS LEAD TO HIM
RED
LINE
A DCI ROBERT KETT NOVEL
ALEX SMITH
OVER ONE MILLION COPIES SOLD

ABOUT THE AUTHOR

Alex Smith wrote his first book when he was six. It wasn't particularly good, but it did have some supernatural monsters in it. His latest books, the DCI Robert Kett thrillers, have monsters in them too, although these monsters are very human, and all the more terrifying for it. In between, he has published fourteen novels for children and teenagers under his full name, Alexander Gordon Smith—including the number one bestselling series Escape From Furnace, which is loved by millions of readers worldwide and which is soon to become a motion picture. He lives in Norwich with his wife and three young daughters.

Find out more at alexsmithbooks.com

RELENTLESS
MEDIA

Printed in Great Britain
by Amazon

46793039R00297